Happy C

With best wishes.

Olivia Rytwinski X

THE ACTOR

OLIVIA RYTWINSKI

'All the world's a stage, and all the men and
women merely players.
They have their exits and their entrances;
And one man in his time plays many parts.
His acts being seven ages.'

William Shakespeare, *As You Like It*

Copyright © 2022 Olivia Rytwinski

ISBN: 9798846248830

PublishNation
www.publishnation.co.uk

For Mike, Aleks & Lily

Also by Olivia Rytwinski:

A Family by Design (2017)
I Never Knew You (2019)
Shadowlake (2021)

Acknowledgements

A special thank you to all those who helped me during the writing of this novel - A J Humpage for her brilliant editing and advice, proofreading and wonderful advice from, Robin Avalyn, feedback and support from, Mark Evan, Kate Trelawny, Kerry Newton, Liz Best and Kath Wilkinson.

The Actor Cast List

Tess Blonski - Actor, single parent, mother of twins. Age 40

Stefan Temple - Business owner of Aztec Imports. Age 53

Judi Temple - younger sister to Stefan, co-owner of Aztec Imports. Age 50

Noah Heath - Tess's ex-partner. Former theatre Stage Manager. Now an electrician. Age 46

Clara - daughter of Tess and Noah, twin to Victor. Age 16

Victor - son of Tess and Noah, twin to Clara. Age 16

Evie Blonski - Mum to Tess. Age 63

Gil Cooney - employed by Stefan and Judi Temple. Age 49

Suzanne - previously worked at Aztec Imports. Age 32

Roddy - owner of the Captain Cook Experience - The Endeavour. Age 46

Heidi Jackson - married to Gavin. Long-term friend of Stefan and Judi. Age 52

Gavin Jackson - married to Heidi. Best friend to Stefan. Age 53

Anna - Noah's younger sister, a teacher. Age 41

Polly - young housemaid to Heidi and Gavin

Mindy and Zoe - actors with the young Tess at Hull Docks Theatre

When I walk along the shore my thoughts flow freely like the water at my feet. Each idea swims in the murmuring waves as they roll back and forth over rocks and sand, clarifying them in my mind, and smoothing any edges that may cause them to cloud, cut or wound. This is why I am drawn each day to the shore - for here is my muse, where my mind's eye grows wider and glistens ever brighter.

Tess Blonski - 'The Actor'

1

Skygale Cottage, Whitby

I stared up at the skylight and into the night, but sleep seemed an impossible dream away. The rain battered the window pane and every now and then the frame rattled beneath another gust of wind. The storm might have been less distracting if my bed wasn't positioned directly beneath the skylight, although during the few days we'd lived here I'd loved gazing up at the sprinkle of stars on clear nights. Touch wood, there didn't appear to be any leaks, which bode well for my nodding off at some point.

'Come on, Tess, you need to sleep,' I muttered.

But however hard I tried to blank out my thoughts and the storm that raged, my mind kept on churning.

This was only our second week in our new home, charmingly named Skygale, a fisherman's cottage situated two hundred and fifty yards up the hill through the narrow streets, from Whitby harbour.

After sixteen years in our previous, more spacious Whitby home, going to bed, waking up and moving around Skygale felt strange still, although with the twins' help, we'd finally unpacked all the boxes and squeezed our belongings into the fitted cupboards or furniture we'd brought with us.

I'd rarely slept alone in sixteen years, other than the occasional night where either Noah, my ex, or I had stayed away for work. My new life as a single parent would also take some adjusting to for our sixteen year old twins, Clara and Victor, who had to get used to living without their dad and me under one roof.

And who was to blame?

The answer, according to Noah and the twins, was debatable, but clear cut as far as I was concerned.

The deluge hammered harder against the skylight and the blasts of wind seemed to have picked up a notch. Sounds of scraping and scratching came from overhead and I visualised a

1

loose tile sliding into the gutter or plunging to the street below. I thought about Victor, asleep in the room directly below mine. On Saturday and Sunday mornings, his alarm went off at five so he could head out on the fishing boat with Roddy, my good friend and previous employer. Surely Roddy would decide against tomorrow's trip unless the storm abated.

If I didn't sleep soon I'd have bags under my eyes for my job interview tomorrow. That was another reason I couldn't nod off. My previous interview had been almost ten years ago with Roddy to be his tour guide for the Captain Cook experience, on a smaller replica of his ship, the HMS Endeavour, and where I'd worked each summer season since. If I succeeded in tomorrow's interview, there would be no out of season downtime. Given my new financially independent status, I needed a job that paid a proper wage and had decent prospects. My years as a part-time worker were over.

I glanced at the bedside clock and sighed - almost 2 a.m. I reached for my phone, plugged in my headphones and found some hypnotic sleep music, then took some long breaths and closed my eyes.

I don't know how long I slept for, until I was catapulted back into consciousness.

A shower of objects landed on the duvet and I felt water on my face, and more alarming, a piercing pain in my belly. I yanked out my earphones and reached for the bedside lamp. Raindrops splattered down on me and around me - fractured and tumbling gems in the lamplight. A cold blast of air rushed in and swept through the room like a phantom keen to make its presence felt and to wreak its havoc.

The pain in my belly intensified and I peered down and saw a shard of glass, about the size of a book cover that poked up from the duvet. I took hold of the glass between my fingers, lifted it slowly, and laid it aside. Then I peeled back the duvet and looked at the soft swell of my abdomen where a pool of blood had formed. I watched as the blood overflowed and trickled down my belly and onto the sheet. With my fingers I wiped away the blood and saw a puncture wound half an inch above my appendix scar.

'Shit, damn, bugger!'

Rain poured through the gaping hole overhead. I climbed out of bed and bent down, gripped the underside of the bed frame and heaved it across the floorboards to the dressing table. I clambered back over the bed as blood dripped and created red smudges against the white of the damp bed clothes. I pulled a tissue from the box on the bedside table and pressed it against the cut, then I headed out onto the landing and down the narrow staircase to the floor below.

All seemed quiet behind the children's bedroom doors, and I pulled the cord on the bathroom light. I felt queasy from the pain and the sight of blood which immediately pooled the moment I lifted the tissue. I squeezed the skin together to quell the flow. The wound didn't appear deep, but the pain seared through me and I felt my head swim. I gripped the edge of the sink and took some breaths until I could focus clearly again. I turned on the cold tap and stretched over the bath for a cotton pad from the jar on the windowsill. Then I dabbed the pad against the wound as I considered the damage the glass could have done had the duvet not taken the impact. I reached into the cabinet over the sink and pulled out a tube of antiseptic cream and a box of plasters.

When I'd washed, dried, winced in pain and dressed my wound, I headed down to the kitchen and grabbed the roll of bin liners from the cupboard beneath the sink. Drawing pins - I'd only unpacked those yesterday and remembered stashing them in the cupboard in the living room, along with playing cards, matches, nail files, and other assorted items. Whether drawing pins would hold bin liners in place was another matter, but I had to try something and I didn't have a hammer and nails. DIY was something else I'd have to take on in my role as sole homeowner. Maybe a couple of buckets placed beneath the skylight, too, would minimise water damage. I grabbed the mop bucket and the washing up bowl and ran back up the two flights of stairs.

Within the space of ten minutes my bedroom had gone from a cosy haven of rustic furniture and pastel fabrics to bloody Armageddon. A screaming wind swirled amidst broken glass; a steady deluge of rain fell through the gaping square. I grabbed my woollen jumper from the armchair and pulled it over my head. Placing the stool from my dressing table beneath the skylight, I stepped up, and standing on my tiptoes reached the open space. Another pain shot through my belly as the wind blew in and rain splattered onto my face, making me blink, curse and spit.

The window frame remained intact so it was likely a tile had come loose and smashed the glass, or possibly a branch had blown over from a tree on the street. The bin liner flapped in the wind, and I kept dropping pins, but when I'd finally secured three bin liners using the entire box of pins the rain no longer poured in, but rather dripped and trickled. I moved the stool aside and placed the buckets beneath.

The bedside clock read 4 a.m. My arms ached and I shivered from the cold clawing at my soaked skin. I pulled off my sopping wet jumper and reached for my nightdress and robe on the back of the door. Clara had a double bed and wouldn't mind if we shared for tonight. I thought I might be able to slip in without waking her. It seemed a better option than one of the two seater sofas where I'd have to scrunch up or dangle my legs over an armrest.

Grabbing a towel from the bathroom I rubbed myself dry, then paused outside Clara's bedroom door. The storm sounded distant and muted and I turned the handle and peered inside. The light from the landing cast across her bed where Clara lay on her side...beside Fleur, Clara's best friend. Clara's messy blonde bob contrasted with Fleur's neatly tied afro plaits. My mind had been so distracted that I'd forgotten Fleur had slept over, even though she'd eaten dinner with us before they headed out to meet up with friends. Neither of them stirred and I looked down at them, as they faced one another, their noses inches apart. I felt a surge of love for my sweet girl and I closed the door silently behind me.

The sofa it was.

2

Saturday

The cries and calls of the gulls started early, always, even on darker mornings. I had become so accustomed to their crooning in the early hours that I barely registered their presence. Often in my dreams they circled the rooftops and made themselves quietly known, but rarely disturbed me from my sleep.

I felt pressure from something on my legs and I opened my eyes. The weight shifted and travelled up over my belly and breasts until a wet nose and tongue tickled my face.

I lifted my hand and brushed a silken ear. 'Morning Digby.'

His round adoring eyes peered down at me and I stroked his smooth white, black and tan coat. When my hand paused he nudged for me to continue.

'I'm still tired, Digby,' I said, and yawned.

A paw pressed my abdomen. 'Jesus H. Christ!' I sat up sharp and Digby leapt down. I pulled the blanket down and saw that blood had seeped through the plaster and formed a rusty cracked pattern on my skin.

I heard footsteps coming down the stairs.

Victor's forehead wrinkled when he saw me. 'You slept down here?'

Digby woofed and gambolled over to greet Victor.

'No choice after the skylight fell on me.'

Victor's eyes widened. 'Jeez, really?'

'Yep. Must have been weak glass or a loose tile and the storm finished it off.'

Victor picked Digby up, held him close and stroked his ears. 'Were you hurt?'

'A shard of glass nicked my tummy. Masses of broken glass and rain. Didn't the storm wake you?'

5

Victor shook his head and put Digby down. 'Not at all. But I looked out and saw branches scattered and rubbish from upended bins.'

I tilted my head. 'Surely you're not fishing this morning?'

'Roddy's not messaged. Besides, the wind has dropped and the sea should be calm enough.'

I folded back the blanket. 'I'll make breakfast.'

Victor grinned. 'Not for me. Roddy brings bacon butties and it'd be rude to refuse.'

I smiled. 'Impossible to refuse, more like.'

At six foot one, Victor was taller than his Dad, and wiry as a wippet. Unlike some of his friends, he wasn't interested in building up muscle in the gym, but he was strong and toned, no doubt as a result of his labouring on the boat with Roddy, hauling in the nets and lobster baskets.

Victor pulled his boots from the rack by the door and sat on the armchair to lace them up. 'Hey, maybe you could ask Dad to fix the skylight?'

'Yes, I was thinking he might agree to board it until I get a glazier.'

'He'd love to help,' added Victor.

'Hopefully,' I said, with a half-smile. 'I'll see if he can come when you're back from fishing.'

Although Noah, the twins' dad, lived in Whitby and they'd still see him, I knew they were both struggling to come to terms with our separation. I felt torn, but angry still at being given no option but to sell and move out of our family home - a home where we'd shared many memories and lovingly refurbished during the sixteen years we'd lived there.

The house sale had resulted in a healthy profit on top of the original purchase, but this had been swallowed up by Noah's gambling debts. Damn Noah and his gambling, and the years I'd put up with him sneaking around to fund his dirty habit.

More than anything, I couldn't have allowed our constant arguing to upset Clara and Victor any longer, even if Noah had promised for the thousandth time that he'd quit gambling. He needed help and until he was prepared to accept that, I knew that nothing would change.

Victor pulled on his jacket and opened the door leading out to the front yard. 'See you later. Oh, and good luck with the interview.'

My tummy lurched at the reminder. 'I'll do my best. Take care and don't forget to wear your lifejacket,' I said, as I always did whenever he set off to the boat. Victor was a strong swimmer, but the tides and currents around Whitby were treacherous, and during the sixteen years I'd lived in Whitby several unlucky souls had lost their lives.

I went to the front window and watched Victor swing the garden gate shut and turn and walk down the street. On his way he waved to the postman who paused outside our house, pulled a letter from the pile in his hands and unlatched the gate.

He dropped it through the letterbox and I bent down to pick it up.

I looked down at the letter in my hand - another from my solicitor. I placed it onto the sideboard amongst the other bills and correspondence I needed to go through. Only a fortnight after moving in, I felt overwhelmed with bills, admin and emails that needed to be paid or replied to.

I headed to our galley kitchen to make a cup of tea. Digby followed me, limpet style, keen to remind me he was ready for his walk.

I looked down at him. 'It's only six o'clock. Surely too early even for you?'

He gazed back up at me with pearly eyes and a wagging tail that suggested otherwise.

I plucked a couple of dog biscuits from the box, threw one across the kitchen floor, which he skidded after, Scooby Doo style, and dropped the other biscuit into his bowl.

I straightened up and pressed my fingers lightly upon my abdomen. On Monday, if it still felt sore, I'd make a doctor's appointment.

With a feeling of dread at what I'd find, I carried my cup of tea upstairs, past Clara's bedroom door and up the second flight to my attic room. When I opened the door and stepped inside, the air felt damp and chilled.

What a mess.

I gave a deep sigh and stepped around the fragments of glass, then peered into the buckets which only had an inch of water at the bottom - the rest had dripped onto the floor and left me standing barefoot in a soggy pool. I hoped it hadn't soaked through to Victor's bedroom ceiling. Damn - I should have put towels down, too. But at least it had stopped raining and the paintwork around the skylight looked undamaged.

Foolishly, I hadn't got around to taking out house insurance. That would be Saturday night's entertainment. Living the single parent's dream. Was it going to be any easier than cohabiting with a gambling addict? No doubt, but I'd have equally as many but different stresses to deal with.

I dressed in jeans and a jumper and my thoughts drifted to my interview that afternoon. I felt certain the only reason I'd been offered an interview was because I was local and expertise round here limited. I was hardly qualified as an Import Administrator. My background was more thespian and hospitality based, although I had spent a long time writing and perfecting my application and letter to give myself the best chance. Prior to having the twins, I'd studied at the London School of Speech and Drama, and for three years after that I'd acted professionally in plays and gone on to tour with the Hull Docks Theatre Company.

After only two seasons I'd fallen in love with Noah, the Stage Manager, and a while later had unintentionally fallen pregnant before we'd even considered, discussed or felt ready to start a family. Fortunately, I'd been madly in love with Noah so although I'd been terrified, equally I'd been thrilled to discover we were expecting twins - a family in one painful and exhausting swoop. The downside was that my acting career had to take a hiatus.

At five months pregnant with my belly already too huge to perform my stage role, we'd made the decision to move to Whitby, where Noah's parents lived, and Noah had set up his own business as an electrician, which he'd previously qualified for as part of his stage management training. After a year he had earned double the money he'd made in the theatre, and with the twins taking up all of my time and energy, we never regretted our move.

I'd always imagined when Clara and Victor were old enough, I'd return to acting, but when the time came, I realised how impractical it would be to perform in a theatre each night. Noah often didn't get in from work until eight and he'd always be exhausted. So when the twins started nursery school, I worked part time in the local tourist information office whilst I studied for a Postgraduate Business and Tourism qualification. Most likely it had been that qualification that had helped me to secure the interview today.

It had been ten years since my last job interview, a fairly informal thing with Roddy, who owned the Captain Cook Experience with his boat, *The Cook's Endeavour*. I'd already known Roddy from the local pub where I'd sometimes joined in the folk evenings with my moderately tuneful voice. Roddy played a mean banjo and we'd been close friends for years. And it was Roddy who employed Victor when he wasn't at school, to help him out when fishing in between tourist seasons.

But I could no longer afford to work only the warmer months and I didn't fancy being a fisherwoman out of season.

The salary hadn't been stated in the advert, but the woman at the agency implied the person who previously filled the role had been well rewarded. In short, I knew this could be a big opportunity for me and I couldn't afford to mess it up.

I felt the twins were mature enough to be more independent before and after school and during the school holidays. They hardly needed me around most of the time, and Victor had become a keen cook and often prepared the evening meals with the fish he caught. He baked bread and cakes too, so they wouldn't starve as long as there was food in the fridge and ingredients in the cupboards. More importantly, I felt ready for a new challenge, a new life, and although I'd loved being the tour guide on the boat, after ten years the novelty really had worn off. I'd miss Roddy and the crew, but I knew we'd meet up, and during music nights at The Anchor Inn.

Downstairs, I retrieved Digby's harness and lead from beneath the coat stand and bent down to strap him in. I only had to move to feel a twinge and be reminded of the wound in my belly. When I showered it had felt tender, but it didn't look deep, and certainly not bad enough to need stitches. Plus, the doctor's surgery wasn't open at the weekend and I had no intention of hanging around for hours at the hospital only to be told to keep it clean. I checked I had a couple of poo bags in my jacket pocket and I set off with Digby down to the beach.

I glanced at my phone - half-past seven. Noah should be awake by now and I dialled his number. It rang out and as his answer message kicked in, he picked up.

'Tess? Everything OK?'

'Yes, nothing to worry about. Well, nothing much.'

'One of the kids?' He sounded on edge.

'They're fine. I wondered how busy you were today. The skylight collapsed last night and there's glass and water everywhere. Would you have time to board it up? It's forecast rain tonight and the floorboards are already soaked.'

'Were you hurt?' I heard the concern in his voice.

'Not really. Bit of a shock though.'

'I've got a job this morning but I could come over one-ish?'

'Brilliant, thank you! You'll need your ladder. The twins will love seeing you.'

'I'd love to see them, too.' And his voice cracked as he spoke.

'Stay for tea if you like.' It was the least I could do, and after all the tension there'd been between us. Hopefully, we'd both manage to keep it friendly and avoid any of the accusations we'd got so used to hurling at one another - or more often, that I'd thrown at him.

His voice softened. 'I'd like that.'

Without deliberate intention, Noah knew precisely how to make me feel guilty. That was probably half the reason I'd stayed with him for so long when my rational brain had told me again and again I should get out. It wasn't as if I didn't threaten separation years ago when his gambling had spiralled out of control.

There were Saturdays he'd spend hours either at the bookies, or in more recent years, online. And his gambling wasn't limited to one sport: horses, football leagues, online poker. I'd grown sick of his lies and when I told him enough, it was finally over, I resolved there would be no going back.

After the sale of our family home, I'd managed to secure a small mortgage to buy Skygale. Noah had the thirty thousand

10

plus debt to pay off, and as far as I was concerned, that was his doing and therefore his responsibility. No way was I prepared to fund his gambling debts. I felt grateful that we'd never married - at least we didn't have the added stress of a divorce to go through. Noah might have earned the larger salary, but he'd spent wildly and irresponsibly, whereas I'd always kept to a tight budget with housekeeping and encouraged the children with their part-time jobs. Victor had begun working with Roddy when he was only thirteen, and Clara had worked a job in the fish and chip restaurant since she turned fourteen. They liked having their own money to be able to go out with their friends and to buy music and clothes.

The breeze felt chilly against my skin and I zipped up my jacket and continued towards the pier and beach.

Clouds drifted across the otherwise pale blue sky and the wind blew through the trees and shrubbery, but thankfully, with none of the force of last night. The storm had travelled on and the air felt fresh and invigorating.

Our street, Captain's Row, already felt familiar. Of course, I knew Whitby and all the narrow streets like the smile lines around my eyes. Parking was limited, though, and most households with two vehicles had to park in the car park down the hill. I was fortunate that the back of our house had one of the few parking spaces, which left very little garden, but we had a small decking area and cobbled yard where we could sit and enjoy whatever weather came our way.

We were overlooked by a hotchpotch of various shaped and sized cottages, but a large parasol would help create some privacy next summer. The previous owners had planted clematis around both the front and back doors and rose bushes lined the short path out onto the street. In our previous home the garden had been more Noah's responsibility and I managed pretty much everything in the house, although he'd lost interest in the garden in more recent years, and I'd taken to mowing the lawn and pulling up the weeds when things grew wild. Our new outdoor areas would be easy in comparison.

Digby, our three year old beagle, tugged eagerly at his lead. A bag of half-eaten soggy chips lay strewn at the side of the footpath and he strained to get nearer.

11

I pulled him to heel. 'Leave, Digby.' That dog could sniff out a morsel from fifty feet away.

Since childhood I'd wanted a beagle and when we'd first brought Digby home as a pup a couple of people warned me that beagles never stopped craving food. Their warnings had proven to be fortelling. At his recent booster appointment, the vet had advised that Digby was borderline overweight and if I didn't get a grip on his intake now, he'd be obese in a year. Since then we'd been careful not to give in to his pleading or leave snacks and plates of food lying around.

After one Sunday lunch in our last home, we'd all drifted away from the dining table without immediately clearing up. That was until I heard Clara shriek for me to come and see. I hurried back in to see Digby nose deep in the chicken carcass, body trembling and tail wagging furiously.

Clara had her phone out and videoed him, whilst laughing hysterically.

'Digby, will you get down?' I called.

He turned his face to me, briefly, before turning back to the chicken with added gusto.

I marched over. 'Right now, young man.' I took a hold of his collar and with much reluctance, he jumped down from the dining table.

'There was enough chicken left for a curry, you cheeky mutt,' I chided.

I wrapped the carcass in a bag and chucked it in the bin. Digby gazed up at me - looking immensely proud and without a glimmer of guilt in his big dewy eyes.

Even before we'd moved house, the beach had always been a favourite spot to walk Digby, especially when the tide was out. When time allowed, I'd march a good couple of miles towards Sandsend, leaving behind most of the dog walkers, who tended to stay nearer the town.

This morning the storm tide had retreated, but frothy tipped waves pounded forth onto the sand a good distance away. The tide had come right up last night, evidenced by a trail of seaweed, pebbles and driftwood lining the foot of the rocks and cliffs.

Digby set off running. He darted randomly here and there, stopped, then sniffed, and cocked his leg against a pile of seaweed, then he bounded up to another dog to check out whether they were more alpha than he was or to exchange a mutual appreciation of one another's privates.

I looked back to the harbour and the wall of the pier that jutted out beyond the cliffs on the far side of the town. The lighthouse at the end, a tower of modest stature and beauty, stood proud and resolute despite its ornamental status. The colourful houses of the town, snugged tight on the rise of the hillside, hugged one another as if deliberately built to foster a closeness between the people who resided there. That sense of intimacy had, I think, gone today, and whilst I'd come to know many of the townsfolk, there were plenty more who preferred to keep their lives and business amongst their own circle, rather than share all their cares and sundry with those around them.

I set off briskly to catch up with Digby and reflected on my phone call with Noah. He wanted to make things work between us - he still believed our relationship could survive despite the troubles we'd been through. But I only wanted us to maintain a friendly relationship and that was mostly for the children's sake.

Unlike the twins, I'd barely seen Noah since the new owners had moved into our old home and I'd moved into the cottage with the twins. Noah had been offered a temporary room at his younger sister, Anna's house, which I think had been done more out of duty than of wanting him there. But they were family and I knew Noah felt grateful. Anna and her husband had three children under eight, and Noah insisted he would soon find his own place so that he could have the twins over to stay.

Could that be reason enough for him to quit his gambling habit and to save the necessary funds or deposit without squandering it away?

Tensions and arguments between us had seemed unrelenting, toxic and all pervasive for months, years even.

As I walked my thoughts drifted back to a Sunday six years ago when the twins were ten and we were to attend Noah's niece's christening at St. Mary's Church in front of the Abbey on the cliffs. I'd dressed the twins in their smartest outfits, gone to a lot of effort myself with my hair and a new dress, wrapped the

13

gift and written the card that I'd taken the time to buy, and when it was time to set off, Noah still hadn't returned from the bookies. I rang his mobile, but he didn't pick up, and twenty minutes before the ceremony was due to start, I walked with the twins into town and made a detour past the betting shop. As expected, there was Noah perched on a stool, staring up at the TV screen with a spellbound expression. Victor rapped on the window and some of the men inside looked our way. Noah, however, remained engrossed in the race.

'Wait here, you two. I'll fetch Dad,' I said, and gave an exasperated sigh, as the blood pounded in my heart and head. I hadn't stopped all morning; I'd cleaned the house, walked the dog, ironed our outfits and prepared some vegetables for the evening meal, whilst he'd sat on his backside gambling the housekeeping into oblivion.

I opened the shop door, marched up to Noah and tapped him on the shoulder.

He startled, swivelling round on his stool. He looked me up and down. 'Wow. You look pretty, my love. Where are you going?'

I rolled my eyes. 'Your niece's christening. Remember? Anna reminded you last night, as did I when you headed out this morning.'

'Oh, shit.' He glanced down at his watch. 'It's too late to get into my suit now. You go on without me, send my apologies and I'll see you at the after party,' he said, then swung back to the screen, to focus on more pressing matters.

'No! You know I can't bear church ceremonies. I'm only going because it's Anna and you know she'll go spare if we don't all make a show of family solidarity. Your mum and dad will be upset, too. It's important to them and it should be important to you, too.'

Without taking his eyes off the screen, he said, 'Please, Tess. Tell them I'm ill, or I've got an emergency job on. They'll understand.'

By now all other faces were on the spectacle of a woman trying to persuade her man to leave. Their patronising grins and sniggers made my cheeks burn and anger whirled through my head.

I'd had enough of the humiliation and I spun round to face them all. 'You think this is funny?'

Someone piped up. 'Yeah. Fucking hilarious, love.'

More sniggers and guffaws followed in surround sound.

'Noah.' I touched his arm. 'Are you coming or are you going to allow these men to mock me and your children?'

'No, love, I'm staying.' He stared at the screen, nodded his head and willed his horse faster. 'I'll make it up to you and Anna, Mum and Dad, too.'

I gave up trying to be discreet and my voice rose. 'This is really shitty, Noah. And you still can't see why I don't think we have a future?'

The room fell silent.

I turned, stormed away and slammed the shop door behind me. I didn't look back as I took hold of the children's hands and we headed towards the old town.

After the church ceremony and in the Anchor Inn, Anna strode up to me at the bar. 'So, where's my brother?'

I looked down at Clara and Victor. 'You go see Gran and Grandad and I'll bring your Cokes over.'

They sensed the tension, and both looked from me to Anna before they turned and walked away. I waited until I saw them greet their Grandparents before I turned back to her.

'I'm afraid Noah was so busy gambling in the bookies that he couldn't make it. He asked me to lie to you, but why should I? That's the truth of it. It was a lovely ceremony.'

Anna glared at me with her chin jutting forwards. 'Seriously, Tess, and you didn't try to persuade him or talk sense into him? Thanks a lot!'

'I hope you're not blaming me for Noah's gambling. He knows I loathe it. No, Anna, it's his problem and he needs to sort himself out. Maybe you can talk some sense into him because he certainly doesn't listen to anything I have to say on the subject.'

Her face flushed and her voice rose. 'You're his partner!'

And I could see she was close to tears.

'It's a woman's job to keep her man on the right track. It's not as if you're usually afraid to speak your mind.'

I sighed. 'I don't want to argue. I can't control what he does, any more than he controls me. But you know I'll talk to him again

15

and I'm sorry he didn't come. I really did try to persuade him. Let's enjoy the party. Everyone else is here and I'll be damned if we should let Noah spoil it in his absence. It's not as if he'll be stressing about it.'

The barman came up to serve me. 'What can I get you ladies?' I turned to him. 'A glass of dry white wine. The largest glass you have. In fact, make it a bottle. How about you, Anna?'

That evening, when the twins and I returned from the christening party, I found Noah in the kitchen preparing dinner. This was a rarity and I knew guilt had driven him to it.

The twins turned on the TV and squabbled over what to watch.

'You could have joined us at The Anchor - I presume the bookies closed at four?'

Noah didn't turn around, but remained with his back to me, as he stirred the pan.

'I'm cooking chilli and garlic bread. I bet the twins are hungry.'

'Probably not. They've been eating iced buns and crisps all afternoon and are hyped up with Coca-cola. I'll eat it though.' I hadn't touched the christening buffet, and had drunk one glass of wine after another.

'You go sit down, love. I'll give you a shout when it's ready.'

'No. I want to talk to you.'

'Let's talk later when the kids are in bed,' he said, his back still to me.

'It won't take long. In fact, you don't need to say anything at all.'

Noah laid the wooden spoon down on the worktop and turned to face me. 'Fire away.' He shifted awkwardly and folded his arms.

I took a deep breath and maintained steady eye contact. 'If you don't quit gambling, both with your time and our money, then I'm leaving you. You've got a week to show me, or that's it. I'm not having our children living with a gambling addict, which is what you are.'

His face paled and he ran his hands through his hair. 'You're wrong.' There was desperation in his voice. 'I'm not an addict.'

'Then prove it to me. I'm so tired of your lies. How do you think I felt today when I had to walk into the bookies and you ignored me and left me and the children to go to your niece's christening alone? I felt humiliated with all those men laughing. Then Anna blamed me entirely for your absence, but most of all I felt disappointed and sad.'

Noah's shoulders drooped and he nodded slowly. 'You're right. I'm wrong and I will prove to you and the twins that I can quit. Give me a week.'

He reached out his arms, and once more as I gave him the benefit of the doubt, we embraced and held one another.

I cried. 'I bloody love you. Quit for me and the kids, but mostly for you.'

And I did love him, deeply. I didn't want to tear our family apart. I didn't want us to leave our beautiful home and the life we'd built together, albeit an imperfect life. It still felt good, some of the time.

After a week or two I felt sure Noah meant what he said and for a while I fell into that deluded state of ignoring the signs - the signs that he had learnt to hide only too well.

But it didn't last long.

I couldn't go back to watching him fool himself each time he placed a bet or spy on his every move and bank transaction. And his betrayal over remortgaging the house without my knowledge or consent had been a deceit too far and an obstacle too high for our partnership to surmount. It wasn't even about the money so much as the trust between us, and when trust is gone what is really left?

My thoughts returned to the present when I heard Digby bark, and I turned and saw him running in wide circles after a grey whippet. Poor Digby hadn't a chance of keeping up with such a lithe and nimble creature, but he gave it his best. If he stopped yapping, he'd have more energy for a better turn of speed.

I looked over at the dog's owner. I didn't recognise him from my previous walks.

He laughed and said, 'He's a trier, I'll give him that.'

The man walked closer and I saw the fans of lines around his brown eyes and generous mouth.

17

I laughed and called over. 'He's trying everybody's patience most of the time.' I was kidding of course - I adored Digby - his playfulness, cheekiness, and the endless affection he bestowed on us and allowed us to bestow on him.

'Are you local?' He squinted his eyes in the sunlight and extended his hand. 'I'm Gil.'

I shook his hand which felt firm but cold. 'I'm Tess. Yes, lived here for years.' I noticed how well built he was, and attractive, with thick, curly greying hair. 'Are you visiting Whitby?'

'Not exactly. I live out past Sandsend at Skarforth. Bruce has a vet's appointment. Nice stretch to walk him first so he doesn't mess up the surgery.'

'I'm going that way later. I've got an interview at Aztec Imports. Do you know them?'

He paused and gave a half-smile. 'Well... you could say I know of them.' He seemed reluctant to say more.

'Then I shall find out more soon.'

He stroked his stubble chin. 'Good luck - hope you get the job.'

'Thanks.' I paused. 'Nice to meet you, Gil.'

'You too, Tess.'

'Come on Diggers,' I called, and threw the man a wave.

He lifted his hand in return, and turned back towards the town.

The wind blustered up from the sea as I walked on, parallel to the surf and the rolling waves. There were no other dog walkers this far out of town and Digby scampered amongst the rocks beneath the cliffs, no doubt sniffing out fish or crabs washed up in the storm. He disappeared out of view and I headed back up the beach. The twins used to love it here with me and Noah and would clamber over the rocks to play hide and seek between the inlets and caves.

I looked down at the patterns and ripples in the sand and stepped over the deeper pools of saltwater left by the receding tide, when a sparkle of silver caught my eye and I paused and crouched down to take a closer look. I picked up the object, shook away the sand and placed it in my palm - one silver hook earring with delicate Celtic swirls above a small Whitby jet stone. It must have been lost recently, such was its shine, and most likely purchased from one of the jewellers here in the town. It was pretty and such a shame to be separated from its twin. I slipped it into my jacket pocket and continued up the beach.

Digby darted between rocks at the foot of the cliff which towered more than a hundred feet to the top and the north end of town. He'd all but disappeared but I noticed his tail wagging wildly. He'd obviously sniffed out something that held his interest, a dead fish maybe, and I climbed onto the rocks and jumped from one to the next.

'Come on, Digby.'

But he didn't raise his head and I heard him whine.

'What've you fo...' I stopped; my heartbeat sounded loud in my ears as my eyes focused on something near to Digby. For a moment I hesitated, afraid of the reality, and I took a deep breath in and stepped closer.

There could be no doubting what Digby had discovered and I stood still, looking down, my breaths jagged and tears already blurring my vision.

A woman, naked, lay face down in the sand a few feet into the cave. Her dark hair straggled across her face which was turned to one side, and her long, slim, lifeless limbs splayed out at ungainly angles. I clipped Digby to his lead, pulled him back and crouched down beside her. I lifted a few strands of her hair from her pale waxen cheeks and her seawashed, salty eyes stared out blankly. Her lips and fingertips had a tinge of blue and there were bruises and scrapes over her skin where her body must have scuffed against the rocks. I saw the height and shape of a woman, but her face revealed her as no more than a child. Might she be a pupil or student from the High School or the College who got caught up in the waves as they battered the coastline? Sometimes the waves washed over the pier and there had been a couple of occasions where those seeking the spectacle of storm-tossed waves had been swept out to sea. But that hadn't happened here in over a decade. And if it had been an accidental drowning, would she be naked?

On trembling legs I stepped around to her other side and when I saw the unmistakable swell of her heavily pregnant abdomen my legs gave way and I dropped to my knees. I gasped and fell backwards at the sight of death. Not one, but two innocent lives extinguished.

My fingers trembled as I pulled out my phone and dialled 999.

I sat down on a nearby rock and turned to face away from the girl. Bile burned the back of my throat, sweat prickled and seeped from my pores and my heart raced ever faster the more I tried to control my thoughts. I'd never seen a dead body first hand, let alone one so exposed and from a death so violent and in someone so young.

Sirens sounded from the town and moments later two police cars drove onto the sands and headed up the beach towards me. I stood on a rock and waved my arms. Within seconds they had pulled up and four officers jumped out and marched my way.

A female officer approached me. 'You found the body?'

I nodded and wiped my hands across my eyes.

I moved aside as she and a male officer approached the dead woman and squatted down beside her.

My legs felt unsteady and I knelt beside Digby and stroked his back. Sensing my distress he nuzzled into me and whined and my eyes stung and welled with tears.

A second female officer stepped closer.

'Could I ask a few questions?'

I stood back up and wrapped my arms around myself. 'There isn't much I can tell you. My dog ran over and discovered her here. If he hadn't, I wouldn't have seen her. I don't recognise her, and I haven't heard of anyone reported missing.'

'How long have you been on the beach and did you see anyone else around?'

'I saw a few people further down the beach but nothing going on here specifically.'

'Anyone you recognised or names?'

'I recognised a couple of faces, and chatted briefly to a gentleman walking his whippet. His name was Gil.'

'And did you walk this way yesterday and see anything suspicious?'

'I didn't come down yesterday, sorry.'

She nodded. 'I'll take your details and we'll contact you if we need to interview you. Do you live locally?'

'On Captain's Row,' I replied, and gave her my name, number and address.

As I turned to leave, an ambulance drove along the sands and I noticed several walkers talking in a group, their curiosity piqued by the unfolding drama. My stomach churned and my mind filled with questions and an overwhelming sadness. What could have happened for the girl to have been either out at sea on a boat or to have got caught up in the storm? Heavily pregnant, too. There was something about her, her nakedness and her swollen belly, maybe even in her lifeless eyes, that told me someone had done her wrong.

The officers began setting up tape and cones to cordon off the immediate area and I moved further back. Two more police vehicles arrived and my stomach turned over and over as they erected a screen to keep the body hidden from prying eyes.

A middle aged gentleman from the group of onlookers came up to me. 'What's happened? Looks bad!'

I nodded, still tearful. 'Yes, I'm afraid a young woman has died. I believe she drowned.'

His hand flew to his mouth. 'Good God! Is she local?'

'I don't know. I'm sorry, I must get home.' I turned away, eager to retreat from the questions and gossip of the townsfolk, who would be keen to hear all of the details first hand. The drowning of a pregnant woman would shock everyone in Whitby, let alone the poor girl's family and friends. Maybe she had a partner waiting for her to return home. I walked quickly. Tears blurred my eyes and the broken skylight and the soreness in my belly seemed trivial in comparison. Death had always seemed to be something distant and clinical and for the aged who'd come to the end of their lives, not a young woman with new life growing inside of her.

As an actor in my teens and twenties, I'd performed plays where the experience of death and the portrayal of the emotional aftermath had been a frequent occurrence. Death added to the drama, but without the full emotional impact of real life. I'd even acted out death in one play by drowning in the bath. A shudder ran through me. Nothing could have prepared me for discovering

21

something of such magnitude and I wasn't even related to the young woman.

I'd ring the police later to see what they'd found out about her. Although I doubted they'd be prepared to share much with me. The image of the drowned woman, splayed out and lifeless, flashed through my mind. I felt a tightening in my throat as if a hand clasped round it and my head reeled as a wave of grief for someone I'd never known made my body tremble.

Who was the girl, and where had she come from? My guts twisted in protest and I hurried towards home.

The past twelve hours had thrown me some horrible shocks. I hoped the rule of threes wasn't at play and that nothing would jeopardise my interview. Maybe I should try to rearrange it for next week when I'd have calmed down. But that might do me no favours if the job was as good as it appeared to be and they had other candidates to interview. I had one other interview lined up, but that was as a tourism Administrator in Scarborough. The salary was far less than I needed to survive financially, and the petrol there and back each day would add to expenses. Noah was supposed to be paying us maintenance, not that we'd seen any evidence of it yet, and my bank account had run desperately low - bills needed paying.

I hurried up the ramp beside the pier with Digby trotting at my side, and up the main street, past the fish and chip restaurants, bars, boutiques and souvenir shops. The shop fronts were opening and the pavements had filled with people going about their business. I could tell by the atmosphere of normality that the news of the woman's body hadn't reached this far yet, and I didn't want to be the one to break it to them.

People might find out that I'd discovered the body and I didn't relish the idea of having to describe the details, which I knew would be asked of me. I'd be approached by the local, even national press, if they discovered who I was.

On the other hand, I knew I'd do anything at all to help the police catch whoever had done this to her - if a crime had indeed been committed.

3

When I opened the front door to the cottage I smelled fresh coffee and toast. The girls were up. Digby's nose twitched keenly and when I unclipped his harness he trotted off to the kitchen to see what was cooking.

'Digby,' Clara called.

I heard Digby woof with excitement at finding Fleur with Clara. He loved nothing more than non-residents visiting, and always pestered them for attention and treats. I hung up my coat, reached into the pocket for the earring and went and stood in the kitchen doorway. 'Is there a coffee going spare?'

'Hey, Mum,' said Clara, looking up. 'I'll make you one.'

'Did you sleep OK?' I asked.

Clara turned to me. 'Yeah. Why?'

I sighed. 'A few dramas.'

Clara's brows pinched together. 'Why, what's happened?'

'A minor matter of the skylight falling in last night. I patched it up and was going to slip in beside you, but forgot Fleur was stopping over. Anyway, I slept on the sofa which was fine.'

Her forehead wrinkled. 'I didn't hear you.'

'You were sleeping soundly. I'm glad the storm didn't wake you.'

Fleur bent down and stroked Digby's ears. 'I didn't hear a thing.'

'And the skylight isn't the worst of it,' I said, quietly.

Clara handed me a mug of black coffee and I took a sip. 'I need this.'

'What else?' asked Clara and I saw the concern in her and Fleur's eyes.

'It's terrible. Upsetting.' My tears threatened and I took a deep breath and swallowed. 'I walked Digby along the beach. We were past the beach huts.' I paused, unsure how to go on. 'Digby... we found a body.'

'What? Not a human?' cried Clara.

'A young woman.'

'No way,' said Clara. She clapped a hand to her mouth, took a step back and leaned against the worktop.

'What if it's someone from school?' Fleur asked, and her voice trembled.

'I don't think so,' I said.

'How do you know if you don't know who she is?' said Clara.

'Because this young woman was pregnant. Quite visibly so.'

'Oh my fucking God,' said Clara. Her cheeks paled and her eyes pooled with tears. 'That's even more horrible.'

I put down my coffee cup and wrapped my arms around her. 'I know sweetheart. The police and ambulance are there and they'll do all they can to find out who she is, and her family, too.'

Fleur picked up Digby. 'I bet Digby was upset.'

'I think he was. He didn't want to leave her side.'

Clara drew away. 'Let's give him a biscuit. I know he's not supposed to, but he deserves a reward. If he hadn't found her, she'd still be lying there.'

She reached into the cupboard and grabbed a dog biscuit from the box. Still in Fleur's arms, Clara fed him and stroked his ears. 'Poor baby. Poor woman. Whitby will be on all the news channels.'

'No doubt,' I said.

'Poor you, too, Mum,' said Clara, and she turned round and gave me a hug. 'Take your coffee and we'll bring you some toast and jam. I bet you haven't eaten.'

'Thank you, darling. One slice will do.' I took my mug and sat on the old armchair by the front window. I pulled my phone from my jeans pocket and felt another jolt of pain. I took some slow breaths as I undid the top button of my jeans and checked beneath the plaster. There was no more blood, but the skin surrounding the wound looked inflamed and felt tender. I buttoned myself up and tapped the local BBC app. No Whitby headline as yet. As Clara's reaction had shown, this would upset everyone in the community. The unborn baby only added two-fold to the tragedy.

My interview wasn't until one, but I headed upstairs for a shower and to dress. As the hot water poured over me, I peeled off the plaster. A bruise had formed and when I pressed the centre, a pain shot through me. But I knew how lucky I'd been. I'd push my bed against the wall. Far better to forgo a starry night sky and avoid being impaled by glass again, even if the chances of that happening twice were slim. Clara had left my toast on my dressing table and I ate that before sweeping the floor once more to ensure no glass remained, then changed all the bedding.

I'd recently bought a fitted blue dress from 'Decadence', our only designer clothes shop in Whitby. The dress cost double what I'd usually spend but I knew how important first impressions could be. I'd picked up a virtually unworn pair of heeled designer shoes from the charity shop that accentuated my legs. I blow dried my blonde curls and pulled them into a flattering updo, then applied foundation and eye make-up to finish the look. I'd already read Aztec Imports' entire website which told me they'd been operating for twenty-three years and a brother and sister managed the business - largely the import of goods such as antiques, furniture, classic cars, paintings and even horses and other animals. All expensive, exclusive items for, no doubt, high spending clients.

I'd never been intimidated by wealthy people, even though I'd never possessed any wealth myself. That was down to my parent's influence. Dad, who was Polish born and gifted at languages, worked as a language teacher in a private school. He'd lived in England since early childhood, and my Mum, also with Polish parents but born in Somerset, worked as a lecturer of Business and Economics at Bath University. Through Mum and Dad's work, and from an early age, I'd met and mixed with monied families as well as academics, and some of their confidence and conversation skills rubbed off on me.

Clara appeared in the doorway and she peered up at the covered skylight before turning her eyes to me. 'You look great, Mum.'

I looked down at my dress and smoothed the skirt. 'I'm hoping to impress them. I only hope they're friendly and don't ask too many tricky questions.'

'Mum?'

'Yes.'

'I need to talk to you about something.'

I sat down on the bed and crossed my legs. 'Of course, darling. What is it?'

Clara sat down beside me, put her hands in her lap and gave a heavy sigh. But before she'd said a word Digby began barking and a man's voice called from downstairs.

'Anyone home?'

Clara smiled and jumped up. 'I didn't know Dad was coming.'

'He's offered to board up the skylight until I get a glazier in.' I stood up too and headed onto the landing. 'We're coming down.' I shouted over the bannister rail. 'But what did you want to talk about?' I asked Clara who was already half-way down the stairs.

She paused and turned. 'Oh, only if Fleur can stay over again.'

'Of course, as long as her parents don't mind not spending time with her.'

'She's gone home so they're seeing her today,' replied Clara. 'They're not very nice anyway. Fleur doesn't get on with them. They're way too strict.'

'In what way?'

'They're always on her case about studying.'

I had firm views on pressuring children with schoolwork, or not, which was my preference.

'They probably think they're doing her a favour.'

'They're not though. Fleur is stressed out.'

'Oh dear. Maybe it's good if she can spend time here and you two can study quietly together. You're doing similar subjects aren't you?'

'Pretty much. Thanks, Mum.'

'Come on. Let's see your Dad. Fleur can stay when she wants - weekends though.' I followed Clara down.

'It's cool you and dad are still friends,' she said.

'I agree. And I want you and Vic to see plenty of him, too.' However, I knew that remaining friends with Noah might not prove easy on either of our parts, even with good intentions.

'Daddy!' cried Clara as we reached the bottom of the stairs. She ran over and flung her arms around him.

'Hope you didn't mind me walking in, but the door wasn't locked,' he said, and looked over Clara's shoulder.

'It's fine. I appreciate you coming.' I thought how smart and fresh he looked.

He'd trimmed his grainy stubble and had a new haircut that showed off his still dark hair framed around fine features, a hawkish

26

nose, half-moon cheekbones and china blue eyes. He wore chinos with a denim shirt. Noah was still trim and handsome and with a lurch in my stomach, I realised he'd have no problem attracting women.

'You look well,' I said.

'I've given up the booze and takeaways to save money,' he said and patted his flat belly.

'I should too,' I said, although I couldn't remember the last time I'd eaten a takeaway. Noah seemed in a good mood. Maybe he was happy to see us, or perhaps there was something else.

'You look lovely. A wedding to go to?' asked Noah.

'Ha ha,' I said. 'It's my interview. I told you about it.'

'You did.' He smiled. 'Feeling nervous?'

'A bit, mostly because I don't know what to expect. I know so little about importing.'

'Maybe admit what you don't know but say you're a quick learner,' said Noah.

'No Mum,' Clara said, still holding her Dad's hand. 'You need to blag it. They'll want someone who can talk their way confidently through tricky situations - that's what employers are looking for. You're good at talking, anyway.'

'Thanks,' I said. 'How do you know that's what employers want?'

'Mr Everington in Economics says so.'

'You mean fake it until you make it, kind of thing. Isn't that old school? Aren't we all supposed to be authentic and open about our weaknesses and flaws these days?'

'I don't know if it's old school, but apparently it works,' she said, and nodded with a knowing glint in her eye.

'OK, then I'll bear Mr Everington's wisdom in mind.'

'Do you want to show me the damage?' Noah asked.

'And I'll make us a brew,' said Clara. 'Tea, Dad?'

'Thanks, sweetheart,' said Noah.

Noah followed me up to the attic.

I heard him sigh and I paused and turned around.

'You OK?'

He nodded and gave a slim smile. 'Sure, but it feels strange visiting your house.'

27

'It'll take some getting used to for all of us,' I replied and continued up the stairs.

We walked into my bedroom and Noah looked around. 'This is lovely.'

'It looked better before last night,' I said, and gazed up at the pinned bin liners. 'But yes, we're beginning to settle. I need this job though.'

Noah stood beneath the skylight. 'You know you don't have to work full time. I can support you.'

'I know you'd like to,' I said, but I also knew this was wishful thinking on his part and in reality I had no other way of supporting myself and the children.

Noah had debts to pay and until they were settled, he couldn't easily afford a place of his own. Besides, I wanted to do this for myself. I'd turned forty a couple of months back; the twins were growing up fast and in two years they'd be away at Uni. I still had time to build a career. I'd thought about going back into professional acting, but I wasn't confident the time was right, what with splitting from Noah and the twins feeling unsettled by it all. The life of an actor meant time away from home, evenings and unsociable hours, and I didn't feel overly confident leaving two teenagers alone to their own devices. I trusted them, but they needed my presence and support.

'Your bed was beneath the skylight?' Noah asked.

'Yes, right up until the glass sprayed down and impaled me. Only minimal damage done. I'd show you the wound but it's beneath my dress.'

Noah looked at me and said quietly, 'I'd like to see you beneath that dress.' His eyes flickered. 'I'm missing being close to you.'

'It'll take both of us time to adjust,' I said.

He came closer. 'We don't have to adjust. Not if we don't want to.'

I shook my head and took a step back. 'Please, not now.'

He let out a long breath.

'Let's talk when we have more time,' I said. But I didn't want to talk about us at all. We'd been through his defending arguments over and over again. I felt emotionally drained still, and any idea of a repeat made me feel ill.

His voice turned testy. 'Fine, if that's how you want it.' He paused for a moment. 'Listen, I didn't want to mention it in front of Clara, but have you heard about the body of a young woman found drowned on the beach? I wondered if it might be a girl from secondary school or college.'

My legs weakened, and I sat down on the edge of the bed. 'Clara knows.' I paused. 'It was Digby and me that found her. Well, Digby.'

'Shit!' He came and sat down beside me.

'Clara's shaken up, and we don't know yet if it's a girl from Whitby or elsewhere.'

His eyes searched mine. 'Have the police interviewed you?'

I nodded. 'I told them what little I know.'

Noah put an arm around me. 'Do you feel OK?'

'Not really.'

Noah drew me close and I leaned my head on his shoulder. He stroked my hair and planted a kiss on my head. 'I love you, Tess. I want to take care of you.'

I straightened up again and his arm slid away.

'I know you do. And I'm glad we can still be friends, for us and the children.'

He looked at me, blinking, and his eyes glistened. 'I'll always want more.'

'We've been through this.' My voice rose. 'And if you can start by paying off those debts and giving up gambling...' I knew I sounded callous but I couldn't back down - not again.

He stood up. 'I have already started,' he replied, his tone defensive.

I looked up at him. 'Good. Keep going and your life will improve no end.'

'I'm doing this for you. I want to make things right between us.'

'Do it for yourself and the children.' I stood up, too. 'I need to go. When you use the ladders, let Clara help.'

Noah gazed up at the blacked-out skylight and sighed. 'Leave it with me. It'll be sorted by the time you get back.' He turned back to me and gave a slim smile. 'Break a leg.'

'I suppose it is a performance, of sorts.'

'It is. And you want an Oscar.'

'I'd settle for a job offer and a half decent pay packet.'

29

4

The Interview

As I drove my old VW Polo up the hill and out of town, then onto the Northern road that followed the coast, I reflected on Noah's generosity to help me out. He'd always been a hands-on and practical partner and father. Maybe not so brilliant at sharing the housework, but he did all the internal repairs and most of the decoration. He'd also done the weekly grocery shopping, which I hated doing. If only he could have quit the gambling, as he'd promised repeatedly, I'd have loved him forever and never have split our family apart.

But he'd long been blinded by his addiction. A part of him saw my leaving him as a symptom that I no longer loved him. Maybe he was right in part. Maybe I no longer loved him enough to tolerate his addiction, as I had ten years ago. I might have been far from perfect, but my faults weren't on the same destructive scale. And Noah rarely complained about them. Either way, they didn't have the same ruinous impact.

Snapping myself out of these thoughts, I turned back to the job. From what I'd read online, Aztec Imports appeared to have a diverse repertoire of import services, and it seemed their focus was more on importing, and less so, exporting. I wondered how Brexit had impacted their business. Had it created more admin, costs and hoop jumping? I wouldn't claim to know much about that side of things, but there had to be government and business information sites to inform businesses on the new processes. The job description had been brief and focused more on professional qualities as opposed to specific skills. My admin skills were on the rusty side, but I could speed type accurately like no one else I knew - something I'd picked up with minimal effort when doing my business qualification. I could speed read, too - another thing that came naturally to me. Although not quite a photographic memory, if I gave something my focus, I could retain what I read, including dates and numbers. If all else failed, I'd sell myself on the skills that had made learning copious lines for my acting roles a breeze. I'd inherited my ability to memorise things from my Mum, along with my pearly blonde curls.

I loved driving the coastal road which helped to settle my nerves. Wind-bent trees dotted the verges, and they leaned in the direction of the cliff-tops and the ocean beyond. Patchwork fields of crops in varying hues spread across the slopes inland and made way to wild heather clad moors in the distance.

Three miles out of Whitby, I headed down the hill and into Sandsend. The tide had retreated and the beach was dotted with walkers and a few kites hung high in the air. I continued over the stone bridge that crossed the stream and curved round to Lythe Hill that led out of the village, and on until I reached St. Oswalds, a charming Norman church.

The drive leading to Lorton Hold was first right past the church. I glanced at the clock. Ten minutes early. Hopefully enough to appear keen and reliable.

As I approached, the house looked more of a castle, with a hexagonal tower to one side and turrets that topped the perimeter of the roof. It didn't look medieval, and I imagined it had been built in the late nineteenth or early twentieth century. The gardens looked beautifully maintained with an array of colourful shrubs planted along the front walls of the castle which softened its appearance. I pulled into a space between a black Porsche and a blue BMW convertible. Both had personalised number plates. Expensive cars, and a sure sign the business was successful. The lawns were freshly cut and striped in the way that Noah and I had never tried to cultivate. Thank goodness I'd made an effort to dress well. My Polo looked decidedly shabby between two shining symbols of affluence.

I rapped the knocker on the front door, glossy black and twice the size of my cottage door, and I stood back. I wouldn't have been at all surprised if a uniformed butler came to the door. I heard a single but obvious cough, and footsteps that crunched on the gravel behind me, and I turned and saw an elegant looking man in his middle years walking towards me. He was smartly but casually dressed in burgundy trousers and fitted black shirt.

'Hello,' I said. 'Tess Blonski. I've come for the interview.'

He smiled and held out his hand, large and long fingered, and his almond eyes, beneath dark scythe shaped brows, glimmered with interest. 'Stefan Temple. Pleased to meet you, Tess.'

I shook his hand. 'Pleased to meet you, too.'

He had a deep voice and an accent I couldn't place, possibly a hint of Italian. He might have been middle-aged but he was good-looking - he'd stand out amongst a group of younger men and not only because of his build and height. He had a slightly hooked nose that suggested intelligence, above full lips. His fair hair, streaked with grey, was swept back and his chin was clean shaven.

His hand held mine - warm and firm. 'You found us OK?'

I noticed he had an expressive mouth - mobile, yet determined. 'Yes, Google maps. Hard to go wrong, really.'

He smiled. 'Of course.' Then he turned the door handle and pulled it wide. 'I know that Judi, my sister and business partner, is looking forward to meeting you.'

I followed him through.

'I can't tell you how keen we are to get the right person in,' he continued. 'Our last assistant had to leave suddenly for family matters. Judi and I have been taking in the slack.'

The entrance hall looked spacious, but light that filtered through from the window left it dimly lit and I felt a chill against my skin. Despite the low light I saw the floorboards had been polished to a nutbrown gleam - no muddy boots came through this way. I spotted a prominent stag's head with long, branch-like antlers above the marble fireplace, and three deer heads fixed in vertical lines on either side. A large gilt framed mirror also hung above the fireplace and there were two carved wooden chairs placed in front. As we walked through, I admired what looked like an antique Ming vase set at the centre of a table. On the walls hung contemporary paintings, mostly of lithe semi-naked women in a neoclassical style. A bold statement that complemented the architectural style of the building and furnishings.

I breathed in a delicious sandalwood scent that filled the air. My heels clicked as he led me down a corridor and into the most opulent dining room I had ever seen, other than those roped off in stately homes. But this was a modernised version - mustard wallpaper with a gold and blue design, a beautiful central chandelier and a twenty foot long dining table that could have seated thirty people, easily. The walls, too, were exquisitely hung with original artworks.

'Judi?' he called through to a room that led off. 'Tess has arrived.'

'I'm on my way,' a confident voice replied.

'Please excuse our casual wear, but we only suit up when necessary.' He appraised my appearance and smiled with appreciation. 'You look exceptionally smart. A great start, Tess.'

How direct. And to my embarrassment, I felt my cheeks simmer. A self-conscious reaction I wasn't used to. 'I like the idea of dressing smartly for work. As you'll see from my application, my last job was as a tour guide on a boat. Fascinating history about Captain Cook, but I had to wear a Captain Cook replica jacket with jodhpurs, hat and riding boots.'

He laughed. 'Splendid stuff! Still, I can see why you might like a change.' He pulled out a chair. 'Let's talk business.'

A woman walked into the room. Immediately, she struck me as a fairer Winona Ryder, and I almost felt surprised when she introduced herself. 'I'm Judi, younger sister of dear Stefan.'

'Younger in years, but altogether maturer in every other respect,' replied Stefan, and when he came closer I noticed a spicy aroma hung in the air.

She gave a half-smile through pursed lips. 'Please don't put Tess off before we've even asked her to sit down.'

'It's important Tess sees our full authentic selves.'

He smiled my way and I noticed how his straight pearly white teeth contrasted against the redness of his lips.

How refreshing, I thought. They both had a sense of humour and I knew from experience that made working with anybody a whole lot easier.

Stefan indicated for me to sit down and they took a seat on either side.

Awkward positioning. I should ensure I addressed them both equally.

Stefan turned towards me and with forearms resting on the table he linked his fingers loosely together. 'Let me tell you about what we do here. I know the job description is brief and that is deliberate because the full scope of our enterprise is wide and might intimidate some.' He paused for a moment but maintained clear eye contact. 'We have supplier links all over the world - some we work with regularly, and others we may only buy from once. Almost exclusively we source and import bespoke items for clients here in the UK.'

'Our clientele are successful folk and use our expertise in buying and transporting because they want the best and they want their goods to arrive quickly, reliably and safely. They are prepared to pay more for our service and therefore we do not get things wrong.' He paused again and lifted a finger. 'Let me rephrase that. We do get things wrong, or at least others in the chain do, but we rectify this as quickly and seamlessly as possible so that our client is blissfully unaware of any hitches. For us, outward appearances and smooth operations for our clients are essential.'

I looked around - the house, the gardens, the cars, the oh so attractive and polished Stefan and Judi. I nodded and smiled. 'You want your clients to feel confident that you'll deliver in every respect.'

'Exactly, Tess,' said Stefan. 'And 99% of the time we do.'

'The other 1% we do whatever we can to minimise the damage and compensate,' As Judi spoke, she lifted her head and her back and neck seemed to elongate a couple of inches. 'Our customer service history is exemplary and our clients leave their testimonials on our website. You may have read some of them?'

I nodded in agreement. 'I did. Impressive, and clearly they value your services.'

'Our client base has expanded over the years because they know they can rely on us,' said Judi.

Judi was precise and firm with her movements, and I thought there seemed something slightly robotic about her. Almost too perfect. She was alluringly correct and restrained, a feminine version of her very masculine brother in appearance but with less natural and fluid confidence.

'Stefan and I have quite literally had to get up in the middle of the night and fly off to resolve issues. Not everything is possible over the phone or by Zoom.'

Her foreign accent seemed more subtle and her queen's English slightly affected. No doubt they'd both received expensive educations.

'Now,' said Stefan. 'I see your background is quite varied and whilst I can see you have an excellent business qualification, we are equally interested in the character of the candidate we hire. How do you think your experience and who you are as a person, can benefit our business?'

I leaned back in my chair and took a moment to consider his question. 'I might not always feel it inside, but outwardly I believe I come across as confident and polite. I'd also say I'm this way with people from all avenues of life. When I worked on the boat I'd talk to the tourists as a group, but often afterwards, some would seek me out to ask specific questions. And our visitors ranged from CEO's, professors, teachers, history geeks, to families, local residents and school children. I knew my subject inside out, too, so there weren't many times I couldn't tell them what they wanted to know, even if they only wanted to sing Captain Cook's praises.

I looked at them both in turn, and Judi, who looked attentive, nodded with encouragement for me to continue.

'It's worth mentioning that I might not be an expert in any business areas, but I do have a near photographic memory and can speed read too. So, anything I need to learn I generally only need to read once or twice, and to understand the intricacies. Oh, and I can speed type, too.'

'My goodness,' said Judi, and formed a steeple with her perfectly manicured hands. 'Didn't you get bored on the boat trips day after day?'

'Rarely. Every trip was different. But I do feel ready for a new challenge.'

'Yes, I'm sure. Repetition day after day is not my thing at all and what we need here is someone who is prepared for plenty of challenges, learning and variety. It's not for a secretary who likes to be spoon fed and type all day.' She added with tightening lips.

I looked her keenly in the eye and smiled. 'Variety, learning and challenge suits me well.' I turned to Stefan and hoped he might be less prickly than his sister.

He tilted his head. 'I see you were an actress for a while.'

He spoke with pitch perfect neutrality, but of course, I knew this to be a question, as opposed to a statement.

I nodded. 'It seems like forever ago now, but I was reasonably good, or at least, I received some great reviews and offered lead parts in the theatre company I worked for. I had to give up touring when my babies, the twins, came along. I don't regret that, but it was an exciting time in my life.'

He leaned in and rubbed his thumb across his chin. 'I see it was the Hull Docks Theatre Company you performed with.'

'Yes, do you know of them?'

He nodded and cupped his chin with his hand. 'As it happens, I've seen a couple of their productions at the Grand Theatre in York. My kind of theatre - none of this pretentious or abstract stuff some insist they enjoy.'

'York Grand is a beautiful old theatre. I performed in John Godber's *Shakers* there in 2004, and *Bouncers* in 2005.'

His eyes twinkled. 'Then our paths have crossed before. I saw *Shakers* in 2004. I remember the year because I went for my thirty-fifth birthday with my then girlfriend. Excellent. And you were in it?'

'I was indeed. I played Nicky, the dancer, aka, waitress. I still remember my monologue.'

'I loved that show. Better than Shakespeare or Beckett.'

'We did get rave reviews,' I said, and smiled. 'Took it down to the West End for a season, too.'

'A shame you had to give it all up,' said Judi. 'If you were that good. Who knows, you might have been on TV and in movies by now.'

'Maybe, but I wouldn't be without my children. They're the best. I know every parent says that, but it's true. They're sixteen and have started sixth form, so they're becoming more independent each day.' I hoped that snippet might win me some brownie points.

There came a knock on the door and we all turned. A face appeared, one that I recognised, but as he stood there and watched us, for the briefest moment I couldn't remember where from. But the moment he spoke I recalled.

He glanced my way and said, 'Sorry.' He looked from Stefan to Judy. Could I have a word with one of you?'

Stefan spoke promptly and quietly. 'It can't wait?'

The man said in a clipped tone. 'I'm afraid not.'

'Do you mind, Judi? I'll chat with Tess and show her the office.'

'Of course.' Judi pushed back her chair and with the slimmest of smiles looked from me to Stefan. 'I'll catch up with you soon.'

When Judi disappeared out of the room, I said, 'Does Gil work for you?'

'You know Gil?'

'Not exactly, but I met him on the beach this morning when walking my dog. He has a whippet, Bruce.'

Stefan scratched the side of his nose. 'Yes, Gil is our buildings, stables and land manager. Been with us a while and lives in the gatehouse. You'll have passed it at the top of the drive.'

'What a small world. And yet, up until last week I had no idea that Aztec Imports existed.'

'Almost all of our business is spread far and wide across Britain, not so much in the Whitby area. We often travel to see clients, or they come here. Our last assistant sometimes accompanied Judi or myself on short trips. Would that be something you might be interested in, family permitting?'

Without hesitation, I said, 'Yes, definitely. The twins' dad lives in Whitby and he loves to spend time with them.'

He leaned forwards and laced his fingers. 'You're a single parent then?'

'Only recently, but yes.'

Stefan nodded, but thankfully his manners didn't permit him to ask more. He pushed back his chair and stood up. 'Let me show you the office.'

I followed him through to a large open plan office furnished with four stunning oak desks positioned against each wall of the room, and an island in the middle with stools around.

'We sometimes hold our meetings here or in the dining room, but mostly in our working living room, through there.' He gestured.

'And do you have a shared customer data system?'

'We do, and it's easy to access and update, for which we can thank Gil who is quite brilliant with IT as well as being handy with all practical matters.'

'Sounds like you're lucky to have him.'

Stefan nodded slowly. 'We are. He's a fine man and a loyal friend, too.'

I liked the way Stefan talked about his staff, respectful and generous with his compliments.

'Do you have other employees?' I asked.

'Not for the business, but we have a cleaner, a gardener and a housekeeper, and you won't have seen, but we have a stable block at the back of the house. Currently, we have four horses and Gil is responsible for their care, too. We have local girls come and exercise the horses, in return for them mucking them out and cleaning their tack. Gil oversees their recruitment. Judi and I love to ride when we have time. There are some bridle paths along the coast down to Sandsend or further north and inland. I don't suppose you ride, do you, Tess?'

'I only learnt as part of my acting training years ago, but I do adore horses.'

A phone rang and Stefan reached into his pocket, turned down the volume, and said, firmly, 'Would you like to see the gardens?'

The interview seemed to be going well, I thought. 'I'd like that.'

'Good to know the whole environment of a workplace. No?'

I nodded. 'Certainly.' I got the strongest feeling he was going to offer me the job. But no, I shouldn't be presumptuous. Who knew how many other candidates they'd be interviewing?

We walked through to the smaller meeting room. Stefan opened the French doors and we headed out into the garden, with rose and hydrangea bushes that stretched along both sides of the lawn. In the height of summer, I imagined the garden must be a glorious sight. A cobbled path led down the middle of the lawn, and as we walked, I breathed in a heady scent of late roses and freshly cut grass. We walked without speaking and I heard his phone buzz again. Stefan had an open and friendly manner, but with an air of confidence that verged on intimidating.

His presence felt large here in his home - his castle.

As we continued, I felt a rush of excitement. Now that I knew more about the role and what it entailed, I really wanted it - with opportunities for travel, luxurious working conditions and surroundings, and people who were passionate and knowledgeable about what they were doing.

At the far end of the lawn, beyond a wall, I noticed a glass topped building - perhaps a greenhouse.

We continued on through a gap in the wall, and a distinct and familiar aroma filled the air. I followed Stefan through wide glass doors and into a modern building constructed from glass and wood and over twenty metres long. The afternoon sunlight streamed through the windows, shimmered on the surface of the water, and dazzled my eyes. There were two white stone statues at either end of the swimming pool. The one closest to me looked like The birth of Venus, standing naked in her shell, and at the far end of the pool stood Aquarius, the water bearer.

I couldn't help myself and turned to Stefan. 'This is quite something.'

His smile widened and his eyes danced. 'Do you like to swim?

'I do. But usually in the sea with a wet suit.'

I felt his arm brush mine and I moved a few inches aside.

'I swim here most mornings, work permitting. It wakes me up. That and a double espresso.'

Exotic plants - palms, bamboo, ferns, cordyline and ginger lily, grew in large ornate pots, and their leaves and flowers cast green reflections and shadows that shimmered upon the glass walls, tiled floor and surface of the water.

I didn't want to sound gushing, but I had to admit I was becoming keener by the minute to secure the job.

'I imagine your clients, when they visit, appreciate the surroundings.'

'They do. And what's more, we have swimwear they can use to indulge a swim, should they wish to. We serve coffee and drinks. It's all part of our customer experience.'

I looked around at the poolside loungers and the crystal water. Talk about perks of the job! A private spa, no less.

I heard footsteps approaching and turned to see Judi in the doorway.

She sounded out of breath. 'Stefan. Didn't you hear your phone?'

'I did. But I wanted to show Tess around.'

Her brows furrowed and she said curtly, 'I'm sure, but I must speak with you.'

'OK,' he replied and turned to me. 'I hope you've seen enough, Tess, but it seems business beckons. Could you see your way back to your car?'

'Of course.' Was that it? Didn't he want to know if I had any questions?

He rested his hand briefly on my arm. 'I'll be in touch. It's been a pleasure to meet and talk with you.'

'Please, Stefan,' Judi said, with greater urgency.

Stefan turned away and without saying more they headed out of the building together. What an abrupt end to the interview and not a thank you from either of them. Still, whatever the problem, they were obviously keen to get it sorted and that was something they had both stressed in the interview. I looked at my watch. I'd been here forty-five minutes and so a decent amount of time for them to get to know me. I hoped I'd done myself justice, given my lack of experience.

After one final look at the water, which looked so inviting, I left the building, closed the door behind me and walked back through the gap in the wall. I saw Judi and Stefan in close conversation just inside the French doors. I wondered if I should go back through the house or find my way round to the front. As I neared, Stefan looked my way and raised his arm in a wave then pointed left, indicating the direction I should go. I smiled and waved back. Judi looked my way but didn't return a smile and I could still discern the concern in her features. Stefan turned back to Judi and continued their conversation in earnest.

I made my way around the side of the house and glanced through the gothic style windows as I went. Each room looked gorgeous and stylishly furnished with artworks, floral displays, opulent sofas, and dressers. The housekeeper had her work cut out given the size and number of the rooms. I hadn't seen or heard any children, but maybe Judi or Stefan had children and they'd flown the nest or were away at school. They both looked to be in their late forties or early fifties, but I'd noticed neither of them wore a wedding ring. Not that that necessarily meant they weren't married or living with someone. Noah and I had never married and I'd always liked the idea of not conforming to what society expected of couples with children. But what an enormous house, a castle, for a brother and sister. Admittedly, they were wealthy, and who wouldn't want a castle, given the choice?

I thought of our fisherman's cottage and couldn't help but compare the two.

A wind rushed past me and rustled amongst the trees that reached over the pathway. Some tendrils of hair came loose from my clip and fell across my face, which obscured my vision for some moments. I swept up my hair and secured it once more.

Walking onto the gravel at the front, I heard a car door slam and the deep rumble of an exhaust as an engine roared into life. I watched the Porsche reverse back and turn in an arch before it surged forwards with gravel spraying in its wake. Stefan was at the wheel, and I saw him glance my way as he drove past. He revved the engine hard and left another cloud of dust as he sped away up the drive. He must have moved quickly to get there before me, and I hoped nothing terrible had occurred to warrant such urgency.

I felt a sense of unease as I reversed my car and glanced back towards the house. I'd never visited someone who lived in a castle. The interview itself had gone brilliantly, but the abrupt ending had left me feeling awkward and in limbo.

5

The petrol gauge flashed on as I headed down the hill into Sandsend and once over the bridge, I pulled into the garage. I thought I'd treat myself to a latte, too. I reached into my handbag for my phone and turned it on. It vibrated and pinged with notifications. I saw I had ten missed calls and several texts, too, all from Clara and Victor. My heart raced - something had happened. Possibly related to the drowned woman. I called Clara and she picked up.

'Mum,' she sobbed.

'What's happened?'

Her words rushed forth. 'It's Dad. He fell off the roof and we're in the ambulance.'

My heart pounded. 'Is he conscious?'

'Yes, but they think he's broken some bones.' She paused amidst more sobbing. 'Lots of them.'

I heard groaning in the background.

'Are you headed to Whitby General?'

'Yes,' she spluttered through her tears.

'I'll go straight there,' I said. 'What about Victor?'

'Roddy came home with him. He wanted to talk to you. They're coming to the hospital.'

'Did you see what happened?'

'I was holding the ladder, but Dad must have slipped. He landed right next to me. It was horrible. I heard his bones snap.' She sounded like she was hyperventilating.

'Take some slow breaths. I'll get there as quickly as I can.'

Petrol could wait. My immediate thought as I turned back onto the road was what if he'd broken his back? Falling from such a height could break anything and everything. And head injuries, too.

'Jesus, bloody Nora!' I cursed as I overtook a car going thirty, and sped out of Sandsend. In less than twenty-four hours, my nerves and sanity had been tested to the full.

6

The moment I walked into the Emergency Department, I spotted Roddy with his larger than life presence and auburn hair wilder than ever. I caught his eye. He raised his arm and I hurried over to where he and Victor stood at the reception desk. Several other people stood waiting to speak to someone.

'Where are they?' I asked Victor.

Victor's face looked pale and I saw he'd been crying. 'They're examining Dad now.'

'Did you talk to your Dad?'

'He lay sprawled in the front garden when we got back,' Victor replied. 'Howling in pain.'

'What about his back? Could he sit up?'

'I think his back is OK,' said Roddy. 'He could move his one arm and he tried to sit up. I told him to lie back down though.'

'What about his head?'

'I couldn't see any cuts or bruises,' said Victor, but he was groaning so much he might have banged it.

I turned to the desk.

'Mum.' Clara ran up to me. Her cheeks were streaked with tears. 'They've taken Dad to X-Ray.'

'Couldn't you stay with him?' I said.

'I came to find you so we can all go.'

She clutched my hand and as the four of us hurried down the corridor to X-Ray, Clara talked non-stop about what had happened and the things Noah had been saying.

'They must have given him strong painkillers as he was rambling. Saying he had to see you. How sad he felt at making you leave him. He kept calling himself an idiot and an addict.'

'Oh dear,' I said, and wondered if maybe he was finally admitting to the problem.

'He's given up gambling. I swear he has. He loves you, Mum,' Clara said, still tearful.

'Dad and I can talk whenever he wants to, but first we need to know how bad his injuries are.'

'I only want you to know what you mean to him, in case he doesn't get chance to tell you himself,' added Clara in earnest.

'He's going to be OK,' I said to reassure her.

But what if he wasn't? What if he had internal bleeding? That was a real possibility.

I'd talked through our breakup over and over with the children, particularly Clara who didn't take her Dad's side, but couldn't understand why I hadn't forgiven him or tried harder to work things out. What Clara didn't know, and what I felt reluctant to talk about, was how for sixteen years he'd been lying to me and had wasted money on his gambling - money we simply didn't have.

I'd been selective with what I'd shared with the twins, mostly because I didn't want them feeling as angry and resentful as I did towards their father.

Yes, I could have been more understanding and forgiving, yet again, but my patience ran dry months ago. I could no longer cope with the stress and upset, and it wasn't as if I hadn't pleaded with him to quit the gambling a thousand times, nor offered to do whatever it took to support him. I'd found addiction groups and encouraged him to go - pleaded for him to go. His reluctance to help himself had been the final cut in our relationship.

No, even if I did still love him, and a part of me always would, I was no longer prepared to tolerate his addiction, not for myself, nor our children, whatever his injuries might be.

When we arrived at X-Ray I stopped a nurse to ask if she knew what was happening with Noah.

'Wait here and I'll find out what I can.'

I thanked her and we sat down.

'How did the interview go?' asked Victor.

'I thought it went well, but it ended abruptly as something urgent came up, so I'm really not sure.'

'Did they say when you'd hear?' asked Clara.

'No. Incredible house and everything, but I'm not overly optimistic. I'm probably the least experienced of their candidates.'

'Don't sell yourself short,' said Roddy. 'I'd reemploy you in an instant.'

'I know you would, Rod. Thank you.'

'Did you tell them you can touch type like lightning?' asked Victor.

'I did drop that into conversation, yes,' I said, with a smile.

'Not many people can do that,' he said. 'Your fingers are a blur.'

'But it isn't a job to be a typist, it's more knowing the ins and outs of importing and financial administration, too.'

'Cross fingers,' said Clara, and she crossed her legs, too.

'They have horses to ride and a swimming pool to use - perks of the job.'

'Oh my God,' gasped Clara, and her face lit up. 'You have to get the job. Do you think they'd let me ride their horses?'

I thought about Stefan's words, "We recruit young people to exercise the horses", but thought better of mentioning that. I hadn't got the job and most likely wouldn't. Better not to raise Clara's hopes, or my own for that matter.

Besides, there were more pressing matters.

'Hey, we'd better ring Anna,' I said, and remembered Noah was staying with his sister.

'I already have,' said Clara.

'Oh, thank you.' And as I spoke, I heard a familiar voice.

'What's he gone and done now?'

I turned to see Anna, who sounded out of breath. Her pink cheeks matched her leggings, headband and the stripes in her white trainers. 'I'd just finished my last tutor session when I got Clara's message.'

'I thought you'd want to know,' said Clara.

'Of course I do, Clara dear.' Her eyes darted from Clara's to mine. 'Do we know the damage yet?'

'We're waiting to find out,' I said. 'He's in X-Ray.'

Anna always sounded accusing in her tone, not in the least like Noah. It didn't matter what she was talking about, whether she was offering to make a cup of tea or talking about the weather, I always felt my hackles rise.

'How did he fall? It was your roof wasn't it?' Her eyes squinted and she gave me a pointed glare.

'I wasn't there when it happened,' I replied, patiently. 'He was boarding up my skylight which fell in during the storm last night.'

'On his own?'

'Yes, on his own.' Which one of us did she think should have been up on the roof with him, I thought? 'But Clara was holding the ladder. I don't think he was on the ladder when he fell. But we'll ask him.'

'That roof of yours is far too steep to be climbing up,' she said, her tone relentless. 'And where were you when it happened?'

'Trying to get a job. And our roof is only like most roofs - slated and sloping,' I said. 'Noah regularly fixes or installs aerials.'

'From what I can gather,' said Roddy. 'It's no one's fault. Most likely rotten luck.'

Anna looked from Roddy to me, her eyes flashed back and forth. 'What's it got to do with you, and why are you even here?'

I noticed the other people in the waiting room had turned our way - their eyes and ears taking it all in.

'Does it matter?' I said, and checked the time on my watch. 'What matters is how Noah is doing and how injured he is. Let's be patient and wait quietly.'

'You'd better lower your voice then, hadn't you,' she spat in an exaggerated whisper, and I noticed how the spittle bubbled on her lips and a few spots jettisoned in my direction.

I stepped back, turned away and took some slow breaths.

'Did you just roll your eyes at me?' asked Anna.

I turned back around. 'No, I didn't. Would you like me to? Do you want something else to complain about? Or, how about we focus on what matters - your brother for instance?'

She pointed her finger at me. 'Noah's only here because of what you've done to him?'

I exhaled slowly, and thought, here we go again. Moments of crisis or stress always brought out the worst in Anna. I could feel my blood rushing and my heart pounding as I tried to keep a hold of my emotions.

'If you hadn't dumped him just when he needed you most, he wouldn't have been on that damn roof and fallen. This is one hundred percent your fault, Tess. And don't bother trying to defend yourself because you know it, and we all know it. You're a selfish stuck up cow and Noah deserves better.' She looked around at the others.

Did she expect them to nod their agreement?

Clara grimaced, and Victor looked at me and tilted his head, awaiting my response.

'If you think that badly of me then he's better off without me and he can move on and find someone more deserving.'

'Oh my God! Can you please stop!' wailed Clara, and she came up and took my hand.

Why oh why did Anna have to be so unkind and vicious? There was something quite absurd about her manner - socially inept even. She often shocked me with the things she came out with. I'd never done anything to offend her, at least not intentionally. I couldn't help but wonder how her students fared with her constant criticism and judgment. It seemed as though she became wound up whenever I said anything, whatever the subject. Many times, over the years, I'd fought with myself not to get upset by her words, but since Noah and I had split, she'd decided it was entirely my fault or I hadn't worked hard enough to support or forgive him.

She started talking again.

'Odd that my brother didn't break his neck - that might have solved many problems.'

'What?' I said, aghast at her insensitivity.

Roddy stepped forwards. 'Shut up, Anna!'

'But auntie Anna,' piped up Clara, her eyes wide and her cheeks pink. 'I'd have lost my dad and been devastated, even if you don't care.'

'Oh for goodness sake, I didn't mean it,' said Anna. 'But how easily he could have from such a height.' She glared at me through narrowed eyes once more.

At a loss how to respond, I put my arm around Clara and gave her a squeeze. I noticed Anna preparing to say more, possibly but unlikely to offer an apology, so I walked away and reached for my phone. No messages, not that I could expect to hear from either Stefan or Judi yet. The nurse we'd spoken to returned and she looked around unsure who to talk to first.

'Are you Noah's wife?' she asked me.

'Technically no, but we are partners. Well, ex partners actually, but only recently.'

The nurse looked confused. 'But you're his closest relative?'

'Like I say, not technically, probably his children or sister, but I'm the mother of his children.' Jeez, my heart was picking up speed like a racehorse released from the stalls. Talk about having to explain myself.

Anna stepped up to the nurse. 'As the twins are minors, I'm his sister and next of kin,' she said without even looking at me. Her expression was filled with concern and her voice softened. 'How is my brother doing?'

'Oh, umm.' The poor nurse didn't know who to address and so looked from Anna to me in turn. 'He has a partial fracture of the radius, and an oblique fracture of the fibula. He fell from a roof, I hear?'

'Yes, maybe lucky a grass landing,' I said. 'Could have been so much worse had it been concrete slabs.'

'I'd say incredibly lucky,' said the nurse. 'We don't believe there are other injuries, but the doctor needs to assess all the X-Rays and give a further examination for internal injuries. He'll stay in overnight, possibly longer. But we'll know more soon.'

I knew exactly how much Noah hated hospitals. Still, he could hardly ignore broken bones that needed treating and setting. 'Thank you, nurse. You've been a great help. Should we wait here?'

'Doctor Myers will come and speak to you shortly.'

Thank God. Serious though his injuries were, they didn't sound life threatening. Although he wouldn't be able to work for weeks, and given our money issues, that was a problem he could do without. I wondered if he'd got as far as boarding up the skylight and then I checked myself for such a selfish thought.

Roddy laid a hand on my arm. 'You OK?'

I nodded. 'Thank you for bringing Victor.'

'The kids were in shock seeing their Dad like that. And Clara watched it unfold.'

'I feel bad that I wasn't there,' I said.

'You couldn't have known. Anyway, Noah's been up on roofs hundreds of times. It's rotten luck, that's all.'

48

'We could really do without this,' I said, and felt close to tears.

'Certainly, but you're both strong enough to get through it. And, it could have been worse…' his words trailed away.

'You're right, Roddy. I'll remember that.' I gave him a hug and drew away. 'Clara mentioned you wanted to talk to me about something?'

He waved his hand. 'Don't worry. Nothing that can't wait.'

'Daddy,' I heard Clara say.

We all turned to see Noah coming through on a gurney, wheeled by two male orderlies and accompanied by a young, rather stout doctor.

'Noah's family?' the doctor asked warmly.

'Yes,' we all chimed together.

'Well, it's great to see Noah has a large support network.'

'The nurse mentioned a broken radius and fibula,' I said.

'Remarkably, that is all, and the bones are pleasingly aligned still. We'll set the bones and keep him overnight.' He looked down at Noah. 'You may be able to go home tomorrow but we'll reassess and see how you're doing pain wise.' He paused and looked at me directly. 'Noah will need support and care over the coming weeks.'

'Actually, Noah is staying with his sister, Anna, just now. Isn't that right, Anna?'

Anna shook her head vehemently, her eyes more startled than a rabbit on speed. 'As you're his common-law wife, Tess, he'll have to stay with you. I've got three young children, tutoring and teaching three full days a week. I haven't the time to care for an invalid.'

I suppressed an urge to sigh. 'Of course. You're right. Noah must stay with us.'

Victor's face lit up. 'Hear that, Clara, Dad's coming home.'

They both beamed, and Clara, protective, clasped her Dad's hand.

Noah gave a sheepish smile.

7

That evening, I still hadn't heard from Stefan or Judi about the job and I feared my heady optimism during the interview had been wishful thinking for a big life change and possibly even lifestyle. But there were more pressing matters to deal with.

After Noah had been settled onto the ward and his bones set in plaster, Anna and I went our separate ways. I understood why she wouldn't want to care for her brother, but given that we'd only recently separated, it felt like a giant step backwards rather than moving on with our lives. But I knew well that situations and circumstances changed and sometimes we had to adapt and compromise.

I invited Roddy back for dinner and when he suggested he'd make a fish curry whilst we recovered from the drama I jumped at his offer. I had plenty of fish in the freezer, and vegetables in the fridge, and Victor offered to help Roddy whilst I went up to inspect the skylight. The bedroom was in near darkness with curtains drawn and a board in place over the skylight. How well it had been secured before Noah fell, I had no idea. Time and weather would tell and a glazier would soon put it right.

I changed into jeans, cotton vest and low-heeled sandals and then headed back downstairs. Fleur had just arrived and Clara was telling her what had happened, and embellished each dramatic detail.

'Poor Dad's coming to stay here while he recovers.' She glanced my way and grimaced slightly. 'Do you think that'll be OK, Mum?'

'It might feel strange, but of course, we all want Dad safe and well again.'

'Where will he sleep? In with you?'

'I hadn't thought so,' I replied quickly. 'He should be near the bathroom, so it'll have to be yours or Victor's room.'

'He should share with Victor. Victor can have the camp bed and Dad can sleep in Victor's bed. That would make sense,' suggested Clara, with her ever practical reasoning, as if she'd already planned it in her mind.

I thought for a moment. 'I agree, that would seem the best solution. We'll have to check with Vic though.'

'Check what?' said Victor as he walked into the living room, followed by Roddy and Digby.

'Dad will have to sleep in your bed so he can use the bathroom,' said Clara. 'You can have the camp bed. Plus, your room is way bigger than mine.'

'Only marginally,' he said. 'Though I'm sure he'd rather be with Mum.'

Every eye in the room turned my way. Even Digby looked up at me with questioning eyes.

No, no, no, my inner voice screamed in my ear.

'Sorry,' I said. 'Just because Dad is coming here to recover, I don't want you having any ideas we'll be getting back together. I want him to be safe and recover, as we all do, that is all. Plus, there's no bathroom on my floor.' Thank goodness, I thought.

'You're a lovely family and Noah will be grateful for your support,' said Roddy. 'I'd have him stay with me, but I think he'd rather be with the people he loves.'

I walked over to Roddy and gave him a hug. 'You're so thoughtful Roddy and a good friend to Noah, too.'

'Sorry if I smell fishy,' Roddy said with a grimace. 'I didn't get a chance to change.'

Victor and Roddy always wore clean overalls over their clothes on the boat, but the smell inevitably lingered on their hair and skin.

'You know it doesn't bother me,' I said. 'I'm virtually immune to the smell after washing the overalls and all the fish we cook.'

Roddy rubbed his hands together. 'OK, you lot. Ten minutes for the rice. Hope you're hungry.'

'I'm starving,' I said. 'I've got a chilled Pinot Grigio in the fridge. Want a glass?'

'You know me.' Roddy broke into a smile. 'Would be rude not to.'

51

'Do want a small glass, kids?'

Clara looked at Fleur and they both nodded enthusiastically.

'Not for me,' said Victor. 'I'm meeting my mates later so I'll have a beer then.'

The twins were too young to drink in bars and often hung out at friends' houses or down on the beach. Victor seemed remarkably sensible, and I hadn't once seen him drunk, unlike Clara, who had already proven to be the wilder of the two.

Given the drama of the day, it didn't appear to have dampened anyone's appetites, and between us we managed to devour all the curry. We also polished off not only the bottle of Pinot Grigio, but a couple of beers, too.

After dinner the girls disappeared upstairs to watch a movie, and Vic headed out to meet his friends, which left Roddy and myself to clear up dinner. I washed the dishes and Roddy wiped the dining table and worktops. He'd been friends with Noah since their schooldays and he'd been more like an uncle to the twins than Anna had been an aunt.

At forty-six, the same age as Noah, Roddy was attractive, well-built and not short of admirers. But he'd never settled down with anyone for long. He'd been with one woman, Maureen, a gardener, for five years, until without warning, she'd broken up with him and promptly moved in with someone else. Unsurprisingly, Roddy had taken it badly and sometimes reminisced about her with regret, but never malice. And he'd been so supportive over Noah when I'd said I couldn't take the gambling, money issues and lies any longer. He hadn't tried to persuade me to try again, unlike others amongst my friends and family, and despite being Noah's best friend and knowing how much it would upset him. He'd seen first hand that I'd gone beyond what most partners would tolerate. And when the time came for us to separate, he'd spent an entire weekend helping me and the twins move into the cottage, too.

'Any news from the interview?' he asked, as he rinsed a dishcloth under the tap.

'Not yet, and I'm feeling increasingly pessimistic.'

'What were they like?'

I thought for a moment. 'Interesting. Not the sort of set up you'd expect near Whitby. Stefan and Judi are striking to look at. Both super attractive, glamorous, and everything about them and their castle home exudes wealth.'

'I don't imagine that intimidated you.'

'You know me. I don't kowtow to anyone. But you couldn't imagine a home more in contrast to our new humble abode.'

'That's what I love about you. Descended from Polish immigrants who didn't have a penny when they came over, now well educated, and here you are, so smart and confident. I wouldn't be surprised if they snapped you up for the job.'

'Thank you, Roddy. I do hope you're right.'

It had gone midnight by the time I'd undressed, brushed my teeth and climbed into bed. I lay down and after I replied to a text from Noah telling me he was in agony and he was sorry for the trouble he'd caused, I lowered the volume on my phone and switched off the bedside lamp.

I slept fitfully and dreamed the dreams of someone overwhelmed and caught up in a maelstrom of situations - frantic house move, a wild storm with shattered windows and splintered glass in my attic bedroom that rocked precariously amongst the treetops, the drowned body of a pregnant child - naked and blue skinned, a handsome stranger leading me round his castle and grounds, Noah tumbling from the roof and lying misshapen and dead at my feet, and when I awoke, I had the stark realisation that he'd be moving in with us. Sweat drenched my skin and I threw back the duvet.

What a crazy dream, but it accurately reflected my stressed out mind and life. Surely this was what becoming a single parent meant, and there would be a difficult period of adjustment as our lives began to fall into place and feel normal again. Money was a massive issue and I urgently needed a well paid job. Furthermore, I could never have anticipated Noah's accident, but it could have been so much worse and for that I felt grateful.

I had no doubt that Victor and Clara would be keen to help out, in theory, but the reality would see me running up and down the stairs with dinner plates and cups of tea whilst trying to maintain the balance between caring for him but not allowing myself to get drawn in emotionally. At this stage we'd have no idea how long it would be before he was up and mobile again, and negotiating our narrow staircase would be a hazard on crutches too. Maybe he'd end up sleeping downstairs with a commode close by. But how would he wash himself?

All these questions swirled and grew in my mind as I showered and dressed. Better not to make too many plans, but to try to stay relaxed and calm, be flexible and find solutions as we went along. Noah was a fairly quiet and undemanding presence as a rule, but who knew what he'd be like as a patient, immobile and in pain. Time would tell, but I wasn't relishing the idea of becoming his carer.

I checked my phone for the umpteenth time that morning. A missed call. It must have rung when I was in the shower. Maybe it was Stefan or Judi. Should I call back? But I didn't need to. The phone rang again and my heart juddered in my chest.

'Tess?'

'Yes, is that Stefan?' Of course it was, I recognised his voice instantly.

'It was a delight to meet you yesterday and I must apologise for the abrupt ending to your interview. As I'm sure you realised we had a pressing matter to deal with.'

'I hope everything is OK,' I replied.

His voice had a clinical tone. 'All is well. Judi and I are used to facing problems and we work quickly to resolve them and move on.'

'I'm glad to hear that.' Was he ringing with a polite rejection? The phone went silent for a few seconds.

'The reason for my call, of course, is to offer you the job. Both Judi and I feel you are ideal for the role. We warmed to you instantly.'

I felt a surge of excitement and didn't hesitate. 'Then I'd be delighted to accept. Thank you! I like the sound of what you do and I feel confident I can work with you both and to the benefit of the business.'

'Fantastic, Tess! When are you free to start?'

8

'Yes, yes, yes!' I jumped up and down like an excited child until a splitting pain in my abdomen stopped me. I took some slow breaths and the pain fell away.

I hurried onto the landing and yelled down the stairs. 'I got the job!' Then realised that Clara would still be asleep - she rarely emerged until eleven at the weekends, and Victor would already be out fishing with Roddy on the boat. Still, I'd share my news later and I knew they'd be pleased for me. I felt pleased for me. It had been the first interview I'd had in years and for a job I didn't stand much chance of getting, at least on paper. Maybe my life was looking up after all the strain and problems of recent years.

I'd start on Tuesday which gave me tomorrow to go out and buy a few smart work outfits. I would drive over to York and make the most of my last day of freedom.

I phoned the ward to find out how Noah was doing. Noah had already called me first thing to say he was missing me like crazy. By his slow speech and overly loving word choices I knew he'd been given strong painkillers. He hadn't been cleared to come home but the ward sister said I could visit that morning, and hopefully the doctor would have done his rounds and made a decision. Not that I was in any rush to bring him home. Maybe I should suggest he'd be safer staying in for a few nights.

I pulled into the hospital car park and searched around for a space. I eventually settled for one that looked a little tight, but once I'd started reversing I felt determined to fit into it. I had to shuffle back and forth a few times to ensure that I could open the door and get out. It left me feeling hot and bothered and annoyed that I hadn't passed it by for a bigger space. When I squeezed out, I caught the eye of the man in the Range Rover in the next space who I hadn't previously noticed. He grinned and winked as though he'd been amused by my efforts. My cheeks simmered.

I didn't smile back and I made a mental note to find a bigger bloody space next time.

I made my way down the main hospital corridor that led to the wards, and passed a heavily pregnant woman in the throes of early labour. She stopped walking, leaned against a wall and braced herself as a contraction held her in its grasp. She bent her head and as the pain eased, she stood up straight and relaxed once more.

When I turned and set off down a shorter corridor, I heard raised voices. A hanging sign indicated the mortuary, and as I passed, I paused and looked down. A few yards in, a young woman wept and pleaded with a man in a white lab coat. They stood in front of the double doors which I imagined gave authorised access to the mortuary. I quickly recognised that she spoke in Polish. My mum had spoken to me almost entirely in Polish for the first five years of my life, even though she was fluent in English. She'd been keen for me to know my mother tongue, and although I rarely spoke it now, even with my parents, I could recall every word and phrase. It appeared the young doctor had no idea what the young woman said and so I approached to offer my help.

I stopped in front of them and they both turned to me.

'Can I help?' I said in Polish to the young woman. 'I can translate for you.'

She swept a few strands of curly brown hair off her tear-soaked cheeks and looked back at me with wide eyes. 'My friend is here. Maria. I heard she's dead, in here, and they won't let me see her. They want proof that I know her. How can I prove I know her when I have nothing to prove it, other than my word?'

Her distress was so clearly genuine, and why would anyone want to see a dead person if they hadn't known them well?

I spoke her words in English to the doctor who listened.

'I'm afraid I can't allow anyone to see her,' he said. 'Authorised bookings and appointments only.'

'But she could be her friend, and you can hear how upset she is?'

The young woman continued in Polish. 'Maria disappeared two days ago and I think it's her they found at the beach.'

My heart lurched. 'She was your friend?' For some moments I tried to frame my words as the drowned girl's body flashed through my mind again.

'It was me who found her,' I said, quietly.

The girl shook her head and spoke again. 'Was she pregnant?'

I turned to the doctor and back to the young woman who awaited my answer. And I thought, why keep the truth from her? She had known the woman and deserved to know.

I nodded slowly. 'Yes, visibly pregnant. I'm so sorry.'

The girl crumpled to the floor, clasped her arms around her and wailed. 'Maria wanted her baby so badly. Even after those men raped her.'

I couldn't take in her words. Had I interpreted her correctly? Something terrible had happened to that girl months before she'd drowned. I crouched down beside the girl, took her hand and looked up at the man.

'You have to let her see her friend. She isn't making this up. You know the drowned woman was pregnant. She can formally identify her which will help the investigation.'

But he shook his head with regret. 'If I could, I would. But under police orders she is only to be seen by next of kin or anyone who can prove they know her.'

I helped the girl to stand. 'Let me come with you to the police and we can say you want to see Maria to identify her. You can tell them what you know about her.'

'The police won't help.' The girl's mascara had streaked down her cheeks and her eyes blazed with desperation.

'They will. The police are investigating who she is and how she drowned. You can help.'

'I can't. I won't!' She turned away from me and ran off down the corridor.

'Wait!' I called, and hurried after her.

The girl glanced back, then sprinted faster still towards the exit.

I called again, praying she might pause and listen. 'I want to help. Please wait.'

She disappeared around the reception desk and all faces turned and watched her, and then me as I followed in pursuit. The girl charged through the main entrance but as I neared the door an elderly couple walked in, pushing a wheelchair seating another elderly woman. For a few frantic moments I couldn't pass, and I stood aside to give them room. The second they passed, I ran outside to see where the girl had gone. I looked left and right and saw people walking to and from the main doors and between cars. And then past several parked cars I spotted a head of curly brown hair and what looked like a silver Mercedes pull up beside her. She opened the car door, jumped in and the car revved its engine and sped towards the exit onto the main road. I caught my breath and tried to catch sight of the number plate, but already the car was too distant to see any detail.

I shouldn't have mentioned talking to the police. It was obvious something illegal or criminal had occurred to the drowned woman. The Polish girl had mentioned her friend, Maria, had been raped, but by who? Men, she'd said - a gang rape? She was an immigrant, too. Had she been staying here illegally, and if so, where?

I pondered whether to go to the police and explain what I'd seen. Not that I'd want the girl to be deported if she were here illegally, but she seemed to be in trouble, too. She'd appeared to get into the car willingly, but maybe she was being followed and controlled. I'd noted her appearance, too. A beautiful girl in tiny shorts, vest top and heeled sandals. Had they been her choice of clothing? But my gut instinct told me something was seriously amiss with the girl and her situation, and the fact she had been close to the girl who had drowned only reinforced my concerns.

Right now, I had to see Noah, but I would ring the police as soon as I got chance.

When I walked into the ward, Noah was in deep conversation with a man dressed in pyjamas and sitting at his bedside.

When I approached, Noah saw me and waved his good arm in greeting. 'Here she is, mate. The love of my life.'

'Hello,' I said. Had he forgotten we'd separated?

Maybe he had banged his head.

'This is Ricky,' he said to me. 'I rewired his entire house last year.'

'Did a damn good job too,' said Ricky. 'All working tickety-boo.'

'He's a great electrician,' I said.

'I was thanking Noah for the tip he gave me on the Cheltenham Gold Cup. I'm not a betting man as a rule, my wife won't allow it, but your Noah won me eight hundred quid.'

'Crikey,' I said. 'How much did you bet?'

'A hundred. Your Noah was bang on the money.'

'Thanks mate,' said Noah. 'Happy to advise, anytime.'

And there he was receiving praise for something that had torn our family apart.

'Actually,' I said, tartly. 'Noah is quitting the gambling. He's accumulated massive debts, so I wouldn't recommend following any more tips of that nature, from anyone.' I couldn't disguise my irritation, then directed it at Noah. 'Have you seen the doctor?'

'I have. Despite the excruciating pain, I can come home because I have a loving family to help me.' Then he added, 'And you know I'm paying off those debts, as I promised I would.'

Jeez, I thought. How much more delusional could he possibly get? Still, now wasn't the time for a confrontation over something I was finally trying to avoid and extricate myself from.

I went to the window which looked out over the main car park. I couldn't help but wonder who had picked up the girl and where they'd driven to.

'Plenty of space in that big house of yours, too,' Ricky said.

I turned around. 'We've moved house recently.'

'Are you still in Whitby?' he asked.

'Noah has moved in with his sister up on Highlands. But with his injuries he's going to recuperate at my new home, a cottage on Captain's Row,' I replied.

Why should I cover up what had happened? This was our reality and the sooner Noah came to terms with it, the better.

Ricky looked confused. 'Well, let's hope you recover fast so you can get back to your job and enjoy life again, eh, Noah?'

'I know Tess will do all she can to make me comfortable. And I'll do all I can not to be a burden. The sooner I'm on my feet again, the better for everyone. Stupid of me to fall.'

'It wasn't your fault,' I said, and sighed. 'Could have happened to anyone.'

He shook his head. 'Loose tiles. Always a hazard to watch out for, so it was my fault.'

I tried to look on the bright side. 'The kids will love having you stay.'

His eyelids drooped with regret, or possibly the medication he was on. 'I'll be making the most of my time with them.'

Was he trying to make me feel guilty about him missing the twins?

But I knew I had no reason to feel guilty - the children were free to see and be with their dad whenever they wanted to. That they'd decided to live with me was their choice, and a choice I was delighted with.

'Oh, I got the job,' I said, changing the subject. 'They rang this morning.'

'Congratulations, love!' said Noah.   'You must have impressed them.'

'I start on Tuesday which means I won't be home so much to help you. The kids will be in and out though.'

'We'll manage. I'll soon be able to walk with the help of a crutch.'

'Are they giving you a wheelchair so we can get you home?'

'Yes, I'm waiting for my medication and a chair, then we're good to go.'

I reached for my phone in my handbag. 'I need to make a call - won't be long. Want anything from the shop, a coffee or something?'

'You can phone from here. No one minds,' said Noah.

'I'd rather not,' I said.

'Why, who are you phoning?' Noah asked.

'I'll explain later.' I didn't want to share with everyone about my being the one to find the drowned woman.

'Secrets eh?' said Noah, tilting his head.

I didn't miss the underlying edge to his teasing. Since we split, he never missed an opportunity to ask what I'd been up to. It seemed he thought I'd dive straight into a new relationship. Nothing could have been further from my mind.

'So, do you want anything from the coffee shop?' I asked again.

'A black Americano would be great,' said Noah.

'How about you, Ricky?'

'I'll admit I'm gagging for a decent coffee. White Americano, thanks.'

When I turned to leave I heard Ricky say in a loud whisper. 'You gotta get her back.'

'You bet, mate,' Noah replied. 'I'm going to make it impossible for her to turn me out.'

I sighed again. He must be high as a kite.

Having Noah to stay was abysmal timing, just as I was trying to detach myself emotionally and about to begin a new job. And yet, what choice did we have? His Dad, recently turned seventy, had been diagnosed with early onset Alzheimer's and his Mum was already struggling physically. And Anna, for all her abruptness and straight talking was herself overloaded with work and child responsibilities. No, I'd take this on the chin, but make it quite clear I was helping him out, not inviting his return into my life.

I found a quiet spot outside the main entrance and dialled Whitby police station. 'Can I speak to your lead officer handling the case of the drowned woman on the beach?' I looked about and checked that no one could overhear me. 'I'm Tess Blonski and I was the one who found her.'

I waited on the line until I was put through to a female officer.

'Detective Walsh speaking.'

'I'm Tess Blonski. I discovered the drowned woman on the beach, and I have information that might help.'

'Can you come to the station?' she asked.

'I'm at the hospital waiting to bring my partner home.'

'OK, let's talk now,' she said.

'Have you identified who she is yet?' I asked.

'Not yet. Seems no one of her description or age has yet been reported missing anywhere in the UK.'

'As I was coming in to see my partner in Whitby General, I passed the mortuary. A young Polish woman sounded distraught and asked to see the drowned woman's body. I know Polish so I understood her. The doctor wouldn't allow it and she became distressed and ran off.'

'Did she name her friend?'

'Maria. Yes, Maria.'

'Did she give a surname?'

'Afraid not. I followed the girl when she ran off but she got into a silver car, a Mercedes I think.'

'Did you see the driver or the number plate?'

'Neither, I'm sorry.'

'What did the girl look like? We should be able to get her on hospital CCTV, too.'

'About 5ft 6. Slim. She could be any age between sixteen and twenty something. Pretty, long curly brown hair, grey eyes, denim shorts, red vest top, heeled sandals. She'd stand out in a crowd because her clothes are too skimpy for this weather. She was crying, smudged mascara.'

'Did she say anything else about her friend, Maria?'

'Yes,' I paused briefly to frame my words. 'She said Maria had been raped. She said, men, plural, so possibly a gang rape, or something that went on with separate men for a while. No wonder the poor girl was so distraught. Something bad might be happening to her, too.'

'Thank you, Tess. Ring me if you remember anything else that might be important - anything at all?'

'Of course.'

I rang off after the officer had given me her contact details and said she'd come down to interview the staff at the mortuary to see what else she could learn. It seemed strange that no one had been reported missing, other than by a young Polish woman who had been too upset to stay and to talk to anyone.

9

Helping Noah up the stairs to Victor's bedroom proved far harder than I'd anticipated. I knew by the moans and gasps for breath that he felt every painful step as Victor and I had propped, and virtually carried him up the stairs. When we'd lowered him onto the bed his eyes were wet from tears and his every feature looked pinched and furrowed with pain.

I propped some pillows behind his back. 'I'm so sorry. We should have made you up a bed downstairs.'

He let out a long breath. 'But then how could I use the toilet? I'll be OK now I'm here, and I'll soon be able to use a crutch to hobble to the bathroom.'

'Did they suggest how best to stay clean given you can't shower?'

'Bowl of warm water, soap, flannel and a towel. Twice a day, if that's OK?'

'Of course,' I said. 'What about clothes and books?'

'Roddy's picking up some loose fitting clothes from Anna's. My laptop and ipad too - that'll keep me entertained.' He looked at the bookshelf and said to Victor. 'You've got a nice full shelf.'

'Help yourself to anything. You can borrow my clothes too.'

Noah forced a smile. 'Thanks, son, but not sure your old dad will fit into your slim fit T-shirts and shorts.'

'Kind of you to offer, Vic, and for giving up your bed,' I added.

On Tuesday morning as I showered and dressed for my first day at Aztec Imports, my stomach fluttered with nervous energy. First day nerves weren't something I was used to.

The previous day I'd driven into York and spent more than I could afford on skirts, trousers, blouses and a couple of jackets. I didn't want to look like a poor relation, and if their clients were spending big bucks, my appearance should reflect the quality service they expected. I wasn't desperately worried about the money because after two months' pay I estimated I'd have paid off the overdraft we'd accumulated since we'd moved in. Noah hadn't given us any maintenance yet, but perhaps I wouldn't need it. The house purchase had virtually been covered by the sale of our larger house, and although there were gambling debts to pay, they were most definitely Noah's. If I could do well in this job my financial independence would be secured. Still, that thought didn't stop my stomach churning as I drove out of Whitby. When Stefan had rung to offer me the job, he'd said my duties might take longer than the usual nine to five some days, but that I must keep a note and take time off in lieu.

'Is that OK with family commitments?' he'd asked.

'Of course,' I replied, and I didn't mention Noah's accident.

'I'm excited to be working with you,' he'd said on the phone. 'I've got a great feeling about having you on the team. You're smart and eloquent, and that you were in the best play I've ever seen didn't go against you either.'

I laughed.

'And you know what?' he added.

'What?'

'I can recall exactly who you were on the stage in York all those years ago. My memory rarely fails me. Your hair was tied up in a high ponytail that swung as you walked and danced across the stage. You had, still have, grace in the way that you move and walk that makes you stand out, and as you did that night amongst the other waitresses. It was you who held my attention for all the right reasons - and I'm sure most of the audience, too.'

I felt flattered. 'Kind of you to say. She was a fun role to play. I love dancing. In fact, I danced in clubs for a while.'

'Really? What kind of dancing?'

'I trained in modern dance and ballet, but this was more chorus type dancing. I did it to earn money as an impoverished student.'

'Of course, I understand,' he said. 'Great experience, too.'

What I didn't share was that the dancing during college had been more along the lines of scantily clad and exotic dancing. I'd never dared tell my parents - Mum would have been horrified, but a couple of my friends in drama school had worked at the same club and my best friend had got me into it. It had been an exclusive club and no back street dive. We earned far more money in tips than we'd have ever earned serving in bars, and it meant I had no debts when I'd graduated, which surprised but pleased Mum and Dad.

Admittedly, it hadn't all been easy and some of the men took their appreciation way too far, but the bouncers had always been on hand to sort out those problems. The club had mostly attracted business men and wealthy types but that didn't mean they had better morals - in fact I'd have said quite the opposite. They thought they could buy more than an appreciative glance with their money and free cocktails.

There had been private rooms where the men and even some women could entertain a private dance, but I'd flatly refused to get drawn into that. The thought alone scared and revolted me. From what I could gather, that had led some of the dancers into high class prostitution. I'd always kept my clothes on, albeit miniscule bikinis. Thankfully, it wasn't a job I'd had to return to after graduating when I became a professional actor with The Hull Docks Theatre Company, a dream job for an acting graduate.

10

Heading down the drive to Lorton Hold, I felt excited that this would be my view every morning - windswept scots pine trees interspersed with oak and beach on my right, and to my left, sweeping grass that drew my eye to the blue-light waves of the ocean beyond with its watery depths and unceasing power and beauty.

Who wouldn't prefer this to a commute to work in a smog surrounded, city office block? I felt a rush of adrenaline, determined to make a good impression this week and felt fired up, ready to take on whatever was expected of me.

Stefan had said I should walk round the back of the house and in through the French doors. When I got there the doors were ajar and I walked through the comfortable meeting room, and into the main office. Stefan stood with his back to me, and talked on his phone. He didn't appear to have heard me and for a moment I cast my eyes over the artworks hanging on the walls - abstract with largely unrecognisable subject matter - colourful and attractive though and they gave the space a sophisticated feel.

I coughed once, and Stefan turned around. He smiled and nodded in greeting.

'I have to go.' I heard him say. 'Tess, my new assistant has arrived. I'll call back.' He tucked his phone into his trouser pocket, walked over and held out his hand. 'Good to see you again, Tess.'

I smiled and took his hand, warm and firm in mine. 'I'm glad to be here and eager to learn.'

'Judi will be down shortly. She was away last night and arrived home a few moments ago.'

'Travelling overnight?'

'Yes, from a client meeting in Edinburgh. First things first, let's get a coffee, or tea?'

'Tea would be lovely.'

He led me through to a small kitchen off the main office, with a kettle and a smart looking coffee machine. A bowl full with shining apples, oranges, bananas and grapes sat on the worktop. 'Mrs. Mills restocks in here. You must help yourself to anything at any time. There's always fresh bread and one or two sandwich fillings in the fridge, too.' Stefan picked up our drinks and we walked through and sat on two armchairs facing one another in the meeting room.

He sat back with his cup of tea in hand. 'I've put together an induction itinerary to ease you in and to help you acclimatise to how we work. I've emailed it to your new email account. I'll text you your email address and that will give you access to our shared documents cloud too. Your password is tessabc1, all lower case.'

He'd written it down on a post-it note, which wasn't necessary, but I took it from him. 'Great. I'll check it out.'

'Your chromebook is on your desk. We have a printer, but we try to avoid printing where we can get by digitally.'

'Time to let the rainforests grow back,' I said.

'Exactly. We're doing our part as an ethical business.'

I looked at the post-it note and wondered if I was expected to change my email password. Was it usual for an employer to know passwords? I had many questions but because this was an independent business, they would have their own preferred methods. I'd leave the email password as it was.

'We have office phones, but are you also happy to use your own mobile phone for making calls and messages? Judi and I have the same for private and business.'

'Yes, I can use Whatsapp or perhaps you use another messaging app?'

'We use Signal for messaging and phoning since Zuckerberg took over. I don't trust that guy.'

'OK, I'll download Signal.'

He took a sip of tea. 'I have an exciting introduction for you today.' He raised his brows and looked at me with insistent eyes.

'Sounds interesting.'

'We're taking delivery of a remarkable show horse from Italy. Gil is at the airport now with the horsebox. I expect him back in an hour or so. We'll give the horse an hour in the paddock to stretch his legs, after which Gil will transport him to his new owner in Oswaldon.' He paused, rested his cup on his knee, and leaned forwards. 'If you'd like to, you can go with him. You'll get to know Gil and meet your first clients. Until then it might be helpful to familiarise yourself with our online systems. How does that all sound to you?'

'Sounds great. What breed of horse?'

'A purebred Arabian - Palomino called Marmaris and a top prize winner. Exquisitely beautiful, and I can't wait to see him in the flesh.'

As we drank our tea, he told me about an upcoming project that involved purchasing a highly sought after painting via an online auction, after which he showed me to my desk. He pulled up a chair and sat beside me, then took the mouse and navigated around the client database and the cloud where the letters and documents were kept.

'Who manages your accounts?' I asked.

'I do,' he said, and cupped his chin with his fingers. 'At one point I hired a bookkeeper, but I can keep on top of them in half the time it took her, and I don't make errors.'

'Did you train in accountancy?'

'No, but I took a course for this software. Because we have few sales but of high value it's relatively straightforward, even the tax elements. We've had Brexit issues to iron out, but the moment Brexit was voted Judi and I renewed our Romanian passports which has made trading within the EU easier.'

'That's smart,' I said. 'It hasn't affected my ex-partner's business too drastically because he works locally, but my good friend, Roddy, says the new fishing regulations are still giving him grief.'

He nodded slowly and thoughtfully. 'I can see you've got a good business head, Tess, even with your artsy background.'

'I read a lot of current affairs and I'm interested in politics and how Brexit is affecting us all. Your family is from Romania then?'

He turned to the window briefly before looking at me directly once more. 'Sort of. My father was born in Romania, but we also have Polish roots with one set of grandparents. Judi and I are a bit of a mixed bag.'

I smiled. 'Well, I am, too, along with a lot of Brits these days. And I like it that way.'

'I couldn't agree more.' He tilted his head. 'I'd say this makes for finer features.'

If it was a compliment directed at me, I didn't acknowledge it as such.

He stood up. 'Pleased to have you on board. Judi thought you'd turn down the role.'

At that moment Judi walked into the office.

'Sorry?' she said with a clipped tone and her ocean blue eyes flashed with annoyance. 'What did Judi think?'

He looked at her. 'I was saying you weren't sure…'

'Oh, I heard you, brother.' Judi walked across the room. 'Take no notice, Tess. I thought no such thing.'

'But you did say it, nonetheless,' said Stefan.

'I was merely suggesting she might have other interviews and offers to consider.'

'Actually, this was my first interview, and decent jobs are in short supply around here. I can honestly say I saw this as my best option.'

'Good to hear!' she said, briskly. And without further comment, she turned and sat down behind her desk. As she opened her laptop her mobile rang. 'Gil. How's he looking?' Judi beamed across at Stefan, their minor disagreement apparently already forgotten. 'Fantastic! Give me a call the moment you arrive.' She hung up. 'Marmaris has landed safely and Gil has him in the van. Back in twenty minutes.'

'Which airport did he fly into - Leeds-Bradford?' I asked her, curious how Gil could get here so quickly.

'We import horses and other large items to Rushmore airport,' she replied and pulled a packet of cigarettes from her handbag. 'I'm nipping out for a smoke.'

'We'll join you soon,' replied Stefan.

'I'm looking forward to meeting Marmaris and delivering him to his new owner,' I said.

Judi's eyes shuttered and she turned to face her brother. 'Stefan?'

'OK with you isn't it? It's an opportunity for Tess to see how we operate.'

69

Judi shrugged, and pursed her lips. 'You knew I'd blocked out my diary especially.'

'But we have other things to deal with.' Stefan paused and his brow furrowed. 'As you well know.'

'I promised Gil I'd accompany him,' she said, and her eyes flicked my way.

'I really don't mind either way,' I said, and felt like I was getting in between them.

'If I didn't need you here, I'd agree,' Stefan said to Judi. 'We'll celebrate tonight to make up for it, OK?'

'Don't suppose I have a choice.' And with cigarette in hand, she turned on her heel and headed out of the office.

Stefan turned to me as though to confide. 'Judi's senses are on high alert. She's done all the legwork, and waded through the legislation and paperwork on this import, plus she's been on tenterhooks for days. But I'll decide how to celebrate tonight and hopefully you can come along too?'

'Yes, I'm sure I can. I'd like that.'

He took a step closer and his eyes swept briefly from my face and down to my dress.

I noticed how his dark brows almost met - an unusual feature I hadn't noticed previously.

'Can I say how professional, but equally, feminine you dress.'

'Thank you,' I said, unsure if I found his nearness daunting. 'I shopped for a few outfits yesterday. It's been years since I worked in an office.'

'What you're wearing and the way you've styled your hair is perfect for how we like to present ourselves and the business.'

The way that his lips and tongue lingered over the words caused butterflies to flit through me. I knew he was only being polite, but being unused to such direct compliments, I couldn't help but feel flattered.

'Come on,' he said. 'Let's join Judi and await Marmaris.'

I pushed back my chair, and with a sweep of his arm, he gestured for me to lead the way. We headed through the French doors and into the garden.

Stefan raised his hand and pointed. 'That gap in the hedge leads to the stableyard and paddocks.'

We walked together along the gravel path to the far side of the lawn.

Beyond the neatly trimmed hedge I noticed the slate roof of a long stone building. 'The gardens are beautifully kept. Do you enjoy gardening?'

'Honestly, no. I mow the lawn because we have a ride-on lawnmower, but our gardener sees to everything else. Judi suggests new plants, and our gardener, Bettina, is knowledgeable and advises us.'

We headed through the gap in the hedge and I heard the rumble of an engine approaching.

Each door in the stable block had its top half secured open. The yard was cobbled and led round to the front of the house between trees still laden with ripened apples.

'Do your horses stop to eat the windfalls?' I asked.

'They do and then froth at the mouth for more,' Stefan said. 'My mount, Zeus, he's a sixteen-hand ebony Welsh Cob, and he's the most gluttonous of them all. He gets it from me.'

I laughed. Did Stefan mean he was greedy with food? He didn't appear to have an ounce of fat on him. I imagined he worked out and he'd told me he liked to swim most mornings. Compared to many middle aged men I knew, he looked trim and the picture of health.

He hadn't mentioned a wife or girlfriend, and I hadn't yet seen evidence of anyone else who lived with them.

Judi strode into the yard. 'They're here.' She dropped her cigarette onto the floor and stubbed it out with her boot.

A large maroon horsebox turned into the yard. We all stepped aside as Gil pulled up and switched off the engine. The door swung open and he jumped down. He beamed our way and saluted. 'The cavalry has arrived.'

Judi walked up to him and rested her hand on his arm. 'Is Marmaris as beautiful as he looked in the video and photos?'

'Far more so,' said Gil, and stroked Judi's hand as they walked to the back of the van. He unbolted the doors.

I stood aside as the three of them lowered the ramp, and a whinny and stamping sounded from behind the internal barrier.

'He's keen,' said Stefan.

'He's been in transit for the past eight hours so needs to stretch his legs,' replied Gil. 'You should have seen him prancing when he came off the plane. I could barely hold him.'

Gil and Judi walked up the ramp and pulled open the internal door, all the while talking to the horse whose ears brushed the ceiling when he lifted his head.

'How big is he?' I asked.

'Fifteen-two which is an inch or two bigger than your average Arabian.'

His coat wasn't so much a palomino yellow as a golden sheen, brushed and polished to a fine lustre. His ears twitched back and forth and his nostrils flared pink as he snorted with curiosity and an eagerness to be released from his confinement.

With Gil leading, Marmaris stepped down the ramp. His neck arched like the morning sun that rose up from slumber and his tail lifted proud and high. He wore a light rug and protective boots on his legs.

'Magnificent! A prince amongst horses,' I said, although my superlatives seemed inadequate for such a divine creature.

'I'll see if he'll eat some oats,' said Judi.

'Good idea,' said Stefan. 'Show Tess where the horse's food is kept.' He turned to me. 'But don't worry, I shan't be asking you to feed or muck them out.'

'I wouldn't mind. I adore horses,' I said, and followed Judi who had headed across the yard.

Judi reached into a large bin and scooped some oats into a bucket. 'This will do. Oats can enliven an already excited horse, but we don't want him arriving hungry at our clients.'

'I've not ridden for years,' I said. 'But as a teenager I rode my friend's pony and had lessons after college.'

'We have a couple of horses you could ride if you want to. Max, our strawberry roan is a lovely ride and steady, too. He's in the paddock. Not the paddock we'll put Marmaris in though. God forbid he should receive any kicks or bites.'

Gil led Marmaris over. Judi placed the bucket on the floor and Marmaris snorted and sniffed before dipping his nose and crunching on the oats.

Gill turned to me. 'I hear you're coming with me to deliver this beauty?'

'If that's OK with everyone, yes.'

I heard Judi give a sniff of disapproval. 'Let's turn him out. I need to get on with other work.'

Clearly, she wasn't pleased that I was taking her place with Gil. But, I could hardly argue, and I wasn't interested in getting stuck in the middle of their squabbles. It seemed clear that Stefan was the senior here, and not only by being the elder sibling.

As Marmaris ate, Gil and Stefan removed his rug and boots which revealed his perfect coat and confirmation all the more. I stroked his silken neck and ran my fingers through his long flaxen mane, all the while inhaling his delicious horsey aroma.

Beside me, Stefan breathed deeply too. 'I never tire of their smell.'

A gust of wind swept through the elms behind the stables, blowing leaves across the slates to flutter down onto the yard. We followed behind Gil and Marmaris who lifted his head, prancing and snorting as his hooves clattered against the cobbles.

'How old is Marmaris?' I asked.

'Eight,' said Stefan. 'We have his digital passport to pass on.'

'What sort of shows does he compete in?'

'Only beauty contests. He is ridden but doesn't compete in show jumping or eventing. He's too precious to get knocked about - rather like a Ming dynasty vase.'

Judi unbolted and swung open the five bar gate and Gil led Marmaris through and unclipped his lead rope. The moment the clip came free, Marmaris turned and lifted his beautiful head in the direction of the horses in the adjacent paddock, and whinnied. He sprung into a canter, arching his back and kicking out his endlessly long back legs. The other horses trotted over to greet Marmaris at the fence, exchanging snorts, squeals and sniffs. Then with another whinny and a swish of his tail he turned and set off at a gallop around the paddock. The sound of his hooves pounding the ground reverberated through me, and I felt my breath quicken and my eyes well with emotion. His magnificence was beyond any creature I'd had the privilege to be this close to before - the fineness of his limbs, the ebony black of his eyes and lashes which contrasted with the golden sheen of his coat, where the well-defined muscles rippled beneath. He thundered past us as we stood mesmerised by his power, grace and movements. He seemed only too aware of our admiration and upped his performance for his audience by twisting his head and back and squealing as he leaped and bucked.

I turned to the others and watched Judi take Gil's hand. Of course, they were romantically involved, and she saw me as a potential threat to their relationship. I'd have to reassure her in a way that was both subtle but definite. I didn't want there to be any tension in our working relationships, or any jealousy, sexual or otherwise.

Gil looked at his watch then turned to me. 'I'll keep an eye on the lad and we can set off at eleven?' He turned to Stefan. 'Does that fit with what you have planned for Tess?'

Stefan nodded. 'The sooner you get going the better.'

'Righto.' Gil looked at me. 'I'll give you a shout when we're ready.'

It was a mild and sunny day despite a northerly wind that blew in from the sea, and wisps of hair escaped from my ponytail and whipped across my face. My hair had always had a will of its own which was why I so often wore it tied back. We headed back indoors and I sat at my desk and opened up my laptop.

I overheard Stefan asking Judi to chat with him in the meeting room. They obviously needed to discuss something in private, which immediately piqued my curiosity. Private secrets. Could it be a family matter or business related? I checked my phone to see two messages from Noah who reassured me he was awake, washed and dressed. He sent me a photo of him sitting up in bed and grinning like a Cheshire cat that so obviously looked forced. I had to smile.

Clara was studying from home, in other words, having a lie-in or watching Netflix, and Vic had gone into school for some lessons. It was helpful that the twins weren't in school full time, and also keen to help their dad, which made me feel less guilty about leaving him in such pain. I didn't reply as all seemed well.

I clicked on Gemini, their customer database system. I was tempted to dive straight in and take a look at who their customers were and what sort of businesses they ran, but Stefan had said I should work my way through the tutorial and I didn't want to risk messing anything up.

I could hear Stefan and Judi talking in low tones in the meeting room until one of them slammed the door to the main office. Stefan's voice grew louder behind the closed door. I tried to focus on the instructions which thankfully seemed straightforward and well-illustrated. The tutorial concluded with how to run a few basic reports.

Being a business administrator and naturally curious, I wondered when I'd be given access to their finance and accounting system. That would show the sums of money they dealt with and probably staff salaries, too. I'd be paid 35k per annum with the potential for bonuses, although Stefan hadn't gone into details. I'd never worked anywhere that included a bonus unless I counted a few free drinks at the local pub and a fish and chip supper to follow.

Eventually, Stefan and Judi came out of the meeting room and Judi stopped by my desk.

'How's it going, Tess?' She blinked her blue eyes and smiled to reveal her perfect pearly teeth that matched her brother's.

I smiled. 'I've gone through some of the database tutorials. They seem straightforward enough.'

'Useful that you've had experience with your husband's business, too.'

'Yes, we weren't actually married, but as Noah's partner I got involved in phoning customers and chasing payments too. Is that ever an issue here?'

'Not often as we ask for payment or a minimum two-thirds up front prior to the service, although we've had occasional issues and negotiated part refunds.' She paused and shook her head as she spoke. 'So you never married?'

'Noah's the father of our children, but we never felt the need for a ceremony or certificate.'

I still found it odd how often people asked about my marital status. 'We're recently separated, actually, although Noah's had an accident so he's recovering in my new home.'

She nodded. 'It's positive you're both still amicable. Neither Stefan nor I have ever married.' Then she added, 'And although it's too late for me, I sometimes regret not having had children. Possibly we've been too married to our careers and our horses.'

I felt surprised by her openness and willingness to share personal information. 'Children are hard work and always a worry, although I love mine beyond anything. I'd say horses and pets are a happy alternative. Equally as expensive, unfortunately.'

From behind us Stefan said, 'That's what I've always said. No sleepless nights, either.'

Judi leaned over and said quietly but quite loud enough for Stefan to hear. 'My brother doesn't have a paternal bone in his body.'

'It's true,' he piped up. 'And I don't mind admitting it. I don't dislike babies or children but I'd never have had the time needed for the business with a family in tow, and neither would Judi.'

'I'll admit, I'm grateful mine are becoming more independent these days,' I said.

'It's good for them to see you in a new career and working full-time,' said Stefan. 'A modern day role model for both of them.'

'I agree,' I said. 'No guilt for this working Mum.' I was feeling more relaxed by the minute, but I did wonder if Stefan had had a word with Judi about making me feel welcome. Her attention and smiling features hadn't seemed entirely genuine.

'Have you accessed our shared diaries yet? Worth looking as you'll be responsible for adding and updating,' Judi asked.

'OK. I'll take a look and see what you have coming up.'

'A busy few weeks ahead, which is why we're so grateful to have you here. And do ask if there's anything you're unsure about, even if it seems trivial. I'm sure you have loads of initiative but I always think it's better to ask than to risk making mistakes.'

'Of course,' I said. 'I don't know enough about how you work to make calculated guesses.'

She nodded her approval and headed back to her desk.

I looked through their upcoming appointments whilst both Judi and Stefan made telephone calls. I respected that they spoke to people - better than sending endless emails, and I knew from experience at home and work that talking generally yielded faster responses.

11

Marmaris had been loaded back into the horsebox and I clambered into the passenger seat. I felt high off the ground after driving my Polo. Gil had seemed friendly the time I'd spoken to him on the beach and more so as he calmly but confidently handled Marmaris. I hoped the afternoon as we travelled together would give me an opportunity to talk to him about the business.

At the top of the drive Gil turned the horsebox north onto the coastal road. A two hour journey each way and maybe an hour there to unbox and settle Marmaris with his new owners. For the first few miles we chatted about other horses they'd brought over from abroad - all show or racehorses.

Gil talked passionately about horses and knew loads about the top breeds and what made one horse a better show horse than another.

'Growing up I dreamed of becoming an eventer, but my parents couldn't afford a donkey let alone a high calibre event horse, and although I got to ride and enter the horses from the local livery yard, I never was successful enough to gain sponsorship.'

'How long have you worked for Stefan and Judi?'

'I'll be fifty next January and I started here exactly eight years ago on my birthday.'

'Sounds like you've found a job you love.'

'I do like it here.' He paused for a moment. 'It's not always easy working for Stefan, well, either of them. They often disagree, but I'm used to how they work. And I get the gatehouse too. It's a beautiful home and Stefan paid to have it decorated throughout last year. You should come up for a cuppa. It's like a miniature Lorton Hold, but without the fancy furniture and fittings.'

'Do you live alone?'

'Yep. I was married until I was forty, then my wife left me and took our boy, Luke, with her.'

'I'm sorry to hear that. Do you still see your son?'

He gave a regretful sigh. 'Not often enough. My ex moved to Cornwall with her new man, and my boy is studying at Exeter Uni.'

'That is quite a distance.'

'I go down when I can.'

The roads seemed quiet but Gil drove at a slow and steady pace - no doubt because we carried such precious cargo. Before long we drove into less familiar territory where the moors and woodlands and occasional farm buildings extended as far as I could see. It was hard to imagine that the industrial towns of Tyne & Wear, County Durham and Northumberland lay beyond the pale horizon.

'Remember when we met on the beach the other day?' I said.

'Small world isn't it?' he said, and kept his eyes on the road.

'You've heard about the drowned woman?'

He glanced at me briefly before turning to face the road once more. 'Yes. The same morning I saw you.'

'The police haven't identified her yet,' I said.

'Maybe they haven't made it public,' he replied.

'You know it was me who found her - well, Digby?'

He turned to me again and his eyes widened. 'I only heard it was a local woman.' He went silent for a moment. 'Have you told Stefan?'

'No.' It hadn't occurred to me during the interview and with so much else to take in.

'Must have been a shock,' he said.

'Awful, and thinking about how devastated her family must be. And then I had this interview later that day.'

'I know you impressed them.'

'I hope I continue to.'

'You're doing great, Tess. Just be yourself.'

'Thanks. I'm feeling good about it so far.'

We turned onto another main road and a phone rang. Gil reached for his phone and placed it on the magnet on the dashboard. 'Hi Judi. I've got you on speaker.'

'All going OK?' she asked.

'Yeah, we're joining the road by Deaf Hill. His lordship's peaceful in the back.'

'Great. Do drive carefully.'

'Of course.'

I discerned a shake of his head - Judi did sound quite controlling.

She continued. 'Stefan rang James and told him you're on your way and should be there oneish.'

'We might stop for a coffee and sandwich but won't be much after one, traffic permitting.'

The line fell silent. 'Judi?'

'Yes, if you need to, fine,' came her curt reply.

'I'll keep you posted. Better focus on the driving,' he said.

Judi promptly hung up.

I hardly needed intuition to hear how uptight she felt, although the cause wasn't clear.

We drove on in silence for a few minutes.

On either side of us stretched moorland, still purple with heather and patches of yellow gorse. We were taking the scenic route as opposed to the motorways which had always been my preference when driving up north. Didn't make the journey a great deal longer, but was far prettier and more interesting.

'Let's play some music. I've got Spotify,' Gil said and handed his phone to me. 'What do you fancy?'

'Do you like classic, rock, indie, pop?' I said.

'Counting Crows? I love their album, August and Everything?' he suggested.

'Nice choice. Noah and I used to play that.'

And I recalled winter evenings snuggled up with Noah on the sofa in front of the log burner, drinking wine, talking and listening to music. Memories we'd never recreate. I felt an ache and a sadness in my gut and I placed my palm upon my abdomen. A sudden twinge replaced the ache and I sucked in my breath. Morning and night I'd washed the wound and used antiseptic cream as a precaution. It didn't appear any worse, but it was taking its time to feel better.

Gil cast a look my way. 'You OK?

'Sorry?'

'You gasped.'

79

'Did I?'

'Yep.'

'A tummy twinge, that's all. Not your driving,' I added, with a laugh.

I looked down at the phone screen, embarrassed, and selected Counting Crows. '*Mr Jones* sprang from the speakers.

After a few moments Gil began to sing along, not loudly, but without inhibition and with a great tone. I turned to watch him and he smiled as he sang. It was such a catchy and uplifting song and I tapped my knees to the beat and joined in. I knew all the lyrics.

'I hope Marmaris is enjoying the musical accompaniment, too,' said Gil with a laugh.

For the first time in weeks my problems faded into the recesses of my mind as we continued along an almost empty road in both directions.

'I'm impressed you know the words,' said Gil.

'I'm one of those annoying people who know all the lyrics to songs. It's one of my very few talents.'

'Well, it's a super talent to have. I make the lyrics up when I don't know them.'

We both laughed.

'That's creative,' I said. 'I'm sure you have other, more useful talents.'

'Mmmm,' he said. 'Actually, I'd say my most useful talent is for tact and diplomacy.'

'Oh? That can be helpful.'

'If I might offer some words of advice with Stefan and Judi, tact and diplomacy would be it. I'm not suggesting you hold back with opinions, but pick your moments and tread carefully. Those who've bravely or naively waded in haven't stayed the course. You seem astute so I can't see that being an issue for you.'

'Kind of you to say. And this is all useful to know. I appreciate the insider tips.'

'You and I are allies. Anyone who isn't the boss are allies.' He turned to me and gave the tiniest of winks.

'Agreed. What happened to the person who did my job previously?'

He looked ahead in silence for a moment before replying. 'I understand Stefan caught her snooping and their relationship deteriorated from there. He didn't dismiss her as such, but she was quick to hand in her notice and leave.'

'I suppose having access to the accounts and diaries etc, one must learn discretion. I'm not interested in anything other than offering efficient and friendly support.'

'Excellent attitude. Keep it friendly but professional in the office environment. We can have a laugh and you can always bounce stuff off me if anything concerns you.'

'Thanks. I will.'

He glanced down at my hands then faced the road ahead. 'Are you married?'

'I'm recently separated from my long-term partner. A single parent with my own home so I have to make a success of this opportunity.'

'Sorry to hear about the separation.'

'It was my choice. Things got messy. Noah's not a bad man, but he has issues he needs to deal with.'

Gil seemed easy to talk to. I could tell by his manner and words that he seemed trustworthy and discreet. I wasn't usually one to share my problems with people I'd just met, but I had a strong feeling about Gil and I usually trusted my inner guide.

'Funny, well, not funny exactly, but I used to be surrounded by partnered or married friends, and now it seems I'm surrounded by singletons,' I said.

'In a way being single is less complicated.' He gave a regretful smile that didn't part his lips. 'I actually prefer it now that I'm used to it.'

'Maybe so.'

After Judi had taken his hand, I'd assumed they were together. Maybe it was only in a casual way. Or, maybe casual wasn't what Judi wanted. Gil obviously didn't see them as a couple.

And I couldn't help thinking that I didn't really want to be single, but the idea of meeting someone new and dating again seemed lightyears away. I had to get comfortable with being single and independent.

Gil was definitely attractive with open and expressive features, and a strong and lean physique. His appearance alone would attract women even before he said anything in his well-educated Irish drawl. His dress was smart in a cool, effortless kind of way. His manner too, appeared calm and he had a way about him that made him a little enigmatic. Still, Judi had her eye on him and no doubt more than her eye.

A track ended and I said. 'Have you listened to Lindsey Stirling? She's a brilliant violinist and she dances as she plays, too.'

'I haven't, but you could look her up?'

I reached for his phone. 'Here's a new one I haven't heard before. *Masquerade.*'

Her melodic violin filled the air and we listened.

'Wow, I love it,' Gil said, as he tapped the steering wheel.

My phone rang from my handbag and I reached down to retrieve it. When I straightened up, my phone slipped from my fingers and as I tried to catch it I somehow managed to flick it between Gil's legs.

'Sorry.' I quickly apologised, but saw that he was already reaching between his knees.

He felt around and then took his eyes off the road to peer into the footwell. He grabbed for the phone just as a pickup van overtook us. The van swung in front of us to avoid a lorry coming around the bend in the opposite direction. The van driver in front slammed on his brakes, presumably to avoid hitting something, and Gil jerked on the steering wheel to avoid crashing into the back of the van.

The horsebox rumbled up the slope of the verge through shrubs and undergrowth.

'Shit!' cried Gil.

I felt myself falling sideways.

Gil turned the wheel to straighten up the horsebox, but the noise of stomping hooves sounded from the rear along with an ear-splitting squeal. The horsebox bounced onto the flat again at the edge of the road, then Gil slammed the brake and we came to a standstill.

I saw a queue of vehicles in front - I imagined a result of an accident or road blockage up ahead. Marmaris continued stomping and snorting and we both unfastened our seatbelts and jumped out. We hurried around to the door on the side of the van, thankfully kerbside. Gil opened the door and stepped inside. I stood back and waited.

'Shh. It's OK boy,' came Gil's calming words.

The snorting silenced and I peered through.

'Is he OK? Can I do anything?'

'Come in,' replied Gil.

I climbed up the steps. Marmaris' ears flicked back and forth, his nostrils flared and I saw a sheen of sweat on his neck.

'Could you hold his headcollar while I check him over?' asked Gil.

I stroked Marmaris' exquisite face and breathed out near his muzzle to show him I meant well. He nudged and sniffed me and his head lowered. 'Good boy,' I murmured.

I heard a car horn sound on the road and hoped that whatever the obstruction was it wouldn't delay us further.

Gil smoothed his hands down Marmaris' forelegs then along his belly and back and to his rear.

'Jesus effing Christ!' Gil cursed.

'What?'

'He's cut - a gash on the inside of his hind leg. He must have caught it with his hoof.'

Marmaris gave me a friendly nudge and his ears pricked forwards.

'Do you have any first aid?' I asked.

'There's a kit fixed to the wall behind you.'

I reached up and unhooked a red box and handed it back to Gil. 'How deep is it?'

'It looks bloody horrendous,' said Gil. 'Not the sort of injury we want to be delivering a horse with that's worth a million.'

'Good God!' I couldn't contain my surprise.

'I might be able to sort it out. There's antiseptic and butterfly stitches to patch him up. There could be scarring but we'll arrange for an equine vet to meet us there. You can look one up as we drive.'

'Of course. I can ring the customer too, to let them know, if you want.'

'Better let me as I've spoken to James before.'

'That makes sense,' I agreed.

Twenty minutes later we were back in the cabin, with a clear road ahead and no sign of what the hold up had been.

'Could have been a tractor or herd of sheep. Or cows, maybe.'

'How odd,' I said. 'I'd never have expected such a sudden hold up.'

'Took us both by surprise, and the reckless van driver too.'

'I feel responsible. I'm so sorry. I'll let Stefan and Judi know this was my fault.'

Gil didn't speak for a few moments.

'No, it's your first day. I've been with them for years and I've made mistakes, but they know and trust me.'

'But I can't let you take the flack.'

'Trust me. I'll talk my way through this. You could listen in and see how I do it. Neither Stefan or Judi are easy, but once you know how to handle problems you'd be surprised how they listen and eventually acquiesce.' He paused. 'Although this will upset them both.'

'OK. I'll listen and learn. And never get my damn phone out of my bag in the car again.'

He laughed lightly. 'Hadn't you better see who was ringing - it might be one of your children?'

'You're right, and thank you.'

It was Noah and he'd left a voice message. 'Please can you buy some milk on your way back. Clara's too busy. Otherwise, I'm in a lot of pain and bored shitless, but surviving.'

I sighed. 'It was Noah. Nothing serious.'

Noah had my sympathy, but ringing to say we needed milk! And Clara - always helpful, but I had to remember she was only sixteen. She wouldn't understand the transition for me to working full-time, being on my own and having Noah to care for, too. I took some breaths and messaged him back.

'I'll buy some. Take care and see you tonight.'

My phone buzzed again. 'Thanks, love. Could you buy some crisps too - cheese and onion?'

12

When we arrived at the stables, Gil impressed me with his friendly manner and Oscar-winning level of tact as he introduced me to the new owner, James Newiss, and went on to explain about the accident en route. Gil played it down as though it were a minor scratch that was hidden from view and would be gone in a day or two. My stomach had turned somersaults as he unloaded Marmaris and proceeded to show the new owner the injury. In fairness, it didn't actually look bad, and there were no traces of blood and only minor swelling. Luckily the cut was in a spot hidden from view unless one peered from beneath. But with a horse of his calibre, I knew how much worse it could have been. James gasped with admiration as he looked into Marmaris' eyes and stroked his face. Then as he ran his hands over his golden coat and down his legs, he gushed compliments about the horse's beauty and conformation.

I felt relieved when the vet I'd rang, Jennie Sweeney, turned up only ten minutes after our arrival. This had seemed to reassure James, too.

Despite her appearance in oversized muddy overalls and wild black hair left loose, she could have been a full-fledged member of the social elite, such was her plummy accent. As she questioned Gil about the accident and he described how he'd treated the wound, she listened attentively then spent some time talking to and stroking Marmaris before opening up her medical bag. With care, she anaesthetised and stitched the wound and even though Marmaris fidgeted and twitched, she had an assertive but soothing manner that seemed to ease his restlessness.

I followed Gil and James, who led Marmaris round to the stableyard and tethered him outside his stable, thick with straw and a full haynet. It was the smartest and cleanest stableyard I'd ever seen. Not a stray bucket, strand of hay or horsehair in sight.

Perhaps they'd swept the yard in honour of Marmaris' arrival. Several horses looked over their stable doors and whickered to Marmaris in greeting. All looked fine boned thoroughbreds or Arabians. Three teenagers, two girls and a boy dressed in jodhpurs and boots came out from a room at the end of the stable block and walked across to stroke Marmaris who lifted his tail and whinnied to the other horses.

'Oh my God, he's the most heavenly horse I've ever seen,' a pretty girl with sleek brown hair said as she stroked Marmaris' face.

'I think Marmaris knows it,' I said. 'He's handsome and proud.'

'We have tea and scones in the house,' James said to us. 'I'd be delighted to celebrate with you.'

Gil turned to me. 'That OK with you?'

Although I felt pretty sure Gil would have preferred to set off back home, I knew what was expected of us. Truth be told, I felt stressed out after the whole horsebox incident, but with some relief that the client appeared to be OK about it. Hardly a good start to my new job and the accident had been my fault. I dreaded Stefan and Judi's reaction when they found out. I felt light-headed; I hadn't eaten a thing since breakfast, so I politely accepted his hospitality.

13

From as early as I could recall, people would comment how much like my mum I looked. My dad, who was olive skinned with black hair, didn't get much of a mention in that respect. Dad's ancestors were Romany gypsies who'd travelled the lengths of Poland, and he'd often tell me stories that had been passed down through the generations, not least some of the horrific atrocities his ancestors had endured during the years of the Nazi persecution. His newlywed grandparents had had a miraculous escape and managed to flee to Sweden, where some of my relatives now lived. In her sixties, mum still wore her hair long and we were both naturally white blonde and our green eyes, long lashes and skin tone mirrored one another. At 5ft 7 mum was above average height and even before I started school it appeared I was going to be tall, too.

Another lasting memory from childhood, which I'd never been quite able to shake off, was Mum's concerns about my fussy eating habits. I'd often refused to eat things if they didn't have the right texture or taste such as cheese or broccoli and other nutritious foods Mum wanted to include in my diet. Which seemed ridiculous to me as I'd eat yoghurt and plenty of alternative fruits and veg. I often wished I had a brother or sister for her to bestow her concern on, but unfortunately for me, I carried the full brunt of her overzealous parenting inclinations. As a result, I grew adept at ignoring her fussing and questions. I'd often go silent rather than justify why I wouldn't eat or do something immediately. I resisted taking instructions from her and became quite rebellious from early on, and once I reached my teens, doubly so.

Dad would comment occasionally, 'Leave her alone. You'll only make her stubborn.'

And I thought, spot on, Dad. Not that Mum listened to him, or me for that matter, if ever I dared to object.

When the twins came along I felt determined not to fret over what they did or didn't eat, and maybe we were lucky with them both, but this had proven to be exactly the right approach. As teenagers they ate almost anything I put in front of them and were keen cooks too, Victor particularly. My poor Mum. In hindsight I realised I'd probably given her a hard time and made her more anxious than she needed to be.

Now, of course, I knew from experience how challenging parenting could be - all too easy to get things wrong.

Another thing with Mum which I realise affected me far more than anything else she did, was her dedication to tutoring me from birth. She wasn't exactly pushy, but almost everything we did together became a learning experience. I could speak Polish well by the time I started school, not that anyone else in my school could. From the day I started school I only spoke English and refused to speak any Polish if my friends asked me to. I didn't want to stand out as different. I knew I looked different though, just as the Malaysian boy in my class did. My hair was and still is the whitest blonde of anyone I know. The only reason I knew I wasn't albino was due to my black eyelashes, and from puberty dark hairs sprouting between my legs and armpits. Besides, I didn't dislike my colouring; I was only conscious that I looked a bit different.

I felt excited to start school. Mum hadn't sent me to any playgroups or nursery sessions and the only friends I'd made had been in our street and the recreational playgrounds, which thankfully I'd been taken to almost daily. I'd been coached on the monkey bars, the balancing ropes and the climbing poles, and so was physically strong and agile. We'd spend a lot of time outdoors - nature walks, climbing trees, and swimming in the sea, only a short distance from home.

My reception class teacher, Mrs Straw, told my parents I was a dream child. She'd even called me her Angel which made my classmates laugh and me want the ground to swallow me up. I didn't want to be seen as a goody two shoes and so I'd play up every now and then to ensure that I got into trouble, had to see the headteacher or be made to stand in the corner. But I wasn't ever malicious, just rebellious, and it was all carefully calculated to ensure my classmates didn't view me as a swot.

One memory stood out in my mind. We had an art lesson and the teacher asked us to paint a vase of flowers for mother's day. 'Use bright colours,' she said. 'Try not to muddy the shades with black or brown.'

Well, this triggered something in my mind and I set to work. The other children chatted and laughed as they drew and painted their flowers, but I focused on the paper in front of me. I felt in a devilish mood and this transferred to great effect onto the page. One or two of my table mates sniggered and made snarky comments as I painted, but I ignored them and said my Mum would like it anyway. 'She likes everything I do.' Which wasn't at all true but it seemed to shut them up for a while.

'Almost break time,' Mrs Straw called across the classroom. 'Can you finish up and we can all walk around and look at what everyone has painted. I stood up and appraised my painting. I felt pleased with the overall result.

Peter, beside me, looked down at my painting as though he hadn't already seen it, then gasped and called out. 'Miss, come and see what Tess has painted.'

'It's OK, Peter. I shall be coming round to look at all of them, Tess's included.'

My classmates stood patiently and proudly in front of their artistic efforts and waited for our teacher's praise. Curious, Mrs Straw began with our table and looked down at Peter's painting with thick green stems and red tipped circular blobs. 'Beautiful, Peter - well done for keeping your colours separate. Your Mum will be delighted.'

She stepped nearer and looked down at my painting. The others at my table giggled.

Peter said, 'Do you think Tess's mum will be delighted with hers, Miss?'

Mrs Straw tilted her head sideways and looked into my eyes, 'What do you think, Tess?'

I shrugged. 'I don't know. I'll ask her when I give it to her,' I said, innocently.

'Does she like sad faces on grey flowers?' Mrs Straw asked with a distinct furrow of her brows.

'What about all the flowers that aren't colourful?' I asked. 'We have brown, black, and too white people, like me, in this country, and they are sometimes sad like everyone else is sometimes.'

'Well, that is a smart way of looking at it. And I like your artistic interpretation. Well done.' She nodded with approval.

She stepped aside to look at the next painting.

'Miss?' I said.

'Yes, Tess.'

'Can I do another painting - one that my Mum will want to hang on the wall?'

She looked into my eyes and smiled. 'Of course you can. You can stay in at lunchtime.'

No doubt the teachers thought me precocious but I don't think it did me a huge disservice at school.

At my first parent's evening Mum and Dad squeezed onto the tiny reception chairs, with myself in between, whilst the teacher proceeded to tell my parents that I was gifted in my language and interpretation skills.

'We can thank Evie for this,' Dad said, turning to my mum.

'Were you aware that Tess also has an exceptional memory? I'm not sure it's photographic, but certainly not far off.'

'Really? No, I didn't know,' said my Mum, beaming down at me briefly. 'How wonderful.'

'Despite English really being her second language, she's ahead of the others in the reading scheme. It seems she only has to see and read a word once to remember it.'

'I told my husband that with Polish words, but he thought I was overstating her abilities.'

I wondered if they'd forgotten that I was sitting there, listening and taking in every word.

'Not at all,' Mrs Straw continued. 'I can see that Tess is naturally receptive in that respect, but it's early days yet.'

I looked from my Dad to my Mum who both looked down at me and smiled. 'Well done,' they said, proudly and in unison.

'And you'll have seen from her painting and drawings and in the way she expresses herself that she speaks and paints from her imagination. Naturally creative and uses nuance to widen her thinking beyond the words or things that are right in front of her. It's unusual in a child so young. I'm delighted to be Tess's

90

teacher and she's popular with her classmates too because she's fun and not too conventional.'

'She gets that from you, too,' Dad said to mum, with a wink.

When Mrs Straw had told my parents that my classmates liked me, that pleased me more than all her praise about reading, my memory and painting, combined.

Throughout my school years, I often felt I didn't quite fit in and so I tried to moderate my behaviour and words so that my peers wouldn't see me as a know it all or different. It seemed to work. I wasn't ever short of friends but having a foreign name and parents in a southern town that was predominantly white and English, made me feel somehow different.

14

From my perspective, James Newiss had seemed delighted with Marmaris.

'A more magnificent creature I have never seen. And look at those jewel-like eyes and ears taking in everything around him. Be assured, Aztec Imports will be on my lips to all who I know, both business and private.'

His words had sounded reassuring and glowing. And the way he'd spoken about horses, it was clear he was knowledgeable and experienced.

On the way home, Gil and I both expressed our relief that the cut, from what Jennie the vet had advised, shouldn't leave a noticeable scar, mostly because it had been well hidden, but also on an area of skin with virtually no hair. The vet bill, although five hundred pounds, was a minimal price to pay for what could have proven catastrophic to the sale.

'Stefan and Judi will want to celebrate tonight. They usually crack open the champagne or sometimes we go out for a meal. Will you want to stay?'

'I'd like to, but I'll check in on the twins first.'

We parked the horsebox behind the stables and headed through the French doors at the back. All seemed quiet and the main office stood empty.

'I'll make coffee,' said Gil. 'I don't know about you but I'm flagging from the driving and stress.'

'I wonder where they are,' I said.

'Awaiting your return.'

I swung around to see Stefan who stood in the doorway.

'All seemed so quiet,' I said.

'I was changing for dinner. I'm ravenous,' he said, with a flick of his eyebrows.

Dressed in well fitted jeans, and another impeccably cut black shirt, he looked like a model straight out of Vogue, and I felt butterflies dance through my insides. I couldn't work out if this was down to nerves after the Marmaris incident or how attractive he looked.

Gil hadn't yet told Stefan about the near accident, but it seemed he had no need to.

'Why didn't you ring me?' Stefan's tone had switched from friendly to accusing, as he directed his words at Gil.

Cool and steady, Gil replied, 'You've spoken to James then?'

'I rang James half an hour ago to see how Marmaris was settling in. I felt embarrassed when he mentioned the accident and the visit from the vet. He imagined you'd have told me and I had to lie and say that I knew.'

'Let's talk next door,' said Gil.

Stefan's eyes narrowed. 'I know all I need to know. James sent me a close up of the injury. We'll discuss how it happened tomorrow. I don't want our evening spoiled.'

'I assume you've spoken to Judi?' said Gil.

'Indeed. We've already had quite enough to deal with today. As James sounded happy then it seems you've talked your way round it. Full explanation tomorrow, OK?'

Gil replied, keeping his composure. 'Or maybe the wound was minor and James is reassured it will heal. But of course, we'll talk tomorrow.'

I admired Gil's manner - so obliging but without a hint of subservience to his boss.

As Gil spoke, I noticed how Stefan clenched his jaw and the muscles rippled beneath his cheeks as if he fought back his response. Then Stefan's expression softened and he turned my way and walked over.

I felt the nearness of his presence and watched the lines around his eyes crease as he spoke.

'I've booked a table for the four of us at La Galerie, 7pm,' he said. 'Can you come?'

Feeling relieved by his lighter mood, I replied, 'I'd like that.'

I had no intention of missing out on dinner at a fine restaurant, or of leaving Gil in the lurch if Judi or Stefan started questioning how the accident had unfolded.

'Excellent. Would you like to go home and change and meet us there or shall I pick you up?'

'It's no distance from home so I'll meet you there. I've always wanted to try La Galerie.'

He reached down and I felt his hand lightly upon my shoulder. 'This is also to celebrate your first day. I'm proud to have you on board.'

I felt the colour rise in my cheeks. Damn, my complexion and my hormones. I'd never been able to disguise a blush, although I couldn't ever recall a man having such an instant and repeated effect on me.

On the way home I visualised rifling through the hangers in my wardrobe. I wondered what Judi would wear. From what I'd seen, she seemed formal and classic in her attire. During the interview, and today, she'd worn smart suit trousers and flat pumps. They suited her slim, boyish figure. I stopped off at the garage convenience store for milk, and Noah's cheese and onion crisps. I also bought butter, cheese, a bag of apples and porridge oats.

When I walked through the front door I smelled cooking and I headed into the kitchen to find Victor stirring a bolognaise. I noticed there were empty packets, onion skins and splashes of tomato sauce across the hob, the back wall and white kitchen worktop. Some of the peeled onion skin had dropped onto the floor and I reached down and picked it up and dropped it into the waste bin. I gave my hands a quick rinse under the tap.

'You're a star, Vic.' I put my arm around his shoulders and gave him a squeeze. 'What a lovely surprise to come home to.'

He turned to me with his wide blue eyes. 'So, how was your first day?'

'Really interesting. I'm going to like it there.'

'That's cool, Mum. There's garlic bread in the oven.'

'I hope you won't mind, but Stefan, my boss, has booked a celebratory dinner at La Galerie. I could hardly refuse.'

'Nice, living the high life.'

'But Dad and Clara will love that you've cooked. I'll clean up when I get in.'

Victor picked up the jar of tomato sauce and tipped some into the pan, which sprayed more across the hob.

I stepped back and checked the front of my dress.

He stirred vigorously, and turned to me. 'Dad's been kinda demanding.'

'Oh, in what way?'

'I think he's bored.'

'Probably in pain too,' I said.

'He kept asking when his next tablets were due. But how am I supposed to keep track when I'm at school?'

'I'll go see him. I'll suggest we write down whenever he takes something. Then we can all help keep track. I imagine he's on the maximum dose of paracetamol or whatever he's been given.'

'Good idea,' said Vic. He lifted the pan of boiling spaghetti and carried it to the sink. 'Oh, and Gran rang. She was surprised to hear you'd already started a new job.'

'Ahh, I hadn't got round to telling her. I'll call her.'

I walked into Vic's bedroom and Noah peered up from his iPad.

He looked terrible. I could see from his pinched features and heavy eyes that he was in pain.

'How did it go?' he asked with a voice that demanded my sympathy.

I turned the chair around at Victor's desk and sat down. 'Really good. They're fascinating characters.'

'It's not the theatre.' He laughed, and then winced in pain.

'No, but I feel I've got to perform well. They're friendly, but their services are so expensive that the customer side might be demanding. Plus, Stefan and Judi are perfectionists which might create its own challenges.'

'That does sound interesting,' said Noah and nodded but without further comment.

'More importantly, how are you? How's the pain?'

'I'm not gonna lie - it's effing horrendous.'

I pulled off a sheet of paper from the writing pad on Victor's desk. 'We'll write down what medication you're having and when. That way you'll keep track and won't overdose.'

I stood up and handed him the paper and pen.

He gave a slim smile. 'Thank you. I should have thought of that myself.'

'I imagine the pain interferes with rational thinking,' I replied.

'Oh, I got your crisps.'

'What crisps?'

'The cheese and onion ones you messaged about.'

Noah grimaced again, but this time with embarrassment. 'Oh dear. I can't even blame a bruised head for that.'

I laughed. 'At least you've still got your sense of humour.'

'Will you eat dinner up here with me? I'd love your company.'

'Sorry, I'm eating out with Judi, Stefan and Gil tonight. Think they want to welcome me into the fold.'

His look of disappointment was palpable. He twisted his mouth and his eyes flickered. 'You mean a double date?'

Noah had never been able to disguise how he felt, although he'd never been a jealous partner. I feared that had changed now he was my ex partner.

'Not at all. It's work,' I said. But I wasn't stupid enough to realise why Noah had thought that, and Judi and Gil were an item, albeit loosely. And truthfully, Stefan was incredibly attractive and apparently single.

I didn't want to admit that to myself, but I could hardly deny the obvious.

He acquiesced. 'It's fine. Don't worry.'

'I'll ask Clara and Vic to come up though. It must feel lonely being up here by yourself all day.'

'It is, but I've seen the kids which is lovely.'

I stood up. 'I must get ready.'

Without speaking, Noah's eyes returned to his screen and I took that as permission to leave.

As I left the room I heard his voice.

'Better not wear anything too pretty.'

I sighed and continued up the stairs to the attic. 'Trainers and tracky bottoms,' I called.

But I knew precisely which dress I was going to wear.

15

By the beginning of sixth form, at sixteen, I'd already chosen my University subject - Performing Arts. In my final year of school I applied, auditioned and was accepted, much to the quiet dissatisfaction of some of my teachers.

Thankfully, after some initial reluctance, Mum and Dad had been supportive.

Throughout my school years I'd excelled in all subjects - there wasn't one I failed at. I don't really know why - it wasn't as if I studied hard. Sometimes, I felt like a fraud for making little effort unlike some of my friends who worked far harder.

My A-Level teachers had expected and encouraged me to apply to one of the top Universities, Oxford and Cambridge even, but I'd already decided that it was acting and drama I wanted to study, not so much in any academic sense, but to perform on stage.

My first real performance role at school, aged six, was playing the newborn lamb given to baby Jesus. I hadn't felt disappointed not to be playing Mary or one of the Shepherds or Kings. The lamb got to sing a solo and dance. Well, the dance wasn't exactly a part of the script, until I suggested it to my teacher.

'What sort of dance, Tess?'

'How a lamb dances of course,' I'd replied as though it was perfectly obvious.

As I'd sung my solo for the first time, I'd gambolled and frolicked around the manger with baby Jesus inside.

Mr Bevan, my teacher at the time, had clapped upon completion. 'Bravo! The best lamb of Christ I've ever had the pleasure to see.'

I think it was Mr Bevan's obvious delight, and subsequently, the audience's, that had ignited a spark inside of me. As a naturally gregarious child, I enjoyed being the centre of attention and didn't worry about being laughed at. In fact, drama or comedy, I threw myself into every role. If ever something went wrong and it got a laugh, so much the better. I was no self-conscious wallflower. In fact, I was probably a bit of a show off.

'You could study Classics or Literature at Oxford. I'm confident you'd pass the entrance exam.' My literature teacher had said.

But why would I want to sit and study texts, and analyse them line by line all day when I could perform and rehearse plays to bring these fine works and characters to life?

As predicted, I received excellent grades in my A-Levels, although that hadn't been a requirement of entry into Drama School. My audition secured that for me. I'd chosen to perform a monologue from *Under Milk Wood* by Dylan Thomas. I'd practiced and perfected my Welsh accent, and my drama teacher, Ms Moore, had tutored me in my rehearsals for the audition.

'If they don't accept you,' she'd said. 'They don't recognise talent when they see it.' She was the kind of teacher to bolster my confidence all the way through.

I felt excited to be leaving Somerset, my home county, and my childhood behind. I was ready for the next step. Mum had been suffocating me with her high expectations in all things, all along really, and the moment I'd escaped her clutches I felt an immense sense of freedom and took full advantage of it.

During the holidays I'd find work and stay with friends so that I could remain in London. It wasn't that I didn't love my parents, I really did, I just didn't miss them hugely and I didn't want to go back to my childhood and my bedroom, where I often felt stifled and hemmed in by the four walls of home and the gossip and small talk of the town I grew up in. In short, I felt desperate to break free. Poor Mum, I know she only wanted the best for me, and I'm sure her pushiness had given me determination and helped get me into Drama School. But as an adult, I no longer needed or wanted her help in that respect.

16

La Galerie

I closed the front door behind me and breathed a heavy sigh.

Leaving the house hadn't proven easy. Noah had needed help with washing and getting to the toilet, and the bathroom had been in constant use. No one had thought to take Digby out, who had created chaos around the house by jumping all over the furniture. He'd brought toys to all of us in turn so we would play with him, and then ran to the front door with his lead and whined. He couldn't have made me feel more guilty if he'd tried.

Eventually, after much persuasion, Clara and Fleur agreed to walk him along the beach.

'We're meeting friends but I'm sure Digby will enjoy that, too.'

'Please keep him away from their snacks and any fish and chips.' Were my final words before they left. The pavements of Whitby were a smorgasbord for seagulls and hungry dogs seeking extra tidbits.

I walked down the steps that led between the houses and into town, and felt oddly self-conscious in my high heels as they clicked against the cobblestones. I couldn't recall the last time I'd worn them, although with straps and buckles they felt secure enough. I hadn't had time to paint my nails; I'd sprayed on a designer perfume Noah had bought me for my birthday, but which I'd barely worn. Getting dressed up to eat out felt indulgent and decadent. I'd washed and dressed my wound, which I thought looked less swollen, but annoyingly, hurt more than when I'd first done it. I poked and prodded it to check there were no fragments left inside and took two paracetamol which helped to dull the pain.

I saw Mum had rung me twice and I called her back as I walked.

'Darling, how are you all?' She didn't pause for my reply. 'So good of you to be supporting Noah after what he's done to you.'

'I don't mind, Mum, and I wasn't given much of a choice.'

'No, I suppose not.' She gave a deep sigh. 'Victor was telling me about your new job. Sounds exciting!'

'Only my first day, but it went really well.'

'You sound as if you're walking - is it Digby?' she asked.

'Actually, I'm meeting Stefan and his sister, my new bosses, for dinner in town.'

'How lovely. Hope they're paying.'

'I expect they'll insist since they're millionaires.'

'Goodness. I told you to go into business, didn't I?' she said, but laughed.

As a business and economics lecturer, mum had tried to persuade me early on that was where the money lay. She'd relented when she saw my passions lay elsewhere and especially when I'd pointed out that she was an educator as opposed to a wealthy entrepreneur.

'My salary is pretty good, so I'm not complaining,' I said. 'They give bonuses too.'

'What's the business called?'

'Aztec Imports. Stefan and Judi Temple. This afternoon I helped deliver the most beautiful Arabian horse you've ever seen, Marmaris, to his new owner. I imagine they'll put photos of him on their website.'

'I'll take a look, my darling. Now, enjoy your evening and don't forget to keep me posted about Noah and your new job.'

When I walked into the restaurant I quickly spotted Stefan sitting at one of the tables in the front window. Gil and Judi sat opposite him with their backs to me. He threw me a wave and I headed over.

Stefan stood up. 'Glad you made it, Tess.'

'Sorry I'm a bit late - dogs and children to sort out.'

'We've only ordered drinks,' he said.

I unbuttoned my coat and Stefan lifted it from my back.

'That's a beautiful dress,' he said, and appraised me. 'It suits you.'

I'd chosen my favourite dress, relatively new. Black chiffon that hung to the knee, a low back and a ruffled neckline and a belt to pinch it in at the waist. I knew it looked good and it was dressy without being over the top. I was glad I'd made the effort. Judi wore a red velvet dress which complemented her colouring. Stefan and Gil wore tailored jeans and shirts.

A waiter appeared with an ice bucket, two bottles and four champagne flutes.

'Your champagne, sir.'

This was an excellent start, I thought, and couldn't remember the last time I'd drank champagne. I'd never been a good drinker, that is, alcohol was something I could only tolerate in small doses. The doctor once told me that it was because I didn't drink often enough, but I knew that wasn't true. So when the waiter filled our glasses I said to myself one glass would be my lot and I'd make it last. With new people I met I'd often explain this so that they didn't try to ply me with more. Unfortunately, this occasionally backfired and they were curious to see how I behaved if I drank too much. I decided to keep quiet and sip slowly. It tasted delicious and certainly superior to my usual glass of wine.

I ordered sea bass with king prawns and vegetables. Everything was cooked and served to perfection and tasted divine. I'd barely eaten all day and after the plates were cleared away I ordered a dark chocolate mousse for dessert. I could see why Judi remained so slim - she ordered a chicken salad and a fruit terrine for dessert. She didn't, however, skimp on her champagne consumption and her voice and laughter grew louder as the meal progressed. She revealed a different, more uninhibited side.

I noticed how territorial she behaved towards Gil, in the way she touched his arm and put her arm around his shoulders. She even leaned in and gave him a lingering kiss on the cheek. To me, his response revealed that he wasn't all that into her, or maybe he was more reserved with his affections in public. She, however, doted on his every word and laughed at all his humour. I found Gil quite witty. Although classically beautiful, I wasn't sure Judi's attentiveness enhanced her appeal. Not that I was an expert, but she seemed a touch too keen, verging on clingy.

Stefan picked up the champagne bottle and moved to top up my glass again. 'There's plenty more where this came from,' he said.

I thought how generous Stefan seemed. Some wealthy types were wealthy because they were tight with their cash. Not so with Stefan. My salary was more than I'd ever earned, too, and certainly more favourable when compared to similar positions.

Between us we'd almost emptied the two bottles.

'I know, but I don't want to feel hungover tomorrow,' I said with a grimace.

'Oh, don't worry about that. Come in later if you like. You worked a long day today.'

I noticed Gil and Judi looking out onto the street and Judi whispered something into Gil's ear. I followed their gaze. A woman stood on the opposite side of the street and looked straight in at us. Even from twenty yards away she caught my eye. She had auburn hair swept up into a high-topped ponytail. She looked glamorous, pretty and petite and wore a black fitted jacket over skin tight red jeans and tall black boots.

I turned to Stefan. 'Do you know that woman out there? She seems to know you.'

Stefan leaned forwards in his chair to look. Calmly, he sat back in his seat again and picked up his champagne glass. Without answering my question he pushed his chair back and said, 'I'd like to make a toast if I may.' He stood up.

Gil, Judi and I took our glasses.

'I was going to make a toast to the magnificent Marmaris but I will reserve that for tonight. However, I would most certainly like to toast a welcome to Tess.'

All three of them turned my way.

'I believe when we recruited Tess we struck gold. From the moment you walked into our home, our business, I felt you belonged. Bright and intelligent in every sense.'

I felt my cheeks burn as people sitting at the other tables watched and smiled.

'Welcome!' he continued. 'I hope you'll enjoy working with us.'

I noticed how he turned to the window for a moment - with his glass still raised.

He turned back to the table and we all clinked glasses.

They continued looking at me, and Gil gave a small nod of encouragement. I realised it must be my turn to say something.

I remained seated. 'Thank you, Stefan. I've had a fantastic first day. Unexpected in some ways, and enlightening too. And most importantly, I'm enjoying getting to know you all and learning about the business.' I paused and looked around at the three of them. 'Thank you for making me feel so welcome.'

We chinked glasses again.

I set my glass back down. 'And finally, do any of you know that woman out there? She's been watching us for a few minutes and doesn't look happy.' I turned to face Stefan.

'That is Suzanne,' he said, through tightened lips. 'Last I knew she was moving out of Whitby so Lord knows what she's doing here. Suzanne used to do your job until she decided to quit last month. She proved to be incompetent then left us in the lurch and didn't even work a week's notice, let alone the month she was contracted to work. A damned nuisance.'

He had a bitterness to his voice that sounded out of character. Or at least from the little I knew of him after only one day. Despite the alcohol I felt a flutter of nerves and hoped neither he or Judi would ever view me as incompetent.

Gil stood up. 'I'll go and see if she's OK.'

Stefan raised his hand to stop him. 'Now isn't the time.'

Judi nodded and put her hand on Gil's arm. 'She left on bad terms, and it was her choice to leave. Good riddance as far as I am concerned.'

When Suzanne caught us all watching her she looked down and wiped her eyes. She didn't look up again and after a few moments, she turned and with head still bowed, walked back down the street towards town.

I felt sorry for her and sensed there had to be something significant that Stefan and Judi didn't want to share with me. 'She looks distressed,' I said. 'Shouldn't one of you talk to her and check if she's OK?'

I looked across at Gil but he kept his mouth firmly closed as though repressing his words. If I'd met her before I'd have insisted on going out to talk to her, but as I hadn't and I didn't know any of the background, I felt I couldn't justify it.

'Suzanne is playing the victim and attempting to make us feel guilty, and gain our attention. If I'd looked her way, or one of us had gone out to her, that's precisely what we're giving her. Neither necessary, nor justified,' said Stefan, quietly, and beneath the dimly lit lamp suspended above the table, the angles of his features seemed more pronounced than ever.

I wanted to ask Stefan what had happened to force Suzanne to leave so suddenly and what had made her come out at night and watch us as we ate and enjoyed ourselves.

A waiter brought coffees to the table and now that Suzanne was out of sight, Stefan was quick to move the conversation away from her.

The restaurant gradually emptied but Stefan and Judi seemed in no rush to leave. I'd given up refusing a refill of champagne and the alcohol enticed me into laughter and to talk more openly.

'So, your husband, sorry, not your husband, your partner, ex-partner is staying in the cottage you've just purchased to get away from him?' asked Judi with a quizzical smile.

'Exactly,' I said with a frown. 'But the accident was kind of my fault and Noah was helping me out. I'm only glad he didn't kill himself.' I giggled inappropriately and the others joined in.

Judi smirked and became forthright in her questions. 'Fortunate indeed. And what precisely did you fall out about? Did he have an affair...or did you?'

'It's more complicated than that. An affair would have ended us years ago, not that either of us has had one, but he has a gambling addiction. So you see, in the end I had no choice but to leave him. I'm hoping my leaving may be the impetus he needs to get help and quit.'

'Mmm, good luck with that,' she replied. 'And should he quit, might you get back together?'

I thought for a moment. 'No. Not now.'

'Why?' she propped her chin on her hand and tilted her head inquiringly.

'Too much has happened. The deceit runs too deep - stealing money from us, in effect. I couldn't risk going back to that, ever.'

'I agree with you,' said Stefan who had been watching me intently. 'You'd be mad to have him back. Stealing from those one loves is an unforgivable crime.'

104

'But love is more complicated than that, surely? You can't simply stop loving someone because they do something wrong,' said Gil.

'That is true,' I agreed. 'But maybe we stop loving someone who doesn't respect us and cannot be honest with us. That's what it came to, eventually.'

Gil nodded agreement. 'I hope you don't mind us asking you such intimate things so soon.'

'I might regret it in the morning,' I replied. 'But right now I'm glad you know more about me. Plus, you're making me feel at ease and I hope we can be friends and confidants, as well as colleagues.'

'Beautifully put, my girl,' said Stefan. 'I've always wanted that with the people I work with. Trust and loyalty comes with openness and honesty. Don't you agree, Gil?'

We turned to Gil who didn't immediately answer.

'It can take me years to trust someone, if ever. But you guys got me early on,' Gil replied, and he put an arm around Judi's shoulders and gave her a squeeze.

Judi leaned in and kissed him on the cheek. 'We might be small in numbers, but we're big on friendship and loyalty.'

I thought back to my other jobs. Other than my stint in the tourist office, I'd always formed close relationships with my colleagues - The Hull Docks Theatre Company, Roddy and crew on the Captain Cook experience. It made going to work easier and more appealing, even if there might be one or two individuals it might be impossible to gel with.

17

When Tess meets Noah

I arrived at The Hull Docks Theatre on my first day of rehearsals, feeling nervous but excited and ready to meet the cast and crew. All the previous day and night my stomach had churned and I hadn't slept until around four in the morning. When my alarm went off I didn't hear it until the girl in the bedsit opposite mine had hammered on my door to wake me up.

Thank goodness she had.

Securing my first post Drama School acting job with Hull Docks had been applauded by my fellow students and tutors. Two of my best friends had already auditioned for and gained roles in the West End and I felt sad to be leaving them and London behind for what I deemed the far less exciting northern town of Hull. However, it didn't take long for me to realise the coastal city had a rich cultural tapestry to enjoy, and the nightlife seemed vibrant and lively too.

On my first day, I'd walked through the stage door at the back of the theatre, as instructed, and quite literally fell down two steps. When I looked up, still on my hands and knees, a man of average height, and well built, and who looked as if he could be an Italian actor dressed from head to toe in black, hurried towards me.

He reached down to take my hand. 'Allow me to help you,' he said, in a broad North Yorkshire accent.

I took his hand and stood up, flustered and red faced. 'Thank you. I was rushing and didn't see the steps.'

'There is a big sign and yellow tape, but it's surprising how often they catch new arrivals out. Are you hurt?'

I brushed down my knees. 'I don't think so. And I won't do it again.'

'True - it's only ever a one way trip,' he said and smiled in sympathy.

I laughed and held out my hand again. 'I'm Tess Blonski. It's my first day.'

'Good to meet you, Tess. I'm Noah, Stage Manager and general dogsbody.'

I knew perfectly well that Stage Manager meant anything but dogsbody, especially in a theatre such as this, and now that he'd introduced himself I recognised his face and his name from the brochure I'd been given when I'd come for my interview and audition.

'Come on,' he said. 'I'll show you to the Green Room. Everyone gathers there before rehearsal starts.'

I followed him down a corridor behind the stage and auditorium and paused in front of a brightly painted green door. 'Are you ready?' he said, with a warmth in his features that showed an understanding for how nervous I might be feeling.

'I think so.'

Noah opened the door and I followed him in. A cast of eight men and women either sitting or standing, fell silent and turned our way.

'Am I the only newbie?' I said, and smiled at the sea of faces.

'This is Tess,' said Noah. 'Go easy on her - she almost broke a leg falling down the back steps.'

There were a few laughs and smiles.

'Those bloody steps are lethal. I'm sure they're designed to ensure someone breaks a leg before performances!' A pretty girl with long black hair said.

'A bit embarrassing, but nothing broken,' I said.

The same girl came forward. 'Embarrassment is something we are all used to here, so welcome to the club. I'm Mia by the way.' She took my hand and shook it heartily. 'Let me make you a coffee. We're all going to need a few shots of rocket fuel to get through today.'

I wasn't so sure - too much coffee gave me the jitters, but she had a warm and encouraging manner.

There were murmurs of agreement all round. I'd heard about our director for my first play, Kim Coleman, a task master by reputation. However, her productions had been consistent hits and huge successes. The play we were putting on was, *Stags & Hens* by Willy Russel - a comedy/drama set in the clubs of

107

Liverpool. I was to play Carol, which wasn't a huge speaking part but as this was my first real professional role, I was more than delighted to be here. I chatted to a few members of the cast and learnt their names. None of us were Liverpudlians where the play was set, although a few of them sounded northern.

I'd been practicing my Liverpudlian accent from the moment I knew which play we'd be doing. Luckily my first boyfriend, Harry, at The Central School had been a dancer from Liverpool. The other students nicknamed him Billy Elliot from the movie and musical.

'But Billy Elliot isn't even set in Liverpool,' Harry had argued to no effect.

In fairness, looks wise he could have been Billy Elliot's older brother.

His scouse accent had been broad and my memory of his voice had helped me to pick it up for this role.

Noah returned to talk to us. 'Kim is here and in the auditorium. Are you ready to meet her?'

'Yes,' we all chorused. And I felt a flutter of butterflies in my tummy.

'We seem to be missing Jessica,' said Noah. 'Have any of you heard from her?'

I looked around and the others shook their heads.

One of the girls, Simone, a tall girl with cropped afro hair said. 'Oddly, I texted her only yesterday and I've not heard back.'

'Strange,' said Noah. 'She's usually an excellent timekeeper.' He pulled his phone from his pocket. 'I'll call her.'

We followed Noah out, each carrying our scripts and bottles of water. I'd dressed deliberately for comfort in leggings, vest and stage pumps, and I'd twisted my hair into a bun. I heard Simone say behind me. 'I hope Jess is OK. She was away with her boyfriend this weekend.'

A circle of chairs had been set up on the stage and we all took seats, along with Noah and Kim.

Kim introduced herself with a short talk about what she'd worked on previously and we all listened attentively. *Stags and Hens* was to be her first production with Hull Docks.

'I hear our leading lady, Jessica, is missing in action. Any luck getting through to her, Noah?'

Noah shook his head. 'Afraid not, but I've left a message.'

The next moment Noah's phone rang and he looked at the screen. He nodded at Kim, and walked up the steps of the auditorium.

As he talked on the phone, Kim asked if we would introduce ourselves and say a few words about the character we were playing.

Noah soon returned and sat down and we all looked at him, expectant. 'I'm sorry to say that poor Jessica has torn her achilles tendon, quite badly. She'll be on bed rest and then crutches for several weeks. It happened late last night as she stepped off the train. He turned to Kim. She can't possibly play Linda and she's devastated.'

There were sighs and murmurs amongst the others.

We all looked at Kim.

'Well, we are devastated too. Poor Jessica,' Kim said, frowning, and paused in thought. 'But the show must go on. Would any of you ladies like to read the part of Linda today, whilst we decide who can play her?'

No one volunteered. Kim turned and looked from one actress to the next in turn.

Eventually I said, 'I'll read her, if it'll help.'

Everyone's eyes turned my way.

I didn't mention that I already knew my character, Carol's lines by heart, and most of Linda's too. I'd been keen to make a good first impression and had spent the past two weeks reading through the play each night, learning my lines and getting into character.

Kim clapped her hands. 'Bravo young lady. Tess, isn't it, first day?'

'But only if no one else would rather read her,' I said looking around. I didn't want to appear pushy but the pause for a volunteer had been surprisingly long.

'OK, ladies and gents. We'll finish introductions first, followed by a full read through of Act One. Then a short break before we move onto Act Two. Any questions?'

By the end of the first Act I was overflowing with adrenaline. I'd loved how everyone read their parts as if they were standing and performing on the stage - putting tension and emotion into each of their lines. The Liverpudlian accents had been mixed but we had a month to perfect them.

We all stood up and headed to the Green Room for tea and coffee.

'A moment, Tess?' Kim said, approaching me.

I felt another flicker of nerves and hoped she wasn't going to criticise my reading.

She waited until the others had dispersed before speaking. 'Have you performed this play before as Carol or Linda?'

I shook my head. 'No, but I have learnt the lines.'

She nodded. 'I wanted to say how delighted I was with your readings. You even gave both of the girls their own personalities. I assume you purposefully gave them subtly different accents too?'

'I suppose I did. I made Linda a little softer, and less broad and bolshy than Carol, who isn't the smartest character beneath her generous nature. Linda is wise without being loud about it, and I hope that came across.'

'It did,' Kim said, twisting her mouth from one side to the other.

'I'm glad,' I replied.

'Would you mind if I swapped your role in the play?'

I felt my eyes sting and couldn't believe what she might be about to say.

'I'm happy to play any part.' Which was true.

'Then I'd like to recast you as Linda, our bride to be. You look and sound perfect for her. The energy you gave her, both characters actually, was marvellous for a first read through - utterly convincing, in fact. I have someone in mind who can play Carol. A real shame about poor Jessica, but I'm sure Noah and the others will agree this is the right move. Not that I care a jot what they think, as long as you are happy to go with the change?'

I couldn't help grinning and I felt my eyes pool with emotion. 'I'd be honoured to play Linda.' And before I could stop myself I clapped my hands and jumped up and down on the spot like a bouncy puppy. Kim threw back her head and laughed.

Whether the other cast members felt annoyed that on my first day with the company I'd been given the main part, none of them expressed that, unless there were mutterings behind my back I wasn't aware of. The fact that I'd known Linda's lines pretty much from the start of rehearsals had, I think, convinced the rest of the cast I could play her well enough. Either way, that first intense month of rehearsals with the company followed by performances at Hull and then for twelve weeks in other theatres, nationally, secured my place with the cast as a friend and performer.

The reviews from theatre critics and audiences were exceptional and most of the cast members had special mentions for portrayals of our characters. I couldn't have been happier even if I did feel exhausted most of the time, and especially after a Saturday and Sunday with a matinee and evening performance.

After meeting Noah on my first day and getting to know him in the weeks and months that followed, I'd got the feeling that he enjoyed my company, although only in a friendship sense. No one could deny his handsome looks with dark skin and hair, fine and strong physique, but it was his generous nature and humour that attracted all of the actors' attention, whether heterosexual, bi or gay. Noah was easy to talk to and never sat alone. There was something about him that seemed special. He was his own person and quietly confident in a way that seemed unique compared to other men I'd met. He was brilliant at his job, too.

What none of us could have known at the time, was that Noah was already gambling, and had been since his teens. He hid that side of him only too well.

Our final two shows of *Stags and Hens* were on a Saturday at York Barbican, which also happened to be Valentine's Day. I'd been sharing a room at Clifford's Tower Hotel with two of the girls, Mindy and Zoe, and none of us had boyfriends.

As we showered and dressed in our hotel room, I joked. 'It's a shame we're not at home to open all of our Valentine's cards.'

'I'll probably struggle to open the front door when I get home,' Zoe said.

'Have you actually sent any?' I asked her.

'Nah,' said Zoe. 'No men have met my rigorous criteria recently.'

Mindy giggled. 'I might have.'

'Ooh, really?' I said.

'Yes, but if I tell you, you must promise to keep it quiet. I'd die if he found out.'

'Let me guess,' said Zoe. 'I assume he's here with us in York?'

'Might be,' she said, and her cheeks reddened.

Mindy played Carol, the part I was originally going to play, and in one of the scenes she had to kiss Robbie, in real life named Jack. I'd noticed that for the past couple of weeks, they weren't so much acting the kiss, which we all knew how to do, as actually kissing one another. It was either great acting or genuine and with feeling.

'I think I know,' I said. 'Is it Jack?'

She shook her head.

'I got the impression you liked Jack, too,' said Zoe.

'Oh, I do like him and he's a great kisser, but it isn't him.'

'I haven't noticed you flirting with anyone else,' I said.

Mindy gave a deep sigh. 'That's because I can't flirt with him. Hard to believe, I know, but I can barely speak two coherent words in front of him.'

'Aww,' I said. 'Then it must be love.'

'It is. Or infatuation. A massive crush anyway,' she said, and she blushed again.

'Did you sign your name on the card?' I asked.

'Yes.' She gave another heartfelt sigh. 'And now I wish I hadn't. I'll die when I see him.'

'No you won't,' I said. 'You're a twenty-first century woman. We have every right to tell a man we like them.'

'I know,' she agreed. 'I'm a feminist, and as you know I'm not shy. The only reason I sent the card is because it's our final night and if I don't do it now then I might not see him for weeks. I've sent a few texts on the pretence of work stuff, but he only replies briefly and super professionally. I feel I'm doomed to love him only from a distance,' she said, with a dramatic sweep of her hair, followed by a mournful shake of her head.

'You have to tell us, and we swear we won't do any nudging or winking when he's around. We are actors and can act as if we don't suspect a thing,' I said.

'OK,' she relented quickly, seeming relieved to share her burden. 'It's Noah.' She took a gasp of air and bit her bottom lip as she awaited our reaction.

The moment I heard Noah's name my stomach did an enormous lurch.

Zoe came over to Mindy and gave her a big hug. 'I've seen him eyeing you up.'

'You mean he looks at me when we're talking?' she said, and groaned. 'That's being polite, not eyeing me up.'

'You're beautiful.' Zoe continued. 'And if he hasn't seen you that way before, as soon as he gets your card the idea and possibilities of you and him will begin to form in his mind.'

'Is that what happens when you send a Valentine's card?' I said. 'I wish I'd known that years ago.'

'Of course it does,' she replied. 'I've tried and tested it.'

'Do you really think so?' said Mindy.

'It's the power of suggestion,' replied Zoe with convincing authority. 'I learned about it in psychology. I read a book about it, too. But you have to do more than send a card. You have to show a keen interest in things he says, respond wittily, throw in little compliments every now and then - be attentive. It's a neurolinguistic technique. Subtly though, not like you're desperate.'

'But I am desperate,' said Mindy. 'Do you think I've left all that too late seeing as it's our last night?' She paused. 'I did send him those texts.'

'Of course it's not too late. Everyone knows people get together at last night parties.'

Mindy chewed her bottom lip, thoughtful.

'I tell you what else you should do. Again, subtly. You should mention how strong he is. Have you seen his arms? Men love that sort of thing - He man protect woman,' Zoe said in a deep voice. 'It's all primitive evolution stuff.'

'Like Tarzan you mean?' asked Mindy with all sincerity.

'Exactly,' Zoe replied. 'I can't wait for the party now. What are you both wearing?' She turned to me.

'I hadn't really thought about it,' I said. 'Does everyone dress up?'

'Of course, this is your first,' said Mindy. 'Yes, we do at Hull Docks. Anything goes.'

'You've got the boobs, Mindy. You must present them well tonight,' Zoe suggested.

'I don't like wearing low cut,' said Mindy looking down at her chest. 'Men stare.'

'I know, but tonight that's what you want, isn't it?' said Zoe.

'I guess. I have got a dress I normally wear a camisole beneath but I could wear it without.'

Zoe nodded with conviction. 'That's the one then.'

I stood quietly aside not wanting to put a damper on Mindy's enthusiasm or plans.

The audience gave a standing ovation as we walked onto the stage in pairs and took our final bows. I couldn't stop smiling and I felt happy but tearful as the curtains finally closed in front of us. The entire cast turned to one another and I could see the joy and emotion in their faces. We hugged one another and Kim and Noah soon joined us.

I caught Noah's eye and he came nearer and held out his arms to embrace me as the others had done. But as he held me to him, and I felt his chest and legs press against mine, I realised this felt nothing like the other hugs from the male members of the cast.

I felt his lips brush my face, so close to my mouth, and still holding me, he said, 'Incredible. I believed every word you said, and I know the audience did too.'

From his control room at the back of the theatre, Noah had watched us every night and no doubt paid close attention to and scrutinised our performances.

As he held me close, I felt conscious suddenly of the gaze from some of the others, and I drew back. Noah still looked at me with eyes that pierced my mind and body and evoked a longing for him to draw me into his arms once more. But at that moment I caught sight of Mindy standing only a couple of feet away, with arms folded, lips pursed and her eyes switching back and forth between Noah and me.

With reluctance, I turned away from Noah and said to Mindy, 'Come on, time to get ready for the party.'

18

But Mindy didn't forgive my falling in love with Noah, or Noah for falling in love with me. In fact she saw it as nothing less than a dreadful betrayal on the scale of a Shakespearean tragedy, that I'd heard her confess her admiration for him only that day, whilst all along believing that I'd had designs on Noah myself. Which wasn't true at the time and I only liked him and had a suspicion that he liked me, too. But I couldn't deny that after that final night when he'd made his feelings for me plainly obvious, it was the only trigger I had needed to fall instantly and deeply in love with him.

And so, despite my best efforts, my friendship with Mindy was no more. This had proven awkward in the next two plays with Hull Docks, but we remained professional, and true to our parts on stage, even if I felt a reserved and distant iciness from her off stage. The other actors, bar Zoe, who understandably took her friend's side, commented along the lines of, 'all is fair in love and war'. This was something I didn't strictly believe in, but it did at least mean that I wasn't completely judged and ostracised by the other players.

Anyone who has ever been in a theatre company will tell you that the other actors and staff become your family, equally or more so than one's own family, when rehearsing and performing together.

'Why don't you come home when you have a holiday?' Mum asked more than once during our weekly phone calls.

'But Somerset is such a long way. Don't worry, Noah is looking after me.' And he was, he did a lot of the cooking early on, whereas I took care of the cleaning. At first, our partnership worked well in every respect, not least in the bedroom where we couldn't keep apart for more than five minutes. Noah was the most exciting, loving and skilled lover I'd known, and he never once failed to please me.

After two incredible years performing with Hull Docks Theatre and touring all over Britain we were to perform our latest production, *It Started with a Kiss*, at The Bristol Old Vic Theatre, not too far from my hometown of Minehead in Somerset. I'd booked tickets for Mum and Dad who were travelling up and making a weekend break of it.

'Absolutely brilliant,' said Dad when we met up in the bar after the performance. 'I think that's the best Godber play I've seen you in, to date.'

'I could hear you laughing and I loved that,' I said, and gave him a hug.

'He was chortling away non stop beside me,' said Mum. 'It's a wonder the folks in the seats behind us didn't complain or kick his seat.'

Dad turned to Mum. 'Trouble is, Evie, my love, you don't know how to enjoy yourself.' He looked across at Noah. 'Too smart for her own good. Tess is smart too, but you'd never know it to talk to her.'

'Hey, shut up, Dad.' But we all laughed. 'I just don't air any pretensions or try to outsmart anyone.'

'Except when they've wound you up the wrong way,' said Noah. He narrowed his eyes. 'I've seen you in action.'

'When?' I said, outraged at his accusation.

He thought for a moment. 'Only the other night after the play when we were all drinking here. You were tipsy and giggly, like you are sometimes.'

'What did I do?' I said, trying to recall any conversations that stood out.

'That guy we were talking to. He leads the youth drama workshops here. He started saying how he'd have interpreted the part you played differently, more subtly - suggesting you played her to extremes.'

'Ahh, I remember him,' I said, nodding. 'Mansplaining to bring me down from my post performance high.'

'Anyway,' Noah said to my parents. 'Tess went into a great spiel about how she'd discussed in length her interpretation of the role with the playwright, John Godber himself, who'd also praised her performance interpretation.' Noah turned to me and continued. 'And then you proceeded to recite the rave review we got from that London critic, where you'd been named for your part. My God, how his jaw fell open at that. Anyway, he went quiet and left soon afterwards with his tail between his legs.'

'I didn't intend to upset him,' I said. 'But I did feel I needed to defend my interpretation.'

'Don't worry. He asked for it, and with the little audience that had gathered around us, he realised he'd made a prat of himself.'

'That's my girl,' said Dad, with a wink.

'Hey Mum,' I said, changing the subject. 'Would you like to watch me and Noah bungee jump off Clifton Suspension bridge in the morning? I've always wanted to dare myself to do one, and they've got a special offer - two for the price of one.'

'You mean you bungee together?' she said, with a horrified expression.

'No, one at a time. They don't do two together - too risky.'

'Isn't it risky anyway?' she said. 'I can't understand the appeal.'

'Neither of us has ever done one, and although I am terrified, I think it's good to try new things. And shared experiences are even better.'

Noah took my hand. 'I'm only doing it because you dared me to. And I could hardly refuse that.'

'You could have,' I said laughing.

He shook his head. 'No way, you'd never let me forget it.'

After a late night and too much alcohol to be taking part in an adrenaline sport, I woke up with a headache.

I swallowed two paracetamol. 'I refuse to cancel.'

'We'd lose our money.' Noah reminded me. 'And I know how tight you are in that respect.'

'You mean thrifty?'

'No comment,' he said, tickling my waist.

I ran my hands under the cold tap and splashed my face with water. 'I'll be fine for it.'

We found Mum and Dad already on the bridge and watching the first jumpers of the day.

117

Dad turned to me and grimaced. 'Looks great fun - screaming their heads off as they plunge headlong into the abyss.'

'Do they come up smiling though?' I said, peering over at the jump ramp and a girl with pigtails standing as stiff as a poker and edging towards the ledge with her arms outstretched. There was a lengthy delay as the safety guy beside her appeared to be encouraging her to jump.

'She's not going to jump,' said Noah beside me.

'She will, watch,' I said.

And I swear I saw the man give her a little nudge in the small of her back, after which she disappeared, her screams echoing along the valley.

'Bloody hell,' I said, and leaned over to see the girl's hands touch the water before she sprang back up again, still screaming like a banshee.

'How's the headache?' Noah said, and draped an arm around my shoulder.

'Fine,' I replied.

Truthfully, it hadn't gone but I felt determined to go ahead.

'I'll jump first if you like,' said Noah as we made our way towards the preparation area.

'Actually, do you mind if I jump first? If I dilly dally I think I might wimp out.'

'I'm more than happy to go second,' he said. 'They take photos and we can frame them for our first mantlepiece.'

'Only if they're flattering,' I said, and doubted they'd be anything but horrifying.

'You'll still look gorgeous, mouth agape and hair flapping.'

'Well, I shan't be smiling for the camera,' I said.

'I will,' he said.

'You're such a poser.'

He grinned. 'I can't deny it.'

'And I'm supposed to be the actor protecting their public image.'

'This is my big chance to perform instead of sitting in the lighting box. I'm not wasting it.'

'You know you can jump backwards?' I said.

He thought for a moment. 'Maybe next time?'

'Let's survive the first time, first,' I said.

118

I turned around and saw Mum and Dad had come closer to get a better view. I waved and Dad gave me the thumbs up.

We were fitted into our harnesses, snug and secure, but by this point my nerves had begun to kick in big time. I watched as a tall, well built man was hauled back onto the ramp following his jump. Far from looking elated and pumped up with adrenaline, he appeared pasty and stood on quivering legs until the safety guys had released him from his harness and he staggered a few feet to the benches. He slumped onto his bottom, and with his friend offering words of support, he dropped his head into his hands.

'OK, who wants to go first?' the safety instructor said enthusiastically, with a smile that was supposed to boost confidence.

I looked over at the man who'd just jumped and he raised his head and some colour had returned to his cheeks. He was talking to his girlfriend in low tones, clearly still in a state of shock.

I stood up, decisively. 'I will.' How difficult could it be to drop and bounce upside down from a springy rope? It was about mind control and taking hold of one's fear and enjoying the new sensations and sights.

The man knelt at my feet and I pushed my bare feet into the padded ankle straps after which I stood up and he connected the straps to the harness. He reassured me that as a fail safe measure there were two straps, but that they'd never had one break or come loose.

I turned to Noah and he gave an encouraging smile. 'Show me how it's done.'

I think I mumbled something in reply as I shuffled towards the edge, but by now I was regretting volunteering to go first. In fact, I was regretting booking it at all. My mind was wrestling between fight and flight, and flight was winning, although I had a fat chance of fleeing anywhere in this get up. Despite a breeze coming in from the river below, my face, neck and palms felt hot and clammy. A few inches from the edge I looked down at the brown swirling water hundreds of feet below.

'Will I touch the water?'

'Not usually, you'll see it up close though,' he said. 'Ready?'

119

I looked directly out in front and the horizon before me seemed to shimmer and pale. My stomach danced a merry tune and I swallowed hard as my toast and marmalade threatened to reveal their semi-digested form.

'Ready to go?' the instructor's voice sounded oddly distant.

I think I nodded, and like a felled tree I toppled forwards to meet my maker. I didn't scream, and beyond a tumbling sensation, I recalled nothing. Not the sky, or the blurred view of the river, nor the cliffs on either side of the ravine.

What I do recall is a voice saying close to me. 'I think she's coming round.'

'Tess, can you hear me?'

I opened my eyes. Noah, Mum and Dad leaned over me, along with a couple of other faces I didn't recognise.

I tried to sit up and felt helping hands assist me.

'I jumped?' I said.

'I think you blacked out. Don't you remember any of it?' asked Noah.

I looked about me and at the faces of those sitting on the benches, all eyes upon me.

'I remember being at the edge and falling...' my words trailed as I tried to remember beyond that.

'You didn't even scream,' said Noah, as if this was something to be congratulated for.

Noah seemed far too concerned about me to do his own jump, or perhaps he took my reaction as an excuse to back out. I imagine had I been in his position, and seeing him go through what I did, I wouldn't have wanted to jump either. Between the instructor, Mum and Noah, they insisted that I be checked out at Accident and Emergency, which seemed an unnecessary and over the top precaution. But given that I had two performances that afternoon and evening, I didn't want to risk any repercussions on stage, and so I relented to their concerns.

Noah turned all official in A&E and insisted I be seen urgently, given that I was one of the main characters in a production.

I felt embarrassed when the receptionist asked me for my autograph. 'I saw your play the other night.' And she placed a post-it pad and pen in my hand. 'It was hilarious and you were amazing, all of you.'

I signed my name and handed it back to her. 'So glad you enjoyed it. It's our last day at The Vic and we're heading to Cardiff tomorrow.'

I still felt shaky as Noah and I followed the doctor into the small curtained room. I described what I remembered and she checked my heart, pulse, blood pressure, oxygen levels, and shone a light into my eyes.

'It's probably fear that made you faint,' she said. 'Your stats seem fine. Have you been having any headaches?'

'I did when I woke up, but paracetamol helped.'

I gave urine and blood samples, and she took them away to be tested.

'I think she's right about fear,' I said.

'But you seemed so brave,' said Noah.

'I was trying to be, but I felt really peculiar as I approached the ledge - a feeling of impending doom came over me.'

'I think we'll quit adrenaline sports,' said Noah.

'Agreed.' I leaned over and gave him a kiss. 'I'll get my thrills on stage in future.'

He grinned and nudged my elbow. 'Or with me.'

'It'll take a few hours to get the blood and urine tests back.' The doctor said when she returned. 'Can you ring for the results on Monday?' And she handed me a card with the lab telephone number.

'Ten minutes til curtains,' came Noah's voice over the tannoy.

I dabbed more blusher onto my cheeks and applied lip liner around my ruby red lipstick. I heard my phone ring from my handbag and leaned down to retrieve it. An unknown number, but I took the risk and answered.

'Is this Tess Blonski?'

'Yes,' I replied. 'Who is this?'

'It's Dr Kobi from Bristol Infirmary. I have the results from a couple of your tests.'

'Is everything OK with them?' I asked, realising that was unlikely given her personal call.

My heart began to thud unnaturally and the lights around the mirror glared in my eyes.

'No need to be alarmed. But I wanted to tell you that we found unusually high levels of HCG in your blood.'

'What does that mean?' I said, unable to disguise the alarm in my voice.

'And along with your urine test, we can confirm that you are pregnant.'

'What?'

'Congratulations, my dear. You're going to have a baby?'

I went lightheaded. 'Oh no! Really?'

'I wanted you to know straight away so that you don't do any more bungee jumps.'

I didn't register anything else from our conversation, but I think I thanked her and told her I had to go as I was due on stage.

19

La Galerie

I looked at my watch. Half past eleven. We'd been at the restaurant four hours but the time had flown by.

'I'd better get back,' I said. 'The twins will be wondering where I've got to.'

'Funny,' said Gil. 'Should be the other way round with teenagers.'

I laughed. 'Yes, the moment they start making a bid for freedom a parent can rarely rest easy.'

Judi's words slurred. 'We haven't finished the champagne yet. I'm not leaving a drop.'

'You two stay and finish the bottle and I'll walk Tess home.' Stefan turned to me. 'It's not far is it?'

'Five minutes up the hill, but I'll be fine walking alone.'

'Up those dark alleys, I wouldn't dream of it,' said Stefan.

I'd never felt overly vulnerable walking home alone in the dark, but Stefan's confidence and physical presence reassured me he was the sort of man other guys wouldn't want to get on the wrong side of.

I reached for my bag and stood up. 'That's kind of you.'

Outside, the street was silent and deserted, which was hardly surprising for a Tuesday night. The harbour lights sprinkled their shimmer upon the calm, black water that lay between us and the far side of town and a distant hush of the waves sounded on the shore. I felt oddly awake given the length and fullness of my day.

'I hope you've enjoyed tonight,' said Stefan.

'It's been lovely,' I said, and felt the nearness of him as we walked. 'I rarely eat at such restaurants and you're all great company.'

'You'll have noticed how close Judi and Gil are?'

I nodded. 'How long have they been together?'

'For a while. Judi is smitten. She's not had the best of luck with men.'

'She's not alone there,' I said.

'Your ex must be a fool,' he said, and paused. 'To let you go.'

'I see myself as the fool for tolerating his problem for so long.'

Stefan murmured. 'I imagine he did his utmost to keep you from leaving.'

'Not really,' I said. 'He didn't quit gambling.'

'Seems a strange addiction. I prefer taking risks to make money the honest way.'

'We all have our faults - our weaknesses,' I said. 'Recognising we have them is the first hurdle, working to overcome them is the second, most important hurdle.'

We started up the steps that led between the houses. The odd light was still on behind curtains and blinds, but most of the houses were in darkness and still beneath the streetlamps. My heels made a staccato clatter above the softness of our breaths as we walked up the incline.

'Too steep after alcohol,' I said.

'How charming it is, though. I've never been up here.' He fell silent for a moment. 'Can I let you into a secret, Tess?'

'Of course,' I replied, feeling a sense of excitement at what he might be about to reveal. 'I like secrets.'

'I must confess that I recognised you as soon as you arrived for your interview.'

'You've seen me around town?'

'I have. You're hard to miss.'

'Oh, really?' I said.

'In a good way, of course,' he added.

'I blame the hair.'

He turned to me and reached out his hand. I felt his fingers brush a curl. 'Beautiful hair, so yes, you stand out for all the right reasons.'

I felt surprised but not displeased by his touch. 'Thank you.' I gestured left. 'I'm down here.'

We stopped at the front gate. 'I'd invite you in for a coffee, but Judi and Gil will expect you back.'

'They'll barely notice,' he replied. 'And I wouldn't mind another coffee, if you're not too tired.'

'Not a bit.' I hadn't expected him to want to come in, and I hoped the others would be in bed. Thank goodness Noah couldn't come downstairs. The sight of a handsome man walking me home from a night out would upset him, and the twins, too.

I unlocked the front door and all seemed quiet. The children had considerately left the light on, or simply hadn't bothered to turn it off. Digby thundered down the stairs to greet me. He liked to sleep up on mine or Clara's bed so I assumed they'd all headed upstairs.

Digby ran straight past me. He jumped up at Stefan and bared his teeth through a growl.

I grabbed Digby's collar. 'Get down, Digby!' I pulled him away. 'We must have startled him.'

But Digby barked and strained to jump up at Stefan.

Stefan took a step back. 'He's a handful.'

'Not normally, but he might be unsettled by the house move and unused to visitors here.'

'I shan't take it personally,' said Stefan.

Digby continued to bark and pulled to reach Stefan.

'I'm so sorry.' I dragged Digby to the kitchen, closed the door and put a biscuit in his bowl. I knelt down and stroked his ears. 'It's OK Digby. Stefan is my new boss. He'll be keeping you stocked up with doggy treats.'

Digby walked away, and sniffed and snarled at the crack beneath the kitchen door.

I held him back as I slipped through the door and closed it behind me.

'He'll keep out any intruders,' Stefan remarked.

Thankfully, he seemed unfazed by Digby's over-zealous guard duties.

'He usually loves pestering visitors for attention. Not like him to growl at them.'

'This is quaint, Tess,' said Stefan, as he looked around. 'And you've only lived here a couple of weeks?'

I noticed the dirty cups and plates left on the dining table along with a half-eaten packet of biscuits. The kids had at least remembered to tuck the chairs in to prevent Digby jumping up.

'It's a bit messy because I've been working. I can hardly expect sixteen year olds to be house proud.'

'But everything - the paintings, the furniture, the ornaments. You have an aesthete's eye.'

'Kind of you to say. I decorated our last home and it was a wrench to move on. I want this to be equally as comfortable.'

Stefan walked over to the bookshelf and ran his fingers over some of the spines. 'Nice reading material, too.'

I heard Digby scratch and push against the kitchen door. He'd wake the whole household if he carried on.

'You'll notice a lot of plays and scripts. I've kept every copy from college and theatre onwards.' I stood beside him and brushed my hand across the top shelf. 'Those are my treasures, notated, dog-eared and loved to death.'

'The only plays I own are Shakespeare's full works. A beautiful vintage collection from a book dealer friend, but Shakespeare's not my kind of drama at all,' he said. 'I prefer contemporary drama - far more relatable.'

'I can appreciate Shakespeare and I've seen some incredible productions and interpretations, but I admit I do prefer to perform in and watch contemporary plays.'

Stefan reached to pick a book from the top shelf and as he did his arm brushed mine. I wasn't sure if this was intentional or not.

I stepped aside. 'Would you like decaf or caffeine?'

'Caffeine. I sleep like the dead.'

'Unlike me,' I said. 'Won't be long.' I headed into the kitchen, gave Digby another biscuit and filled the kettle.

I felt a frisson of excitement. I couldn't deny that I found Stefan disarmingly attractive. During my time with Noah I'd had a couple of crushes, but nothing I'd ever dreamed of acting upon. But I was single now, and Stefan seemed intelligent and fascinating, and all the compliments he gave me made me think he might like me too. But, as he was my employer there was no way I'd get involved romantically. Still, there could be no harm in building a friendly working relationship and enjoying his company.

When I returned to the living room, I found Stefan flicking through a book. 'This is a favourite of mine. I read it at University, not as part of my course.'

126

'Ahh, Madame Bovary,' I said. 'It made quite an impression on me.'

'Yes,' Stefan said with thought. 'A beautiful yet tragic story. I found Emma Bovary utterly appealing for her passion and her futile attempts to suppress the immensity of her feelings.'

'Too self-destructive though,' I replied. 'She makes too many bad decisions, which grated on me.'

'I usually read over lunch, mostly non-fiction though. Jordan Peterson, have you read him?'

I scrunched up my nose. 'He doesn't appeal. But I know he's popular and people seem to like his ideas.'

'He's controversial, I agree. But reading a real book gives my mind a break from work - a refreshing midday shower.'

I handed Stefan his coffee and sat down beside him. 'Books are escapism in its finest form. Fiction is my preference though.'

'I learned masses from books growing up - far more than from most of my teachers,' he said, and his brows furrowed.

'I agree about learning for oneself. If you're motivated, learning comes easily.'

'I couldn't wait to leave school,' Stefan continued. 'A while later, University was better for me. The professors appreciated independent thinkers.'

'Where did you study?'

'I studied Business and Economics at Bath, as a mature student in my late twenties.'

'What a coincidence! My mum is a professor of Economics at Bath. Do you remember her?'

He thought for a moment and rubbed his chin. 'Professor Blonski?'

'Yes, Evie Blonski. She's taught there for thirty years.'

He pinched his bottom lip between his thumb and forefinger. 'I don't think so.' He shook his head slowly. 'Does she look like you?'

'Hold on.' I stood up and walked behind the sofa to the dresser. I picked up a photo frame of myself standing between Mum and Dad at a wedding. I was fifteen at the time and stood shoulder to shoulder with Mum, who was only a year or two younger than I was now.

I sat back down and passed the photo to Stefan.

He held it up and studied it for a moment then turned his eyes to me and handed the photo back. 'The likeness is uncanny - you could be twins. Except you have the edge in prettiness.'

'That photo doesn't do her justice. My Mum is still far prettier, but yes, everyone comments on our likeness.'

'But no,' he said, shaking his head. 'If your Mum had taught me, I'd remember.'

'Would have been funny and cool if she had, and she could remember you too,' I said.

He took a long sip of coffee. 'At Uni I was setting up my new business and so working and studying at the same time was full on. I was a bit of a boring swot so don't imagine I stood out. But a degree from Bath added to my credentials.'

And I thought, swot or not, his presence and striking looks alone would have made him stand out.

'Bath is a top Uni and not easy to get into. I loved Drama School, my uni alternative, but I found school limiting. The teachers wanted to mould us, rather than allow us to shape ourselves,' I said. 'It felt liberating to study drama where individual expression was encouraged and expected. As long as we arrived at rehearsals on time, of course.'

Stefan turned to me and with a look that made me dizzy, said, 'You moulded yourself admirably.'

I bit my bottom lip. If those words had come from another man, I might have thought them too much, but the way he said it, and the way he lingered over each word whilst he looked directly into my eyes, gave me an unbearable thrill.

I felt a glow deep inside and gave a flirty smile in return.

My phone rang, which startled me.

I stood up and went to retrieve it from my bag. When I saw it was Noah calling, I hung up.

I texted him. "I'll see you on my way up."

I muted the volume and sat back down. I imagined he'd heard Digby barking and me and Stefan talking. Awkward, but I'd done nothing wrong.

We chatted about my first day at work and he asked about my childhood and my parents, but when I enquired about his family in return, he drank back his coffee and glanced at his watch.

'I should get back.' He stood up. 'I'll see you tomorrow?'

128

I laughed and stood up too. 'Absolutely, if you'll have me.'

'After lunch I have to visit a client in Saltburn-by-the-Sea. You could come too, meet a loyal client and learn more about what we do.'

I unlatched the front door and held it open. 'I'd like that.'

'Excellent, thanks for the coffee.' And without warning, he leaned down and kissed me briefly on the cheek before he turned and walked away down the garden path.

When I closed the door and stood there for a moment I could still feel the lightness of his lips on my skin.

All seemed quiet up on the landing but I popped my head through Victor's bedroom door. Victor was fast asleep beneath his duvet, but Noah lay propped up by pillows. The air in the room smelled sweaty and stale. In the morning I would open the windows to allow some fresh air to circulate.

To avoid waking Victor I went and stood close to Noah. 'Have you been OK?' I whispered.

'In pain and bored shitless, otherwise...' He shrugged, and looked about as miserable as I'd ever seen him.

I sat on the edge of the bed. 'So sorry.' I took his hand. 'Hopefully the pain will ease soon.'

'Yeah, in a month or so.' He looked at me directly and with an accusing tone said, 'Who were you with?'

I released his hand. 'My new boss, Stefan.'

'I thought a few of you were going out?'

'Yes, but he insisted on walking me up the hill.'

Noah sniffed. 'How gallant. What does he look like?'

I sighed. 'He's my boss, older than us.' I stood up. 'If you don't need anything I'll go to bed. I need to be up early.'

'You're being a little hostile. Have I said something to upset you?

I shook my head. 'You can't keep track of my movements, you know that.'

He nodded and exhaled slowly. 'I'll see you before you leave?'

'Of course. I'll bring you breakfast and a bowl of warm water to wash yourself.'

Victor stirred and mumbled beneath his bedclothes, and I turned to leave.

I showered quickly, blow dried my hair and fell into bed. I felt sleepy but satisfied with my first day.

My phone vibrated on the bedside table.

I reached over. I was surprised to see a message from Stefan.

"Thanks for a wonderful evening, Tess." Beneath was a photo of him looking relaxed and ridiculously handsome.

Bad thoughts came into my mind and I tried to push them aside. It's your first day. He's your boss. Get a grip.

Should I reply?

I typed. "I had a lovely time, too, thank you! A delicious meal and eaten in great company." I pressed send and turned my phone to silent.

20

My alarm clock woke me at seven. I'd never found mornings easy and the champagne headache made me regret those extra glasses, as I knew I would. But despite the fuzzy head, I felt enthused about my second day at work. If yesterday was a typical day, this had the potential to be my dream job. I headed downstairs to make a cuppa. Clara was saying goodbye to Fleur who'd obviously stayed over again.

She closed the front door and I gave her a hug. 'Sorry I barely saw you yesterday.'

'I was fine. And it's fab having Dad to chat to. How was Aztec Imports?' she asked.

'Better than I could have hoped. Stefan, Judi and Gil are all so kind, and interesting, too.'

Clara opened the curtains and sunlight poured through to light up her bobbed fair hair. 'That's cool, Mum.'

'They've got stables and horses and I think you might be able to ride them.'

Her features lit up. 'Seriously? What are their horses like?'

'Beautiful. They have local teenagers help out and ride them so I'll mention you and Fleur once I've settled in.'

'I'd love that, and Fleur would too.' Her eyes and nose crinkled and she cupped her cheeks with her hands.

'I thought you might. Can you believe they have an indoor swimming pool, too, which I can use?'

'Bloody hell. Are they millionaires or something?'

'They must be. Super successful anyway.'

'Cool. I better go shower,' she said. 'Biology first period.'

'Does Fleur's mum mind her staying over midweek?' I asked, conscious that Fleur seemed to be here more often than not.

'It's fine. Anyway, her mum's on night shifts this week and her Dad is away in London, so it's better than Fleur being alone.'

'OK.' This was new. Fleur didn't usually stay over midweek, although now they were in sixth form, they only had to go in for their lessons.

I prepared eggs on toast for myself and Noah then sat on the end of his bed as we ate.

Noah ate but didn't speak much, other than to ask if I had a hangover. He gave a disapproving huff. 'You seemed drunk when you came in.'

Don't rise to it, I said to myself.

I set my empty plate on Victor's desk and opened the window to freshen the air. Victor stretched and sat up. He looked heavy-eyed and full of sleep. 'Morning.'

'Sorry if we woke you,' I said.

'It's fine. I've got lessons this morning.'

Conscious of the time, I said, 'I'd better get on.' I leaned down and gave Victor a kiss on his head.

'Roddy said he'd try and pop in later, and I thought I'd ask if he could help me to the bathroom for a proper wash,' said Noah.

'That's kind of him,' I said. 'He's a good friend.'

Noah sighed. 'At least he hasn't taken sides, yet.'

'Roddy's not that sort of person,' I replied.

'We'll see.'

Noah obviously felt down, and who could blame him? I would have to try and think of some distractions for him, or at least spend some time talking with him in the evenings. But was that even a good idea given we were supposed to be separated? New books - he used to love reading. I'd recharge my Kindle and suggest some decent novels.

When I walked into the office, Stefan and Gil sat together at Stefan's desk, talking intently. They glanced my way, said hello, then continued quietly - almost at a whisper.

Clearly they didn't want me to overhear.

'Have you got drinks?' I asked.

'I'd love a coffee,' replied Stefan, without looking up.

Gil turned my way. 'I'm OK, thanks.'

When I returned with our drinks, Gil had gone. I set Stefan's cup on his desk and he picked it up and raised it to his lips. 'God's nectar, and precisely how I like it.'

'Great. What would you like me to help with today?'

'Do you write?'

I thought for a moment. 'I can write. I mean, I was reasonably good at English and essay writing at school, twenty odd years ago.'

'I've asked Gil to email you the best photos of Marmaris he took yesterday. You'll have seen on our website we have a news section that we regularly add to. It's our most viewed page and I know some of our clients love seeing their purchases presented in all their glory. It reinforces the value and price of their goods and prompts us to be recommended to more clients, which is how we gain most of our new business. I wondered if you could write a piece on Marmaris? Where he came from, his breeding, his top prizes and where he's living now, but only the area, no specific location. Goes without saying to leave out any mention of prices or the scratch on his leg.'

'Of course,' I said, and imagined there was still some tension between Gil and Stefan. 'I'll have a go, and Gil gave me lots of useful background during our journey.'

'If you read some of our other news posts you'll get an idea of the tone to use. Judi wrote the last one, but her diary is full so it'll really help us out.'

'I'll draft and share it with you both?'

'Excellent. Spend a couple of hours and then I have something else planned for your induction.'

He gave a playful lift of his eyebrows, which made me curious as to what he had in mind. Last night he'd mentioned going to visit a client up the coast, perhaps that was it.

I sat at my desk. Writing a blog would be a challenge - the important thing was to keep it lively, word tight and relevant. I went over the day in my mind and a few of the conversations with Gil and James Newiss. I'd add a few soundbites. Customer quotes gave a post authenticity.

Stefan called over. 'I'll show you how to upload it, too.'

Yesterday, I wondered why Gil had taken so many photos, and now I knew. Any opportunity to promote their business brand, and Marmaris happened to be the most photogenic creature most people would have set eyes on.

We worked at our laptops until Judi came in with combed wet hair and a bright expression. 'That's sixty lengths of the pool. Not bad going with a hangover.'

'You must be a strong swimmer,' I remarked.

'I used to compete, years ago,' she said. 'Now I enjoy it purely for leisure.'

'Did you enjoy competing?'

'Loathed it,' she said without hesitation. 'Dad and my coaches thought I had potential, and I probably did, until I grew to hate the early mornings, and the competitions when my every stroke, turn and timing would be scrutinised.'

'By the coaches?' I asked.

'Not so much the coaches.'

'Judi, dear. Get yourself a coffee and add sugar to it,' said Stefan.

'That I do need,' she agreed.

'And did you swim, too?' I asked Stefan.

'Yes, but never competitively. I competed with the horses. Did well, but once I hit sixteen I told Dad I was giving up competing and only riding for leisure.'

'Your dad sounds quite the taskmaster.'

A darkness came over Stefan's face. 'Ambitious for his children, like many parents.' Then he added, 'I can't deny that I'm competitive, but only on my terms.'

When he didn't elaborate further I turned back to my screen.

Judi returned with her coffee and disappeared into the meeting room with her laptop.

I read through what I'd written and tweaked it in a few places, then inserted a handful of the best photos and emailed the file to Judi and Stefan.

Stefan got up and walked through to see Judi, and I opened up the cloud to read a few more of the recent letters and documents to familiarise myself. There was a business strategy for the current financial year, which I saved to my desktop. How thorough they appeared.

A word file stood out amongst some excel files and with an unusual name that didn't give much away. P21. I clicked and opened it up. At the top it read, 2021. Beneath were a list of names - first and surnames. What struck me was that the names, without exception, were all female. Many of them were foreign sounding. Were they female clients? Gertie Pawlak, Sandy Gorski, Bernadette Duda, plus many more. I read down the list and back up again.

I didn't hear Stefan approach from behind - he must have come back in through the meeting room at the rear.

'How's it going?'

I startled and clicked to close the file. Even though I had full access to their files, I felt as if I'd intruded on something I shouldn't have seen.

I clicked on the newsletter folder. 'All good, thanks.'

He stopped at my desk and watched me as I opened the newsletter I'd created.

He leaned in closer and I felt his breath brush my hair. 'Need any help or got any questions?'

Had he seen the file I closed?

'No, I'm coping so far.'

'OK.' He lingered over the word and I sensed an edge of doubt in his voice.

He went and sat down and read from his laptop. I noticed how he glanced my way every now and then.

Stefan held responsibility for the finance files so maybe he'd saved it in the wrong folder. I had no intention of asking. Perhaps he might even view or track the files I accessed and ask me about it.

After a few minutes he walked over to my desk and pulled up a chair. 'I like what you've written, Tessa.' He paused and looked at me. 'You don't mind my calling you Tessa do you?'

'No one has ever called me by a different name before, other than the occasional insult,' I said with a laugh.

He tilted his head, slowly, as if to give weight to what he was about to say. 'Is it wrong of me to do so?'

'I don't suppose I mind,' I said. 'I quite like Tessa.'

His black flecked eyes continued to scan mine. 'Were you christened Tess?'

'My parents are first generation heathens. I wasn't christened at all, and on my birth certificate I'm plain and simple, Tess.'

He gave a winsome smile. 'I must contradict you. Plain and simple are words I could never associate with you, heathen or otherwise.'

135

I laughed. 'I'll take that as a compliment.' I watched him as he read and pondered if I preferred being a Tess or a Tessa.

He turned to me and his brows flicked upwards again. 'You have a natural writing style and an unpretentious tone. Clearly expressed and with a varied vocabulary, and a mixture of sentence structures to keep it fresh. I'm pleasantly surprised.'

'I haven't written much in ages, so I'm pleasantly surprised, too,' I said.

He gave a satisfied nod. 'Judi will like it.'

'I hope so.' Instinctively, I felt that Judi might be the harder partner to impress. Time would tell.

'One minor alteration,' he said. 'More of an addition.'

'Oh?' I said.

'Gil shared the photos with me, too. Could you open them up?'

I opened the file and the thumbnails appeared.

Stefan leaned in closer to the screen. His shoulder brushed mine and I caught a whiff of his aftershave.

He pointed to the screen. 'That one there.'

I clicked. It was a photo of me standing in their stableyard beside Marmaris as I stroked his face. I'd already decided against including myself, but had included one with Gil and Judi. 'I could insert it if you like?'

'Yes, it's a lovely shot. Wonderful expression.'

I laughed with light self-deprecation. 'Marmaris or me?'

'Both of you. One's eyes cannot but fail to be drawn in,' he said.

'Well, Marmaris looks stunning and I've no objection to including it.'

'Excellent,' he replied, and straightened up. 'I hope I haven't embarrassed you.'

'Not at all,' I said, although my cheeks simmered.

'I give praise where it's due. I love the quotes you've included. A really nice touch.'

'I'm glad I paid attention when James was speaking.'

He gave an appreciative smile. 'Attentive and observant, I like your style.'

21

Stefan and I stood together at the front of Lorton Hold. We were to travel fifteen miles to a client's house in Saltburn-by-the-Sea to help purchase a painting. There would be an online sales auction and Stefan would be placing the bids.

'You'll find this fascinating and exciting,' Stefan said to me. 'You'll be off screen, but Heidi, the client and family friend won't mind you observing.'

'Who is the artist - anyone I'd know?'

'A Croatian artist, Corina Petrovak. The sort of art I'd love to hang in my home. Let me know what you think of her work.'

'I'll look her up,' I said. I might be no art buff, but I could appreciate paintings and different styles.

'The question I have is what mode of transport should we use?' His eyes danced and he turned to a shining blue motorbike beside his car.

'You mean the motorbike?'

'Pillion, if you'd like to?'

I looked down at my skirt and heels. 'Wearing these?'

'I have some women's leathers that would fit you. What size are your feet?'

'Six.'

'Judi's a six, too. But if you prefer the car...'

'I've never been on a motorbike. Are you steady?'

'Of course,' he said, with a laugh. 'I wouldn't ask if I wasn't. Huge respect for speed and other road users, too.'

'Then I'd like to,' I said, without thinking further. 'I'm sure it's quicker, too.' Hopefully not too much quicker, I thought.

Stefan found the leather trousers, jacket and boots and pointed me in the direction of their downstairs bathroom. 'I think they'll fit, but if not we'll go by car.'

I hung up my skirt on the back of the door, tried on the leathers, and stood in front of the bathroom mirror. They fitted perfectly, although the trousers were on the short side.

When I returned to the front, Stefan had dressed in his leathers too.

He appraised me with unashamed eyes. 'They look like they were made for you. But more essentially, they'll protect you.'

'They feel heavy,' I said, and stretched my arms out in front.

'You won't notice when you're riding. Better zip it up though,' he said.

I fiddled with the zip and pulled it up, but it stuck below my breasts.

'Need some help?' he asked.

'The zip's caught,' I said, and wiggled it.

I felt his hands upon mine and I let my hands fall to my side. Slowly, he lowered the zip and then pulled it up over my breasts.

'It is quite snug on you.' His eyes lifted to mine with a distinct sparkle.

I breathed in and my wound twinged beneath the leather waistband. I released my breath. 'I can still breathe so we're good to go.'

'Almost.' He picked up a gleaming red helmet off the saddle and passed it to me. 'Let me show you how to fit it.' He lifted his own black helmet, raised it over his head and pulled it on from the back and lowered it down. 'That's the easiest way.'

I followed his cue. It felt surprisingly light.

Stefan reached beneath my chin and clipped the chin strap. 'How's that - not too tight?'

'Do I look like a caged hamster?'

'A little.' He laughed. 'But so do I.'

'We just need to spin our wheels,' I said.

He laughed again. 'Tandem style.'

We stood on either side of the motorbike - a Yamaha, polished to perfection.

'You'll need to sit forwards as close to me as possible and keep your arms around my waist at all times. If you feel an itch, ignore it. Try not to move your weight but keep your head slightly to one side and looking forwards, that way you can see any bends coming up.'

Stefan mounted first.

Butterflies fluttered through me as I lifted my leg over the saddle, sat forwards and put my arms around his waist. It felt such an intimate thing to be doing with a new boss. Riding pillion required huge trust in the driver. I'd only known Stefan a couple of days, but I sensed I'd be in capable hands.

He switched on the engine and the revs rumbled through my seat and spine and up through my arms to my fingertips.

Stefan turned slightly. 'You OK?'

I nodded. 'I'm good.'

The coastal road looked weirdly unfamiliar from the back of the bike. It wasn't so much the speed that we moved, which I couldn't gauge to be either faster or slower than I normally drove, but the new perspective, the nearness to the tarmac and the shapes and blur of the passing trees and buildings. After a few minutes the strangeness of being so close to Stefan faded and as I began to relax a feeling of euphoria crept through me, making my nerve endings tingle and my breaths come quicker. His back felt broad and strong, and even through his leather jacket I could feel the firmness of his abdomen and the subtle sensation of the movement of his muscles as he leaned into the bends. I wondered how aware he was of me pressed against him. I felt excited to be experiencing something so thrilling and with someone I was fast growing to admire and respect.

When we headed into Saltburn-by-the-Sea, we turned off an avenue of large and expensive looking homes and through some tall iron gates. Apple and pear trees still laden with fruit lined either side of the drive. We pulled up in front of a red brick Victorian Villa. Even from the outside I knew it would look amazing inside. The gardens appeared to be just the right side of impeccable with flourishing flowerbeds of colourful plants. Opulent curtains, hooked to one side, framed each sash window, complete with vases filled with flowers, which all added to the appearance of taste and comfortable affluence.

I swung my leg over the motorbike, unfastened the clasp and lifted the helmet over my head. A welcome breeze caressed my skin and I ran my fingers through my curls.

Stefan turned to me. 'How was that for your first time?'

I let out a breath. 'Thrilling! If I'd known how safe I'd feel I might have done it years ago.'

'I didn't go too fast?'

'Not at all.' I didn't mention the other feelings I'd had. I needed to digest those first.

'We're meeting Heidi and her husband, Gavin. I've known them for years. They're wonderful people, but neither of them are overly confident bidding for art online and last time they tried without me, Heidi lost the painting she'd set her heart on. It's a relatively new way of dealing and buying art with a different feel to being in the physical auction room. Equally as tense. Sometimes it's a matter of luck and usually the client decides what price they are prepared to go to, but sometimes one needs to risk edging a little higher to outbid the competition.'

I heard a woman's voice call out and I turned.

'Stefan, darling.'

A statuesque, glamorous woman with auburn hair cut into a neat bob, and a red dress that accentuated her Amazonian figure, walked towards us.

We hung our helmets on the handlebars and walked to meet her. Stefan and Heidi hugged and kissed briefly on the lips.

Heidi turned to me with an inquisitive gaze. 'I didn't realise you were bringing someone, Stefan.'

'I'd like you to meet Tessa,' he said. 'She started with us yesterday.'

Heidi held out her hand. 'Delighted to meet you.' Her eyes moved from my face, down the length of my body and up again.

'Lovely to meet you, too,' I said, and shook her hand. She had a surprisingly assertive grip.

'Fancy making Tessa ride on the bike, Stefan. You are a naughty boy.'

'Not at all. I gave her the option to come by car.'

'Of course you did, darling.' She turned to me and winked.

'It was fun,' I said.

'Indeed. Stefan is an accomplished rider. I've had the pleasure myself.' She paused, tilted her head to one side and looked directly at Stefan. 'Let's go inside. We've time for a coffee before the auction and we must talk tactics.'

'Is Gavin about?' asked Stefan.

'He's away for a couple of nights. I'm sure I mentioned it.'

Stefan shook his head. 'No, you didn't.'

The interior was even more beautiful than I'd imagined. Every item of furniture and ornament and painting had been perfectly positioned and not a book or cushion appeared out of place.

We sat in the office, which was more like a sumptuous living room, but with two gorgeous antique desks. As we drank our coffee, Stefan and Heidi discussed the painting, the bidding process and the prices. Their exchanges seemed intimate, given the subject matter, and I got the distinct impression that they'd been more than client and customer in the past. Heidi all but excluded me from the conversation, and I had no doubt she'd have preferred Stefan to have come alone. She spoke eloquently, seemed charming and confident and I found it hard to believe she couldn't bid perfectly well on her own.

However, I was curious to see the painting in question, how the bidding worked and to see Stefan in action.

When the auction room sprang to life on the monitor, Stefan looked up the numbers and names of those who'd joined. The auction room itself was located in Rome. I mused how much nicer it would be to travel there, but could understand the convenience of bidding remotely.

Heidi turned to me. 'This is the second time we've bid live in an online auction room. 'It's an experiment in a way. Usually these auctions take place over a few days or a week, and bidders can increase their bid or pull out at any time.'

'Like Ebay?' I said.

'Yes, I suppose it is,' said Stefan.

'It's why I asked Stefan to help. He's wonderfully calm under pressure.'

I looked at Stefan - a picture of cool composure.

'Forty-three of us are currently online,' he said. 'And I imagine a good proportion are after this painting, given that it's the big showpiece.'

I sat on a chair a few feet back but close enough to see the auctioneer on the screen. When it came to the painting Heidi wanted, the auctioneer began the bid at ten thousand euros. I couldn't believe the sums of money they were dealing with. This was a whole different world to the one I was used to. And how did people find these sums of money to spend on one piece of art to hang in their home? I could see why Heidi wanted it though. It wasn't huge, but such an original style - surrealist.

In the painting a beautiful, dark-haired ballerina in a blue tutu and ballet shoes sat in front of a chessboard, on a beach. Her expression looked reflective. In the swirling sea behind her several ballerinas danced upon the waves in ballet shoes. The chess pieces were also ballerinas, in different poses. Sea water poured off the side of the chess board. It was exquisite, colourful, wildly imaginative and expertly painted.

The previous painting sold for a staggering one hundred and eighty thousand euros, and neither Heidi or Stefan showed any surprise at the amount. When the bidders wanted to put in a bid they had to enter their price via a bidding inbox, then confirm to ensure they weren't placing an unrealistic bid. Heidi sat close to Stefan and they talked quickly and quietly as the bidding progressed. Heidi seemed excited, expectant and nervous all at once. Stefan was quick to enter a new bid and Heidi nodded her approval each time.

'There are two of us now,' I heard Stefan say, with his eyes fixed on the screen.

Heidi twitched nervously, but Stefan remained otherwise composed. His only appearance of tension was in the way his fingers quivered over the mouse in readiness. Of course, Heidi had far more at stake emotionally and financially. The auctioneer's voice grew more animated and louder, and called out each bid until there was a pause, when Heidi bobbed up and down and reached out and clasped Stefan's knee.

Finally, the auctioneer raised his hammer and brought it down. 'Sold to Heidi Jackson of England.'

Heidi leapt up off her seat and shrieked. 'Yes, yes, yes! Stefan, you are a miracle worker.' She leaned down and wrapped her arms around him.

He grinned at me over his shoulder. 'Happy to oblige, milady.'

But there was no hiding the look of relief in his eyes.

Heidi straightened up. 'I'm delighted, Stefan, thank you!' She turned to me. 'Tessa, would you help me fetch the champagne, and we'll leave Stefan to finalise the purchase?'

'Of course.' I stood up. 'I'm so pleased you got your painting.'

'It didn't quite reach my maximum price either.' She clasped her hands together. 'I do believe Stefan has the coolness of an iceberg.'

'I was on the edge of my seat, quite literally,' I said.

I followed her through a magnificent dining room and into the largest and most beautiful kitchen I'd ever seen. Expensive, uncluttered, but homey with rustic kitchen utensils, dried flowers and wall hangings on display. I could only compare it to my galley kitchen in our new home which seemed shabby and cramped in comparison.

Heidi picked up a tea-towel from the central island, and folded it neatly before placing it beside the sink.

I'd never wanted to earn more money than I needed and that was probably a result of my modest but comfortable upbringing in a three bed semi-detached in Minehead. My bedroom did have a sea view if I stood on my bed and peered between the two houses at the end of the back garden. But now that I'd seen Stefan and Judi's house, and then yesterday, the glorious home and stables where we'd delivered Marmaris, and today, this Victorian palace, I could almost understand why those who had money were keen to keep hold of it, and even to gain more.

Heidi tutted and ran her hand over the wooden worktop before she walked across to the doorway. 'Polly?' she called, then waited a moment before calling again, 'Polly!'

I heard a distant voice call in reply and a few moments later a young woman hurried in. She looked no more than sixteen and wore a short, fitted maid's dress, and her nut brown hair had been plaited and pinned up.

'Polly, I distinctly asked you to keep the kitchen spotless, and look what I found.'

I glanced over and spotted a few crumbs on a chopping board. Nothing that would concern anyone in our home, or most homes, but clearly Heidi had high standards.

The girl hurried to the sink and ran water over a dishcloth. 'Sorry, I thought I'd finished in here.'

She had a distinct foreign accent, which I thought sounded Russian. She was short and slim, almost waif-like, and as she wiped up, Heidi turned to me and shook her head with dissatisfaction.

'Please don't worry on my account. You should see the mess my son makes when he cooks for us.'

'Ahh, but you don't pay him to clean, I imagine,' Heidi replied.

The girl finished, rinsed the cloth and turned to Heidi. 'I'll get back to the ironing.'

'First, can you collect the coffee cups from the living room?' Heidi instructed, with neither a please or thank you.

'Of course.' The girl nodded and glanced at me briefly before she hurried out of the kitchen.

There was something about Polly that made me feel uneasy. It could have been the timidity in her expression, or the pallor of her skin, and that she had dark circles under her round brown eyes.

'What is your business, Heidi? Other than purchasing valuable pieces of art.'

'Oh, the art is a hobby, but we sometimes resell them at a profit,' Heidi replied. 'Our business is hospitality and event management. It's exclusive and niche and not on a large scale. Like Stefan and Judi, we cater more for individuals and small businesses. We host here sometimes, but more usually elsewhere.'

That might explain the help of a maid, I thought.

'That sounds fun,' I said, and pictured glamorous parties, with fancy canapés, waiting staff, chilled champagne and cocktails.

'I suppose it is,' she said, but she sounded unenthused. She pulled a champagne bottle from the fridge and set it on a silver tray with three flutes. She turned to me. 'I can understand why you got the job with Aztec Imports, well, with Stefan.'

'Oh?'

'Yes, you see, you're charming and beautifully presentable to clients.'

'Hopefully I'll be an administrative asset, too.'

144

'I shouldn't think you'll need to worry too much about that side of things,' she said, and picked up the tray.

'But that is what I'm employed for.'

'Of course, but if I may be so bold to say, not the main reason Stefan recruited you. I really shouldn't say this, but you are one of a few attractive ladies to have taken this role. And they rarely last longer than a year.'

I didn't hide the edge to my tone. 'I can assure you I'm well qualified for the job and I'm here for no other reason.'

If she could be forthright then so could I.

'Quite so. I'm only trying to make you aware that Stefan and Judi like things doing their way... or not at all.'

'And you've known them a long time?'

'Oh yes,' she gushed. 'Stefan and I are close.'

I couldn't help but think that close friends didn't try to warn off a new employee in their first week. The woman on the street outside the restaurant came to mind. Suzanne had been my predecessor. Pretty, certainly, but why had she been upset and watching us?

Gil hadn't revealed much about her. Possibly he hadn't known the full details, or he'd been reluctant to open up. Maybe he'd been told to keep the finer details quiet.

'I appreciate the heads up, but I'm more than capable of deciding for myself what is and isn't the right job for me.'

'Quite. I can see that. Stefan can be utterly charming. You wouldn't be the first woman to fall for him.'

My voice rose in defence. 'This is my second day, and I don't know what you're suggesting but...'

'Please,' she said. 'Let's leave it there. I am only saying that a woman forewarned is a positive thing. Believe me, I should know.'

I didn't trust myself to reply politely and suppressed my response as I followed her from the kitchen to the living room. As we entered the room I heard a scuffle and a squeal and saw Polly scrabbling around on the floor.

Stefan stood close by.

'What's happened here?' Heidi placed the champagne tray on the coffee table and frowned down at Polly.

'Nothing to worry about,' said Stefan. 'A cup slipped off the table as we were tidying them up, didn't it, Polly?'

Polly glanced over her shoulder. The poor girl looked flushed and her eyes darted about. 'I'm really sorry.'

'For goodness sake,' said Heidi, irritated. 'My best coffee set, and now we're a cup short.'

'I'm sure it can be replaced,' suggested Stefan. He picked up the other cups and placed them on the tray.

'You're the expert,' said Heidi with a hint of sarcasm. 'Perhaps if I give you the details, you or Judi can find me another cup or two, or a whole set if it doesn't come alone.'

'I'd be delighted to,' said Stefan, in a calm and unruffled manner.

Polly placed the broken pieces on the tray, straightened her skirt and smoothed down her hair. She picked up the tray and with her eyes cast downwards she walked out of the room.

'You didn't say anything to upset Polly, did you Stefan?' Heidi asked.

'Of course not,' Stefan protested. 'I initiated a conversation and offered my help. Hardly my fault that she's clumsy.'

'Mmm.' Heidi's eyes narrowed. She opened her mouth to say more, then seemed to think better of it. Instead she picked up the bottle of champagne and placed it in his hand.

'Does Polly live locally?' I asked.

Heidi turned abruptly. 'She lives with us, dear, rather like our daughter did until she flew the nest ten years ago. She's our surrogate daughter, in a way.' She tilted her head as she spoke.

'Oh,' I said. 'But she wears a uniform and cleans and cooks for you?'

'Exactly, and gets well looked after for her services,' Heidi replied.

How strange talking about her as if she was a daughter, when it seemed clear she was being treated like a skivvy. I wondered how much they paid her. But I didn't feel I could enquire further without sounding like I was prying.

I considered Heidi's comments back in the kitchen and the way she talked to me as though I was inexperienced in work, life and love. She might be married but judging by the tension between her and Stefan I strongly suspected there was or had been far more to their relationship than friendship. And how generous of her to share her knowledge and wisdom with me after having only just met me.

The pop of the champagne cork made me start and I watched Stefan fill the glasses with the expertise of someone who'd done so a thousand times before.

'The deal on the painting is complete,' he said. He handed a glass to Heidi and one to me. 'Payment made and I'll be talking to them tomorrow about packing and delivering your precious cargo.'

'Then let us raise our glasses to a splendid job done. I knew you'd do this for me, darling. You and Judi must come over for dinner when the painting has been delivered and hung.' Heidi was all lightness and smiles and it seemed she'd moved on from the coffee cup incident.

We all chinked glasses and I took a sip of champagne.

The bubbles fizzed on my tongue - precisely what I needed to take the edge off my irritation with Heidi. 'I appreciated the opportunity to listen in,' I said. 'I learned a lot.'

'Your presence alone was a help, Tessa,' said Stefan.

I almost laughed until I realised by his expression that he was completely serious.

Instead, I smiled and drank more champagne. My first week was becoming a mixed but surprising experience. As the alcohol took effect my mood softened. Heidi's words seemed evidence that she either viewed me as a threat to her relationship with Stefan, or that she had genuine concerns combined with no tact. But I was a single woman now, and I didn't take lightly to being warned off someone. I'd form my own opinions and all that I'd seen of work and Stefan so far showed favourable in my eyes.

'Come over at the weekend with Gavin,' Stefan said to Heidi. 'We can swim and then drink and dine.'

Heidi's face lit up. 'Gavin was only saying we hadn't seen you both for weeks. We'd love to.'

There seemed to be no separation between business and pleasure where Stefan was concerned. Was this how Stefan and Judi conducted business with other clients? Or perhaps Heidi and Gavin had a special business relationship with Aztec Imports.

I'd barely eaten since the morning and the booze went straight to my head - a pleasant feeling that despite Heidi's interference, left me feeling optimistic. We finished the bottle and I noticed that

Stefan had more than one glass. I hoped it wouldn't impair his control of the bike. He certainly looked stable enough as we got up to leave, unlike me, who tripped down the front step.

Stefan reached for my arm. 'Steady there.'

I chortled. 'I don't often drink during the day.'

He kept hold of my arm. 'We don't make a habit of it either.'

'I do though,' chirped Heidi. 'Any excuse to celebrate.'

Stefan let go, and we left the shadow of the house and moved into the late afternoon sunshine.

I turned to Heidi. 'Lovely to meet you and thank you for your hospitality.'

'My pleasure, Tessa dear. Do remember our little conversation, won't you?'

Stefan turned to me and without waiting to be out of earshot, said, 'What conversation was that?'

'Well,' I paused. I didn't want to drop Heidi in it or to let Stefan know that she'd warned me against getting close to him.

Heidi chimed in. 'I mentioned to Tessa that you and Judi are workaholics and not to expect the same of her.'

'Heidi is right,' Stefan agreed. 'But rest assured, I wouldn't dream of asking you to work longer than you're contracted to.'

I caught Heidi rolling her eyes.

She stepped closer, leaned in and kissed Stefan on the lips. 'Take care, my darling.' Heidi returned to the front door and remained watching us as we mounted the bike and set off.

Stefan threw her a wave, but I kept my hands firmly about his waist.

We didn't usually suffer the drag of rush hour traffic along the coastal road, but there were far more cars than during our journey here. We approached the rear of a combine harvester that held up another car in front of us and Stefan edged towards the white line.

He called back, 'Hold tight.'

The engine throbbed and the exhaust roared beneath us as the bike picked up speed, and we darted past the car in front and continued on past the combine harvester. The stretch of road ahead looked straight and clear and we raced on until all around me became a blur. The wind rushed past and I felt at one with the bike and Stefan. My heart and blood settled into a steady but quickened rhythm as instinctively our bodies moved together with the bends, slopes and inclines in the road.

'That was exhilarating,' I said, when half an hour later we headed through the French doors and into the office.

'You're a natural,' replied Stefan

'All I did was hold on.'

'Trust me. I've had pillion riders tense up, shift and shuffle and that can make riding the bike trickier, and riskier too. I wouldn't have kept to that speed if I didn't feel secure with you.'

'It was incredible. I can't wait to tell the twins. Not that I'll be encouraging them to ride motorbikes.'

'Indeed, if I had children I'd keep them well away from motorbikes and fast cars. But as I don't, I've no need to play the role model.'

'I can see how that could have its advantages,' I said, and grinned.

'It isn't that I never wanted children. It's more that I never found the right woman,' he said, with a slim smile of regret.

I noted how his words contrasted with what he'd said when Judi had mentioned children.

It also seemed impossible to believe that Stefan hadn't been flocked by perfect women his entire life. Maybe he was particular about who he chose to get close to.

'I wouldn't be without the twins,' I said. 'But I try not to think about my acting career if I hadn't had them.'

'Didn't you want to continue?'

'Strangely no, as I'd been so driven to succeed in the theatre beforehand. Motherhood did something to me. I was quite young and I did find having them overwhelmingly exhausting. They took up every spare moment, physically and mentally, and I couldn't imagine leaving them. Once they started school, it got easier, but I wanted to work around the school runs. I guess I was born to be a full time Mum and that satisfied me.'

'Nothing to regret. And had you pursued acting, you wouldn't be here now, so I'm the lucky one.'

'Kind of you to say. And I'm still young enough to build a career, even if it isn't on the stage.'

'One needs to perform in all areas of life, so I'm certain your acting skills won't ever be wasted.'

22

Late on the Friday afternoon of my first week, Gil came into the office. I hadn't seen either Judi or Stefan, who'd been visiting a client in Newcastle that needed their help with some jewellery imports. From what I understood, they wanted Stefan or Judi to travel overseas as their buying agent because they couldn't travel themselves.

For most of the day I'd drafted promotional updates and an online newsletter to email to customers and to add to the website. I hadn't found it easy, but I had access to their photo library and a list of recent and ongoing assignments which I used as the basis to build on.

Gil sat down at Stefan's desk, propped his chin on his hands and sighed.

'You look ready for a rest,' I said.

'I am, but I doubt the weekend will be restful - horses don't take days off.'

'Have you got any horsey enthusiasts to help?' I asked.

'Yes, but they'll need supervision. How's it been anyway, are you coming back next week?'

I nodded. 'I've loved every moment. I don't think I could have asked for better employers.'

'They do have their moments,' Gil said, but with a dry tone.

'Actually, I've been meaning to ask you and I hope you won't think I'm prying, but you know outside the restaurant on Tuesday, that woman who watched us from the other side of the street?'

'Suzanne?'

'I'm interested to know what happened between her, Stefan and Judi? Only so that I can avoid making the same mistake.'

Gil stood up then came and perched on the edge of my desk. He sighed and spoke almost at a whisper. 'I don't know the details, but I got the impression she became infatuated with Stefan, obsessed even. He hadn't encouraged her.'

My heart began to beat in an unnatural rhythm, and I took a deep breath. 'Were they in a relationship?'

'I believe she wanted more than a working relationship, which Stefan resisted.'

I thought about how young and attractive Suzanne looked. 'I suppose working closely with someone one is attracted to can confuse boundaries.'

Gil nodded. 'Indeed, and that isn't necessarily a bad thing if both parties understand what the relationship means, if that's possible where attachments and emotions are involved.'

I thought about Gil and Judi. Did Judi know the boundary with Gil and what happened when one of them decided they no longer wanted to be intimate or met someone else? It seemed wiser and safer all round to keep working relationships platonic, and especially if one was not the boss or manager.

'Now you've told me that kind of makes sense. Sad though.'

'Don't most relationships end in sadness? With one partner or the other being unhappy, or even devastated?'

By the distant look in his eyes, I imagined he spoke from experience.

'If she was infatuated with Stefan I don't understand why she would leave? Wouldn't she have wanted to stay so she could see him?'

'I didn't ask too much but I understand there was a bust up between Stefan and Suzanne when Judi and I were out, and when we returned she'd gone. Stefan refused to talk about it but was fuming that she'd left them in the lurch.'

'Was Judi more forthcoming about what happened?' I pushed to find out more.

'Unfortunately, Judi and Suzanne didn't get on.'

'Why what happened between them?' I replied, thinking forewarned is forearmed.

'This might sound strange, but Judi complained a lot about Suzanne's attire.'

'Why, didn't she dress smartly enough?'

'More that Judi thought she dressed provocatively.'

'What? Skirts too short and low-cut tops, kind of dress?'

'Exactly, although Suzanne looked amazing, and professional, in my view. She always looked good.'

'OK, so Judi was jealous?'

He scraped a hand through his hair. 'She can be a little insecure, in that respect.'

'Well, I appreciate you being open,' I said.

'Anytime. I think we can be honest with one another.'

And I could tell that he meant it. 'Yes, I'd like that. So, Suzanne is still nursing her wounds and is upset that her role has already been filled.'

'Stefan believes she won't bother him again. She's married with young children and she won't want her husband to get wind of the reasons she left.'

'And yet, there she was on Tuesday night,' I said. 'Sounds messy. But she's better off out of it if Stefan didn't want to take the relationship further.'

'Mmm,' murmured Gil, without saying more.

I heard the front door bang shut and voices.

Gil stood up, alert. 'They're back.'

'I hope you didn't mind my asking,' I said.

He went and sat on a stool at the central island. 'Anytime. I may not have the answers, but I'll help when I can.'

Judi walked in looking unusually cheerful, followed by Stefan.

'A good day?' I asked.

'Excellent,' Judi replied and without elaborating, walked up to Gil, put her arm around him and kissed him on the lips.

Stefan came over and glanced down at my computer screen and then back at me. 'How have you got on today?'

'Good. Three pages of text and photos. Spoke to several clients and I've left a few messages on your desk and forwarded a couple of emails. I'll send you both a link to the newsletter and you can let me know if you want any edits.'

'Excellent, Tessa,' said Stefan, and nodded his approval.

'Better read it first,' I said. Although I felt fairly confident it read OK.

'You know we have Heidi and Gavin coming over on Sunday for a swim and drinks,' said Stefan. 'I wondered if you'd like to come and bring the twins, too. I'd like to meet them.'

I thought for a moment. 'I don't think I've got anything on. I'll ask them. Clara's fixed to the hip with her best friend at the moment so she might not want to, although she does love swimming and horses.'

'She can bring her friend along and they can see the horses, too.'

'That's really generous, thank you. I'll text you later.'

23

'Of course we want to go,' declared Clara, and grinned with enthusiasm.

'What about Fleur?'

'She'll defo want to come. I'll call her,' said Clara, and dunked her bread in her soup.

'This is your best recipe yet,' I said to Victor sitting opposite me. 'What did you say was in it?'

'We made it in Home Economics last week, but I ate it all at school. Smoked mackerel, leeks and potatoes.'

'It's lush,' said Clara, as she spooned another mouthful.

'I'll go see if Dad wants more,' said Victor.

'At least his appetite seems normal despite him feeling miserable,' I said.

'Actually, he's been cheerful today. Not demanding, and reading when I went to see him.'

'Maybe he's getting used to keeping still and in less pain. Not easy for someone who's usually so active.'

'He's reading a book and joined an online forum for people on bedrest,' said Victor.

'The sounds depressing,' said Clara. 'Aren't they all decrepit and waiting for the grim reaper?' She cupped her chin. 'I wonder what they talk about.'

'Probably the easiest way to spend a number one or number two,' said Victor.

Clara giggled. 'It's easy for men, surely.'

'Only if it's a wee,' said Victor. 'Not so easy to have a poo in bed.'

I laughed, and Clara shrieked.

'Stop it, Victor' I said, and laughed harder.

'Most likely it is the basic needs they talk about,' said Clara. 'They're taken away from you the moment you have a serious

154

accident or illness. Little things like the toilet can become major issues.'

I almost spat out my soup. 'Stop!'

'So immature, Mum,' said Victor with disapproval, followed by a snort of laughter.

'I'll wash the dishes as punishment,' I said.

Victor might have been a keen and excellent cook, but he hadn't yet mastered the art of cleaning up during or afterwards. He'd use every utensil within reach and the hob looked like he'd lost half the contents of the saucepans. Still, a small price to pay for a willing chef and delicious food.

I sat cross legged on the end of Noah's bed as he ate his second bowl of soup and we chatted about our days.

'Don't you think it's irresponsible riding pillion when you have children?'

It wasn't like Noah to be judgemental and I realised I'd been insensitive telling him. Hardly fair when we'd separated and he was restricted to his bed and in pain with broken bones.

'It was fun and I can't imagine you'd have turned down the opportunity. I'm free to do as I please, remember.'

'Mmm,' Noah muttered and his eyes narrowed. 'I'd like to meet this Stefan.'

'I'm sure you will one day.' I sensed Noah was already suspicious of the relationship.

My phone pinged beside me and I glanced down. A message from Stefan. I felt a flutter of adrenaline.

'Who's that?' asked Noah, and peered to see.

'Oh nothing, Judi at work. I'll read it later.'

'I'm enjoying that *Hamnet* you recommended,' he said.

'I thought you would. Best novel I've read this year.'

He picked up *Hamnet* from the bedside table and laid his hand on the cover. 'I'll have it finished by tomorrow.'

'Plenty more where that came from.'

'I saw the gambling addiction book you uploaded,' he said.

'And will you read it?'

'I've read the first chapter. I'll read it after *Hamnet*.'

'That's fantastic, Noah. It has real life accounts.'

'Maybe I'll write my own one day,' he said.

'Writing can be therapeutic. Tackle the problem whilst you're resting and at the same time you could journal - describe how you felt when you gambled, and now that you don't.' That's if he wasn't still gambling, I thought. I never could tell when he was or wasn't, and so much of it was done online.

He nodded, thoughtful. 'Maybe I will.'

I didn't say more. Any help he accepted had to meet him halfway. But I felt encouraged to see him reading and revealing a more positive state of mind.

I stood up and picked up his tray. 'I'll go and change.'

'And see what Judi wants,' he said.

'Judi?'

'She messaged you?'

'Oh yes. I must be tired,' I said, covering my petty lie.

'I hope they won't keep bothering you out of hours.'

'I doubt it.' I paused and framed my words. 'They've invited me and the children over to swim in their pool on Sunday. They're having a client over for drinks and dinner.'

'Nice, but do you really want to spend time with your boss in your free time?'

I gave a noncommittal shrug. 'I'll see how it goes. We needn't stay too long.'

In my bedroom I listened to Stefan's video message. 'Hope you can come on Sunday. Have you asked the twins?'

I recorded a quick video message. 'Hi. Yes, Clara and her friend, Fleur, but Victor is busy. I'm looking forward to it.'

I pressed send. Maybe video messages were how he liked to communicate. It did seem more personal. I played his video back a few times. He had a sensuous and insistent tone and the way he lowered the phone and looked down made it feel intimate.

A text reply came. "Fantastic! Don't forget your swimsuit."

I pulled my bikini out from the bottom drawer, closed the bedroom door and removed my work clothes. I put it on and stood in front of the mirror. Thankfully, it was fairly high waisted and covered my wound which still felt sore. I'd applied Savlon several times a day but the redness hadn't yet receded. If anything, the skin around the wound appeared angrier each time I looked. I'd give it a few more days and if there was no

156

improvement I'd make a doctor's appointment. Then I reached for my hand mirror, turned around and peered at my behind. Not bad. Round but with only minimal cellulite. I could thank my mother for my genes and being naturally leggy. 34D breasts, still nicely full even after breastfeeding.

I tried to imagine what Stefan might look like in his swimwear. Speedos? Probably not his style.

Clara walked into my bedroom. 'I'm wearing my new bikini.'

I turned to her. 'Bikini might be stretching the description.'

'Don't you think it's suitable?' she asked and stood in front of the mirror.

The white triangles that barely covered her buttocks and budding breasts were tied with strings. She looked lovely in it but almost prepubescent for her sixteen years - just as I had at her age.

'How about a sarong, to wear around the pool?' I suggested.

'I could do. Although I doubt Fleur will wear one.' She paused for a moment. 'I wish I had Fleur's figure.'

'And I'm sure she'd love to have yours. It's often the way when we compare ourselves to our friends,' I said.

'Maybe,' said Clara, thoughtfully.

'It's nice that you are so close,' I said.

Clara's face lit up. 'Fleur's the bestest friend I've ever had.'

I went to my dressing table and opened the drawer. I pulled out a crumpled pastel pink chiffon sarong. 'How about this?'

Clara threw it around her back and tied it above her bikini top.

'It suits your colouring,' I said.

'You mean whiter than a snowman?'

'Not at all. You're a beautiful young woman.'

'Are you wearing that one?' she asked.

'I thought so.' I turned sideways in the mirror. 'Or should I wear a costume for modesty?'

She shook her head. 'No, it looks fab on you.'

'Thank you, sweetheart.'

'Some mums would never wear a bikini, but I guess you were an actress and so body shy isn't in your makeup.'

I laughed. 'As long as I won't embarrass you.'

'Get away,' she replied.

The front doorbell sounded.

'That'll be Fleur,' said Clara and she ran out and down the stairs.

As I dressed, the sound of Clara and Fleur chatting excitedly travelled up the stairs.

Victor shouted up. 'Mum have you seen my wallet?'

'No,' I called back. Victor could never find anything. Even when it was right in front of him. 'Try your jacket pockets and school bag.'

'I've checked all of them - everywhere!' came his reply.

'I'll come down.' I sighed. I wanted to plonk down on the sofa and watch a movie. It had been an exciting but exhausting week.

I went downstairs to the living room.

'It's nowhere,' said Victor, sifting through the piles of papers on the dresser.

'Maybe it slipped down the side of the sofa or got kicked under a piece of furniture. When did you last have it?'

He scrubbed his hand through his hair. 'I'm sure I left it in my jacket pocket, but it isn't there now.'

We traipsed up to his bedroom and I knelt on the floor and searched under the beds, then rummaged behind piles of books and files and other miscellaneous stuff.

'What are you looking for?' asked Noah.

'My wallet. I already told you,' said Victor, impatient.

'It'll turn up,' said Noah.

'I need it now. And I want to get some cash.'

'I'll lend you some,' I said, 'and when you find your wallet you can pay me back.'

'Thanks. But I'm worried I've lost it.'

'Maybe you should ring the bank and stop your card,' I suggested.

'Sorry I can't help look,' said Noah. 'Why don't you give it until Monday to see if it turns up?'

'I don't know. If he's lost it on the street, anyone could be using it for cashless payments, or worse.'

Victor looked at his watch. 'I've gotta go. Can you text me if you find it? Mind if I borrow a tenner?'

'Course, my bag's in the kitchen.'

'Thanks, Mum. I've never lost my bank card before.'

'You'll have to be more careful where you leave your wallet,' I added.

Victor's voice rose. 'I don't need a bloody lecture.'

'I'm hardly lecturing you,' I said.

'And I'm always bloody careful.' And with a glare at Noah and then me, he marched out.

I heard him stomp down the stairs.

'I was only trying to offer advice,' I said to Noah.

'He'll calm down. The good thing about Vic is he never holds a grudge.'

I nodded. 'We're lucky. Not many teenage boys are so helpful and kind. You know he's cooked every night this week to help me out, and you, too.'

'Given up his bed and his privacy, too,' said Noah.

'Exactly. I hope people never take advantage of his good nature.'

24

'Sorry I can't come,' said Victor. 'I've still got this essay to finish and I'm knackered after fishing.'

'It's fine, Vic, and it's helpful to have someone here to keep an eye on Dad.'

We parked up in front of Lorton Hold.

'It's a castle!' Clara said. 'You never told us it was a castle.'

'It isn't medieval. It's only a century old.'

She peered out of the car window. 'Have you been up onto the turrets yet? Do you think they'd let me? I could take some awesome photos.'

'With me posing in them,' said Fleur.

'In your swimsuit,' said Clara with a laugh.

'No chance,' replied Fleur.

We all clambered out with our swimming bags. 'Let's see how we get on first,' I didn't want to dull their excitement, but felt reluctant to take any liberties with the Temple's generosity.

Stefan had messaged first thing to say that we should walk round the back to the pool area. Although the pool was fully enclosed and covered, the day felt mild and the skies, untypical for the north east coast, almost clear of clouds.

'Are there changing rooms?' asked Fleur, as we walked across the gravel to the path that led down the side of the house.

'I believe so.'

Clara gazed about. 'They must have a gardener. It's amazing.'

'They do,' I said. 'A lot of land to look after.' I heard voices and as we neared the pool I recognised Heidi's high pitched laughter.

When we walked through the doorway, Stefan looked up and came over.

He ushered us to where Heidi and Gavin sat. 'Come and meet my friends.'

Heidi remained seated, but Gavin hauled himself out of his chair as Stefan introduced us. Gavin shook my hand, then turned to the girls.

'Well, this is a delightful surprise. Three mermaids to bathe with us today.' Gavin turned to Stefan who stood beside Clara and Fleur. 'You didn't warn me we'd be surrounded by nymphs.'

'You know how I like to surprise,' said Stefan, with the smallest of winks.

Gavin held out his hand to Clara and when she extended hers in return, he took it and lifted it to his mouth. He planted a kiss on the back of her hand. 'Wonderful to meet you, Clara.'

He let go of her hand, then Clara turned to Fleur and quite openly grimaced.

When Gavin moved to take Fleur's hand, Fleur took his hand, shook it quickly and released it just as fast. I wasn't embarrassed, but impressed and amused by the girls' reactions. I was far less impressed by Gavin's behaviour which bordered on sleazy. Entirely different generations and expectations, I mused.

Unlike Heidi, impeccably glamorous and in amazing shape, Gavin was of average height, but equally as wide. A more rotund man I couldn't recall meeting and he showed no inhibition with his enormous belly, which spilled over and all but obscured his swimming shorts. He did have a full head of brown hair, which I imagined he coloured due to the mismatched and abundant grey hair on his chest. As Gavin turned and walked back to his recliner, he gave the impression of a slow loris - his limbs were heavy and he moved in slow motion. Facially, he looked a similar age to Stefan and Heidi, but perhaps he had arthritis or his size hindered his movements. Judi and Gil lounged side by side on recliners in their swimwear, each with a glass of something in hand.

'Let's get you some drinks,' said Stefan. 'Are the girls allowed a little sparkling wine?'

Clara and Fleur grinned at one another.

I smiled. 'I should think so. It is a special occasion after all.'

Stefan directed me and the girls to the bottom end of the pool and we traipsed down the steps to the changing rooms.

No detail for aesthetics, quality and comfort had been spared. The changing room had open showers, private changing cubicles and a row of sinks with vases of dried roses, gypsophila and cornflowers, and well lit mirrors above. Wooden shelving had been stacked with plush folded towels and an array of shampoos and toiletries.

Fleur's dark skin, courtesy of her African father, looked stunning in her red swimming costume.

'Mum insisted I could only come if I wore this. She's suspicious of new people.'

'Well, she isn't here and so she is right to be protective,' I said.

'I don't mind,' she said. 'I hate being ogled, which is what always happens with my chest.'

'You have no idea,' moaned Clara. 'I'd rather have your figure than mine. I don't even need a bra yet. What sixteen year old doesn't need a bra?'

'I'd say you do need a bra now,' said Fleur.

'Yes, I think Fleur is right,' I agreed. 'Besides, I was the same as you and look at me now.' I adjusted my bikini top.

Back at the poolside the girls jumped straight into the water and Judi and Gil got up and went for a swim, too. Stefan retrieved some inflatable balls, dolphins and lilos from a room off the pool and threw them into the water for the girls to play with.

I joined Stefan, Heidi and Gavin, who sipped their drinks and chatted round the table.

Stefan wore loose fitting swim shorts but it was clear he worked out. He didn't have any excess fat, and my eyes were drawn to the tufts of hair between his nipples. When I lifted my gaze, he caught my eye.

I felt my cheeks glow and I raised my glass to my lips. Why on earth did I keep blushing? Perhaps they were hot flushes. Whatever they were, he made me feel self-conscious - too intensely aware of his physical presence. I hadn't felt so strongly attracted to a man since I'd met Noah. I might be a free agent but I realised that celibacy wasn't going to suit me for long.

'Is your husband working today, Tessa?' asked Gavin.

'No, my partner and I are recently separated,' I said.

'Ahh, but Tessa has kindly taken him in as he fell off her roof and broke a leg,' said Heidi.

'His arm too, so he's in a lot of pain,' I said. 'And it was my skylight he was fixing.'

'I'm sure he's grateful for your support,' said Gavin with a wink. He reached over and topped up my glass.

I felt mildly irritated by his wink, which seemed to imply I was providing more than platonic support. 'Our son Victor is kindly sharing his bedroom,' I added.

The sun blazed through the glass roof and I felt myself getting hotter and hotter.

I stood up. 'Think I'll take a swim.'

'I'll join you,' said Stefan. 'It's the greenhouse effect in here - encourages us to swim, and why all these plants are flourishing.'

I walked to the side of the pool and sensed Stefan's eyes following me.

He came and stood at my side.

'It has the feel of a tropical oasis,' I said.

'Intentionally,' said Stefan. 'It makes swimming here all the more inviting, but without any of the snakes and mosquitos.'

'Relieved there are no snakes,' I said, with a laugh.

'This is the deep end,' he said. 'Want to jump?'

I dipped my toes in the water which felt surprisingly chilly. I grinned and nodded. 'The water doesn't feel tropical but, OK.'

Stefan took my hand in his and turned to me. 'After three?'

We counted together then leapt off the side and plunged into the water. We released hands and I sank down until my feet touched the bottom. I pushed off the floor and when my head bobbed up above the surface I wiped the hair and water from my face.

I gasped. 'Is it heated?'

'Not much,' he replied. 'It's more invigorating that way.'

'I'll race you to the far end,' I said, and set off at a crawl.

Stefan quickly pulled up alongside me and I swam as hard as I could until we reached the other end.

'Wow. For someone so dainty, you're a strong swimmer,' he said.

I laughed. 'Like your Dad, my mum was a stickler for swimming lessons, so at least I'm safe from drowning.'

He trod water. 'Judi's prepared food for us today. She's a wonderful cook.'

I propped my arm on the side of the pool. 'I imagine Judi is accomplished at anything she sets her sights on.'

'She is very driven, that is true,' said Stefan, resting his elbow on the side of the pool.

'Victor loves cooking. I wouldn't be surprised if he goes into that line of work. If not, he'll make his partner in life extremely happy.'

'A tough profession to work in, but plenty of scope for success. And what about Clara? What's her passion?'

I followed his eyes to Clara and Fleur as they splashed and clambered onto lilos. 'I'm not sure yet. She's not sure yet. She loves art, sport, maths and science, so quite a mixture. She's bright without much effort.'

'Does she get her brains from you?' he asked, turning back to me.

'Her Dad is incredibly smart, so lucky genes, I think.'

The girls threw a beach ball between them with plenty of squeals and laughter.

'Sixteen is a funny age,' I said. 'Still children in many ways.'

'Indeed.' Stefan thought for a moment. 'Judi and I were left to our own devices at that age. Mother and father were away most of the time. We boarded at a school near York and didn't see them much during the holidays. Our nanny, sports coaches and private tutors were more like parents.'

'Sounds a bit lonely for you both.'

'Maybe, but we had each other, and in many ways we had complete freedom. I used to stay with friends in the holidays, go to all night parties. Dabbled with things I shouldn't have. In short, I grew up fast.'

'How about Judi. Did she miss your parents?'

'Yes, though she'd never admit it. She's developed a tough exterior. You might have noticed?'

I nodded. 'I have. And where do your parents live now?'

'In Australia. Melbourne, I think.'

'Don't you visit them, or they come here?'

He gave a visible shudder. 'Not for the past decade.'

'Wouldn't you like to?'

'Not at all. They'd drive me insane after a day of listening to them bicker and snipe at one another. I've no idea why they're still married.'

'Mummy?'

Clara's shriek made me look over. I saw her clinging to the side of the pool as Fleur climbed out beside her.

Clara beckoned me over. Her eyes darted about.

I swam over and as I neared I noticed a red tinge to the water. 'Are you bleeding?'

Clara looked down. 'Yes, loads of it.' She began to sob.

'It could be your period. You should get out.'

Fleur returned with a towel and held it up. 'Climb out, Clara.'

Clara pulled herself up and I noticed a ribbon of blood trickle down her inner thigh. Fleur wrapped the towel around Clara's waist and I climbed out too.

Heidi walked round the side of the pool. 'Is Clara OK?'

'I think it's her period - her first.' I turned to the girls. 'Let's go to the changing room.'

Clara wept as Fleur put an arm around her and led her away. I followed behind and Heidi walked with me.

'I have some pads in my bag,' she said, then added, 'You'd think I'd be past all that by fifty-two.'

'Thank you, Heidi.'

We hurried down the steps and Clara disappeared into the toilet. Fleur sat on the changing bench.

'Are you OK?' I stood behind the door.

'It is my period,' she sobbed. 'I've been waiting for years and it starts when I'm swimming.'

'Unlucky timing, my love.'

'I'm mortified,' she moaned.

'Becoming a woman is something to celebrate,' chimed Heidi.

There came a louder sob.

'Clean yourself up. Heidi has some pads you can use and we'll go up and have more sparkling wine,' I said.

'I don't want anyone to mention it. I won't come up otherwise.'

'Of course,' I said. 'I'll let them know and we won't talk about it.'

Heidi reached down and pushed some pads under the door.

Fleur came over with a bundle of Clara's clothes, and pushed them under the door, too.

'Thank you,' I heard Clara say quietly.

'Do you want me to stay or shall I go back up?' I said.

'I'm fine. I'm in shock, that's all.'

'I understand, darling,' I said.

'I want Fleur to stay though.'

'I'm not going anywhere,' Fleur replied. 'I know how I'd have felt if that had been me in the pool. I started at school and that was bad enough.'

I touched Fleur's arm lightly. 'You're a wonderful friend, thank you.'

Fleur smiled. 'Clara's a wonderful friend, too.'

Heidi and I left the girls alone and headed back up to the poolside.

I couldn't see either Stefan or Gavin.

Gil and Judi sat at the table with towels wrapped around them. They both looked over.

'Is Clara OK?' asked Judi.

'She's fine,' said Heidi.

I walked over to them. 'Do you mind if we don't mention anything? Poor Clara's embarrassed - she's started her first period.'

Judi sympathised. 'Poor girl, and in a pool, too.'

I noticed how her eyes travelled up and down me as she spoke.

'My first period came during a maths lesson,' Heidi said. 'I was only ten and one of the first in my year. Children can be so cruel and I got teased for days.'

'I remember first seeing the blood myself. Quite a shock initially. And Clara is so late in starting, too.'

'We soon adapt. It's in a woman's genes to adapt to changes in her body and environment,' said Judi.

I nodded slowly. 'I think you're right. Must be how women got to be so strong, mentally and physically. We're survivors despite the pressures stacked against us.'

Judi laughed. 'The only reason I'm still here. Oh, and because I have Gil.' She gazed at him with adoring eyes and took his hand with a protective grip.

I turned around. 'Where are Stefan and Gavin?'

'They needed to discuss something,' said Judi, and she released Gil's hand and got up. 'And I must check on dinner. Can you help me, Gil?'

'Sure,' he replied, genial.

'You relax and drink more,' she said to Heidi and me. 'We shan't be long.'

Heidi and I collected our drinks and sat back on the loungers. I watched Judi head out, followed by Gil. I sighed and took a long drink of my spritzer.

'I hope you won't mind my asking,' said Heidi. 'What was the reason you split with your partner?'

I felt taken aback by the directness of her question.

'And now you have him back with you again?' she continued, not waiting for my reply. 'Gavin and I have had some ups and downs and almost split a couple of times, but we've always resolved our squabbles. Life is easier with a long term partner, even with their faults.' She gave a slim smile.

'It's complicated,' I said, unsure whether I wanted to continue.

'Life is complicated. Being a single mum won't be easy and especially with two teens who need their Dad.'

She really was being quite persistent.

'Noah's had a gambling problem that's got steadily worse. I've supported him, forgiven him more times than I can remember, but I couldn't take any more. Addiction affects the whole family, and the children particularly.'

Heidi sat forwards, keen to find out more. 'And has he sought help for this?'

'Only half-heartedly. He barely accepts he has a problem, although my leaving him has hit home.'

'What treatments has he tried?'

'Treatments for gambling?' I asked.

'Yes.' Despite us being alone, she leaned in to confide. 'I myself have had one addiction, and ultimately it was hypnotherapy that got me through it. My life became a misery for years. The guilt, the lies, the overthinking everything. My guilty conscience couldn't cure me. I needed something powerful to alter my neural pathways.'

'Sounds intriguing. I hadn't considered hypnotherapy as a cure for gambling. Is it costly?'

'My therapist, Jameel, now also a friend, doesn't come cheap, but he's the best in his field. I'll give you his business card and if you or Noah contact him, let him know I recommended him. I can't think of one person who he hasn't helped or cured. It really is life changing stuff.'

I realised I'd been judging Heidi for being interfering and bossy, but not only had she passed on some emergency sanitary protection for Clara, she'd also sounded supportive over my problems with Noah.

I imagined her therapist would be costly but it would be worth talking to him.

The girls emerged from the changing rooms, both in their pretty dresses and wet hair neatly combed. They walked over, their arms linked.

'Are you all right sweetheart?'

Clara nodded. 'Is the pool OK?' she said, and she turned to where she'd climbed out.

'Nobody would ever know,' I said.

She sat down on the end of my sunlounger and rested her hands on her knees. 'Where are the others?'

'Gil and Judi are preparing food, and Stefan and Gavin are talking business somewhere,' I said.

Fleur touched Clara's hand and said, 'We heard voices down in the changing room. We wondered if there was a men's changing room.'

'No, that's the only one,' replied Heidi. 'Although I've heard voices travel down from up here. That'll be what you heard.'

Fleur turned to Clara. 'They sounded closer than that. Whispers.'

Clara nodded. 'Yes, a lot closer.'

Heidi reached into her handbag and pulled out a lipstick and mirror. 'Well, we were up here, so it could have been the wind that you heard.'

A feeling of unease came over me and I wasn't sure why. I rubbed my damp palms against my legs and took another sip of my drink.

We weren't all up here. Where had Stefan and Gavin disappeared to? There were loungers at the far end of the pool where they could have spoken in privacy.

Stefan shook Clara's hand and gave her a hug. 'Delighted to meet you both.' He turned to Fleur and gave her a hug, too. 'You must come back and use the pool anytime you like. It doesn't get enough use.'

I noticed how neither of the girls minded Stefan hugging them, despite their earlier reactions to Gavin.

Clara said, 'Thanks for letting us see your horses and stables too. It's been brilliant fun.'

'And remember you can help with the horses,' added Stefan. 'Check in with Gil first.'

Clara turned to Fleur, her confidence recovered after the pool incident. 'We'd love that, wouldn't we?'

Fleur nodded with enthusiasm. 'Thank you, Mr Temple.'

'Stefan, I insist,' he replied.

The girls smiled and chatted as they made their way back to the car.

'What a lovely afternoon, thank you,' I said. 'Judi is an incredible cook. Are you sure I can't stay behind and help with the clearing up? Judi must be exhausted.'

'Between you and me, Judi loves to cook but she doesn't do any of the donkey work. Our housekeeper looks after that.'

'OK, if you're sure,' I said.

'I'm only glad you enjoyed yourself.' His eyes remained fixed upon mine. 'From my point of view the afternoon has been all the more pleasurable because you were here, and your delightful daughter and friend.'

'Thank you. I'll be back again...' I glanced at my watch. 'In fourteen hours.'

'I've enjoyed getting to know you better. And if you don't mind my adding, you looked sensational in that bikini. Really, Tessa. Stunning.'

169

'It's not often I get the chance to wear it.'

Stefan leaned down, and with his hands resting on my arms, he kissed me lightly on the lips.

I felt surprised, but at the same time, not so surprised.

I'd been aware of how his eyes had followed me during the afternoon, and he'd gravitated towards me to talk, even sitting beside me during dinner.

I also got a definite sense that Heidi didn't approve of him bestowing his attention on me, but she had her husband with her, and both Stefan and I were single. She'd even tutted when he'd sat beside me at the dining table. I imagined she'd expected him or wanted him to sit with her. As for working together, nothing of any note had happened between us. Perhaps it would, perhaps it wouldn't, but I couldn't deny how he made me feel - even thinking about him.

Stefan was undeniably delicious.

25

I heard raised voices even before I'd opened the front door and walked into the living room.

Clara turned to me. 'Why's Vic shouting?'

I heard a door slam and footsteps thundered down the stairs.

Victor stopped at the bottom of the stairs and looked at the three of us. His cheeks were flushed and his eyes wild and red rimmed.

I stepped closer. 'What's happened? Is Dad OK?'

'Oh, Dad's OK! But he won't be by the time I've finished.' Victor's lower lip quivered.

My heart pounded faster. I'd never seen Vic so enraged and upset. It took a lot to make him lose his cool.

Victor went to the sofa and lay down, covered his face with his hands and cried - his body heaved with emotion.

I knelt down on the floor beside him. 'What on earth has happened?'

He sat upright and spoke through his tears, 'At least I know where my bloody bank card is.'

'What do you mean?' I said, but already suspected the worst.

'Not lost, but stolen by my own Dad.'

I felt a fury build inside of me as I took Victor's hand. 'How much?'

'Cleared it out,' cried Vic. 'Five hundred and seventy pounds. Which leaves me with three pounds and eight fucking pence precisely.'

'Christ! I'm so sorry.' Every fibre in me wanted to run upstairs and yell at Noah for being an effing bastard. For being one shitty dad.

'He's the one who'll be sorry,' said Vic. 'It's fucking bullshit!'

'I'll go talk to him,' said Clara, and she set off towards the stairs, her eyes wide and her jaw set firm in readiness for confrontation.

Victor had worked so hard to earn that money, money that Noah could earn in a couple of days.

I hurried over to her. 'No, Clara. Let me talk to him.'

With reluctance, Clara paused and stood aside.

As I walked up the stairs I don't think I'd ever felt so enraged and disappointed with Noah. To lie and abuse our finances was one thing, but to steal from his own son? He disgusted me. My feelings had swung from pity upon him falling and breaking bones and being confined in bed, to fury that bordered on loathing. Seeing our son all wound up and sobbing had forced me to see Noah for what he was, for what he'd become and for what his pathetic addiction had turned him into.

I stood behind the closed bedroom door and took several long breaths. Then I turned the handle and walked in.

Noah sat in bed, his face turned towards the window. I walked around the other side and glared down at him. 'How could you?'

He lowered his head into his hands. 'I'm sorry.'

'You're nothing but a pathetic liar and thief.'

'I know it.'

'Why, Noah? Don't you even attempt to engage your brain before continuing with this lunacy?'

He lifted his head, but couldn't look me in the eye. 'I'm sorry. Will Vic forgive me?'

'You're not sorry so why should Vic ever forgive you? Perhaps if you pay him back the moment you have the cash to do so then you might be in with a chance of clawing back some sympathy.' My heart pounded and tears stung my eyes. 'He'll never forget though, and the sad thing is you've lost his respect. He's always looked up to you...'

Noah's face crumpled and his shoulders shuddered as he sobbed.

'Don't you dare feel sorry for yourself.' I continued my tirade. 'You need some bloody resolve to kick this. You're close to destroying every relationship that's ever meant anything to you.'

Noah's sobs intensified and he couldn't look my way.

But I couldn't hold myself back, and my face and head burned with anger.

'How are you going to beat this? If you'd only accept your problem and seek help, then you might be in with a chance of saving yourself and what little remains of your relationships.'

'I've tried everything, you know I have.'

'Then you haven't tried hard enough. I forgave you over and over again and then we welcomed you into our new home and this is how you repay us. The sooner your leg is healed the better, so I can get you out of my house and out of my life.'

He looked at me briefly before he lowered his head in shame once more. His tears flowed drop after drop. A pitiful sight, and I prayed that the damage he'd caused had finally sunk in.

'I'll forgive you for when you've returned Vic's hard earned money. Until then, I can't bear to look at you.' I swung around and left the bedroom.

Victor refused to share his room, and without saying a word to his Dad he packed away his camp bed and carried an armful of clothes down to the living room. We pulled the sofa forwards and positioned the camp bed behind it. The living room looked even more cramped and cluttered than before, but I could only sympathise.

'Dad won't have your room forever and as soon as he's better and more mobile, he'll move back in with Anna.'

'Are you going to tell her what Dad did?' asked Vic.

I thought for a moment. 'I'm not sure that would help. I don't want her refusing to have him back and I don't want to sour their relationship - Dad needs his family more than ever.'

'True,' said Vic with a thoughtful look. 'I was saving that money to go camping in France next summer.'

'I know, my love. If Dad doesn't pay you back by then, I will. I should be able to afford to.'

'I don't understand how he managed to use my card. Surely gambling sites send those annoying verification codes.'

'I don't know, Vic. But sad to say, I expect your dad knows ways around these barriers.'

'He's sick,' said Vic.

'Yes, I'm afraid he is. I lost it with him big time up there, and I don't feel good about some of the things I said.'

'He deserves it. I lost it with him too. And maybe he needs a massive reality check.' Recognising that I was close to tears, Vic reached out his arms and hugged me.

'I love you and I'm sorry your Dad is being such a dick.'

'If he was only being a dick I could cope with it,' said Vic, with a small smile. 'Stealing my earnings, not so much.'

'We will get through this, Vic. I promise.'

That night, I slept, but only fitfully, and when my phone pinged at two am, I reached over to read the message.

My tummy fluttered. A message from Stefan.

"I can't stop thinking about you."

I stared at the words. I saw he was still online. I put the phone down, unsure how or whether to reply. I picked it up again and typed. "We hardly know one another and you are my employer."

He typed a quick reply. "I know. But being near you makes me happy."

Had I flirted with him? No, I'd only been friendly and responded to his words. If anything I'd tried to hold back on being overly friendly. I'd tried to repress the attraction I felt developing within me. I'd only known him a few days. With Noah, we'd worked together for months before acknowledging our attraction and getting together.

Yet, I had to admit to myself that I'd never experienced such an instant and overwhelming connection with a man before.

"I like being near you, too." I typed the words that did little to express the real physical and electrifying sensations he evoked in me. I pressed send and held my phone against my chest half expecting him to reply again.

After some time I fell asleep and in the morning I saw there were three new messages from him. Two were songs and I played them. Both were '70s ballads I'd heard before and with poignant lyrics. His third message said, "These remind me of you. Sweet dreams."

Sitting there alone, I felt like a teenager experiencing my first monumental crush. But one that was reciprocated and led by him, and with the potential to become something, rather than a painful longing from afar.

How could this be happening so soon after my separation?

And for some moments, in a dreamy daze, I pictured a future with Stefan, lying in bed with him at Lorton Hold - his castle. Swimming together in the pool. Holding hands with him as we walked Digby, or riding the horses side by side along the coastal paths. Some relationships did happen quickly and out of the blue and still lasted a lifetime.

Love could happen in an instant. But, I knew, so could infatuation.

We couldn't choose who we were attracted to and when that attraction was mutual and no other parties involved, where was the harm? He was thirteen years older than me, but he looked incredible, and he was fit, driven and intelligent. And more importantly, he seemed a generous, interesting and thoughtful man.

Even so, I knew I'd be a fool to allow my emotions to get carried away.

I'd take it slowly, be careful and not rush into anything I might end up regretting.

26

'I'm not cooking for Dad,' said Vic, as the three of us crammed into the kitchen to make our breakfasts.

'He can't exactly cook his own can he?' I said. 'If I'm here I'll sort him out and I'll pack him a sandwich for lunchtime, but if he needs a drink or help with something, can you rise above your frustration and help him out? It'll help me out, too. And I'll cook the evening meals.'

'While he sits on his backside all day and you're out at work? Hardly seems fair.'

'But you know Dad would be working if he could,' said Clara, and showed her sympathetic side, as she always did.

Her ability to see both sides here was heartwarming.

'That's right,' I said, and put an arm around Victor. 'I know he has faults. OK, he has one bloody great big fault, but let's help him recover and then he can return to work and pay you back. And me too.'

Victor huffed and shrugged me off, clearly unconvinced.

I had time to take Digby for a run on the beach and when I returned, wet and windswept from a showerburst, Clara and Victor were bickering about whose turn it was to wash up the breakfast things. The kitchen didn't have the space for a dishwasher and we were all tired of the washing up routine.

I couldn't wait to get out of the house - the atmosphere felt as strained as before Noah and I had separated, and I prayed that Vic and Noah wouldn't have any more bust ups while I was at work. I doubted Vic would go near him unless he had to and Clara seemed fairly even tempered about it all, most likely resigned to how her dad was or tired of the never ending drama and arguments.

The last thing I'd said as I'd left the house was. 'Keep your wallets and bank cards on you at all times - don't even leave them down here.'

'What a sad and sorry state of affairs,' I heard Clara say.

She was spot on. Sad and sorry, indeed. And I felt my throat tighten with emotion.

When I walked into the office, Gil, Judi and Stefan were talking around the central island.

'We have a Monday morning greet to talk about what we have planned for the week. Stefan beckoned me over. 'Come and join us, Tessa.'

'I like your dress,' Judi said, and peered over her reading glasses. 'I have one similar. Where was yours from?'

I pulled out a chair and sat down. 'Thanks. Only our local charity shop. They sometimes have barely worn designer clothes and I got lucky.'

I detected a sniff from Judi but then she tilted her head and smiled.

I'd put on a green, fitted, business style dress and wore it with sheer tights, black pumps and a short black blazer.

'You could wear anything and look good in it,' said Stefan.

'Then I'll wear a sackcloth and wellies tomorrow.'

We all laughed and Judi said, 'You can help muck out the stables.'

But I couldn't help feeling flattered by Stefan's words.

The morning passed quickly as I rang clients and scheduled appointments. Some of them were to be held over Zoom, but most required a visit from either Stefan or Judi. It seemed they liked to talk to clients regularly face to face to discuss upcoming and future purchases.

'It takes up an inordinate amount of our time but it's the best way to keep working relationships strong and intact. Visits often result in new jobs and we don't want our clients thinking they can receive a better service elsewhere,' he'd added. 'Plus, it's a good opportunity for you to introduce yourself and for them to know who is new to the team.'

We had the clients' mobile numbers listed and I was surprised how many of them answered first time. I'd expected to have to leave voice messages. But most seemed keen to talk and to set up meetings. The majority of their clients were men, which left me slightly disappointed. Surely plenty of women had their own salaries to purchase large value items? A few asked about Suzanne and I replied that she was moving out of the area as Stefan had mentioned.

Mid-morning Judi and Stefan set out to meet a client to discuss the transportation of some furniture from Indonesia. The client had purchased a new property and wanted it furnished almost exclusively from one overseas supplier.

The day was mild and sunny and at lunchtime I took my sandwich out to the front of the house where the garden stretched as far as the cliff tops. I walked across the lawn and between some elm trees that led to an expanse of land left to grow wild. The summer grass had turned to long yellow stalks and dried wildflowers - thistles, teasels and poppies, remained standing, and breathed in their final days of the warmth and sunlight.

Young trees, recently planted, lined either side of a dirt path that meandered through the grass, their leaves now faded and yellow. A breeze rushed in and rustled through the trees and for a moment or two it sounded reminiscent of distant voices, indistinct yet searching for something, or someone, perhaps. Being so close to the sea and high up on the cliffs made me feel separate from anything work related. Hidden amongst the trees and tall grass, away from the house, my home and Whitby, felt liberating and invigorating. I sat down and inhaled the air and soaked up the atmosphere.

Until my phone buzzed from my pocket.

I got up and walked on so that I could capture the seaview. It was my lunch break and the message could wait for now. During the morning I'd received two texts from Stefan - the first asking if all was going OK and to call if I needed him for anything, the second was a photograph of him in the car. Judi must have driven. His message said, "Don't forget to take a lunch break and I hope you're missing me".

He talked as if we were already an item. Such intimate words and tone. But it didn't annoy me, rather, it pleased and excited me. I decided that if it was him messaging me again, it wouldn't hurt to make him wait. My feelings towards him were growing by the hour, with our every exchange, whether it be with words or a look. All my problems, Noah, our finances, Victor and the bank card, seemed diminished, to disappear even, whenever I thought about Stefan.

I felt swept along by desire, and I couldn't hold back from feeling this way. I didn't want to hold back. It felt as though I'd reached a momentous juncture in my life where the route to my future had forked abruptly. New experiences, adventures and love lay ahead, and maybe even a new life and home.

The wind swept in from the sea and in front of me the grass swayed and blurred the edges between the land and the waves that lay far below.

The cliff top fell away suddenly and I gazed out at the endless blue expanse to the horizon and to white crowns that flickered upon the surface then faded beneath the sun. I spotted three boats each separated by wide expanses of water - pale silhouettes that appeared unmoving. I crept closer to the edge and crouched down on my knees. I'd never been afraid of heights, and I felt a thrill run through me as I peered right over and down to the rocks below and the white froth of the waves that rolled forwards and backwards over the stones, softly sounding from up here. There came a crumbling sound; loose stones and soil fell away only inches from my face and tumbled down to the rocks below. But the earth beneath my bones felt safe and solid.

On the beach, to the right, I spotted a ramp, twenty feet or so long, that sloped down to the shoreline. If Stefan owned a boat, there had to be a way to reach the shore. I stood up, stepped back from the edge and headed further down the slope to look for a way down to the beach. A hundred yards or so further on a trodden path in the grass led to the cliff and a flight of steps, partly concealed by bramble bushes. Carefully, I pulled the brambles aside, taking care not to snag my tights. I peered down the steps which looked treacherously steep, but had a handrail on either side. With the rocky cliff face to my left, I proceeded down. I paused and looked over the rail at what appeared to be a boathouse at the top end of the ramp. I stepped onto the beach and walked over stones and sand and up some steps onto the ramp. Up close the boathouse smelled freshly painted in sea green. The double doors were bolted but discovering they were unlocked, I yanked back the catch and pulled the door ajar.

I had the strangest feeling I was being watched, and I paused, turned around and looked back along the beach and up the steps to the cliff tops.

Would Stefan and Judi mind me coming down here? Neither of them had said I couldn't walk around the grounds, although no one had mentioned a private beach. What a mystery and surprise.

I felt a thrill of adventure and discovery that reminded me of my childhood and exploring the secluded bays close to home with my friends.

I opened the door wide to allow more light and stepped inside.

And here she was, named on the side of the bow in metallic blue, Amphitrite, the goddess of the sea. She was a shining white and blue speedboat, twenty or so feet long, mounted on a wheeled frame. I walked along the side and looked inside. The boat had wooden benches along the port and starboard, and in the middle a plastic crate full of what appeared to be metal chains. I walked round to the stern, stepped onto the frame and clambered into the boat. I crouched down and reached into the crate. It contained chains and what looked like lockable cuffs.

A chill ran through me and as I climbed off the boat, questions reeled through my mind. I'd seen hundreds of boats in Whitby harbour, sailed on the smaller boats, and worked on one with Roddy for years, but I had never seen anything such as this. How could I bring it up with Stefan or Judi without them knowing I'd been down here and snooping around? Or maybe I'd be upfront and ask Gil outright - watch his response and listen to what he had to say.

It couldn't be easy getting the boat down to the water without a vehicle of some kind. I left the boathouse and secured the bolt on the double doors, then walked to the bottom of the ramp to where the waves rose in and back again. I sat down on the sun warm concrete, unwrapped my tuna sandwich and took a bite. My stomach felt hollow but my appetite had vanished.

The moment Stefan came into my mind's eye butterflies swarmed my insides. All thoughts of him excited me, but at the same time I found these new feelings unsettling, too. Despite his warmth and openness with his words, he seemed beyond my normal sphere of experience in a way that I couldn't fathom. He was well educated, eloquent, a successful business owner and millionaire with a castle for a home. But it was his manner and how he spoke to me that had elicited such an intense reaction.

The sun felt hot on my legs and I was tempted to take off my shoes and tights and dip my toes in the water. I turned around and looked back up to the cliff and the steps I'd come down. It felt like a secret hideout. I could skinny dip and no one would ever see me. Maybe they used the boat to import goods? It wouldn't carry large items but it could be used to bring things in from ports further up the coast or even out at sea. There had to be a rational explanation for the chains and cuffs and I felt determined to clarify what purpose they served. Maybe Judi, Stefan or Gil were into some strange sex stuff. But on a boat? And if they weren't used for sex, then they had to be used to stop animals or people from moving - from getting off. My mind spun with the scope of possibilities.

I wrapped my sandwich back in its foil. I felt anxious and it suddenly seemed wrong being here.

By the time I'd jogged back up the steps, my heart pounded and my breaths came fast. I stopped at the top to look out at the ocean and to catch my breath, when a sudden gust of wind swept in from nowhere, slammed into my back and pitched me forwards towards the edge. I staggered, recovered myself and stepped back several feet. Overhead, thick clouds rolled and formed and I turned and looked out where rain clouds accumulated casting black shadows over the sea's surface. I marched back up the slope, but half way up, and still breathing hard, a revolting and overpowering stench filled the air. I instantly recognised it - a dead creature. I knew the odour from walking Digby who, being morbidly curious, sniffed out corpses of any kind. And far worse, the young woman on the beach. Although I guessed that she must have died not long before Digby found her because I hadn't detected any hint of the aroma of decay, and her body had not yet bloated.

I drew my jacket collar over my mouth to quell the stench, and continued up the hill.

When I reached the top of the slope something made me stop and pause. The smell had dissipated. But what had died that could give off such an overwhelming stench? I turned around and felt my skin prickle as I retraced my steps towards the bushes and trees that lined the cliff edge. I covered my mouth and nose, but the smell permeated through, becoming more gross and nauseating with each step that I took, until my reflexes kicked in and I gagged. I saw something brown and stick-like protruding beneath one of the bushes and amongst the grass and forget-me-not blue flowers. With shaking hands, I pulled the foliage aside.

Two black, hollowed out eyes stared up at me. Maggots crawled from its eyes and across the carcass as flies buzzed. It was a young doe, her legs rigid and outstretched, and her ribcage protruded through decayed hide. Poor beauty. She must have fallen ill and laid down here to die. How had I not noticed the stench as I'd walked past only twenty minutes beforehand? But the pounding in my heart eased with relief for it to have been the death of a creature who'd suffered a natural death. I don't know what I'd expected to find but the deaths of the young woman on the beach and the unborn child in her belly, continued to haunt my thoughts and shadow my every step.

I glanced at my watch.

I hurried back up the slope and when I started along the path towards the house, my phone pinged.

A text from Judi. "Tess, I rang the office but no reply. We're setting off in half an hour or so. Is everything OK?!"

I typed a reply. "Just eating my sandwich in the garden. Heading into the office now if you need me."

I walked faster with the distinct knowledge that Judi had been checking up on me.

I hadn't taken a full hour, which I was entitled to, but I got a definite sense she wasn't pleased I hadn't answered the office phone.

All in all, an eventful, if unsettling lunchtime.

Back at my desk, images of the drowned woman and the young doe remained with me. Two messages arrived from Stefan that could have been combined, which asked me to look up the best prices and products for a new laser printer and a laptop, as his had become unreliable. The tone of both emails was impersonal and purely instructional, not the sort of friendly communication I'd already grown to expect from him.

The unusual file with the list of girls' names came to mind. With no one around to interrupt me, I clicked on the finance folder and scanned down the list of files. It had jumped out at me before but I couldn't see it anywhere. Stefan must have noticed it had been filed in the wrong place and moved it elsewhere.

Later, when I heard the Porsche crunch over the gravel I expected Stefan and Judi to come straight into the office, but other than the front door opening and banging shut, the house remained quiet for some time.

I worked on through the afternoon and tried to resist the temptation to think about Stefan.

When I came back to my desk from making a cup of tea, I heard a click followed by a faint whirring sound and I looked about me. Neither Judi or Stefan's laptops were on their desks.

Had it been the printer or the coffee machine, perhaps? Although, it didn't sound like either of their usual noises. I put my cup down beside my laptop and wandered over to Stefan's desk. The whirring seemed louder at his end of the office, but still too indistinct to pinpoint. And then an odd and uncomfortable thought entered my head, and I don't really know what prompted it. Had the office been fitted with security surveillance, or even microphones, strategically placed to keep an eye on the place so that Stefan or Judi could view it remotely? They'd returned in the afternoon, as far as I was aware, but there would be times, like this morning, when I'd be alone in the house and office. As a private business, internal surveillance cameras may not be seen as an invasion of privacy. Was I being paranoid? Possibly so, but I hated the idea of either being watched and unaware, or of being caught doing something I shouldn't, snooping, for instance. I would have to behave and act as though I was always with someone.

I wondered, too, if they had the capability to track all that I did on my laptop - every click, word typed and website visited. Some employers did that. Employees had been sacked for browsing or shopping during working hours. I knew of a friend of Noah's who'd lost his security guard job for looking at adult websites on his phone, and a hidden security camera had captured everything. Not that I would do anything like that but I had phoned the kids a couple of times. Christ, I thought, feeling paranoid at work wasn't a pleasant feeling. But was it only paranoia or could my feelings of unease be justified? They seemed to know I wasn't at my desk as I'd walked down to the beach. Maybe there were cameras down there, too. I turned around and looked about, and tried to look nonchalant and natural. And then I noticed that the whirring noise had stopped and I sat back down. Unfounded paranoia or not, wise to play it safe.

At a quarter past five I tidied my desk, washed and dried the mugs left in the sink and then headed out through the meeting room and French doors. Of course, the good thing about running your own business was having the freedom to come and go from the office.

I closed the doors behind me and heard footsteps. I turned and saw Gil with his dog, Bruce.

Bruce sniffed my feet and I bent down to stroke his ears. 'It's been quiet in the office today.'

Gil nodded. 'I've been busy with the horses.'

'Must be nice having all this land to walk Bruce,' I said.

'Yeah.' He paused, unsmiling. 'I walked him down to the private beach.'

Should I mention I'd been down at lunchtime? Maybe he'd seen me head down earlier. 'Actually, I explored a bit at lunchtime and ate my sandwich down there. Hope that's OK?'

He gave the smallest of nods, but I noticed his brows pinch together.

'Nice boathouse,' I paused. 'And a beautiful boat.'

He blinked several times in succession. But if I wasn't supposed to go in there he didn't say as such.

'Indeed. Barely gets used though. Too much effort to launch.'

'Nice to swim down there on hot days, I imagine,' I said, and wondered if I should be direct and ask about the chains.

Gil turned and gazed out over the garden then without looking my way said, 'Stefan prefers we use the pool for bathing.'

His tone seemed oddly detached and nothing like the man who had spoken so freely with me only days before.

I hesitated before replying. 'Easier and warmer, too.'

Gil turned back to me but I noticed that he wouldn't meet my eye. 'Indeed.'

'Have I done something wrong, Gil?'

But he didn't immediately reply and the air seemed charged between us.

He looked down at his feet and scraped his boot through the gravel. 'No, you're fine, Tess.'

'Well, I'll get off.' I gave a brief smile as I walked round him and started along the path.

'Tess?'

I turned back.

He took a step closer and dropped his voice. 'It's better if you don't go down to the beach or boathouse. Sometimes the tide reaches the cliffs and it can be treacherous.'

'Oh, I didn't realise,' I said, innocently. So this was the problem, I thought.

Gil's face relaxed. 'It's for your own safety.'

'OK, no problem.'

How strange, I thought as I walked to my car. The sea had reached the driftwood left by high tide, but there appeared to be a good several feet of remaining beach beyond that. And today the sea had been calm and the tide was well back.'

It only raised my suspicions about the real purpose of the boat and the mysterious chains and cuffs.

27

When I closed the front door and entered the living room, all seemed quiet, eerily so. I hung my jacket on the coat rack and was about to head up the stairs to see who was in when I heard the familiar thumps of Digby coming down the stairs to greet me. He bounded over, jumped up against my legs and whined to be let out. He followed me through to the back of the house and I let him out into our small walled garden. I looked down and noticed the ladder he'd ripped in my tights. 'Thanks Digby...' I called over as he relieved himself against the pear tree.

I returned to the living room and checked my phone. Two texts from Victor.

"I'm staying with Roddy for a few days. So pissed off with Dad." Second message. "Sorry. I've got clothes and my school books. I'll call later."

So this is what Noah had done to us. He was tearing our family apart. I felt tearful and tired and I slumped onto the sofa.

Poor Victor. He'd been upset and angry and who could blame him? Maybe some distance between him and Noah would be a good thing for Victor right now. I doubted he'd told his Dad - that would be my job.

Digby scampered back in, leapt onto my lap and licked my face. 'All right. Let me change first.' He leapt off and scampered to pick up his lead.

On the landing, Clara came out of her room. 'You heard about Victor?'

I felt a lump in my throat, swallowed and nodded, aware that Noah would likely overhear us. 'You OK, love?'

'I'm fine, but I have Physics and Chemistry homework for tomorrow.'

'I'll cook tea when I get back from walking Digby - he's desperate.'

'Sorry, I've not had chance to take him.'

'It's fine, love. I need some space and air.'

When I walked into Victor's room Noah looked up.

'I hear my son has gone to Roddy's. Not exactly loyal of my supposed best friend.'

My voice became tart. 'I'd say quite the opposite. Roddy's supporting your son when he needs time away from his own family.'

'All right! I feel guilty enough without you piling it on.'

'Good. Maybe you need space to think and reflect too.' I didn't bother to hide my disdain. 'Do you need anything?'

He patted the bed beside him. 'Please, I want to talk to you.' He reached for his glass of water and took a sip.

I sat down and waited for him to speak.

He reached for my hand and held it in his. 'Despite my accident, which couldn't have come at a worse time and I realise it was entirely my fault, I'm grateful that you are kind enough to let me stay with you after everything. But I also hoped that it might give us two an opportunity to try to put aside our problems. I know I've blown it with Vic, for now, but can't you and I try to resolve our issues?' His eyes watered and pleaded with mine. 'I still love you, Tess, and I always will. I've never cheated on you or barely looked at another woman. Isn't that something to be grateful for? So many men are unfaithful and I'd never do that to you.'

He stroked my hand and his eyes searched mine - the eyes of a man I'd known for so long.

I closed my eyes and instead of seeing Noah, Stefan came into my mind's eye, with a face that evoked in me a completely different reaction. To force my feelings for Noah again seemed an impossibility.

I looked back at him. 'You might not have been unfaithful, for which I'm thankful, but neither have I, and I've never harped on about how grateful for my loyalty you should be. And on top of that I haven't betrayed you in any way, financially or emotionally. I could go on, but I'm afraid I'm ahead on all fronts. If you'd have quit gambling like I pleaded with you hundreds of times, and I have serious doubts that's ever going to be possible, our relationship might have stood a chance. I'm sorry, but us as a couple is in the past. I'm tired of giving you chances.'

His eyes filled with tears, and gently, I pulled my hand away from his.

'I'm exhausted by it all.' And without waiting for his reply, I stood up, walked out of the room and closed the door behind me. I thought I heard Noah speak, but I didn't turn back.

Digby pulled relentlessly on his lead as we headed down the ramp and onto the beach. I let him off and he ran headlong across the sand towards a cluster of seagulls who flapped and squawked around something. Most likely scavenging for dead fish. I looked out at the rising tide and two surfers that rode the waves, and I inhaled the salty air.

After the bank card incident, Noah's presence at home felt stifling and his stubborn persistence in believing we still had a future, on the day our son moved out to get away from him, struck me as beyond delusional. Were the painkillers affecting his mind or did he genuinely believe the things he said? Maybe delusional thinking had been his thing all along and only now was I beginning to see the full scope of it. Either way, I felt relieved to be out of the house and away from him.

Digby ran hither and thither amongst the seagulls which flew up and back down again, unprepared to give up their meal. I jogged over and the gulls squawked and rose up again, and scattered the air. Digby sniffed the opaque disc of a jellyfish, pecked and peppered with holes, and I clipped on his lead and led him away.

The beach was almost empty of people and we continued on for some time until I glanced up to see I'd drawn level with the rocks and cave where the young woman's body had lain. I felt a shiver run through me and I crouched down and gave Digby a cuddle. Since that morning ten days ago, the girl had never strayed far from my thoughts and I'd had several disturbing dreams that played out different scenarios around her demise, but all linked to the weeping Polish girl at the mortuary.

Following my discovery of the body, there had been a flurry of news coverage, along with reporters and journalists who had visited the town to scavenge for information and local gossip and opinions, but already the interest of where she'd come from had waned. Thankfully, and by some miracle, my name had been kept out of it and the twins had been discreet with their friends.

Surely the police had made some headway with discovering the girl's identity? As I stood and stared at the rocks, my eyes blurred, and an image, or perhaps it was a memory, came into my head, of a figure, a man who stepped over the rocks and jumped down onto the sand before he headed towards me up the beach. I blinked and rubbed my eyes and the rocks sharpened back into focus and the man's image vanished. Had I seen that figure on the rocks on the same morning Digby had discovered the body? Had that man seen her pale and lifeless body amongst the seaweed but walked away? And why would anyone choose to do that? Or was my mind confused and playing tricks on me?

My phone buzzed and I retrieved it from my pocket.

"Sorry I missed seeing you today. I got your details about the computer kit. Thank you, Stefan."

Did that mean he missed me, or did it mean he'd wanted to talk about work stuff?

A minute later another text came. "Are you free to meet for a drink tonight? I can drive over."

I could already feel my heart thumping into life and the flood of relief to hear from him again in a friendlier tone than earlier that day. If I'd felt tired before, his message revived me in an instant.

"I'd like that. What time?" I glanced at my watch. Already a quarter to seven.

"Eight o'clock OK?"

"I'll be ready."

He replied with a red love heart.

I called Digby and we jogged back along the sand towards town, my mind working over if I had time to cook tea and shower as well as dress.

'Do you really think it's a good idea to be going out on a date with your boss?' said Clara, and fastened on me with her gimlet-eye.

'Technically, I'm single. He's also single. There shouldn't be a problem,' I replied, and stood in front of the mirror above the fireplace to apply some lip gloss.

'Seriously, Mum. Because it's one of the first rules of employment. Even I know this.'

Clara was right, of course. 'Maybe more so today, but it's how I met your Dad. Things were and still are different for our generation. We don't take these new rules to heart.'

'Really?' said Clara, unconvinced. 'Dad wasn't your boss. Stefan is and so in a position of power.'

I turned back to her. 'I know all this. Believe me, darling, I can take care of myself. I always have done.'

She chewed her bottom lip. 'I know, but it seems so fast, that's all.'

'It's only a drink, nothing serious.'

'I won't tell Dad or Victor.' She clasped her hands together and bit at her thumbnail. 'Dad would be upset.'

I wondered if she realised how judgemental she sounded. I gave a heavy sigh. 'Your Dad should have thought about this two years ago when I told him it was the gambling, or me. He made his choice.'

'I know, but it's an addiction. He can't just stop.'

I saw Clara's eyes mist over and I took her hand. 'I do have an idea that might help him. It might help all of us.'

'What? Gambling anonymous?'

I shook my head. 'He tried that, remember? No, something more radical. I need to make a call first, and talk to Dad.'

'Sounds interesting, Mum. You still love him don't you?'

'Of course I do, he's your dad. He's a wonderful person in every other respect.' I gave her a hug and drew back. 'I do understand how difficult this has been for you and Vic and it's what made leaving your dad such a wrench. I really did try.'

'I know you did, and I doubt I'd have had the patience that you showed him.'

I felt the need to defend myself. 'Which is why I really need some relaxation now.'

Who was I trying to fool? I found Stefan insanely attractive.

'I'll say this, Mum. Stefan seems like a fast mover which isn't always the sign of a reliable man.'

'One could say the same of women,' I remarked.

'It's only what I've heard and read.' She shrugged. 'But I hope you have a nice time.'

Clara had never had a boyfriend. At least not one that I knew of. Not even in primary school. In fact, she'd shown little interest in boys at all and seemed happy with her girlfriends and having boys as mates. And then as I slipped my arms into the sleeves of my denim jacket I suddenly wondered if boys weren't going to be her interest at all. Had I missed seeing something all too apparent? What if she was suffering the turmoil of her confusion inside and hadn't had the courage to tell me for fear I might be upset or reject her. I would find a reason for us to sit down and talk and give her an opportunity to open up.

My thoughts were interrupted with a short toot of a horn and I pulled the blinds apart. Stefan threw me a wave from the open window of his Porsche. I felt the rumble of the car engine in my stomach, or was it a shudder of excitement?

I closed the passenger door and turned to Stefan.

He lifted his glasses onto his head and fixed his eyes on me. 'You look lovely.' He dropped his gaze and further down to my bare legs.

My eyes were drawn to his parted lips, deep red, and to the shining tip of his tongue as he ran it slowly across his lower lip. I felt a strange tingling in my own lips as if his mouth had brushed mine.

Was it possible to fight desire when it hit and when the attraction was so clearly mutual and there were no other people standing in the way? I'd never been in such a position before where my logical mind told me I should hold back, but at the same time I felt a distinct sense of joie de vivre, something that had been missing from my life for too long.

We hadn't driven far before Stefan pulled up outside a row of townhouses that led up the hill to the park and natural history museum at the top end of the town. I looked out and wondered why we'd stopped so soon.

He turned to me. 'I have a flat I usually rent out. It's charming and it's empty at the moment. I have chilled wine - a Chateau d'Yquem.' He gestured to the back seat of the car.

'Oh, OK.' I nodded and felt a bubble of nerves inside of me.

The flat was on the first floor of a four story red brick terrace. I'd seen how much these sought after properties and flats sold for on the rare occasions they came up for sale - they were eagerly snapped up within a few days. I followed Stefan around the back and up a flight of stone steps that led to a pretty entrance porch with a terracotta pot of grape vines that grew up around the doorway and a plaque on the wall that named the flat - Treetops View.

The interior was impeccably and tastefully decorated and furnished in Scandi style decor and colours - pastel hues, natural wood furnishings, white fabrics, hessian fibres and jute carpets. Far from feeling unlived in, it felt homely, and I inhaled a woody pine aroma. Stefan showed me through to the living room and I walked to the window and looked out over the gardens and to the road beyond where we'd parked. I'd walked and driven up this hill countless times and often gazed admiringly up at these graceful town houses. It looked costly to rent out, or maybe it was a holiday let which would earn them even more revenue. Stefan returned from the kitchen with wine glasses and a corkscrew.

'I hope you don't think I've bought you here to seduce you,' he said, his eyes securely on mine. 'It's only that I feel comfortable here and we can relax and talk more freely.'

My heart pounded. 'Not at all,' I said, unsure if I felt relieved or disappointed that he didn't want to seduce me. 'It's a beautiful flat.'

With a deftness of hand he pulled the cork, raised it to his nose and sniffed it before he poured the wine into two glasses.

He handed me my glass then sat beside me. 'Let's drink to your impressive start with Aztec Imports. I've had several assistants over the years and I can't think that one settled in so effortlessly.' He raised his glass and chinked mine. 'At this rate I'll be giving you a pay rise to ensure you stay with us.'

'I'm enjoying the work, and I'm only glad you're finding me helpful,' I said.

He took a sip and placed his glass on the coffee table. 'And how did you find today, working alone in the office?'

'Plenty to do. The hours passed quickly.'

'And you went to explore at lunchtime, I hear?' He gave a half-smile followed by a frown.

Had Gil been talking to Stefan? I'd done nothing wrong, and yet my stomach twitched with nerves.

I looked him directly in the eyes. 'Well, I did head out for some fresh air and to eat my lunch.'

His eyes narrowed. 'You discovered our private beach?'

If he knew there was no point in my lying. 'I hope that was OK? I wasn't away from my desk for long.'

He nodded in thought. 'I really should have mentioned that the steps down are unsafe.'

If he was trying to make me feel guilty or scared I wasn't prepared to submit.

'I didn't feel they were unsafe,' I said, playing along.

'But if you'd tripped, I'd feel dreadful and responsible.'

'Not a problem. I won't go again.'

'We had a dog fall from those steps. Gil's previous dog.' Stefan swatted away a wasp that buzzed around our glasses. It landed at my feet and he flicked it away with his boot. Then he raised his glass and took a long drink. 'Judi was walking the dog at the time and was devastated.'

'That's awful. They are steep.'

'Exactly. Too easy to trip and fall.'

He set his glass down and rolled up the sleeves of his shirt to his elbows. I couldn't help admiring his long fingers and powerful wrists as he reached into his pocket. 'But onto lighter matters.' He pulled out a small red box. 'A small token of my thanks. It's not a bribe, only a gift of friendship and appreciation.'

There could only be jewellery in that box, from Victoria's Jewellery in town, I noted. 'I hope it wasn't expensive,' I said, and felt awkward and undeserving. Nonetheless, as I looked down at the box in my hand, I felt curious to see what was inside.

'Open it,' he said, tracing a forefinger carefully over one eyebrow.

I prized the lid open and gazed down at a beautifully crafted round black stone of Whitby jet, nestled in a ring of clear stones and set in gleaming silver.

'It's beautiful.' I looked up at him. 'I don't know what to say.'

It seemed an overly romantic gift from a man I hardly knew. A ring of all things!

His eyes danced. 'Don't say anything. But do try it on.'

My fingers were slim and I suspected it might be too loose, but when I picked it out of the cushion, I noticed that it looked on the small side. I slipped it onto the middle finger of my left hand and held it up. 'How did you know my size?'

'I didn't,' he replied. 'But I saw you had slim fingers and with the jeweler's help we selected a size.'

'I've only ever admired their jewellery from the window.'

'It suits you.' He took my hand and looked closer. 'The jet looks perfect against your skin.' He lowered my hand to my lap. 'I've worked with Joshua and Victoria. You'll see that Judi wears a jet ring sometimes, and earrings too.'

'I did notice. When we ate at La Galerie.'

'I'd like to see you wear it every day. I love to buy my friends gifts if I think it's something they'll appreciate.'

Being given a ring by your employer could hardly be considered a normal gift. I'd never been given a ring before. Not by friends or family, or even by Noah, although I'd hinted many times that even though we weren't married we could still wear rings to symbolise our love. He'd joked that he didn't like wearing jewellery and I'd been satisfied with buying my own, albeit far less expensive rings than my new one.

Stefan reached over once more and took my hand. He raised my hand to his mouth and kissed the ring.

I felt his lips, soft and cool, against my skin. The situation was becoming stranger and stranger but I couldn't help but go along with it. It felt novel and exciting and I had never shied away from new experiences. It felt delicious to be in his close company.

He kept hold of my hand and pulled me up and led me to the window.

'I love to stand and look out across the lawn, to the treetops and down to the road. So different from our view at Lorton Hold, but I think almost as lovely. Whitby is a very special town, don't you think, Tessa?'

I looked out. 'I've lived here for sixteen years and I've no desire to move. I love Whitby's history - the smuggling, the fishing, links with Dracula, Whitby jet.' I glanced down at my ring. 'The streets and houses. The town has so much character. But mostly I feel this is my home, even after all my troubles with Noah and our separation.'

'Almost separation,' said Stefan with a tilt of his head.

'He'll recover and move out,' I said.

'You're too kind to him. But I can see you're a kind woman, and I admire that.'

'I couldn't abandon him, even after everything. And the children still need him.' I felt a flurry of anxiety about Victor. 'Life is reality to work through. No point in fighting it, but in finding the best path.'

'And what a generous and poetic heart you have.'

'I hope so, although I have been told I'm too trusting and naive. I don't think so though. Oddly, Noah is one of those who said that to me and he's been the biggest deceiver in my life so far. But the way I view it is, I trust until proven otherwise.'

'Other than in respect to Noah, and it sounds as if you have the full measure of him now, I'd say trusting is a quality, not naivety,' said Stefan. 'Too many lose that openness when they grow into adulthood. I prefer people who care and are unafraid to show it.'

'And what do you care about?' I asked, and looked directly at him.

His brows furrowed, thoughtful for a moment. 'If I told you, I'm not sure you'd believe me.'

'I'm sure I would,' I said.

He waited a moment. 'Zależy mi na tobie.

'You speak Polish? You said you care about me.'

'I do, in both respects. I spent five years in Gdansk during my twenties, which I'll tell you more about at some point, and...' he paused. 'I realise we haven't known one another long, but I've never felt as drawn to someone so instantly as I am to you.' He paused and took a breath. 'If I may confess, I can't stop thinking about you - not even when I'm working. Everything about you fascinates me and distracts me. Not least that you're one, if not the most beautiful woman I've ever seen. How could I keep these feelings platonic even if I am your employer?'

I looked into his eyes, intense and unblinking. His words sounded genuine and full of warmth and passion. But in my head I hesitated. Despite feeling an enormous physical attraction towards him, it felt too soon and too fast for me.

I told him that I liked him, too. 'Ja tez cie bardzo lubie. But we mustn't rush.' Even though, in truth, I ached for him to touch me.

Undeterred by my hesitancy, he cupped my face in his hands and leaned down to kiss me. I stepped back, but he took my hands without any force, and slowly drew me to him. I felt his lips upon mine, warm and sensual. I leaned into him and returned his kisses, cautiously at first, and then with an urgency I couldn't restrain.

He moaned softly and moved his hands down to my waist. Then he lifted me off the floor and sat me upon the windowsill. We kissed again, and when his tongue flickered against mine, I opened and lifted my legs and was filled with a longing for him to be closer, still. He lifted the skirt of my dress and I felt his fingers linger upon and caress my inner thigh, then gently slip inside my knickers. He touched me so tenderly as we kissed, and I responded like a bird released from her cage after too long confined.

'My God, Tessa. You feel divine.'

'So do you,' I said, barely able to speak.

For a moment he paused, and with his face only inches from mine he held me with his eyes and his breath fell like a caress upon my skin.

'Don't stop,' I said.

And without another word, he pulled my knickers down over my legs and ankles, drew my legs apart and knelt down between them.

I felt his mouth, warm and urgent upon my skin, as he moved closer. 'I want to see you and taste you.'

His lips tantalised and nipped my skin. His tongue probed and flicked and created sensations that made me melt and quiver and drove me into a frenzy.

196

If there was one thing one should never judge a man on, but which I'm afraid to say that I had, was the tenderness and attention they showed when it came to giving themselves to pleasure. Not only for themselves, but to a woman's sensual and most intimate pleasure. And Stefan took that element of lovemaking with not only wild and selfless abandonment, but with the finest expression of feeling and skill I had ever had the pleasure of experiencing. If there was one way for a man to seal his attachment and his future fate with a woman, this surely came close.

I gripped the edge of the windowsill with one hand and with my other I ran my fingers through his hair, until my breaths came faster and I was lost to him, to our lovemaking, and the moment.

Stefan stood up and unfastened his belt and trousers then kissed my mouth again. I drew my arms out of my jacket and cast it to the floor. He placed his hands on my shoulders and lowered the straps of my dress so that the dress dropped below my breasts. For a moment he stopped kissing and gazed down at me, before he lowered his face and hands, then cupped whilst he kissed and teased me. I pulled his jeans over his hips and gazed down at his arousal. He clasped my hips and when I tilted my pelvis I felt his hardness touch and press against my lips and slowly enter my core - already overwhelming sensations rippled through me. I moaned, then gasped and drew him closer.

Stefan reached behind me and pulled the strings of the blind. The room darkened but I could see the blackness of his eyes as his gaze penetrated my mind until he was all that I could see and breathe, and all that I could feel. He thrust deeper and I felt myself respond with a desperate need to keep him close to me - inside of me. And sensations began to rise and build in me again as he pulsed back and forth.

'You want me?' Stefan asked, and his gaze blazed into mine with a demonic ferocity. 'You want me harder?' He breathed the words.

'Yes,' I whispered. And I did want him. In that moment I was lost to what my mind desired and my body craved.

Within minutes a primeval need had driven me to sensations I hadn't known before. I felt consumed as my blood pounded and pleasure exploded through me, again and again. I cried out and clutched his shoulders as he shuddered his seed inside of me.

We remained there, holding one another, euphoric, damp with perspiration and still tingling from the remnants of pleasure given and received. I felt the afterglow of the most glorious sensual pleasure I'd experienced. And my senses still pulsed with gratification.

I'd never made love with a man so spontaneously and quickly, and I hadn't ever expected to. And certainly not tonight. There had been no one since I'd met Noah eighteen years ago, and prior to that only two other men, each of whom I'd dated for weeks before sleeping with them.

Stefan drew away and looked down at me. 'My sweet love. I felt your exquisite pleasure as though it were my own.'

My eyes watered and I laid my hand on his cheek, too choked with emotion to speak.

He smiled. 'Are you thinking good thoughts?'

I nodded. And despite that we were no longer making love, I felt my body pulsate with pleasure once more. 'I still feel you.'

He moved a curl away from my face and as I leaned my forehead against his I felt his hand between my legs.

'I want to touch you,' he said.

I closed my eyes, and gasped again.

He kissed me long and slowly on the lips. 'You are the most beautiful and heavenly creature, and now that I've fallen for you there's no going back.'

'I feel like I've landed in paradise.' And I meant every word.

His eyes searched mine. 'When did you last make love?'

'A while ago, but it's you and how you make me feel.' I kissed him on the lips. 'What about you?'

He gave a small shrug. 'I honestly don't remember. A while ago, like yourself,' he said, and kissed me in return.

He fastened his trousers then he took my hands and helped me off the windowsill. I lifted my dress straps onto my shoulders.

Stefan watched my every movement with an intensity that I found unnerving and thrilling at the same time.

He buttoned and tucked in his shirt. 'Have you heard the word apodyopsis?' he asked.

I shook my head. 'Is it English in origin?'

'I believe so, although rarely used.'

'What does it mean?'

He raised his brows and gave a slight smile. 'It means to mentally undress someone - you, who I find irresistible.'

'Oh!' I couldn't help but smile.

'From the moment I saw you, but overwhelmingly when I saw you beside the pool. I'd never have guessed you'd had children.'

I laughed. 'I hate to shatter illusions, but with the twins, I was the size of a hippo.'

His mouth curled up at the sides. 'Impossible! The gentle curve of your stomach, your sweet breasts, your peachy arse. You are perfection in every sense - perfect for me.'

'I notice my imperfections,' I said. 'Don't we all?'

'Imperfections! What are those?' he said, then added, 'You must have men forever begging at your heels.'

'Other than my close male friends and relatives, I keep men like that at arm's length. Anyway, I haven't been single until now…'

He put his arm around my waist and guided me to the sofa. 'Let's drink more wine. I need sustenance.'

'You definitely deserve it,' I said with a giggle, and felt a sensual glow deep inside of me.

'You're still flushed my love, which pleases me,' he said, and ran his fingers down between my breasts. 'I'm sorry I was quick, but you're insanely desirable.'

I stood on tiptoes and kissed his lips. 'You were far from selfish on that score. Besides, once should lead to more times.'

He wrapped his arms around me. 'Of course. My beautiful, Tessa.'

When I arrived home, well past midnight, I paused outside Victor's bedroom and popped my head in. The room appeared dark and silent and I headed up to bed relieved that Noah was asleep and hadn't heard me come in so late.

I messaged Victor. "Sleep well, Vic. I'll call you first thing. Love you, Mum."

28

After that wild and unexpected evening in his flat, Stefan featured constantly in my thoughts, even so that I imagined his face whenever I closed my eyes. I replayed our lovemaking over and over in my head, like a beautiful melody on repeat. Even caring for Noah no longer felt like a chore. My mind and body ran high on hope and full on desire. I couldn't admit to myself that I'd fallen in love. Or was it infatuation? But no, it seemed like the real thing. I'd never felt so primed to understand how wonderful life could be. In only a couple of weeks, my life had gone from constant anxiety and high level stress, to the closest it had been to bliss throughout my forty years.

The following day, Stefan had to travel to France, but I lived for the moments when we spoke each day about work and in the evenings when we video called.

That in itself proved to be a new and enlightening experience for me.

He phoned me late on Friday night from the home of a business connection in Lyons. He sprang to life on my screen; sitting in bed, broad shouldered and bare chested, with a dark stubble across his chin and with his hair delightfully disheveled.

'I miss you madly, Tessa. I can't stop thinking about your lips and your velvet skin next to mine. Will you let me see you?'

I giggled. 'You mean now? Here?' I'd heard about people doing this sort of thing and always thought it sounded unappealing, sleazy and awkward. Where was the pleasure if you couldn't touch and kiss the other person?

'Unbutton your shirt and pull it over your shoulders?' he said. 'But use one hand to hold your phone so that I can see you.'

I glanced across at the closed bedroom door. 'Are you certain no one can see us?'

He chuckled. 'How could they? I'm the only one here and I'm guessing you're alone, too?'

'OK,' I said, and held my phone up with one hand and undid the buttons of my nightshirt with the other. I pulled the shirt off my shoulders, all the while watching Stefan, as he watched me. He stared and I saw him move his hand beneath the bedcovers.

'Will you caress your beautiful breasts? I want to watch you squeeze and tease your nipples and I can imagine my fingers touching you.'

I felt myself becoming aroused and I did as he asked.

I saw his hand moving below the sheets. 'You're my angel. Would you like me to pull the sheet off, so you can see me, too?' he asked.

'Yes,' I said, unable to slow my breathing.

Without inhibition, he pushed the sheet back and my eyes fell to his erection, nestled in thick black hair. I felt both shocked and thrilled at once.

'Pull your duvet back so I can see you too,' he said, his eyes drunk with lust.

He watched me, unblinking. We watched one another. I felt intoxicated and lightheaded.

I drew my knees apart and slid my hand over my abdomen and down between my thighs. At first I felt self-conscious but I saw in the way that Stefan touched himself that he enjoyed what he saw.

'I want to see closer,' he said.

I leaned over and propped my phone against the folded duvet.

He didn't seem to notice the plaster on my belly as we teased one another with our eyes, our sighs and our touch.

'Imagine your hands are mine and my hands are yours. I feel close to you, my beautiful girl. I can taste you with my tongue and inhale your sweet aroma.'

His words made my imagination take over and I felt him beside me, his lips touching and kissing me, as I looked into his eyes, near and yet far.

I lost all sensation of time and place, and afterwards, I lay back exhausted and euphoric. He stayed on the line and we talked, neither one of us wanting to say goodbye.

It was hours later, as the first gulls called to one another over the rooftops and deserted streets, that I rolled onto my side, hugged my pillow and fell into a deep and immersive sleep.

The following morning when I pulled on my robe and headed downstairs, Victor was seated on the sofa, drinking tea with Roddy.

'I thought everyone would be up,' said Victor, sounding disappointed.

'I was worn out so I slept in.'

'Must be tough working full time again,' said Roddy.

'It is quite a shock to the system,' I said. I went to sit beside Victor and gave him a hug. 'So lovely to see you. Please tell me you're back for good.'

'Sorry, Mum. I've only come to pick up more clothes and stuff.'

'Don't worry. The lad's fine at mine and he's no trouble,' Roddy reassured me.

'Are you getting into school on time?' I asked.

'Roddy's been driving me in. I'm staying in all day and walking home. It's fine. Easy.'

'You didn't fish this morning?' I asked.

'No, we decided we deserved a morning off.'

I nodded. 'Good thinking.'

Roddy stood up. 'I'll chat to Noah and leave you both to catch up.'

'He'll be glad to see you,' I said.

'I hope so, and he doesn't see me as switching loyalties.'

I sighed. 'He has to change, Roddy. He can't continue like this.'

'I've been telling him for years. Only he has the power to change himself now.'

Victor tutted and looked down at his hands, clearly unconvinced anything would change.

I took Victor's hand. 'I have an idea that might help your dad. I'll let you know more when I can.'

He looked at me, with an expression that questioned. 'Anything has to be worth a try.'

Victor and Roddy stayed a couple of hours and after they left I looked around at the house. It looked a complete shambles, and

I dressed in jeans, T-shirt and trainers. As I finished hoovering the stairs, Clara finally emerged, but still looked sleepy. She switched on the TV and lay back on the sofa.

'Do periods always make you feel so tired and miserable?'

'They can, yes,' I said. 'And we need to take special care of ourselves. Eat healthily, relax and sleep when we want to. I'll buy some multivitamins with iron which you can take during your period and for a few days afterwards.'

'But I'm relieved I've started at last. I must have been the only girl in the entire upper school who hadn't.'

'I'm glad you have too, sweetie. The doctor thought it would be soon.'

By late-afternoon I'd hoovered the entire house, dusted, put two loads of washing on and hung it out in the back garden. I prayed it wouldn't rain. I'd filled the supermarket trolley to bursting and squeezed it into the kitchen cupboards and fridge freezer, by which time I felt ready for a nap. Instead, conscious of all that still needed doing, I cooked king prawn pasta and took a bowl up to Noah.

While he ate, I sat on the end of his bed.

'How's the pain?'

'Easing, I think. My arm hurts but nothing like as much, and the leg pain comes and goes. At least I can get to the toilet and back independently now.'

'Yep, no one wants help in that department,' I said.

'How's Vic - he didn't speak a word to me?'

'Have you spoken on the phone?'

'I've tried calling and I've sent messages of groveling apology. I only hope he'll forgive me.'

'I hope so too, but you have to show and prove you won't do anything like that again, and pay him back pronto.'

Noah's eyes grew damp and the lines on his brow deepened. 'I loathe myself for what I've done to him - to all of you.' He twirled his fork around the pasta.

'I believe you,' I said, and paused. 'Look, I have a suggestion. Something that might help.'

Noah looked up again from his bowl. 'What is it?'

'But I need to know if you genuinely want to get better - put this whole mess behind you for good?'

'You know I do. I've been fighting it for years. It's become a part of who I am, a part I need, but loathe and detest.' A tear rolled down his cheek and I sensed he spoke from the heart and like any addict who wanted to destroy their demons.

'Good.' I nodded. 'I've spoken to a hypnotherapist who was recommended to me. His area of expertise is addiction and I've read and heard first hand testimonies to suggest he's extremely effective.'

Noah snorted. 'I expect he charges handsomely for this service?'

'Not excessively, and he can do it by video call. But what is the cost to your future, Noah? Your relationships? What about Victor?'

Noah stabbed a prawn with his fork, looked up and nodded slowly.

'But you have to believe it will work. If you're resistant, hypnosis is useless.'

'I'd be willing to give it a try,' he said.

29

When I awoke on Sunday morning the sky was clear and blue despite a brisk and chilly wind that blew in through the vent of my newly glazed skylight. I was keen to make the most of the fine weather for October and my one real day off. Sitting at an office desk for most of the day felt too inactive and I wasn't used to that. My new job had also short changed Digby, and although he wasn't alone all day, he didn't get the usual miles for his walks, and neither did I.

My phone rang as I set off walking, but by the time I'd retrieved it from my pocket, whoever it was had rung off. I headed down the ginnel steps into town, past the fishing boats moored in the harbour, then over the swing bridge that spanned the water to the south side of town.

I looked around and my mind and body felt in a strangely elevated state - the fisherman's cottages, the shimmering tide, the iron railings and cloudless sky seemed sharper and more illuminated. My footsteps felt light upon the pavements; I'd been bitten by love, lust or infatuation.

A message pinged from Mum. "Darling, give me a call when you've a minute." But Digby had other ideas and pulled me along. I slotted my phone back into my pocket. I'd call her once we were out of town.

I loved Whitby, but for its traditional and picturesque feel I preferred the south side of town. Despite the many tourists, especially during the summer months, I never tired of walking the narrow cobbled streets or gazing into shop windows. I paused outside Victoria's Jewellery and down at my new ring. The black stone blinked up at me like the eye of an owl in moonlight. The Romans had believed that jet was a magical gemstone that could protect the wearer, deflect the evil eye and drive away snakes. I wasn't particularly superstitious but I loved the symbolism and the stories I'd heard over the years.

Since Stefan had slipped it onto my finger I hadn't taken it off, other than to drop it into the palm of my hand and to gaze upon it from all angles. At night alone in bed it made me feel closer to him - as though he could see me and knew I was thinking about him. I was amazed that Noah hadn't noticed and asked where it came from, and I hadn't even thought how I'd reply with a plausible excuse for wearing a ring that a man - my employer, had given to me. I wondered if I'd subconsciously covered it up when sitting in Victor's bedroom - quite possibly.

If Noah asked where it came from, I'd have no choice but to lie, for now. He'd already voiced his suspicions over my working relationship with Stefan. When he'd asked where I'd been on the Monday night I'd lied and told him that we met up with a client at the White Rose Hotel and I'd be given time off in lieu. Clara told me Noah had questioned her and she'd had to lie and say she didn't know. It felt wrong and deceitful but I didn't want to upset him any more than he already was about our separation, on top of his injuries and being confined to the bedroom.

I walked past the Kipper House on Abbey Row and inhaled the delicious smoky aromas, whilst making a mental note to stop and buy kippers for dinner on my way home. I started up the steep steps that led to the cliff tops and to the church of St Mary's, and beyond that, the Abbey ruins that stood statuesque, yet stark, and a shell of its former grandeur. At each step I became aware of the sound of footsteps that grew closer from behind. Always conscious of those walking near to me, I turned and glanced quickly over my shoulder.

A woman.

A face I recognised.

My heart juddered as I continued upwards. I paused on the footpath at the top - should I continue or wait and talk to her?

I turned around and faced the woman with her piercing blue eyes and thick, auburn hair, golden in the sunlight.

She didn't speak but tilted her head slightly and looked into my eyes with an intensity I found disconcerting.

'Hello,' I said. 'I recognise you.' I smiled to soften my words. 'You worked for Stefan and Judi?'

Her eyelids drooped and her lips quivered as if she might be about to cry.

'Do you mind if we talk? Suzanne isn't it?' I said.

'How do you know my name?'

'I saw you outside La Galerie and Gil told me.'

She nodded. 'I thought it might be you from the restaurant as I followed you up. Not that I was following you,' she added.

I gestured to the row of benches in front of the gravestones and we walked along the path a short distance. I sat down and she sat beside me, whilst Digby fussed around her, eager for some attention.

'He likes you,' I said.

'He can probably smell our pet rabbit.'

'Oh, yes, he's a big fan of rabbits. Any small animals, actually.'

She stroked his ears. 'He's sweet.'

'It's a coincidence I should see you,' I said. 'But I'm glad that I have.'

Her eyes narrowed a touch as she looked back at me - she seemed to be forming words in her mind.

'Do you live up here?'

'Our cottage is past the allotments.' She gestured. 'I had to get out for some air.'

She clasped her hands together in her lap and I saw how she twisted her ring round and round her finger.

'How long did you work with Stefan and Judi?'

'Fourteen months to the day,' she said and shook her head with regret. 'But I should have left long before that.'

'Were you unhappy there?'

She sighed and I got the strongest sense she was going to reveal something I wouldn't like.

'As you've approached me, may I speak in confidence?'

'Please do,' I replied, and I felt a pulse throb in my temple as a million thoughts raced through my mind.

'I've seen you around town before,' she said. 'And we came on your boat tour a while back. You were the guide.'

'Yes, for ten years.'

She paused a moment before continuing. 'I did think about calling Aztec Imports and hoping you'd answer.'

'Oh?'

'After my experience, I feel you should know what you're getting involved with. If you choose to ignore what I tell you, that is entirely your choice. And please know that this isn't driven by jealousy. I only wish someone had warned me when I started. Before I got...' she paused again, 'emotionally involved.'

And now that she was there beside me, and about to tell me something I knew would be difficult to hear, I felt an urge to stand up and walk away. But instead, I remained seated, with my nerves on high alert and my blood racing in anticipation.

From what Gil had said, Suzanne had fallen out with Stefan. She'd had feelings for Stefan - become obsessed. And if that was so, how could she be objective? She was attractive, young and petite, but there was a deep sadness in her features and etched along the fine lines on her face. Her eyes appeared dull and her lips red and full, but downturned, and even her soft unblemished skin had a grey pallor. Everything about her body language and countenance seemed jaded and uneasy, in someone so young.

'I'm married,' she said. 'At least, for now. Stefan knew this when I started there. You're so pretty and I know he'll want you. He can't resist the appeal of making an attractive woman fall for him.'

She looked at me and paused as if waiting for me to say something.

I think she half-suspected that I was already involved with Stefan. But I had no intention of confiding my feelings for him yet, even though she seemed willing to confide in me.

'Are you married?' She looked down at my hand. Her eyes fixed on the ring on my middle finger.

'No, my partner and I have recently separated.'

She nodded. 'Then it will be easier for him to get close to you.'

'What do you mean?' I said.

She shrugged as if sharing the obvious. 'Stefan is a master in seduction. Or how I think of him now, a predator - a psychopath. Surely he's begun his seduction? Not only did he flatter and love bomb me with compliments from day one, he made me feel special in a way that I'd never experienced or imagined possible before. He's handsome, has an easy and superficial charm and is intelligent too, of course. I had no idea he'd done this many times before. How could I have known? I came in blind. I loved my husband, my first love, and had never considered being unfaithful, but although I resisted, Stefan persisted and pursued me until I finally fell for him like a brick sinking into the murky depths of a swamp. In hindsight, I was a fool, more foolish than a teenager infatuated by their first love. But by the time he got through to me, every fibre of me wanted to believe the things he said. Which I now know were lies. I admit that I loved him and grew addicted to him, to his words, the thrill I felt from his attention, that I came to crave and need.'

Her eyes searched mine.

But I gave nothing away.

'I don't know if this is making any sense to you, but you must know that Stefan isn't what he seems.'

I nodded. 'Go on.' But my voice cracked. I needed to hear everything she had to say, even though each word that she confessed twisted and coiled agonisingly through me.

She let out a breath. 'He is a man incapable of either honesty or loyalty. Not for a month, a week, a day, a minute. I learnt too late that he is always on the prowl for his next lover - his next victim. He said he loved me with what I thought to be genuine sincerity. I wanted to believe him. I know that I loved him.'

My heart thudded out of rhythm and for some moments my head and vision swam. I closed my eyes and took some breaths. When I opened them again she was staring down at my hand.

'Stefan gave you that ring?'

I nodded and raised my eyes to hers.

She uncovered her hand and I saw a ring, not dissimilar to mine.

'Are you OK?' she said.

I shook my head and my eyes flickered.

'He's already got to you, hasn't he? When he gave me this ring, I'd been there for weeks. He said it was to symbolise his commitment to me and my career, and my commitment to him and the business. Later, to secure his grip on me, he told me it would be for our future together. And like a fool again I believed him. I wanted to believe him. He kept talking about all the things we'd do when we were finally living together.'

'Maybe you and he weren't right for each other long term, what with you being married.'

A flush appeared about her face and throat. 'Stefan isn't right for anyone long term. Not even short term,' she said, with bitterness. 'He's a bachelor and childless for a reason. I've no doubt he's devastated countless women's lives. He's probably persuaded women into having abortions so he doesn't have any responsibility for a child, or the women he impregnates without any care or thought. I might not be pregnant, but right now my life is a train wreck and I'm trying my best to fight through the wreckage. I've got no job, and likely soon, no marriage. And it was all a damned lie. Fabricated by Stefan. He took over my mind and I became his puppet. And now the strings are cut, I feel useless and I'm falling apart.'

My lips felt numb and I could barely form the words to speak. 'Why were you outside La Galerie?'

She nodded once. 'I'm not a violent woman, but I wanted to hurl a brick through that window. I wanted to damage his head as much as he damaged mine. I wanted to wipe out that evil, shallow and insincere smile once and for all.'

'You need help and support,' I said quietly.

'I'm seeing a counsellor, alone.' She scraped her fingers through her hair. 'My husband doesn't know about the affair. He thinks I'm going off the rails, and most days it feels that way.'

'I'm so sorry,' I said, but my words sounded weak and inadequate.

The lines on her brow tightened. 'There are other things, too. I should go to the police, but Stefan threatened to tell my husband if I made trouble. He still has that hold over me. And my husband is not the sort of man to tolerate an affair. He's already a jealous and suspicious man, and who can blame him when he has every reason to be?'

My heart raced faster still, and I felt hot, sick and dizzy. Sitting here beneath the blue, chilled morning sky, the harbour and the huddled rooftops below blurred in front of me. I pressed my fingers to my eyes and then turned again to the face of this woman who could be me - who in effect had been me up until a few days ago. Only minutes earlier, I'd woken up, walked Digby up the steps, and I'd felt excited and full of energy, as if my life had turned the page to an incredible new chapter in a book. But in the last few moments, the future that I'd already pictured and framed in my mind had distorted, collapsed and died.

'You said you should go to the police.' My voice quavered. 'Is there criminal activity you know of?'

'Nothing I could prove or link them with directly. But conversations here and there, serious issues with imports. Irate clients threatening legal action, violence or far worse. Be hyper vigilant and keep your ears and eyes tuned.'

Who and how many women had Stefan been with for a week in France, I thought? He'd told me his visit was entirely work related, to purchase items of jewellery and rare antique ornaments. None of which I'd seen evidence of upon his return. The accounts weren't my remit and I hadn't been given any photos or details for their online news page - something Stefan was usually quick off the mark with.

'I can see you're in shock,' she said.

'I don't know what to think, yet,' I replied.

'You mustn't tell him I've spoken to you. I don't want him thinking he has any power to upset me.'

If that were the case, I wondered why she'd waited outside the restaurant so obviously for him to notice her.

'I wouldn't. I won't say a thing,' I said and stood up. My legs trembled beneath me and I felt a horrible urge to cry. 'I need to go.'

'And please don't mention to anyone that I had an affair with him.'

I shook my head and rested my hand on her arm. 'Trust me. I know the damage that could do.'

She wiped the corners of her eyes. 'Thank you. Would you like my number, in case you want to talk again?'

I nodded. 'Please. I'm glad I know why you left. Gil seemed hesitant.'

'Gil is a kind man, but surely you've noticed how they both have him in their grasp?'

'They have something over him?' I said.

She nodded. 'Be careful what you share with him. He's loyal to Stefan, unswervingly so.'

'He is sleeping with Judi so his loyalties are complicated.'

'Gil doesn't love Judi,' Suzanne scoffed. 'I'd be surprised if he even liked her.'

'What do you mean?' But I only wanted to hear her views - I'd seen and heard enough to realise it was more of a one-sided relationship.

'She loves him, I think. She treats him like a pet and throws him treats, buys his clothes, takes him on city breaks. But he's only sleeping with her because he can't easily get out of it.'

'She's attractive, there's no denying that.'

'She can afford to look good. She's had a zillion cosmetic procedures.'

I couldn't help but think Suzanne sounded bitter and unkind now. But maybe she had reason to be.

'I can't take this in. I need time...'

'Watch them together.' She went on. 'I'm no relationship expert, thank goodness I'm seeing one now, but I can read people.' She sighed, then added. 'Usually. If only I'd read Stefan from day one, but he bypassed my brain and went straight for my blood.'

And hearing Suzanne's words made me feel like a prize idiot. She was eloquent, passionate, sharp minded and smart, but from the little she'd told me I could see how her life had been devastated.

She continued. 'I fell for his lies. As I'm sure many women he targets do, too. If he was on the stage for his mind games and seduction antics he'd win an Oscar. I don't so much feel foolish, as furious.'

'Furious because eventually he rejected you?' I asked. I knew this was a blunt and possibly cruel thing to say, but could that be the truth?

'Yes, I'm angry that he said all those things to suck me in, only to spit me out when I became impossible to control. I confronted him about his lies. And yet, what is truly sick is that even now I half expect to hear from him again. To receive one of his midnight messages or videos. He got into my head like a drug.' Her eyes filled with tears and for some moments she looked away. She turned back to me and her voice softened. 'Maybe you'll be more resistant to his charms.'

But I already knew that I'd been no less taken in by him than she had.

Before we parted, Suzanne apologised again for upsetting me, then she turned and walked away. With my mind in a daze I headed over the stretch of grass to the cliffs and followed the path along the edge that led away from town. I felt dizzy as I bent down and unclipped Digby's lead, and as I walked, my head swam and felt separate to my body.

"He is a man incapable of either honesty or loyalty. A master in seduction." Those had been Suzanne's words.

If she hadn't sounded so genuinely upset, insightful and coherent, I'd have dismissed her words as coming from a rejected lover. But her openness about the affair and concern for my feelings had shown without any doubt that she spoke the truth. At least, the truth as she perceived it.

I was glad I'd spoken to her, despite her revelations leaving me feeling sick and devastated.

My stomach roiled, and waves of nausea kept coming, over and over. I'd made love with Stefan with barely any hesitation, and willingly. Like a delusional, sex-starved animal I'd thought nothing of following him into that empty flat, putting on the ring he'd bought me and feeling flattered that he must surely be falling in love with me to bestow so much of his precious time and attention. I'd felt enthralled and captivated each time we kissed and touched one another. I'd re-lived those delicious moments over and over again in my mind, and not only in my head. Each time I thought about how he'd made me feel, those feelings had returned and made me crave his touch. And that time we video called intimately. I felt sickened and confused by my behaviour that night which seemed so out of character and which had taken me way beyond my usual comfort zone.

Had it been something to feel guilty about? Right now I had no idea what to think. But it wasn't so much the physical connection with Stefan that held me captive. In only a few days he'd delved deep into my psyche, just as he had evidently done with Suzanne. The excitement I'd felt at receiving his messages each night, working together in the office and in the way that he looked at me, making each moment rich with meaning and anticipation - attentively, boldly and without inhibition, and with

213

sensual curiosity, had awoken in me a passion I couldn't control. When we'd swam together in the pool last Sunday I'd begun to feel like we were a couple as his hands and skin brushed mine as we swam, which I sensed had been intentional, and with each look and glance my way. The memory too of riding pillion along the coastal road and feeling physically close with my body pressed against his. All of those images, and at the same time, feelings of closeness and intimacy flashed through my mind. The thought of them being snatched away made my legs weaken, and I slumped onto the grass beneath me.

Digby sat down and whined beside me as I wept. He nudged my face and I turned and stared out at the horizon, not really seeing anything other than a blurred, sad and lonely future. I'd been in the job for two weeks, and in that brief time my troubles had magnified a thousand times.

Are we ever free to choose our desires? I read that somewhere and I knew it to be true, or at least true until we are finally forced to make a different choice. Even after weeks, Suzanne was still in knots about Stefan. He'd all but destroyed her. If only I'd approached him, desire and love, with greater caution. But my feelings had been explosive. He'd deliberately done that to me, manipulated my feelings, knowing that his seduction strategy would work because he'd honed this on other women looking for love, or maybe not even looking, but a husband or a partner would be no deterrent.

My heart thudded and my face pricked and burned as an overwhelming sense of panic built up inside of me. What might be the consequences of what I'd done? I'd plunged headfirst into a relationship without thinking it through. I'd been swept along with the excitement of believing he had fallen for me and that love at first sight with a handsome and wealthy, middle aged and never married bachelor was perfectly possible. But I knew it had only been lust, on his part, or a desire to seduce a reasonably attractive woman, and to make me want and love him. Sadly for me, I'd felt more than this. I'd already envisioned far more than was healthy or realistic. I couldn't undo any of it, least of all these feelings I'd already developed.

But what should I do?

If I admitted to knowing all the things that Suzanne had told me, he'd tell me that she was jealous, deluded and lying. Whichever way I viewed the situation, my job, and more essentially, my salary, was in serious jeopardy.

I remained there and listened to the waves as they swirled against the rocks below, their watery sounds lifted by the breeze. I gazed out to sea as the white tipped waves rolled forth, one after another. And the gulls soared up and down from their nests upon the cliffs.

Stefan was the first and only man I'd thrown caution aside and jumped into bed with, or more accurately, onto the windowsill of his lair. If only the sex hadn't been so incredible. His seduction had been swift and he'd gone straight for the jugular. I'd barely had time to resist, although the thought had crossed my mind, half-heartedly and fleetingly. We hadn't even used precautions. If I fell pregnant that would be a monumental disaster. Hopefully, at forty years it was unlikely to happen after only one reckless and unprotected occasion. And how was I supposed to work with him now and turn away his advances? Would my rejection jeopardise our working relationship and my position there? Of course it would. Was he also the sort of man who if he didn't get what he wanted, would cause trouble? And would I be able to resist?

Yes, without a doubt.

There was no chance of my being made a fool of again.

30

All of Sunday and most of the night I'd either raged silently and sobbed in my bedroom or fought the urge to cry. Clara had caught me red eyed and sniffing into a tissue as I peeled and chopped the vegetables for dinner and I'd lied and said I felt upset about Victor staying with Roddy.

She'd put her arm around my shoulders and told me Victor would come home soon.

I'd opened a bottle of wine with dinner and drank every drop during the course of the evening, hoping that it might numb my sadness, or at least help me to sleep better. I was wrong. The alcohol only made me feel more wretched than ever.

I couldn't stop turning everything over in my mind. And then I recalled Stefan telling me he'd studied at Bath Uni and that Mum must have tutored there at the time.

I tapped out a text. "Hi Mum, I would have phoned you back but it's a bit late. I've been thinking, Stefan Temple, my employer, studied business and economics at Bath Uni twenty odd years ago. He was a mature student, late twenties. Do you recall tutoring him?"

I didn't expect her to reply until the morning, but a minute later my phone buzzed with a text.

"Hi Tess. Does Stefan remember me?"

I replied. "I showed him that wedding photo with you, me and Dad, and no, he didn't."

She texted. "I don't recall a Stefan Temple, but I've taught thousands of young men so hardly surprising. And my memory isn't what it used to be. Ha ha!"

"No worries, Mum. He maybe had other tutors."

"Yes, we were a sizable faculty even back then."

I texted. "I'll call you for a chat soon. Night night xx." I put my phone on the coffee table and dropped back on the sofa.

Other than my own misery, which I felt I deserved for being impulsive and naive, something else weighed on my mind - something that Suzanne had said that I couldn't shake off. She'd mentioned she wanted to go to the police, but she had no solid evidence to incriminate them, and on top of that she worried about Stefan taking revenge and telling her husband about their affair. Could that have been merely a ruse for revenge on Suzanne's part, or could it be that Stefan and Judi were operating in illegal imports hidden behind their visible legitimate imports? In the fortnight I'd worked there, I'd learned plenty about the sorts of items they transported, how they imported them and who their clients were. I'd spoken to many of them on the phone and they'd all seemed pleasant, and their requirements legitimate - at least on the surface. But there was something else, too.

Stefan kept a tight control of the finances, to the point where I wasn't allowed access to the accounting system. In fact, I'd barely seen their transactions other than some excel spreadsheets. Not that I had a problem with that - there was plenty of work to keep me occupied. But as a business administrator, I should be given access to the accounts, and because I wasn't and after what Suzanne said, I had suspicions they could be hiding something. If that was the case, there had to be a reason for doing so.

I needed to keep the job though, at least until I could secure another position.

The following morning as I stepped out of my car, I looked up at Lorton Hold and saw it not as the fairytale castle I'd first encountered only days before, but rather a fake facade behind which lurked evil monsters and liars, and specifically, one that ruled and led the rest.

With trepidation in my steps and nerves that darted through my insides, I walked around to the back and took my place in the office.

'Hello Tessa.'

At the sound of his voice, my heart bounded to life and I turned in my chair and saw Stefan in the doorway.

'Morning,' I said, and feigned a smile. 'Good to be back from France?'

He walked up to my desk and sat on the corner. 'Couldn't wait to get back - to you.'

He raised his eyebrows playfully.

My stomach turned a somersault.

He leaned closer and whispered. 'I want to show you something at the stables.'

I sat back. 'A new horse?'

He took my hand and pulled me up. 'It won't take long.'

'I must nip to the toilet first,' I said, and felt apprehensive about what he planned on showing me as well as wondering how best to respond to any physical advances.

I stood in front of the bathroom mirror. I'd purposefully dressed in plain and loose fitting trousers and blouse and worn no make-up to try to cover the dark circles beneath my eyes. I'd scraped my hair up into a tight and unflattering ponytail.

Stefan took my hand and without speaking led me into the hay barn where he closed and bolted the door behind us. He turned, drew me to him and kissed me full on the lips. Within moments I felt his hands upon my blouse as he undid the buttons and caressed my skin beneath, he murmured, 'My God! I'm never leaving you again. The thought of having you again has driven me insane.' He grabbed my bottom. 'Each night I fantasised about fucking you on that window ledge.'

Despite all that I had resolved during his absence, every part of me still desired him physically.

But, I drew back. 'Not here. Gil might interrupt us.' I wondered why he hadn't taken me to his bedroom.

'No. Gil and Judi are out. We're completely alone.'

'But we don't have protection?'

'Aren't you on the pill?'

'No, I was careless at your flat, but Noah had a vasectomy years ago. I could easily get pregnant.'

His eyes narrowed and I saw a distinct flash of anger pass across his features. 'Damn! Then we'll do everything but, for now.' He grabbed my hand and crudely pressed it against his bulging trouser front.

And to my shame, I allowed him to push me back amongst the hay, and without a lack of enthusiasm on my part, we kissed, touched and gave pleasure to one another. But how often could I use contraception as an excuse if he produced a condom, and would I be able to resist?

I'd play whatever game I needed to. If he was going to use, manipulate and dump me, I felt strong enough mentally, and prepared to do exactly the same to him in return.

Even so, when we returned to the office, my appetite satisfied temporarily, I felt guilty, weak and confused. My head felt wracked with suspicion and jealousy that he'd been with another woman in France, possibly more than one, and that alone should have been enough to refuse to make love again. But, I would put my confused feelings aside and bide my time as I worked to uncover the truth of what really went on behind the smooth and glossy exterior of Aztec Imports.

In the office, Stefan approached me, and with his fingers he removed a strand of hay from my hair. 'Slight giveaway, my love.'

'My hair isn't dissimilar to hay so hopefully any more will remain camouflaged.'

'Your hair is like woven silk,' he said, and trailed his fingers through my ponytail and down to my bottom. 'You really are the sexiest creature I've ever had the pleasure of… knowing,' he drawled.

'And I imagine there have been a fair few,' I said, and heard the edge in my tone.

He shook his head and rolled his bottom lip over his top. 'Surprisingly few for a bachelor of my years.'

A most convincing liar, I thought.

'And how about you, Tessa. Have you had many men take their pleasure with your heavenly body?'

'Surprisingly few for a woman of my years. You are my fourth.'

His eyes widened. 'Then I feel honoured. You're practically a virgin.'

I couldn't help but laugh. 'I did give birth naturally to twins, so I hate to shatter your illusions, but nothing terribly virginal about my lady garden.'

He burst out laughing. 'I adore your humour, my love.' His gaze lowered. 'But I adore your lady garden far more.'

'Stop it.' Then I added, 'I've been fortunate to have known few but all loving and loyal men.'

Oh, the irony.

Judging by Stefan's features, the irony had missed its target.

I wanted to avoid any intimate talk as much as possible. If I wasn't at work and if he wasn't my boss, I would end the relationship today. But I knew if I did, he could be resistant and angry, and it would end his trust in me in an instant and I'd never discover more about the extent of their imports.

'Would you mind making me a coffee - and yourself?' he asked, when seated back at his desk. 'I have a proposal I'd like to put to you.'

'Oh?' I said.

'Don't worry. I'm certain you'll like it, and it's not a marriage proposal,' he chuckled at his joke.

'Phew!' I said, although I decided nothing he could say would surprise me much.

I placed our coffee cups on the table and pulled up a chair, keeping a decent gap between us. I stirred my coffee cup and watched as the steaming, nut-brown liquid swirled in circles until it slowed and settled.

He swiveled his chair round to face me. 'If I asked you to come away for two nights, for work, do you think the twins and Noah would manage without you?'

I really didn't like the idea of going away with him - that would complicate my already conflicted feelings and could thwart any attempts to put a distance between our intimacy.

Nevertheless, I couldn't flatly refuse. 'Maybe. When, where to and what's the job?'

'On Wednesday, to travel to the Netherlands and pick up a consignment.'

'Just us two?'

'Judi's volunteered to hold the fort here, but we'll be using Gavin and Heidi's yacht to travel and they'll come, too.'

'A yacht with cabins?'

'Yes, *Nikita* is the queen of yachts. What do you think?'

'What's the consignment?' I asked, hesitant to commit.

He tilted his head from side to side as though he had a crick in his neck. 'It's confidential. So I can't go into details, yet.' He reached for my hand. 'But it would be wonderful to have your help.'

Why so cagey? What lay behind his reluctance to share details?

I realised this could also be my opportunity to discover more.

'Sounds interesting. I'm sure I can get away for a couple of days with some preparation at home.' I leaned over and placed my other hand on his knee. 'And it would give us more time together.'

Two could play at his wicked game.

31

On Tuesday morning as I prepared breakfast and coffee for myself and Noah, Mum rang.

'Can I call you tonight, Mum? I need to get to work.'

I heard a heavy sigh from her end. 'You get ready and I'll talk. After you'd texted Sunday night I meant to call you but your Dad has the flu and a chesty cough so what with work and looking after your Dad I've been run ragged. I ended up calling out of hours care and thought I might have to take him in.'

'Oh no, is he OK?'

'Most likely a chest infection. He's got an appointment this morning and I imagine he'll be put on steroids and antibiotics.'

'Sorry, I should have rung you. Tell Dad I'll speak to him tonight.'

'He'd like that,' she said. 'But, that isn't why I'm calling.'

'Oh?'

'Your boss, Stefan Temple. After we texted, I went onto the Aztec Imports website.'

'And did you recognise Stefan?'

'Instantly. He has distinctive features - still extremely handsome.' Mum sniffed. 'Seeing him triggered a memory - a most distinct memory. I did tutor Stefan and if you showed him that wedding photo then I'm surprised he didn't remember me. Although I doubt he'd want to draw attention to having known me.' She stopped talking.

'Why?' I said, and wondered what she might be about to divulge.

She sucked in a breath. 'I didn't often receive inappropriate attention from the young men back then, but I'm sorry to say Stefan was one of the rare exceptions.'

'What? He flirted with you?'

'Far, far worse, my darling. He'd hang around after lectures or come to my study on the pretext of asking me a question that couldn't possibly wait. I told him repeatedly I was happily married, despite your father almost driving me to having an affair more than once. I jest, of course. But Stefan continued to pursue me. I'll admit to having been a touch flattered by his persistence, but I saw through his charming exterior, plus professors seeing students is a massive no-no as far as the University and I am concerned. After he'd tried it on with me, I'd notice how he'd always have the pretty girls buzzing around him, hoping for his attention. But I had him well and truly sussed from the outset.'

My heart hammered in my chest. 'I can't quite believe he was that predatory,' I said, as I tried to digest her words.

'There's something else, too.'

'What?'

'His name wasn't Temple back then - his surname was Dudek.'

'What? But he and Judi are both Temples.'

'Makes you wonder, doesn't it?' said Mum.

'Why would they change their name?'

'Not an easy thing to do, and why bother unless you have something to hide?' said Mum.

'But he gave up chasing you?'

'He didn't give up so much as he left the University prematurely.'

'He told me he got his degree.' Another lie, I thought. 'Do you know why he left?'

'I remember being told he'd been thrown out for unacceptable behaviour, but it wasn't revealed publicly. Looking back, I wasn't surprised. He was a loose cannon in every respect and if he'd tried it on with me, I doubt he'd have been easily discouraged by the younger ladies' refusals. I really should have flagged this up at the time.'

'It was a long time ago, and maybe you weren't encouraged to flag these things up like everyone is today.'

'Yes, you're right there.' She fell silent for a moment. 'When I go to work this afternoon, I'll ask around some of the oldies.'

'You mean there are others who've been there as long as you have?'

'Ha ha,' she said. 'Some of us are genuine antiquarians, but I'll let you know what I discover.'

'Please. At the very least he sounds like a serious womaniser,' I said, but didn't reveal the full extent of my concerns.

'Has he tried it on with you?' she asked suddenly, her voice full with alarm. 'My God, I doubt he's changed, only probably a whole lot smoother and more successful with his seductions.'

I felt my face redden with embarrassment. 'No, Mum. He can be charming, but the relationship is purely professional.' I lied outright, defensive, and my fraudulent voice sounded thin to my ears.

'Good. Please keep a wide berth in that respect. You're a beautiful woman and any man would want to get to know you better. The fact you're single now and he's a...' she stopped. 'Remember, you're in charge of what you do and don't want. Is he married?'

'No,' I said. 'Apparently never been married, has no children, or been in a long term relationship. Nor his younger sister for that matter, and she's super attractive.'

'Hmph! Why am I not surprised?'

'Marriage isn't for everyone,' I said, and wondered why I still felt the need to make excuses. 'Let me know if you discover more?'

'You'll be the first to know. Now, you get to work and I'll check on your Dad who's having another coughing fit upstairs.'

'Yes, go!' I said.

We hung up. My phone was damp from my sweaty palm and my legs felt weak. For some moments I leaned against the kitchen worktop and tried to make sense of mum's words. Twenty odd years ago and as a mature student Stefan had tried it on with my Mum, a thirty something married woman. Mum had been beautiful and still was at sixty-three, but there weren't many students who'd have the gall to try and seduce their older eminent professor, and especially after she made it clear she was married and not interested.

When I took Noah his coffee and porridge, I knew that he wanted to chat, but my mind was still spinning from Mum's revelations. I felt fragile and tearful and wanted nothing more than to give in to my feelings, curl up under the duvet and have a good cry, rather than head into work for a man who I realised I knew too much, but at the same time, too little about. I could see no easy way out of the mess I'd got myself into. Did I want to quit my job and already as a single parent, succumb to social benefits? Not a chance - at least, not without a fight.

32

The Yacht at Staithes Harbour

'We'll be fine, Mum,' said Clara with confidence. 'Fleur will look after me and I'll look after Dad. And we promise to walk Digby.'

Anyone would think she was delighted to have the house to herself and her friend for a couple of days, I mused.

'You're a gem,' I said, and gave her a final hug in the doorway. 'I'll phone you and you can message me or Roddy if there are any problems. The yacht has WiFi so I should be contactable.'

'Oh, I messaged Gil about me and Fleur going over to help with the horses.'

'When?' I had serious concerns about letting Clara anywhere near Stefan, Gil or Lorton Hold.

'This weekend.'

'Can we talk about it when I get back? I don't want you going over in the meantime.'

'Why? You were dead keen before.'

'I know, but please do as I ask.'

Her smile evaporated and she shrugged. 'Fine.'

I sighed. 'I would rather be there the first time you go up, that's all.'

Stefan and I stood side by side and looked out at Staithes harbour where Heidi and Gavin had moored their yacht, *Nikita*. The tide was in and the water high against the harbour walls where a number of small recreational boats and yachts were moored amongst several fishing vessels. One superyacht stood out as grander than all the rest. It looked well over twenty metres in length and stood twice the height of most of the other boats. The sun had risen above the horizon, reflecting and glinting upon the larger yacht's windows and exterior giving it a polished and pristine appearance.

'Is that theirs at the end?' I asked, unable to hide my surprise.

'Yes, that's the gorgeous *Nikita*. Have you travelled on a yacht before?' Stefan put his arm around my shoulder and squeezed me closer.

As we stood there I couldn't help but wonder that anyone watching would think we were partnered, not boss and employee about to head off on a working trip. I repressed an urge to shrug him off.

'The most glamorous sailing I've done is a day ride on the smaller *Endeavour*.' I pulled out my phone and found a photo of the boat I'd worked on for ten years. I felt a sweep of nostalgia for the job to which I'd devoted so many days out at sea. 'I did take the occasional nap on the benches with an anorak for a pillow.'

'It is charming though, and I can imagine how much the tourists adored you.'

I laughed. 'Well, they didn't jump ship half way.'

It was rare for such a magnificent yacht to moor even in Whitby - a much larger harbour than Staithes. 'You and I move in very different circles. But I'm prepared to give Nikita a shot.'

He squeezed my arm. 'We're moving in the same circles now, my love. It's only a pity it's not warmer. You'd look sensational lounging on the deck in that bikini. I'd have to grab you every five minutes and take you to my cabin to make love to you. In fact, I'll do that anyway.'

I suspected it might be impossible to avoid sleeping with Stefan, without revealing my motives, so I'd brought my own condoms. Could I fake pleasure? If I could control my emotions it wouldn't be too difficult. The 'if' was a big if, though. As an actor, previously used to taking on a different persona, I felt sure I could take on my most challenging role to date, where real life became the drama and every word of dialogue had far more at stake than a memorised script.

I was a natural actor when a tricky situation demanded it. And I knew this wasn't something to be proud of, but it became a skill I'd call on. I knew others did this, too. But what I could say in all sincerity was that it hadn't been something I abused to try to manipulate or deceive people in a cruel way, but I had used it to my advantage, such as complaining about a service or product where I wanted my money refunded, and during childhood being able to get round Mum and Dad when they didn't or did want me to do something.

Could it be that Stefan had the same skills, but because of his dark personality, he used it to deceive so that he could get what he wanted from people, to seduce women into falling in love and sleeping with him, and in an equally corrupt way, to manipulate people in business and for financial gain?

This was my opportunity to find out exactly what sort of 'special' imports they were dealing with. Maybe the trip would turn out to be all above board, but at the very least I'd get to know more about Stefan and his privileged pals and get paid for it - plus it was my first, and probably last, opportunity to travel on a superyacht.

When I caught sight of Heidi and Gavin on deck I had to stifle a snigger. They wore matching outfits - navy slacks, classic beige deck shoes and Breton striped tops. Heidi wore a red scarf around her head and a full face of bright make-up, complete with false eyelashes. She looked good though - pretty and glamorous.

Gavin sat with his legs up on the bench and held a cup of coffee in one hand and a cigarette in the other. 'Welcome aboard *Nikita*, dear friends. Ready for our next adventure?'

Heidi glided across to greet us, all smiles and arms embracing. She turned to me. 'Let me show you to your cabin.' She then turned to Stefan and I thought I detected a wink. 'You're in your usual cabin.'

I assumed Heidi promptly allocated the cabins to ensure that neither Stefan nor I might imagine we would share one. I had no complaints on that front.

Once on board, *Nikita* had a striking presence and was without a doubt the sleekest and most elegant boat I'd seen up close. A few people had strolled along the harbour wall and lingered to appraise her. I saw Gavin standing proudly with another cigarette in hand and one leg propped up on the side, as he talked to them and answered their questions. I doubted he was sharing the details of what we were picking up, something I too had yet to learn.

The varnished wooden decks gave the boat an open and airy appearance, but with sturdy rails around to keep passengers safe. The interior was equally glossy and contemporary, and at the same time, surprisingly tasteful, with Art Deco design details on the furnishings providing an elegant ambience.

I followed Heidi down a short staircase and along a narrow corridor to the back of the yacht. She opened the door to a small cabin with a single bunk below a porthole. I peered through and saw the water level a few feet below.

'Come up when you're ready and we'll eat breakfast,' said Heidi. 'Then we'll set sail.'

'Thanks. *Nikita's* a beauty and it's generous of you to invite me as your guest.'

'We are working, and we always try to combine leisure with work. It makes life infinitely more palatable.'

'That's true and nice to have the opportunity.' I caught Stefan's eye behind Heidi in the corridor and he flicked his brows playfully. I knew exactly what he had in mind and my stomach fluttered with nerves.

I turned back to Heidi. 'Who's your skipper?' I wondered if they hired someone.

'We are of course, darling. Gavin loves playing Captain.'

'She's quite a size to manoeuvre.'

'She's surprisingly graceful to manoeuvre,' said Heidi. 'Do you have good sea legs?'

'I was out most days on *The Endeavour* for ten years, so yep, I'm still upright, compos mentis and with a stomach of iron in a force 10 gale.'

'Excellent! Just like me,' replied Heidi.

I'd checked out the shipping forecast for the next few days and apart from some moderate wind and rain there looked to be nothing to deter a boat like *Nikita*. I unpacked a few toiletries and made my way back up to the deck where Gavin was preparing for departure. He straightened up and pressed his palm into his lower back as though it gave him trouble, then he inhaled a deep breath of sea air.

He turned and saw me watching him. 'Stefan and Heidi are out back preparing breakfast. I'll be along shortly,' he said.

'Aye aye, skipper.' I smiled and gave a salute. 'I'll go batten down the hatches before we get underway.'

Gavin looked at me askance for a moment and then guffawed with laughter. 'Glad you know the ropes, lassie. Happy to have ye aboard.'

I saluted again, then clicked and turned on my heels. I wandered down to the kitchen and lounge area, to be greeted by a mouthwatering aroma of fried bacon, and where Heidi and Stefan stood shoulder to shoulder with their backs to me.

They didn't hear me enter.

'We'll rendezvous with Gil at the fort and transfer the goods,' said Stefan. 'Not sure of timings yet.'

'Hi,' I said.

They spun around in unison.

I noted their surprised expressions. 'Sorry, did I startle you?'

Heidi regained her composure and smile. 'Not at all, dear.'

Stefan leaned against the worktop and folded his arms.

'This kitchen and living room is bigger than my fisherman's cottage,' I said, and I ran my fingers across the wooden worktop. 'And what a magnificent view.'

The glazed doors to the rear of the boat were open and a salty breeze swept in from the sea and through the harbour entrance. It had only been a few weeks since my final guide boat excursion, but seeing the open ocean from here made me long to be out on the water again.

'Tessa,' said Heidi. 'Would you tell Gavin bacon sandwiches are ready?'

I found Gavin up in the control room. He sat at the wheel, but his shoulders were hunched and his breathing sounded unnaturally laboured.

I walked closer. 'Bacon butties are served.' But he didn't reply and I could see how he clutched his palm to his chest. 'You OK, Gavin?'

He could barely speak and breathe and scrunched up his eyes, clearly in pain. 'Angina...spray.'

I turned swiftly and raced back below deck. 'Quick, Gavin needs his angina spray.'

Heidi dashed towards me. 'He should always have it on him.'

'He hasn't,' I replied.

Stefan and I hurried behind Heidi.

When we entered the control room, Gavin had turned in his seat and his face appeared relaxed once more. 'I found my spray in my trouser pocket. Sorry.'

'Goodness me, Gavin!' said Heidi, and clutched her ample bosom. 'Don't do this to me.'

'Sorry, my love,' he said, and gave a sheepish smile.

She put her arms around him and pressed her cheek against his. 'You gave me such a fright.'

He kissed her on the lips. 'I'm fine now.'

'Phew,' Stefan said quietly to me. 'His angina attacks are becoming frequent.'

We left Heidi and Gavin talking and walked out onto the deck.

'He seems young for angina,' I said. 'How old is he?'

'Fifty-three, same as me. We were roommates at boarding school.'

'Oh, lifelong friends then?'

'Heidi and he were childhood sweethearts,' he added. 'Started seeing each other at sixteen and have been together since. He was the golden boy every girl wanted to date.'

'I'd have thought that would be you,' I said.

He thought for a moment. 'You might find this hard to believe, but it wasn't until I'd left school that girls began to seek me out.'

'Or you seek them out?' I said, unable to resist.

'Truthfully, I've never been one for chasing women,' he said. 'I'm more inclined to seek friendship with women, and men alike. I prefer intelligence in a woman to beauty. If something happens romantically, then it's a mutual coming together of minds.'

'Really?' I almost laughed at the delusional, or was it a deliberately dishonest way that he spoke. 'That's lovely, Stefan. Rather like you and I. A mind connection prior to anything physical.'

He kissed me briefly on the mouth. 'Exactly so, my love.' Then he added, 'Although now that I've had you, I can barely focus on anything other than your kissable lips and peachy arse.'

He took hold of my hand and called into the control room. 'Shall we bring breakfast up to you?'

'It's OK,' replied Heidi. 'We're coming now.'

Without a word, Stefan released my hand.

So, he didn't want Heidi or Gavin to think we were together, in any intimate sense. That would make these two nights easier. But why wouldn't he want Heidi to know? Either way, I knew I'd have to play my relationship with Stefan with thought and caution and not get swept along by any more of his bullshit.

The sea was calm and sun-drenched as *Nikita* sailed between the harbour walls, and despite my concerns and reservations, I felt the spirit of adventure rise up in me. I pulled my sunglasses over my eyes and zipped up my hoodie against the breeze that swept over the glistening, undulating waves.

How I'd missed the feeling of riding upon the ocean playground - my mind and body felt strong as the deck beneath my feet rose and fell. Cotton wool clouds overhead puffed smoke signals in the breeze as we sailed into open waters, in no great rush it seemed. The horizon seemed impossibly serene and the palest of blues.

I stood at the bow, held the rail and gazed down at the rolling foam as the boat split the water to allow our passage.

Stefan came up and stood beside me. 'Feels like the ultimate freedom, doesn't it?'

'I have to give you credit,' I replied. '*Nikita* is a fine excuse to use for work.'

'It makes business sense too,' he said and rested his hand over mine.

'I'm sure.' I turned to face him directly, determined to find out what work we'd be doing. 'So, where exactly are we sailing to, and why?' I felt a spasm in my left eye and my eyelid flickered and I thought it must be visible. Nothing must give away my distrust.

'So curious, my love,' he replied, and looked at me closely. 'Don't you trust me?'

'Of course I do.' My eye flickered again and I ran a finger over my eyelid.

'OK, Miss curious. We're heading to No Man's Land Fort, eight miles off the Dutch coast. Have you heard of it?'

'No. Have you been before?'

'Only once. It's unused but previously featured in a couple of movies and sporting events.'

'I assume we're authorised to moor up there?'

'I know the owner.'

Of course he did. 'How exciting! I'll look it up.'

'Already got the Wifi code?' Stefan said.

'Only because of the twins,' I said. 'I am curious to know what we're picking up, though.'

'I'll tell you more later. It's a little unusual, but you'll understand when I explain.'

I squeezed his hand and leaned into him, 'I look forward to finding out.'

'It's a little sensitive and the fewer who know, the better.'

'But Gavin and Heidi know?' I said, and tried to disguise my growing frustration.

'Yes, because we're using their transport.'

'OK,' I said, realising my persuasive powers were getting me nowhere. 'I love a mystery to solve.' But I suddenly felt unsure and out of my depth.

I recalled Suzanne's suggestion of illegal activity, as well as the boathouse and the mysterious chains down at their private beach. If he wanted to avoid revealing what they were importing, I felt damn certain something had to be amiss.

I'd taken a risk coming along.

Drugs? No way did I want to get involved in anything illegal, but equally, it could have been precisely what Suzanne had been concerned about.

I had to know.

Heidi had been quick to change the subject when I'd asked her about what we were picking up.

Stefan reached down and squeezed my bottom. 'You really do have the most delectable derriere. Later I shall devour you.'

'Only if you let me return the favour,' I replied, and ran my tongue suggestively between my lips.

He moved his hand round my hips and between my thighs. 'You've made me hard, my love.' He took my hand and pressed it against him. 'What should I do about it?'

I lowered my eyes. 'I do want you, Stefan,' I said. 'But Heidi will notice we've disappeared.'

'She might indeed. But I'll have you later. My anticipation will only make it all the more exciting.'

I smiled. 'Maybe for now one of us should check on Gavin and help out?'

'Let me. You stay and enjoy the view,' he said, then added. 'Although I leave you with deep reluctance.'

I watched him walk away and my thoughts went into overdrive. So much to take in and I must stay hyper alert - listen to every word spoken, every nuance of meaning, and be aware of every facial expression and movement. I had no doubt that today and tomorrow would reveal much about Suzanne's suspicions, now also mine. I got the strongest sense that Stefan wanted to involve me so that I too would be incriminated and therefore he'd have his hold over me. A bargaining tool, should I cause any trouble, like Suzanne with her husband.

I wondered, too, if that was what Stefan and Judi had over Gil. Tonight Gil would be the delivery man - about as involved as it gets. Stefan had the finances, Gavin and Heidi were tied in with their glamorous appearance, and *Nikita* gave the guise of a leisure trip out to sea. And what of me? Stefan wanted me as his paid accomplice and whore, nothing more, and no doubt would cast me aside when it suited him or he set his sights on another pretty woman.

But if I contacted the police, what could I realistically say, other than I felt suspicious and they should investigate him? No, Stefan was too smart for that - he'd have taken care to cover any tracks that led to illegal activity.

I felt the engine rev and the yacht pick up speed, and I turned around and looked back at Staithes and the snug fisherman's cottages and townhouses that rose up the hillside until they finally shrank from view to become a blur of distant dots. How I longed to be back amongst those distant dots.

33

Dusk fell and the clouds overhead turned thunderous grey, and blood orange streaks hung over the horizon. I spotted a large structure in the distance, a shadowed silhouette, with what appeared to be a curved outer wall. It had to be, No Man's Land Fort. I remained leaning against the rail, swaying with the movement of the boat, and as we approached I could see the pale, windblown stone with three rows of windows - all unglazed, some with bars, and a tall watchtower to the left. There looked to be a jetty or pier to the right of the fort. The sea had grown blacker beneath darkening skies, and during the last hour of our journey, choppier too. I watched the waves spray up against the walls of the fort.

The closer we got the more mysterious the fort looked. It must have been built during a war but against which army? It looked to pre-date WWI and WWII. I'd imagined the fort would be built on a small island but there appeared to be no land in sight and no rocks to suggest an island beneath.

'Tessa, come up here.'

I turned around to see Heidi leaning over the rail on the upper deck. I walked round and up the steps to where she greeted me with a smile and a whisky tumbler. She'd changed into a navy blue catsuit and a coordinating navy hairband that swept her hair off her face. And then I noticed her earrings, and the single earring I'd found on the beach the morning I'd discovered the drowned girl, came to mind. It was at home on my dressing table. Heidi wore almost identical earrings, with the signature jet stone.

She held out the tumbler. 'To celebrate our arrival.'

'Thank you.' I took the glass. 'They're beautiful earrings. Did you buy them in Whitby?'

She reached up to her ear and smoothed the tip of her finger over the black stone. 'They were a gift from a friend.'

And would that friend be Stefan, I felt tempted to ask?

'I had a pair quite similar, but I lost one,' I said, and watched for her reaction.

Heidi tilted her head. 'That's a pity.'

'I lost it on Whitby beach only the other week. Little chance of my finding it again.' I shrugged. 'Buried in the sand by now.'

Heidi took a slow mouthful of whisky.

'The fort looks amazing,' I said, taking a sip myself. 'Have you been before?'

She nodded, gazed over at the fort and said vaguely, 'Once or twice.'

'I'd love to know what we're picking up,' I said, confidingly, and hoping our whisky moment might loosen her tongue.

'When the delivery arrives you'll learn more. Rest assured, you'll understand why I couldn't say more before.'

'Could it be drugs?' I asked with a playful lift of my brows.

She shook her head emphatically. 'I'm against anything of that nature.' And she drank back her whisky.

'But it might be illegal?'

'Please, don't fret, Tessa. All will be well.'

I felt patronised and furious with all of them. She might as well have patted me on the head. And as she hadn't denied my question of an illegal import, my suspicions skyrocketed.

I wondered again why I'd agreed to come along. I hadn't expected them to be so cagey and evasive. I'd barely spoken to Stefan all day. He'd either sat beside Gavin at the wheel in the control room, or disappeared below deck. I imagined he'd done so to avoid more probing questions from me.

'How's Gavin doing?' I asked.

'He's good. Only a blip, as happens sometimes. He's loved the sail over.' She lay her hand on my arm. 'I hope you have, too?'

Jeez, I thought, talk about smoothing over reality.

But in reply I said, 'Honestly, I could get used to this. It's been heavenly.' I looked around me and spread out my arms. 'This is living the dream.'

'You must come away with us again. We go further when time allows. Honfleur, Dieppe, down as far as Brittany occasionally, where we can really enjoy the sun, sand and sea.'

She might as well have added sex, but I refrained from further comment. She must have conveniently forgotten I was a single parent of two teenagers.

'Don't you bring Polly along to help with the food and drinks?'

Heidi gave a dismissive wave. 'Oh, it's easier without her here, trust me. Last time I brought her along, she got seasick and kept moping about and weeping. I've got no time for that sort of behaviour,' said Heidi.

Not an ounce of compassion, I thought. 'At least she can have a rest for a few days which I'm sure she'll appreciate.'

Heidi's eyes grew wide. 'Not with the list of jobs I've left for her. I don't want her slacking off.'

The wall of the fort loomed large and the rumble of the engine dropped to a steady hum.

'This is the tricky part and the choppy sea won't help,' Heidi said.

'There's no buoy to moor with and use a dinghy?' I asked.

'Far better. We slip into the harbour which is snug, but secure.'

And as she spoke the engine growled and the yacht swung right.

I stood at the bow as Gavin slowly but expertly manoeuvred *Nikita* into the harbour, which had no doubt been built for smaller vessels.

Stefan came down and we jumped onto the pier and secured the yacht with ropes to the moorings.

'Do we get to explore?' I said, and looked up at the vast structure.

'If you like, although it's treacherous in places,' replied Gavin, as he secured the gangplank and walked down to join us on the jetty.

'Feel free to take a look around,' Heidi said to me. 'But tread carefully. Dinner will be an hour.'

'I'll come with you,' Stefan said, then added quietly, 'To make sure you don't escape from me.'

My stomach did a somersault at his remark. Did he hold suspicions about my loyalty?

Maybe he was more intuitive than I'd given him credit for.

'You can give me the grand tour and show me the interesting bits,' I said, with a flirty, and I hoped, reassuring smile.

With Stefan leading the way we climbed several steps from the jetty into a low-ceilinged, dark and damp windowless room with a stone floor. A little daylight filtered in through the open doorway to guide our way, and at each step my trainers splashed through puddles in the seaworn indentations. Stefan kept a tight hold of my hand and led me through a gap at the far end of the room and into a short and narrow passageway with more steps at the end. Saltwater and seaweed lined the floor and walls and their aromas lingered in my nostrils and throat. The light returned the further we ascended until we reached the top step where the space opened out to a mezzanine floor that circled the entire interior wall of the fort. From within it looked even more cavernous than I'd envisaged and it appeared to have been recently refurbished with sturdy floorboards and iron railings.

I peered over the inner railing to where seawater covered the floor below, then lifted my eyes and gazed up forty feet or so to the open skies, which had darkened now that evening approached.

'This place is incredible,' I said. 'What a shame it's unused.'

'Did you ever watch the TV show, *Fort for All*, where teams competed against one another?'

'Yes, I did! I thought I recognised it from somewhere.'

In fact, I'd already Googled it, and more precisely, our exact location. The more naive or surprised Stefan thought me, the less he'd suspect hidden motives, hopefully.

'They cancelled the show when a contestant fell into the sea from up there.' Stefan pointed to the tower and continued talking as though he were the official tour guide. 'She died, as did one of the other contestants who jumped in to rescue her. It isn't the safest of buildings and was originally built for war and cannon fire.'

'How tragic,' I said. 'But it is a spectacular fort. Probably safer and easier to explore in daylight.'

'We won't be hanging around tomorrow.'

'Oh?'

He stopped, turned to me and took my hand. 'Do you trust me, my love?'

My pulse began to pick up speed. 'Of course, why wouldn't I?'

'Because tonight especially, it's vital that you do. What we're taking on requires absolute trust and loyalty.'

'It's not illegal is it?' I gave a nervous laugh.

'No, because all parties are cooperative, willing and paid well.'

My skin prickled and my heart pounded faster, and for some moments my vision went into a spin.

If the import was legitimate, we wouldn't be sneaking around at a fort in the middle of the North Sea, and instead we'd have moored in a port and be clearly visible to the authorities.

I felt sure he'd sense my spiralling anxiety. 'I feel like a pirate.'

'A dangerously sexy pirate,' he said, and pulled me to him. He looked intently into my eyes - the way he'd done to summon my attention from the start. 'In the short time I've known you, you've come to mean so much to me. I'm falling in love with you, Tessa.' He leaned in and kissed me on the lips.

On the surface I responded to his kiss, but inside my thoughts ran riot and threatened to give me away.

As I gave in to his kisses, I felt oddly detached from where we stood, and nostalgic for home, a place where I felt safe with people that I loved. Being with Stefan, Heidi and Gavin felt dangerous, lawless and dirty, and I strongly feared things were about to get a lot worse.

Stefan lifted my T-shirt and slipped one hand into my bra and pushed his other hand through the waistband at the back of my jeans and squeezed my buttock. 'Touching your skin, even looking at you, drives me insane,' he said, close to my ear. 'I want you.'

But his words and his touch only felt mechanical and unnatural.

He pulled the button and zip of my jeans and a gut wrenching pain pulsed through my belly.

I went rigid and held in my breath.

He didn't notice my discomfort. 'You could be a lingerie model. I'll buy you some silk underwear and peel it off you with my teeth.' He eased my jeans over my hips but I placed my hands over his.

'We can't.'

'I won't go back without fucking you first.'

'But I have my period.'

'You think that will stop me?'

Damn. I hadn't got my period but I thought that would deter him.

'I've got cramps and I'm bleeding heavily.'

He pulled my top back down and his eyes narrowed. 'OK, but you won't hold me back tonight.'

I couldn't decide if he was being playful or genuinely annoyed. His tone and blazing eyes suggested the latter.

The pain in my belly subsided, but I resolved to clean the wound as soon as I returned to my cabin. I'd been dressing it daily, but there hadn't been any signs of infection and I thought the redness had lessened.

I brushed my fingers over his cheek and continued down his neck. 'You know I want you, too?'

'I've never desired a woman like I do you.'

I wondered how many of these lines Suzanne had heard and been desperate to believe. I felt torn. Despite all that I knew and learned of him, physically, a part of me still desired him, even as my rational mind screamed in my ear - he's a sleazy lying bastard, he'll say anything to brainwash you and get what he wants.

'I'll make it worth your wait,' I said, and kissed him only long enough to deceive him in return.

I knew he wanted me physically, but only in as much as he wanted to make love to any attractive woman early on. But there was no doubt he'd soon need a fresh challenge, move on, cheat and lie behind my back, if he hadn't already. That was all he was capable of even if I was his current target. At forty years I might not have been overly experienced with men, but I wasn't stupid, either. I'd only known him intimately for two weeks and already I felt confused, hurt, betrayed and more than anything, angry. Noah's face flashed into my mind. What a contrast these two handsome men were, both flawed but only one with a warm and genuine heart.

Stefan had fed me a cocktail of drugs from day one, that aimed to betray my rational mind. If only he didn't arouse me physically with one missile-accurate look, or a few well scripted and rehearsed lines, whilst at the same time I wanted to punch his nose and yell how much I loathed him.

'Stefan, Tessa!' Heidi's voice echoed around the walls.

'Up here,' called Stefan, releasing me.

'Dinner,' she called.

'I'm ravenous,' he called back. His voice dropped to a whisper. 'But I'd far rather eat you.'

I placed my finger on his lips. 'Later, my love.'

I rested my knife and fork on my plate. 'That was delicious, Heidi.'

'You really are the finest cook I know,' said Stefan. 'And how splendidly presented, too.'

'Better not tell Judi,' said Heidi, but she glowed with pride and delighted in his words.

'I wouldn't dare,' said Stefan, and confided a smile.

What a smooth talking snake, I thought. He took every opportunity to faun and flatter a woman. Yes, the food was tasty, but his words sounded sycophantic and slippery.

'I enjoy Heidi's cooking rather too much,' said Gavin, and patted his round and well nourished belly.

'I do keep it nutritious, unprocessed and low fat, though,' said Heidi.

Really, I thought? There hadn't been anything remotely low fat about tonight's meal. A rich cheese and bacon sauce and pasta with huge portions of oil-soaked roast potatoes. We'd had bacon butties at breakfast and lavishly topped pizzas with a minimal salad garnish at lunchtime. Not what I'd have cooked for my partner if he was Gavin's size and suffered from angina. In fact, not what I'd cook for myself unless I wanted to pile on the pounds.

Stefan poured us all more wine for which I felt grateful. My nerves were on high alert and still with no idea of what to expect overnight.

'What time are you expecting your delivery?' I said, and tried once more to glean some details.

'Most likely midnight or soon after,' said Stefan. 'But I won't wake you.'

'Oh, but you must.'

'No,' he replied all too quickly. 'The fewer people the better.'

I shrugged. 'I might be of help.'

And my curiosity soared to stratospheric levels.

I knew I wouldn't sleep for a minute. Delivery expected from midnight onwards in the black of night. This reeked of smuggling. If it were drugs I'd be devastated. I might not have led a blameless life but I was fairly puritanical about drugs after having seen first hand at College how illegal substances had destroyed two fellow students' lives.

Still, I had to know the full extent of who and what I was involved with. Or maybe…, hopefully, I'd be proven wrong in my suspicions, and Suzanne's too.

I helped Heidi wash and clean up and I noticed Stefan and Gavin soon disappeared.

'I'm having an early night,' said Heidi. 'We'll be busy tomorrow.'

'Will you be helping with the delivery?' I asked.

'I doubt it,' she replied evasively, then reached into a cupboard for some glasses, no doubt to be filled with more alcohol.

A further attempt to placate me.

She pulled a bottle of rosé from the fridge and unscrewed the cap.

'I'll knock on your door early tomorrow. You should get a good night's rest.'

Clearly she thought I should remain in my cabin until told to come out.

She poured two glasses and placed one in front of me.

I picked it up but with no intention of taking another drop of alcohol. Interesting that Heidi, that all of them, saw me as the placid and obedient type. Still, that impression would suit me well.

When I returned to my cabin I phoned Clara who reassured me all was well, then I washed and changed into pyjamas. I felt restless and on edge, and I sat on the floor and held a glass against the closed door to listen for movement or voices. I hadn't seen Stefan or Gavin since dinner and they hadn't been in the control room when I'd gone up to say goodnight. They'd maybe headed onto the pier or fort to talk and make plans privately - secretly.

I heard footsteps approach along the corridor. Probably Heidi heading to her cabin. A door opened and clicked shut. I checked my phone but there were no replies to my texts. I'd already taken several photos of the yacht's interior, discreetly, and took one of myself now in my cabin in my pyjamas, that recorded the time taken. I knew that even by being here, any criminal imports or activity could instantly incriminate me.

I heard voices and listened closely. Stefan and Gavin talked in low tones, and I caught Stefan saying, 'I'll wake you.' The rest was indiscernible. I heard someone enter Stefan's cabin next to mine and the door closed. I felt troubled by the myriad of possibilities that lay ahead and I sat on my bunk and stretched out my legs. But there could be no chance of me sleeping through whatever they had planned.

I heard a door open nearby followed by a tap on my door. I got up to open it, but I already knew who it would be. Without saying a word Stefan slipped past me and closed the door softly behind him.

He put his arms around me and pulled me close. 'Thank God I've finally got you alone.'

I repressed my instinctive response and I gently but firmly pushed him away and stepped back. 'We can't.'

He took my face in his hands and gave me a long and lingering kiss. 'Blood doesn't stop me. I need you.'

I tried to pull away from his grasp. 'I have cramps. Men don't understand. I'll be fine tomorrow.'

With a jerk he released me. 'I'm beginning to think you don't want me.'

'You know I want you. But I'd hate to mess up Heidi's sheets.'

'She won't care,' he said.

'I believe she does.' I looked directly at him. 'Heidi cares a lot.' Would he realise I was talking about him, not the sheets?

Whatever his interpretation, his eyes flared. He gripped my arms and shoved me backwards onto the bunk.

My head smacked against the headboard and I felt a painful jar in my neck.

He glared down at me. 'I thought you were different, but you don't fucking care either.'

He swung round, left the cabin and slammed the door behind him.

I hadn't expected a violent response. I felt the pressure of his hands still on my arms and when I rolled up my sleeves I saw red marks had already formed. My hands trembled and I pressed them between my thighs and tried to calm my breathing and the panic that was building in my head. Surely I was acting in a melodrama with my audience as the other players. Everything felt too bizarre to be my reality.

How dare he push me because I refused him? If I'd been anywhere but on the yacht miles from land I'd have fought back, kicked him where it hurt and run away never to look back. My eyes filled with tears, but I wiped them away and swallowed back my fury.

Now I knew the sort of aggressive and violent person he could be when he didn't get his way. And maybe my refusal would turn him off me, and more importantly, keep him at a distance. I got up and checked the catch on the cabin to see if it had a lock, but no, he was free to walk in whenever he wanted.

Once more, I checked my phone for messages. Nothing, and the battery was running low. I plugged it into my portable charger.

There came the sound of voices nearby, imperceptible and whispered, followed by a woman's shriek and giggling. I pressed my ear to the door. I reached for my hoodie and pulled it over my pyjama top, laced up my trainers, then opened the door a crack and peeped into the corridor. All seemed quiet and I made my way up to the deck. A breeze had whipped up and waves lapped and bubbled against the sides of the boat. The dark shadow of the fort loomed tall in front of me and I thought, if it weren't for that, we could almost be in Whitby Harbour with the lights, bars and fish restaurants nearby.

The cry of a lone gull that circled overhead reminded me how alone I was here with these people - people who I barely knew, and who the more I got to know, the less I wanted to. Their glamour, smiles, smooth words and wealth had impressed me initially, but it didn't make them better people. In fact, the reverse appeared to be true. They seemed oh so confident in their abilities, business dealings and opinions, but I finally saw it for what it was - self-centred arrogance.

I'd always been confident with people, and Stefan and Judi didn't intimidate me, but they did make me see those I knew well in a far kinder light, like Roddy, so wise and generous, and successful, too, despite having had a humble upbringing without a university education. And Noah had a kind and loving heart, despite all the upset and trouble he'd caused us.

I wondered if he'd gone ahead with his first hypnosis session scheduled for today. I hadn't messaged him to ask how it had been and he hadn't messaged me about it either. Oddly, he hadn't messaged me at all.

Despite the late hour, I felt angry and restless and my heartbeats grew heavier as I became conscious of the space and emptiness that surrounded the yacht. I'd lived on the coast for most of my life, but what an unfamiliar and disconcerting place the ocean could be. The tide washed in and waves did as nature and the weather dictated. Humans, for all their parasitic destruction and consumption, couldn't control the oceans. We could enjoy the riches of the sea - its beauty, nourishment and wildlife, but mostly we polluted and contaminated wherever we went. We interfered with wildlife by overfishing, transporting goods and sailing for leisure, but we would never delay or prevent the tide and its never-ending journey back and forth across our planet. I felt comforted with the knowledge that for all that we were, the sea and the land would be here long after I'd gone and long after all of humanity, whenever that might be.

I walked soundlessly to the front of the yacht and looked out over the jetty wall at the shadows across the ink-black ocean. Overhead, distant stars sprinkled the sky and the crescent moon glowed pale beyond the clouds that curtained its sheen. A light glimmered somewhere in the distance. I stared at it and tried to work out if it was moving or static, until it flickered like candlelight and disappeared.

I headed down to the lounge area and looked around. A more impeccable space I had rarely seen - so neat, contemporary and spotless. One of the seat cushions caught my eye because it looked misplaced in one corner. Something compelled me to walk over and set it straight to complete the neatness of the room. When I lifted it off its base I noticed a gap of about five inches wide, rather like a pocket between the two compartments of the base. There were two objects nestled deep inside and in the semi-light I couldn't make out what they were. I knelt down and reached inside. My hand met something hard and in that instant I knew what it was. My thoughts spiralled. With care, I lifted both objects and placed them on the floor in front of me.

I looked down at the handgun laid on its side beside a carton of bullets. I slipped my phone from my pocket and took a photo for evidence.

There were three possible reasons for hiding the gun - for it to be close to hand should they feel threatened or if they needed a bargaining tool, or worse, to deliberately snuff out someone's life. I could throw it overboard, along with the bullets. And then I had a better thought. I stood up and checked under the other sofa cushions. Beneath the cushion at the far end of the sofa I found another similar pocket. I picked up the gun and the carton of bullets and tucked them inside.

My mind and heart still raced and as I returned to my cabin, I took some long and steadying breaths. When I passed Stefan's cabin I heard noises - shuffling movements, low voices and the faintest of moans. A female moan that could only have been Heidi.

My face grew hot and I felt nauseous. Unsure what to do, I leaned against the corridor wall. Stefan and Heidi were together, fucking, and only earlier he'd said how much he desired me and loved me! For all Suzanne's words of warning, I don't think I'd fully believed him capable of sleeping with someone when he seemed so into me and with our relationship so fresh and exciting. My refusal of him and his subsequent anger and frustration had only sparked him to seek gratification elsewhere. What a bastard.

Anger surged through me and I wanted to storm into the cabin, catch them at it and hurl abuse at both of them. And what about poor Gavin in his cabin? Was he aware of the affair?

Heidi's moans intensified and it seemed she didn't care who overheard her. Maybe she wanted me to hear, and Gavin, too. Sleeping with another woman and right under my nose proved how little Stefan valued me. They obviously hadn't just got together. Their relationship went way back. And I recalled when Heidi had warned me against getting close to Stefan. And yet here she was doing the exact opposite of her thoughtful advice. What a hypocrite. And as for Stefan, I felt enraged, but at the same time grateful for Suzanne's warnings. Stefan was a monster of the most despicable kind. Handsome, smooth tongued, witty and intelligent on the outside, he knew precisely how to manipulate a woman and delude those he wanted to impress and seduce. He'd been doing it before and since he'd attempted to seduce my mum.

In the past half-hour everything had become all too horribly clear.

Furious tears spilled down my cheeks and I stumbled into my cabin and fought an urge to slam the door behind me. Instead, I closed it quietly and leaned against it. What other horrors would I face before I could return home to my children and turn my back on Stefan and Aztec Imports forever?

34

The Delivery

Some time later, I became aware of the rumbling of an engine close by and water lapping against the sides of the yacht.

Were we on the move?

I climbed off my bunk. Voices and movements sounded from above, or possibly the pier. Heidi and Stefan had asserted I shouldn't get up but I had no intention of waiting in the cabin like their well behaved servant.

I left the cabin and headed to the upper deck.

I saw another boat, a smaller vessel, moored at the end of the pier while people moved about and talked in low tones amongst beams of torchlight. For some moments I hesitated, before I walked down the boarding plank and stepped onto the pier. I moved towards the group gathered beside the smaller vessel, and paused. I could make out Stefan's voice and Gavin's figure, and it had to be Gil helping someone, a young, slight woman, off the smaller boat. From here the vessel looked identical to the boat I'd discovered at their private beach.

I stood back silently in the dark.

Stefan jumped off the smaller boat and helped another young woman - tall and slim. And then Gil climbed back onto the boat, disappeared for some moments before two other women stood up with him and were assisted onto the pier.

Were people the delivery - young women in the darkness of the night, miles from the mainland? My heart shuddered and I knew this to be a far sicker and more heinous crime than I'd expected, but one I should have anticipated. When I'd first seen the chains and cuffs, alarm bells had sounded, but not loudly enough for me to investigate, report or take action. How naive and deluded I'd been. I should have questioned Gil or Judi to understand their purpose. And I should have confronted Stefan directly.

Where were these women to be taken and where would be their destinations and positions? I couldn't look on in silence and I walked towards the group.

Stefan and Gavin turned to me in unison.

'Wait for us on the boat, Tessa,' Stefan instructed.

'I'm here to help,' I said, trying to rouse enthusiasm into my tone.

'We don't need help. Go back!' he said, with a firmness that gave no room for manoeuvre without my giving myself away.

I turned and walked away but only so far that they couldn't see me. I heard words but nothing specific. The group walked up the pier towards me and I hurried back over the boarding plank onto the yacht and down to the lounge. I sat on the corner of the sofa, beneath which I'd stashed the gun. God forbid I'd need to protect myself or anyone else with it. I'd only ever fired a blank from a revolver on stage, although I'd done so many times and it had looked and sounded real enough.

I heard footsteps and voices and Heidi and Gavin entered the lounge followed by Stefan, Gil and four young women. Heidi smiled at me as though nothing untoward or unusual was happening. In stark contrast, Gavin appeared agitated and his face glistened with beads of sweat.

Stefan gestured for the young women to sit on the chairs or sofa with me. I tried to keep my face neutral but inside the blood pounded in my ears and a renewed feeling of confusion and panic grew inside of me. This was a crime and I was involved whether I wanted to be or not. I looked at each of the young women in turn. Without exception, their faces looked pale, tired and drawn, but their eyes darted from one face to another to reveal their unease. One of the girls was tall and beautiful, with curly brown hair that fell to her waist. Another girl was petite and fine featured with pixie cut blonde hair, while another girl looked about my height, strong looking and dark skinned - she had a voluptuous figure and her skimpy clothes only enhanced her curves. The fourth auburn haired girl was of average height and build, but from her face, she looked the youngest of them all. She was exceptionally pretty with intense brown eyes, and I noticed how her hands trembled in her lap.

Did they even know why they'd been brought here?

All would soon become clear, I hoped.

Beside me, two of the girls shivered, and they clasped hands and clung to one another. I caught their eyes and I gave them what I hoped to be a reassuring smile, but they didn't smile in return. To them, I was the enemy, one member of the gang responsible for them being here and for their future fate and destination. Gil stood on guard by the stairs to the upper deck. But he looked awkward with neck and shoulders tensed and concern deepened the lines on his face. When I attempted to catch his eye he deliberately looked away.

How could he have let himself be drawn into something so depraved?

The four girls looked so diverse in appearance revealing the beautiful variety of humans, and yet I had no doubt they would be treated as nothing more than slaves and vessels - one dimensional and female, whose purpose was to serve in whatever way deemed fit by their owner.

And yet, here I was. But I also knew without hesitation that had I known the sordid depths of Stefan's plans, I'd have divulged all to the authorities and been well away from here. Still, I felt determined to help these young women in whichever way I could.

None of them could have been much older than sixteen. Three of the four looked underfed, gaunt almost, and all of them wore clothes too light for a night journey at sea. I felt wracked with guilt for even being here.

'I'll fetch the drinks,' said Heidi, and she sparkled with enthusiasm.

I wondered who she was trying to impress.

Stefan smiled at her. 'That would be splendid. Then I'll talk through our plans.'

Plans? I looked at him but he stared straight through me as though I were invisible and insignificant.

Heidi, our charming and glamorous host, filled glasses on a tray and busied herself handing them round. The girls each took a glass and drank thirstily as if they hadn't touched fluids in hours. I took a glass and a sip - gin, with a splash of tonic.

When Stefan spoke almost fluently in Polish I could barely breathe. The girls turned to him and listened. I understood every word, even with his many mistakes.

Stefan welcomed them. 'Witam, przyjaciele. I thank you for travelling from your home country to be with us here. I hope your journey was restful and pleasant. Before you move on to your new homes in Great Britain, you will spend the night here with us, relaxing and enjoying yourselves on this millionaires yacht. So please drink up and we will take our places.'

Places? What the heck did he mean by places?

My feelings of revulsion towards Stefan soared. Here was not a man, but a hideous monster.

These girls can only have come out of desperation, and judging by their appearance, they'd travelled for too long in poor conditions. What they needed urgently was food and water, warmer clothing and a safe place away from here. Where were their bags? Surely they'd been allowed to bring clothes and other belongings? Perhaps their luggage was aboard the smaller boat?

Of course, Stefan knew something of the Polish culture, and the hardships that so many young people and their families suffered. Far from having sympathy, he was prepared to exploit them for whatever he could use them for. Did he have no feelings or conscience at all? With his poker player face, he seemed more the mannequin than a living and feeling human. His expression had become that of a man wearing a mask over a carefully concealed personality that revealed only the barest minimum of what it meant to be a real, breathing, human. Beneath his smooth exterior I realised his mind had been rewired differently to most people. But what had happened to make him this way? And Judi, notably absent from tonight's atrocities, seemed different. Messed up and damaged, yes, not likeable, but sensitive in her own way.

I noticed Heidi and Gavin eyeing the girls in turn, assessing their worth. Gavin wiped his face which dripped with sweat and he trembled with what appeared to be grotesque anticipation.

Surely they weren't singling a girl out to serve them in their home? They had Polly, and judging by their behaviour here I wondered what additional duties Polly had been expected to perform. Maybe they planned on replacing her.

Gavin stood up and lumbered across the floor and stood in front of the petite blonde girl beside me. Without speaking he reached down, took hold of her wrist and pulled her up. She didn't resist, but when he cupped her chin to get a closer look, her eyes grew wild with alarm. He acted as though he was buying a horse at the market and her eyes darted to the corner of the room, quite unable to look him in the eye.

I wanted to jump up, push Gavin aside and scream my objections, but I knew that timing would be crucial.

Heidi approached the young black woman and held out her hand. 'Hold my hand, dear.'

So, the plan was to pick a companion and test them out before they moved on. Would Stefan and Gil do the same? Gil's arms were folded and his mouth formed a hard line. His body language told me he felt as sickened as I did. But he'd known of their plans and had still assisted them.

Stefan came and stood in front of me.

'I'm sorry we don't have any young men, but given you're bleeding I know you'd have to decline,' he said loudly and with a sneer. He gestured to the auburn haired girl. 'You have this girl to keep you company in whichever way you prefer. Is she to your liking?'

My heart ached at the look of terror in her features.

'Indeed she is.' My tone was as soft and fluid as I could force it, until a burning pain shot through my abdomen. My eyes watered and I looked away to hide my discomfort. I took some breaths and the pain subsided.

I wondered how much English each girl spoke or understood.

When I turned back, Stefan looked into my eyes. 'I knew you were my kind of girl.' He gave the smallest of nods. 'Our sort.'

Clearly, he knew nothing about me - nothing at all. This drama grew darker and more sordid with each scene.

I forced down a mouthful of gin and swallowed hard. I wished I'd brought painkillers to get me through until I could see my doctor. When Stefan turned away and sat beside the tall, dark haired girl, I lifted my hand to my chest and felt the hard outline of my mobile phone in my pyjama pocket.

I watched Gavin lead the blonde girl out of the lounge. She took small steps and looked down but she didn't resist and it seemed the girls knew why they were here.

I stood up. 'Where's Gavin taking her?'

'Somewhere private,' Stefan said, and he put an arm around the tall girl's waist.

My stomach heaved and acid burned the back of my throat. I turned to Heidi, who hadn't shown a flicker of concern as her lecherous husband had disappeared with the girl. 'Heidi?'

'It's all fine. It's what the girls came over for.' She turned to the girl beside her. 'What's your name?'

'Helene,' replied the girl who bravely maintained eye contact with Heidi, probably seeing her as the lesser of the evils in the room.

Heidi turned to me. 'Helene will keep me company. We may only talk…'

'Oh, so you speak Polish?' I asked, but I already knew her answer by the way she'd spoken in English to the girl.

'One doesn't only need words to communicate,' she replied.

'I'll finish my drink.' I went and sat down beside the auburn haired girl and turned to her. 'My name is Tess. What's your name? I won't touch or hurt you,' I said in Polish.

'Sienna,' she replied, her voice barely audible.

My heart wept at the uncertainty they faced and that I faced, too. I wanted only to reassure her that I would help her and her friends.

Stefan began talking to his chosen girl in Polish. He hadn't even asked her name. Maybe he preferred them nameless, or perhaps he liked to choose their names, the way he'd already altered mine. Stefan put his hand on her bare leg and I saw how he blatantly moved it between her thighs. Her whole body went rigid and Stefan picked up his glass and raised it to her lips. She turned her head to decline but he tipped the liquid into her mouth. She gulped and swallowed and the drink spilled down her chin and onto her vest.

With his face inches from hers, he slowly wiped his fingers across her lips. 'Better?'

Her chin quivered and she didn't reply. Stefan cared nothing for her vulnerability or fear.

When he took her hand and stood up, the girl resisted until Stefan reached for her arm and hauled her to her feet. He said in low Polish tones. 'Do you want to go to your new home or would you rather return to your family with nothing to contribute?'

Blackmail. To perform lewd acts with him and God knows who else in the future, or resist and be sent back to poverty.

'I do want to go home,' she replied quietly.

'I'll take care of you. Is that clear?' His tone left no room for argument.

Unless someone stood in to defend her or she fought back, what choice did she have?

I watched, feeling sick and horrified, as he forcibly led her towards the stairway that led to the cabins.

As I turned to the girl beside me, an ear splitting scream came from below, followed by a terrible wailing that sent chills through me. I jumped up and ran through the doorway that led to the cabins. Stefan and the girl were at the bottom of the stairs. I hurried down and saw the blonde girl, taken by Gavin, now half-dressed and talking through gasping sobs. I caught some of her words.

'On the floor, collapsed...'

Heidi appeared and shoved me aside. 'What's happened?'

Stefan ran to the end cabin, pursued by Heidi.

The girl who'd been with Stefan clasped the blonde girl to her, protective.

I dashed into my cabin, grabbed a jumper and passed it to the blonde girl. She took it gratefully and pulled it on. When Heidi began to scream I hurried down the passageway, and from the doorway I saw Gavin sprawled on his back and filling the space between the bunk and the wall.

I watched on as Heidi slapped Gavin's cheek, which looked pale and lifeless. Stefan pressed his fingers to Gavin's neck to search for a pulse and when he looked up at Heidi and shook his head she fell upon Gavin and sobbed. She breathed into his mouth and after a few moments she knelt over him and began chest compressions.

But I saw how she floundered and didn't know the way to resuscitate.

'Move Heidi! I'll try,' Stefan ordered.

'I'll call the coastguard - they'll send an air ambulance,' I said.

Stefan swung around and held up his hand. 'No!'

I pulled the phone from my pocket.

Stefan jumped up, lunged towards me and made a grab for my phone. 'Put that away.'

'Stefan?' Heidi cried. 'Help me.'

She pounded Gavin's chest.

I held my phone out of his reach. 'Gavin is dying and needs help.'

Stefan's eyes flared. 'Give me your phone.'

He made a grab for it again and I jumped back. 'Listen, I won't call if you help Gavin.'

Stefan turned back to where Gavin lay. 'Move, Heidi.'

Sobbing, she scrambled back.

Stefan grasped Gavin's ankles and with considerable effort, hauled his bulk into the larger space. He knelt beside him and began to compress his chest. Then he tilted Gavin's head back and breathed into his mouth.

With both Stefan and Heidi distracted, I reached for both girls' hands and mouthed, 'Let's go.'

They needed no further encouragement and we sprinted back up to the lounge where Gil stood guard over Sienna.

'Where's Helene?' I asked Gil.

'I thought she came down after Heidi.'

'I didn't see her.' I turned to Sienna. 'Where's Helene?' But she shook her head. She either didn't know or wasn't prepared to say.

I turned to Gil. 'You must have seen where she went?'

'I didn't. I came down to see what had happened and when I came back up she'd gone. She can't get far.'

I ran to the sofa and reached beneath the cushion for the gun.

I turned to Gil. 'There's been a change of plan. Gavin's dead, his heart I think, unless Stefan can resuscitate him. He won't let me call for help but I'm going to. It's probably too late. Don't try to stop me.' I lifted the gun and pointed it at Gil. But I had no idea if the gun was loaded. 'Are you prepared to help these girls?'

Gil held his hands up. 'My hands are tied. But yours aren't.' He nodded at the gun. 'Be careful with that.'

'I want the key to your boat.'

'I don't have it,' he replied.

'Course you do.'

He shook his head. 'No, I don't.'

'Come with us, Gil.' But I already knew I wasted my breath. And I had no intention of hurting him.

'I'm taking the girls. Don't try to stop me...or us.' I jabbed the gun in his direction. 'I will use it if I have to.' I paused, and for a few moments he looked back at me, but without animosity or threat. 'But I don't think you want to. I think you want to help, or at least, not stop us.'

He gave the smallest of nods.

'This isn't the first time, is it?' I asked.

'No, but it will be my last.'

I wanted to ask him why - why he stayed loyal to Stefan. But the girls needed help, and fast.

'I'll go and help Gavin,' Gil said, decisively. 'You stay with the girls.'

'What about Helene?'

'I'll find her,' he replied. 'She'll be hiding somewhere on the boat or the pier.' Then he turned abruptly and headed through the doorway to the cabins below.

I knew Stefan would come back up soon. Maybe he'd revive Gavin, but I doubted he'd try for long, and he wouldn't risk losing the girls.

The moment Gil disappeared, I turned to the girls. 'Quickly.'

Without speaking they ran with me to the upper deck, and one by one, we stepped down the boarding ramp and onto the pier.

The girl who'd been with Gavin touched my arm. 'I didn't do anything to him.'

'I know. But did he hurt you?' I asked.

'He pulled off my clothes and touched me. Then he began breathing funny and clutching his chest, and collapsed.' She began to weep again.

'It's not your fault. He is to blame.' I turned to the girls. 'Wait here one moment.'

I sprinted to the end of the pier to the smaller boat. I jumped on board, activated the torch on my phone and looked to see if the key had been left in the ignition or lay close-by. As I suspected, no key to aid our escape. 'Damn!' I climbed back onto the pier and raced back to the girls who stood huddled together. I looked towards the fort and gestured. 'We must hide and I'll message for help.'

'What will happen to us?' asked Sienna.

'You'll be protected by the authorities the moment they know why you were brought here,' I said. 'You're victims of trafficking.' I turned and pointed back at the yacht. 'They're criminals. But first we must hide.'

35

Would Gil be true to his word and find and protect Helene? Or would he tell Stefan we'd fled the yacht before he could find out for himself?

From what I'd seen of the fort earlier, there'd been rooms tucked away that could conceal us. I held the gun in my pocket and motioned for the three girls to go in front. I followed until we reached the top step at the entrance to the fort.

'Tread carefully. There are sheer drops, pools of water and holes.'

With hands outstretched, we splashed our way through the narrow room I'd come through earlier with Stefan, now pitch black and covered with several inches of freezing water, then up more steps onto the mezzanine that circled the interior.

I pulled out my phone which lit up the few feet around us. No signal. Damn!

'I don't want to go further,' said Sienna, and she let out a sob beside me.

I stopped and held out my hand. 'I'll help you, but we must stay quiet. If Stefan hears us, he'll find us.'

I felt a cold hand reach for mine and I clasped it in return. I saw the whites of Sienna's eyes inches from mine and sensed her fear within as her breaths came quickly and sounded above the thudding of my heart.

I turned and looked behind me, and in the darkness there seemed no sign or sound of anyone approaching. For now, it seemed Stefan remained on the yacht with Gavin.

The blonde girl came forward and said. 'I worked nights - my eyes are sharp. Let me lead with you.'

I nodded. 'Good.'

'Use your hands,' she said. 'Stay close.'

As we passed a gap in the wall, I heard the swell and hush of the ocean below, and above that the wind that echoed through the fort like voices chanting a mournful song.

We drew alongside another gap in the wall and I thought I detected a pale and distant light out to sea. Another boat?

'Keep moving,' I whispered, and their feet shuffled behind us.

'Is he dead?' asked Sienna who still clutched my hand.

'I think so, but they might save him,' I whispered in reply.

How could I contact anyone without a signal, or in return anyone be able to contact me? Maybe I could find the girls a hiding place and sneak back to the yacht for the WiFi? Yes, that might work.

At the far end of the fort, we came to a narrow flight of steps that led to the upper level.

'Follow me, and hold the rail,' I said.

We climbed the dozen or so steps onto a narrower mezzanine. As I turned to the others a voice echoed through the building.

'Tessa?'

My heart thundered and I clasped my phone against me to conceal the light.

'I want to help you,' Heidi cried. 'Gavin is alive. Where are you?'

I heard her footsteps echo along the floorboards below.

'Stefan forced us to do this. Where are you?' she called, insistent, and her voice grew more desperate as she neared.

Surely Stefan was with her?

And could Gavin really be recovering?

'Please, Tessa!' Heidi cried in a feeble and apologetic tone.

'We must hide from them,' the blonde girl said in Polish.

She was right, and my instinct told me to keep moving. Heidi would survive whether she was with us or not, and right now I wanted Heidi nowhere near us.

'Keep going,' I whispered. But I was all too conscious of the sounds of our footsteps upon the floorboards.

The blonde girl tapped my hand. 'A room.'

I turned her way and I felt my way into the dark space. 'In here,' I whispered.

I felt a rush of cold air against my skin and through my hair, and could make out the faint outline of a window. The room, no bigger than five by five feet, felt chilled and cramped, but if we remained still and silent it would conceal us. I edged closer to the window and peered out. Above the sounds of the waves that rose against the walls of the fort below, I caught another sound.

I leaned over the window ledge and craned my neck through the gap.

Fifty or so metres away I saw the distinct lights of a vessel. It seemed to be moving nearer. My heart bounded when I recognised the men inside the dimly lit cabin. There was Roddy with his long hair tied back, and Victor, tall and wiry. I pulled my phone from my pocket, activated the torch and beamed it in their direction.

The day before sailing out on the yacht, I'd shared my concerns with Roddy. And when I'd discovered precisely where we were headed, I'd messaged Roddy who'd replied that the location for the rendezvous seemed too remote and suspicious to be above board.

Thank God I had shared my reservations with him.

Clearly, he'd been concerned enough to risk setting out after us. I waved my phone back and forth until finally Victor and then Roddy looked our way, and *The Endeavour* made a swift turn in our direction.

The girl by my side leaned through the gap. 'I think there's a ladder.'

I reached over the ledge and touched a metal rung. I leaned further and shone my phone. 'Yes,' I whispered. I pulled on the metal frame which seemed secure.

The Endeavour rose up and down on the waves and came close to the fort.

I turned to the girls and whispered. 'Do you feel strong enough to climb down a ladder to a safe boat below?'

They murmured their agreement.

'The men in the boat are my son, Victor, and my good friend, Roddy. They'll help us and take you to England, and away from these evil monsters.'

I watched the boat attempt to line up against the side of the fort, or as close as they could safely get.

A familiar figure appeared on the deck below.

'Roddy,' I called. 'We're coming down.'

'Careful,' he said. 'You don't know how secure it is.'

'It might be tricky for them to keep the boat close to the wall. Be careful,' I warned the girls. I helped the blonde girl onto the ledge and held her as she lowered herself onto the ladder. I heard Roddy encouraging her from below.

I leaned over and watched her descend the ladder, until finally, I saw her draw level and make a nimble leap onto the deck.

The two remaining girls were eager and quick to follow their friend. I feared for Helene hiding somewhere, but prayed that Gavin's collapse or Gil's help might prevent any immediate harm to her.

'Tessa?'

I spun around.

Heidi stood in the doorway and beamed a torch in my eyes. 'Where are they?'

'Don't try to stop us,' I warned.

'You have to return with me,' she pleaded.

'No way.'

'But you have to.' There was a desperation in her tone.

'Why?'

'Because Stefan's threatened to kill Helene if you don't.'

'Gil said he'd protect her.'

'Stefan and Gil had a fight and Gil's locked in the engine room.'

'Can't you let him out?'

'Stefan has the keys and Gil's injured.' She grabbed my arm. 'You have to help me.'

'Why should I?'

'Stefan wants you back. You don't know what he's capable of.'

'Yes, I do know, which is why I'm never going back.'

The whites of her eyes pierced the darkness and she gripped my arm. 'You don't know him. He'll stop at nothing to get what he wants.'

'He sent you to persuade me?'

'If you go he'll never leave you alone. He knows where you live and you'll give in, again and again.'

I replied with resolution. 'I'm not you, Heidi.' I pulled her hand off me and clambered into the gap. Then I felt Heidi's hands on my arm, and she hauled me back inside. Adrenaline burned through me as I struggled against her grip, and we both stumbled. That's when I heard the metallic clunk of the gun hit the floor.

I froze.

Heidi looked down at the gun.

Without hesitation, I shoved her back as hard as I could and heard her body hit the floor. But I ignored her cries and instead grappled for the gun, located and clasped it and shoved it in my pocket. Then I clambered through the gap and reached for the ladder with my feet.

I'd only taken three rungs when I heard a creak of metal against stone, and the ladder rocked beneath me as one side tilted away from the wall. My feet slipped and for some moments I hung on by my hands alone. I swung both feet and secured a rung, but I sensed in seconds the ladder would come away from the wall. I scrambled down, taking two rungs at a time and with each step the ladder wobbled precariously. I glanced over my shoulder and saw Roddy on the deck six or so feet beneath, just as I heard a terrible scraping and felt the ladder come loose from the wall.

I screamed and made a leap for the deck.

Roddy didn't move aside but instead held out his arms. I crashed headlong into him and we sprawled onto the deck. I heard a thunderous crash beside me as the ladder landed.

I lay across Roddy with my face pressed into his neck. 'Are you alive?' I whispered.

'Course I am you daft lass.'

I lifted my face and looked into his eyes. 'You're a lifesaver.' I kissed him quickly on the lips then scrambled to my feet. I reached out my hand, which Roddy took, and I hauled him to his feet.

'Are you sure you're OK?' I said.

He pulled his coat straight and paused for a moment. 'I am now I know you're OK. That was way too fucking close.'

'You're not kidding,' I said, then we turned to where the ladder had crashed, and swung out over the side of the boat. Thank God it hadn't landed on us or the girls.

Roddy marched up to the ladder, lifted one end, and in a single powerful motion, pushed it over the side. 'A bloody death trap.'

'But it did help us down first,' I said.

'I know how much you like to make a stage entrance, but that was just showing off.'

I grimaced. 'Stop it!'

'Tessa!'

I looked back up to see Heidi's dimly lit face peering over the ledge.

'Don't leave me here.'

'Go back to Gavin,' I called. Heidi's loyalties didn't stray beyond Stefan's grasp.

The Endeavour's engine rumbled and we turned away from the fort. The three girls sat huddled together on the bench.

I hurried with Roddy into the cabin.

Victor, who had hold of the wheel, turned to me. 'Are you OK? Who are they?'

I hugged him as he steered the boat. 'We must take them somewhere safe. They've been trafficked from Poland. There's still one girl on the yacht, Helene.'

'We should help her,' said Victor, and he handed the wheel over to Roddy.

'Thank God you both came,' I said.

'I knew it would be illegal,' Roddy turned to me and said firmly, 'I should have stopped you coming.'

'But I had to come. Let me off at the pier so I can find Helene. I'll bargain with Stefan.'

Roddy shook his head. 'Too risky. I alerted the Dutch coastguard. They'll be here soon.'

'By boat or helicopter?' I asked.

'Both.'

The radio sprang to life. '*Endeavour, Endeavour*, come in.'

Roddy picked up the radio. 'Come in, over.'

'We're twenty minutes away by chopper. Boat will be longer, over. Stay away from the fort and yacht,' instructed the woman at the other end of the radio. 'I repeat, stay away.'

I turned to Roddy. 'I'm not waiting. Take me to the pier. Stefan will listen when I say the guards are coming.'

'No chance,' said Roddy. 'Who knows what stunts he'll pull.'

I grabbed the wheel. 'Trust me.' I pulled the gun from my pocket.

'Jesus, Tess! Where did you get that?' asked Roddy.

'I found it. I can't tell if it's loaded.'

Roddy held out his hand. 'Let me see.'

He took it, and pointing it away, pushed open the cartridge to reveal the barrel loaded with three gold-tipped bullets.

'I won't fire it,' I said. 'I'll only use it to bargain for Helene. They have another boat. Please, Roddy, take me to the pier and move away with Victor and the girls. But stay around so you can come back for us.'

He shook his head, still unconvinced.

'We have no choice,' I pleaded.

'What if you're hurt? You have Clara and Vic. I'll tackle Stefan. I've nothing, and no one to lose.'

'Stefan doesn't know you so you're a threat. I can get through to him.'

I knew by Roddy's expression, he doubted my judgement and wrestled with his conscience, but after a moment he switched off the cabin light, gripped the wheel decisively and swung *The Endeavour* towards the pier.

The engine quietened as we neared the yacht and I looked out to see if anyone was visible.

Other than the sounds of the sea, all seemed quiet - eerily quiet.

'Vic, look after the girls until the Coastguard arrives,' I whispered.

'Let me come with you,' Victor said.

'No, stay here.' I took his hand. 'I know what I'm doing.'

Roddy cut the engine and steered the boat alongside the pier.

I staggered as the bumper scraped against the wall.

Surely Stefan had heard the ladder rip away from the wall of the fort, or Heidi yelling at me. Had he heard our approach?

I reached out and gripped the ladder on the wall of the pier. *Nikita* loomed large and tall thirty feet away on the other side of the pier and I climbed the top two rungs and stepped onto the wall. With no stars or moon visible, I prayed I'd be concealed by darkness. I kept low and trod softly until I reached the boarding ramp. I detected no movement, shadows or sounds on the upper deck, but I figured that Heidi had returned by now and told Stefan of our escape and whereabouts.

Why weren't they up here preparing to depart, or out searching for us? The smaller speedboat at the end of the pier appeared still and empty.

My heartbeat thundered in my ears and sweat prickled my skin as I crept in silence. I walked up to the control room to find that it, too, was empty. I headed down to the living room, lit up but similarly deserted.

My forearm shook with my hand firmly on the revolver grip and finger pointing down past the trigger.

Were there other weapons hidden on board?

No doubt about it.

I wondered if it might be safer to hide the gun. If Stefan saw it, he'd perceive me as an immediate threat. By now he'd already believe I was. I moved cautiously through the doorway to the top of the stairway and crept down to the cabins. The door to Heidi and Gavin's cabin stood open, and the light was on.

Where was the engine room with Gil locked inside? Heidi had said Stefan had the key.

With the gun concealed behind my back, I approached Heidi and Gavin's cabin and peered inside, half expecting to see Gavin upright and recovering on the bunk. But instead I saw his lifeless form in the same position as when Stefan had tried to revive him. I opened the door wide and stepped closer. Gavin's lifeless eyes stared up at me. My hand went to my mouth as I stifled a sob. Heidi's husband of thirty years had died, and yet immediately afterwards she'd come to find us, had lied about his recovery and tried to persuade me to return with her to placate Stefan.

I jumped as a woman's cry shattered the silence, followed by a man shouting. I darted into the passageway. More screams and thuds came from behind the closed door where I stood.

Then above this, Stefan's growling tone. 'Shut up!' More cries followed. I twisted the door handle and it swung open to a scene that will never leave me. The girl, Helene, cowered on the bed and Stefan knelt over her. He held a knife inches from her chest. I glanced at Heidi, who leaned against the wall, sobbing.

If Stefan touched Helene with the knife, I wouldn't hesitate to shoot him. Anger coursed through me to see the brutality with which he threatened the girl and the terror in her eyes.

'Drop the knife, Stefan,' I said.

Stefan swung round to face me. Blood dripped from his nose and his eyes looked red and swollen. 'I knew you couldn't stay away from me for long.'

Helene saw her chance and rolled away from Stefan, leapt off the bed and darted to the corner of the cabin.

I drew the gun from behind my back and aimed it at him. I watched the surprise register in his eyes, but he barely flinched.

'Put the gun down, my love,' he said. 'Guns are dangerous in inexperienced hands.'

'Only when you put that knife down,' I replied, with a calmness that disguised the fury that boiled inside of me.

He wiped the blood from his face with the back of his hand. 'I won't hurt her, or anyone. I only wanted her to do as I asked. After all, I am offering her and her friends a better life. Where have you hidden the girls?'

Hadn't Heidi told him? Or had she, and he was calling my bluff?

'In the fort.'

'Why?'

'They're terrified. They think you'll hurt them. They came with the promise of honest work.'

'Are they really that naive?' Stefan scoffed. 'Are you that naive?'

'How could I have known you were trading girls? I'd never have come.'

'It makes no difference. You're one of us. And you should know I look after all the girls who come and work for me, including these girls.'

And I thought - he means he deceives them, says he cares and sleeps with them, then discards and passes them on for more men to exploit and abuse. Nothing less than evil and criminal exploitation.

For a moment I paused, my mind torn between threatening him or playing for time before the Coastguard arrived.

'Yes, I am with you, and I want to stay. On condition you don't hurt any of these girls. That's all I ask.' I lowered the gun and walked up to Stefan. 'You know I want to be with you, don't you?'

His eyes narrowed. 'And yet your loyalties appear divided.'

'I want what's best for you, and myself included.'

He took hold of my wrist but without force. 'Take me to the girls. We'll bring them back here together.'

Stefan turned to Heidi. 'Keep the girl here.'

He held out the knife to Heidi, and with reluctance and a trembling hand, she reached out and took it.

My God! That was how much he trusted Heidi and the hold he knew he had over her. I had no idea what was going through Heidi's mind. Safer to expect nothing of her, but to assume the worst.

The part I played could go either way for us, but would Stefan be willing to trust me?

And who was really fooling who?

'The gun isn't loaded, Tessa. By all means bring it if it makes you feel in control,' said Stefan.

And another lie that spewed from his mouth. He knew damn well it was loaded.

'We might need it to persuade the girls that we mean them no harm,' I said, realising the irony of my words.

'We're in the middle of the ocean so their options are limited.'

'They might risk swimming and drowning rather than come back,' I said. 'We must be kind but persuasive.' I looked at Helene, huddled and terrified in the corner of the room. 'We shouldn't leave Helene here. It's not fair on Heidi.'

Stefan nodded, then spoke to the girl in Polish. 'Come with us to find your friends.'

Her eyes flitted between Stefan and me.

'You'll be safe,' I said.

Slowly, she came and stood by my side, and the sound of her sharp and shallow breaths reminded me of my responsibility to protect her. Despite Stefan's previous threats and presence, she seemed to trust me, and I would follow through with her trust whatever it took. I glanced towards Heidi. But whose side was she on? And how could she appear so outwardly normal with Gavin lying dead next door? Was she in shock? My head reeled with questions, but I kept a cool exterior.

On the upper deck, I scanned round to see if *The Endeavour* was in view, or for any other lights. Roddy must have sailed to the far side of the fort. And why was the coastguard taking so long?

I deliberately held back and Stefan led the way down the boarding ramp and onto the pier. If I were stronger, I'd have wrestled and pushed him into the water - that would give us time to get away.

From the top of the ramp I raised the gun. 'Stefan?'

He turned around. 'What are you doing?'

'If you come closer I'll fire.'

He lifted his hands up. 'I already told you it isn't loaded.'

But he knew otherwise and the tension in his voice betrayed him.

I tilted the gun, braced myself and fired above his head. The bullet blasted the air and echoed through the fort as Stefan threw himself to the ground. My ears numbed with a ringing sound, but through it came Stefan's voice.

He stumbled to his feet. 'I love you. You fucking know I do.'

I laughed. 'Is that why you were fucking Heidi, you bastard? Back away from the ramp, or I'll shoot and won't miss.'

He raised his hands again. 'Gil will return the girls. We'll bring them back here together - you and me.'

'And where is Gil?' I asked.

'He's here somewhere.'

'And more lies,' I spat. 'You've locked him up. You've hurt and locked your friend away.'

'I made a mistake bringing you along,' Stefan went on. 'You're far more than I thought you were. You're strong and smart and I admire you for that. I thought you wanted to be with me?'

'I'm not your fool.' I jabbed the gun. 'Not like the others. Now back off.'

He took a step towards the ramp. 'You want to protect the girls? We'll protect them together.'

'Put a foot on that and I'll shoot. Don't make me do it.' I held my arms out rigid with the gun aimed his way and my finger resting on the trigger. My hands shook and I thought I might lose my grip. In my peripheral vision I sensed movement at the front of the yacht. And then beneath my feet I felt the rumble of the engine as it sprung to life.

I watched confusion sweep across Stefan's face.

The yacht began to inch away from the pier wall and Stefan made a lunge for the ramp.

I aimed the gun low at his legs and fired. My shot missed and rang out, deafening me again.

Stefan tripped forwards, but gained a grip on the ramp as it came free from the pier. He clung on by his hands and swung his legs to try to gain a hold.

'Help me,' he called.

But I only watched - willing him to plunge into the water.

The yacht moved into reverse between the walls. With one more push, Stefan swung his leg onto the ramp and clawed his way up. I climbed onto the edge and rammed my heel down on his fingers.

He yelled and his hands slipped an inch, but still he clung on. I looked into the blackness of his eyes and saw desperation, but more than that, I glimpsed the evil he could no longer disguise. I perched on the edge, stretched out my legs and as he attempted again to climb up, I thrust my foot beneath his chin and with a final yell, he plummeted into the water and disappeared beneath the surface.

Helene grabbed my shoulders and pulled me back onto the deck and when I stood up and turned around, I saw Heidi sobbing nearby. She stumbled forwards and leaned over the edge of the yacht and down at the water.

I leaned over, too, and in the darkness could make out Stefan splashing about as he struggled to gain a hold on the harbour wall.

'He'll drown,' cried Heidi.

I saw she still held the knife and with no resistance, I took it from her.

'He won't drown,' I replied. 'But he will be arrested.' I raised my arm and flung the knife over the far side of the yacht

Distraught and defeated, Heidi's legs crumpled and she sank onto the deck.

Still gripping the gun, I ran up to the control deck to see who was steering.

Victor turned around, his hands firmly on the wheel and his eyes wide. 'Did you shoot him?'

'No, but he's overboard, where he belongs.'

Victor adjusted the steering to keep *Nikita* steady in reverse.

'Do you know what you're doing?'

'Not really.' He turned and grimaced. 'But I'm trying to steer this monster of a yacht without destroying her and us in it.'

The yacht shuddered as she scraped the pier wall and Victor adjusted the wheel.

I peered through the window and spotted *The Endeavour* on the far side of the harbour wall. I could just see the girls' outlines as they watched on from afar. They were safe and so was Helene, and I felt a wave of relief. I'd done what I needed to do and with the help of my friends.

I heard yelling and saw that Stefan had climbed onto the pier. He stormed along the wall, and raged and ranted obscenities into the darkness. He'd finally lost control of those he'd so carefully manipulated and coerced to carry out his dirty work.

I ran back down to the deck to where Heidi muttered incoherently between sobs. Helene looked on at Stefan, who appeared to have lost his mind, as he cursed my name from the pier. All of a sudden, he turned and ran towards the speedboat. But who had the keys?

I knelt beside Heidi, and her eyes followed Stefan.

'This is the most vile and cruel thing I've seen or experienced. And to think you and Stefan thought I'd go along with it.'

Heidi scraped her hands through her hair. 'This was all Stefan's doing.'

'You're his accomplice. He couldn't have done this without you.'

Slowly, she looked about her as though she searched for the right words to say. She couldn't even meet my eyes.

'I had no choice,' she said feebly.

'Yes, you did. And what about Gavin?'

She seemed to revive her senses briefly at the mention of his name and finally she lifted her eyes to mine. 'He's been ill for so long.' Then she lowered her eyes again and wept.

So she'd been expecting Gavin to die, and not only that, she'd allowed him to come out to sea and hook up with a girl, no more than a child, who had been forced into being with him. Was the girl supposed to have been a farewell gift from Stefan? And Heidi herself had appeared only too willing to take advantage of the girls.

I felt sick and revolted by all of them.

The yacht swung away from the pier and towards *The Endeavour.*

I turned to Heidi again. 'Stefan has poisoned you all.'

No wonder Judi had chosen to stay at home. No excuses though - she would have been aware of and involved in the planning and execution of the whole operation.

Above the thoughts that raced through my mind, I detected another sound. I turned and spotted a light that pierced the night sky, and grew brighter as it approached.

Was the pier wide enough to land a helicopter?

Heidi looked up. 'You knew they were coming?

'I knew this must be criminal.'

She grabbed my hand. 'Isn't losing my husband enough for you?'

I pushed her hand away. 'You knew exactly what you were doing. And this isn't the first time. Stefan fooled me initially, but I soon grew suspicious. And Suzanne warned me, too.'

'Suzanne is only the tip of the iceberg,' said Heidi, and her voice shook. 'Stefan's left a mountain of shattered hearts and lives.'

I stood up and scanned up and down the pier for Stefan. The smaller boat was still moored and I wondered if he'd fled to the fort to hide.

I turned back to Heidi. 'And the pregnant girl washed up on the beach? I saw Gil on the beach that day.'

Heidi nodded and fresh tears fell. 'Another of Stefan's victims, and I cannot bear to think about that unborn child, a baby that I believe was Stefan's. So many times I've wrestled with my conscience. We tried to reason with Stefan, but he wouldn't back down and my hands were tied.'

'Your hands aren't tied now. You must share all that you know with the authorities.'

But I doubted Heidi was capable of honesty, or only selectively so.

Now that their crimes had been uncovered, I figured Heidi would do her utmost to incriminate Stefan whilst minimising the extent of her own involvement. I might be no detective, but I imagined how their minds worked - with deception, lies and self-interest at the fore.

Whatever else they'd been involved in, and I felt certain tonight's crime was only one amongst many, this alone would put them all away.

36

The following afternoon, still feeling shaken by the dramatic and disturbing events of the previous night, I gave my statement and evidence to the police. Afterwards, I was allowed some minutes to talk with the young women who sheltered in comfortable rooms in a safe house nearby, but under close guardianship. Each girl spoke with emotion of her relief and appreciation at being rescued, which made me cry, and before I left, they each hugged me in turn. I discovered that the petite blonde girl who'd been molested by Gavin had only recently turned sixteen - the same age as Clara. What she'd endured and gone through would leave its mark on her, and on all of them. And their ordeal wasn't yet over as they had to await further questioning before being allowed home or granted safety, here.

All four had wanted to escape the poverty of their lives in their home country for a better life, and to be able to earn and send money to their families. But from what they told me, they'd been deceived and lied to about the work they'd be doing and the money they'd earn in the UK. During their transportation they'd been locked up for three days in the back of a truck, hungry and with barely enough water to stay hydrated. By their accounts, even Gil, with assistance from the truck driver, had chained them in the boat and only given them minimal sustenance.

In the interview room at the station, I'd sat opposite two officers - a young man and a senior officer in her middle years, Detective Walsh - who'd been leading the investigation into the drowning of the woman on the beach. Initially, they questioned me as if I, too, were involved and implicated, but it seemed the girls had openly exposed Stefan, Heidi and Gil, whilst citing me as their rescuer, along with Victor and Roddy.

They recorded my interview, but I watched the young male officer take notes as I spoke.

'I find it extraordinary that you were the person to discover the pregnant woman's body on the beach on the exact same day that you had your interview with the Temples,' said Detective Walsh.

Her tone and narrowed eyes revealed her mistrust of the extent of my involvement.

'I can't explain it either,' I said. 'But however strange the coincidence, it happened. When I spoke to the police, I mentioned I'd met Gil on the beach that morning, but I couldn't have imagined he'd be connected. Now I don't believe that was a coincidence. He'd told me he was taking his dog to a vet's appointment. You could check if he ever attended any appointment. Heidi said she believed Stefan was the father of the drowned woman's baby, so he had to have been involved in her death. Probably responsible for her murder, too.'

Detective Walsh nodded. 'OK, a matter we will be discussing further with these people. Although whether we will ever locate Stefan Temple is another matter.'

'Maybe he's still hiding in the fort,' I said. 'There are hidey-holes and it was pitch black.'

'Every inch and corner has been searched, and during daylight, so that is unlikely,' she replied. 'Do you know if Stefan is a strong swimmer?'

'Oh, yes, extremely,' I said. 'Although surely too dark and cold and he wouldn't have known the direction to swim.'

'Then he may have drowned,' she replied. 'In which case we may never find him, unless his body is washed up by the tide.'

'Have you considered that someone, an ally, picked him up - a boat that none of us saw?'

She shook her head. 'Unlikely, given that neither the skipper of *The Endeavour* nor the coastguard spotted another vessel.'

The realisation that Stefan might have escaped prosecution sent another wave of nausea through me.

'I assume you've questioned Judi Temple?' I said.

The officers looked at one another before turning to face me once more.

'Judi hasn't been located either. Her car is missing and we understand from Gil Cooney that she'd been visiting a client.

We've used his phone to try to get a response from her, but so far, nothing.'

'Then you must realise that Judi may have been aiding Stefan to escape and that's why he hasn't been found?' I said, stating what seemed obvious.

'I don't know how she could have,' said the young officer. 'Do they have another boat?'

'Not that I know of, but that doesn't mean she doesn't know people who do and who could have stepped in or been nearby to help. They have money and wealthy friends and connections.'

The young officer listened attentively and scribbled more notes.

'We'll locate her soon enough,' replied Detective Walsh.

'Good luck with that,' I said, 'I can't understand why she wouldn't answer the phone to Gil. They're in a relationship, unless she'd been forewarned by him or was already out of the country. They use the private airport at Rushmore.'

I feared now that Stefan and Judi had disappeared into the untraceable ether and outwitted every one of us - every one of their victims, as well as the authorities. Stefan had altered his surname to Temple since his student days, and who knew if he had other pseudonyms or identities he could call on if needed. He had the money, connections and more essentially, the deviousness to do so.

'Rest assured, we won't let up until they're found,' Detective Walsh said. 'What we unearth may warrant a life sentence for Mr Temple, Dudek or whatever name and guise he may go under.'

I felt doubtful, and worse still, fearful. My phone buzzed on the table in front of me. I saw it was a message from Mum with the first line, 'Important!'

'Do you mind if I read this?' I said, and looked up.

They nodded agreement and I opened the message.

"My darling, I discovered Stefan Dudek was thrown out of Uni for setting up a prostitution ring with students - young women who could earn him money by selling their services to wealthy businessmen in Bath. He hadn't recruited more than a handful of students, but the disclosure and witnesses resulted in Stefan receiving an immediate suspension. It's all on police records."

I handed the phone to Detective Walsh. 'More damning evidence.'

What if Heidi was right when she warned that Stefan refused to let go of someone he wanted to keep in his life? If he was alive, as I strongly suspected, what might happen if I became one of those people?

'Do you know of any other women from overseas who may be linked to Stefan - perhaps you saw or heard something whilst working? Telephone conversations, files, conversations between him and Judi, Gil or the Jacksons?'

And the list of girls' names came to mind - the list from the computer file I'd spotted in the finance folder and that subsequently disappeared. A list that had seemed peculiar at the time I'd stumbled across it.

I nodded slowly and rested my hands on the table. 'A list of names of women who may have been trafficked, although I have no details or proof. Had I even suspected the Temples of any criminal activity at the time I'd have come to you, but I didn't make the links.'

'Do you recall where you found the names precisely or any of the names listed?' asked the male officer, with his pen poised.

I nodded once.

And as I spoke, and remembered every single name in full and in the exact sequence that they had appeared on the screen, the enormity of what I spoke caused my throat to tighten and my eyes to fill with tears.

'Nadia Pawlowski
Carin Wozniak
Wynne Zajac
Gertie Pawlak
Sandy Gorski
Bernadette Duda
Helena Krol
Sabrina Nowicki
Daisy Jablonski
Maria Wojcik
Ova Adams
Ulrika Madsiar
Maddie Klinger

Carmen Janus
Apollonia Hofman
Bella Kaplya
Sixteen females in total.'

'Both officer's eyes remained fixed and unblinking right up until I'd spoken the final name. And I could see by the firm line of their mouths and how they swallowed that they struggled to digest my words.

'How can you remember them?' Detective Walsh asked quietly.

'I don't know, but I can.' I gave a small shrug. 'When I saw these names, I thought it strange and out of place, with them all foreign sounding and female, rather like my surname and my family heritage.'

The two officers exchanged a sceptical look.

'I can repeat them, and you'll hear the same names,' I said.

'And do you recall seeing or hearing any other details that could link the Temples to illegal foreign imports - and more specifically, people trafficking?'

I shook my head. 'I don't think so, although I wasn't given access to the accounts, which Stefan insisted he handled.'

'We've seized laptops from Lorton Hold and the Gatehouse, and have Gil Cooney and Mr and Mrs Jackson's phones, which I'm certain will reveal more,' the male officer said.

'Have you searched the Jackson's residence in Saltburn? When I went with Stefan they had a foreign speaking maid, Polly, and there was something not right about her position in their home and in how Heidi treated her. She may be unpaid or trafficked. Plus she may be able to help with the investigation.'

The younger officer nodded. 'OK, thank you.'

What happened to the sixteen girls on the list? Could they be traced to homes in the UK? Would the police be able to force Stefan and Judi, if or when they located them, and Gil or Heidi, to reveal their whereabouts?

I talked through the events and details from yesterday and I knew that my statement would match what the girls, Roddy and Victor had said, as well as my messages and phone calls to them, too. I had serious concerns about what Heidi and Gil would say. They may still protect or back Stefan and Judi despite everything that had gone on. Both Heidi and Gil had been duplicitous and were up to their necks in guilt and culpability. I also imagined they'd want to present themselves as duped and controlled by Stefan. And for sure Judi knew every detail of the plans, too. The fact she'd stayed away didn't absolve her in any way. I strongly suspected that Heidi and even Gil would do their utmost to incriminate me.

But what saddened and distressed me the most was how Judi and Heidi had thought nothing of betraying their gender.

37

Late that evening I stood in the shower and hoped the water might wash away some of the sadness and stress of the past few days. I reflected again on my fleeting but devastating relationship with Stefan. I wanted to banish all thoughts and memories of him from my mind. If only that were possible. I didn't want to end up feeling emotionally wrung out like Suzanne, and unable to let go of the memories, despite knowing that was the only right thing to do. I felt angry and tearful periodically, and so I'd contacted Noah's hypnotherapist to arrange an initial session to see if he could help me in any way. I no longer worked for Aztec Imports, given that there were no business owners - Gil had been detained and there was still no trace of Stefan or Judi. I hadn't been paid any wages either and money was already tight.

I squeezed some shower gel into my palm and rubbed my hands together to form a lather. I moved my hands over my shoulders and breasts to my waist and the small puncture wound which looked almost healed over. I smoothed my finger carefully around the wound before placing my finger at the centre. I pressed gently until a searing pain tore through me and I cried out. My head swam and I staggered and fell against the wall and slumped to the floor of the shower.

I looked down and saw fresh blood oozed from the wound. And I noticed that the tip of my finger bled, too. I wiped the blood from my finger and spotted a pinprick. Feeling light headed still, I stood up and stepped beneath the flow of water to wash away the blood that had dripped down my belly and between my legs. I moved aside from the flow of water, then with my thumb and forefinger placed on either side of the wound, I squeezed the skin. I watched as an object about half a centimetre long protruded from the wound. I stepped out of the shower and went to the cabinet over the sink and reached inside for my tweezers.

I took a deep breath in and with the tweezers in hand I pincered the object, then slowly drew it out.

'Jesus Christ!' I said aloud.

I held up a two centimetre long, two millimetre wide splinter of glass streaked with blood, which can only have remained lodged inside of me since the skylight fell in three weeks ago. No wonder the wound hadn't healed and I'd experienced intermittent pain. I wrapped the glass in a piece of toilet roll and set it on the side of the sink. Could there be more inside still? I sponged away the blood that seeped out and pressed a cotton wool bud against the cut. In contrast to before, I felt nothing, not a twinge or any tenderness. I looked down at the tissue wrapped around the glass on the side of the sink.

Did I want to keep a painful reminder of these past three weeks - traumatic, sad and troubled in every sense? I picked up the tissue, dropped it into the toilet and pressed the flush.

'Good riddance!'

38

'OK, you two. I know you won't be keen, but we need a family chat,' I announced. 'We have things to talk about, and Dad especially.'

Clara stood up and surprised me by saying, 'I'm up for that.'

'I hope this family chat won't be as horrible as the last,' said Victor. He paused and turned from Clara to me. 'Or will it?'

'Of course not,' I said, and remembered the tears and emotional fallout after I'd told the twins their father and I were separating. 'A lot has happened the past few weeks and we need to air anything we feel we want to share.'

'Come on then,' said Clara, and she turned and jogged up the stairs.

'OK, Vic?'

He nodded, but I saw the reluctance in his features. Poor Victor. Events over the past few weeks had been more than any teenager should have to face.

Clara carried her bean bag in from her bedroom, I perched on the desk stool and Victor opened the window and stood leaning against the windowsill with his arms folded.

'Who'd like to go first?' I turned to Noah.

'Me, if that's OK?' he said, and looked from Clara to Victor in turn.

They nodded in unison.

'I'll keep it brief.' He let out a long breath then turned to Victor. 'Firstly son, I want you to know how terrible I feel about stealing your bank card and your savings to spend on my addiction. I'm so sorry.'

Victor nodded once and his mouth set in a firm line.

Noah continued. 'Secondly and importantly, I've managed to sell my road bike, and I've transferred the money, plus fifty pounds interest, back into your account.'

We all looked at Victor who's features melted. He straightened up and walked over to Noah. Without speaking he leaned down and wrapped his arms around his Dad, who in turn hugged him back with his one good arm.

I looked at Clara and we exchanged smiles.

Vic really was such a wonderfully forgiving person, I thought, and hearing Noah accept full responsibility with an apology and acknowledgement of his problem filled me with hope.

When they drew apart, Noah said, 'I know I don't deserve that, but I hope that I can win back your respect and love in time. Thank you, son.' And Noah's eyes glistened with tears.

'Thanks, Dad. A shame about your road bike but you can always borrow mine.'

'Give me a month or two and I might take you up on that.' He looked down at his leg in plaster and frowned. 'And thirdly, as you know I've been having some hypnotherapy to help me tackle the gambling. I admit to having felt dubious initially when your Mum suggested this, but I tried to keep an open mind. And it is my being open minded that has given me the biggest breakthrough yet. Jameel says he rarely treats individuals who are as receptive as I've been. I'm not suggesting I'm special or anything, but what I am saying is that I believe I'm cured.' He looked at the three of us in turn. 'I don't expect you to understand or even to believe this sudden turnabout, but I ask that you give me some time to prove it to you. I'm not asking for us to live together again. Trust must be earned and I hope eventually, it will be.'

As he spoke, tears filled my eyes. I could see that Noah believed what he said, and meant every word. His sincerity couldn't have been clearer to me, when I compared him to all the many times he'd denied his problem and lied to me. The steadiness of his voice, the directness of his gaze as he spoke made me feel more optimistic about his future.

I went to sit beside him on the bed.

Noah reached across for the box of tissues. He pulled one out and handed it to me and then one for himself.

I felt choked and emotional for all the right reasons.

'Would either of you children like to say something?' I said eventually and with a distinct wobble to my voice.

Clara stood up and clasped her hands in front of her. 'I have two things to say. The first is easy.' She paused. 'The second will be tough.' She took a deep breath.

When I'd called the twins up to talk with their Dad, I hadn't imagined either of them would have big announcements and my thoughts floundered as I considered what she might be about to say. Clara knew I'd been out with Stefan, but beyond that she didn't know the full extent of our involvement, and given that Noah was still hurting from the split I hoped she wasn't going to say anything that might fan the flames. Surely not?

She stood there and seemed to hesitate, as though choosing her words.

I felt more anxious than she looked. 'What is it darling? We'd all like to hear.'

'OK. I wanted to say how proud I am of Mum. Finding that poor pregnant woman on the beach was a horrible shock, then she started a new job, which I know she had high hopes for, but that ended up bringing her a whole heap of stress and upset. But look at you here - so strong, and I know how you've tried to keep up a brave face for us, despite everything going wrong.' She smiled and gave the smallest of nods that suggested she knew I'd been through far more than she would reveal. 'If it hadn't been for Mum, those four girls could be anywhere by now and going through all kinds of abuse.' Her voice cracked at the weight of her words.

'I only did what anyone would do,' I said.

She wiped her eyes. 'I don't believe that, Mum. You were super brave and smart and the police know it, too.'

'Thank you, Clara. My biggest regret is that I wish I'd shot Stefan in the leg to prevent him escaping. Until he's locked up, no girl or woman he goes near is safe.'

'The police will track him down,' said Clara.

'I hope you're right,' I replied. But I didn't share her optimism.

'And Victor, too,' Clara continued. 'What a real life hero my bro is - insisting on going all that way with Roddy and not knowing what they'd find when they got to Mum, helping to rescue those girls from that fort, and even with guns firing and helicopters whizzing overhead, steering that gigantic yacht away from that vile pig, Stefan. All my friends think Vic is amazing.'

'What?' said Victor, and his cheeks reddened. 'You've told your friends at school?'

'Well someone had to. You're too modest to share. Anyway, I could hardly not tell them, they were desperate to know the details and you were being all cagey.'

'You know I don't like blowing my own trumpet.'

'Well in this instance, you should. You're brilliant,' she said, proudly.

'Dear Clara,' said Noah. 'That is lovely of you to say. And it's all true.'

'But Mum's the real hero,' said Victor, looking at me. 'Those girls would be slaves by now if it wasn't for her.'

'He's right,' said Clara.

'Thank you, my darlings. A joint effort, I'd say. But until Stefan and Judi are found and convicted, I won't rest.'

By now I was feeling so emotional, I had to grab another tissue.

'There is one more thing,' said Clara. 'And I hope you'll all understand because I'm literally shaking.'

We all looked at her and I saw that her hands really were shaking.

'Don't worry, my love. Nothing you say could shock me, or any of us. Not after all we've been through the past few weeks.'

'OK,' she took a long breath in. 'You know Fleur?'

'Of course we know her, she pretty much lives here,' said Victor.

Clara looked at Victor and spoke boldly. 'Well, Fleur is more than my best friend. She's my girlfriend.' She paused and her cheeks grew pinker. 'I guess what I'm trying to tell you, is that I'm gay.'

Victor was the first to speak. 'Oh, I already guessed that, sis. But that's brilliant. I'm so glad you've told us at last.'

Clara looked at him and shook her head lightly. 'But I'm not sure I really knew myself until a few weeks ago.'

My heart thundered, but I smiled to reassure her. 'It's all good, my darling. I've been so wrapped up in my job, settling into our new home, and all our troubles, that I didn't

282

acknowledge what I realise I should have seen. In truth, what I probably did see. Now that you've opened up to us, of course it's clear how close you both are. And that is simply wonderful.'

'Really?' her face crumpled and she gave a gasp of relief now that she felt free of the burden she'd been holding inside.

I jumped off the bed, hurried over and wrapped my arms around her. 'Finding someone we like and want to spend time with is special and it doesn't matter what sex they are if you make one another happy.'

'Help me up,' said Noah.

I turned around and saw him struggling to lever his plastered leg over the side of the bed. Victor hurried over and handed him his crutch and we both helped him up. Victor and I stood close by as Noah took a couple of tentative steps towards Clara. She came forward and they met halfway.

I felt nervous about making my own announcement, and seeing the three of them so upbeat and welcoming of one another's news made me reluctant to interrupt. Perhaps I'd be better speaking to Noah first and then the twins.

But the issue was forced when Clara turned and said, 'So Mum, what's your news?'

'Oh, I'm sure anything I have to say can wait a day or so,' I said, and thought Noah's and Clara's news was quite enough for everyone to digest for today.

'No way,' said Victor. 'You were the one to call the family conference so we're going nowhere until you say something.'

'OK.' I looked from one expectant face to the next, knowing that what I said would impact all of them. What I couldn't anticipate was how well they'd take it. 'As you know, my departure from *The Endeavour* to Aztec Imports couldn't have been a more disastrous move - possibly the biggest mistake of my life.' And I thought, in more ways than they could ever imagine.

'But you didn't know what an evil bastard Stefan was,' said Victor.

'No, Vic, but I should have used my intuition. The whole set up seemed too good to be true, and of course, it was. The red flags were flapping in my face from day one.'

'So what will you do now? You'll need a job of some sort,' said Clara.

I nodded. 'Since that horrendous night last week, I've been reflecting and giving my future a lot of thought, and I've decided I need a radical change, once more. So, I've been busy contacting theatrical agents, and on Friday I went to visit two in Newcastle.'

'Ahh, so that's where you were,' said Vic, with a sly smile.

'Yes, sorry I was a bit cagey, but I didn't want to jinx anything.'

'How did you get on?' asked Noah, expectantly.

'Well, it seems I'm not over the hill with regards to parts in theatre and TV, and after my audition with Mike Polling, agent to several well known names in the industry, he rang me earlier to say he wants to take me on.'

'OMG, Mum! That's amazing! Who else does he agent for?' said Clara.

'I can hardly believe it, Ewan Campbell, Shona Horgan, James Malloy, plus several more well known names.'

'Bloody hell, Mum, you must have impressed him,' said Clara.

'Hard to believe after so many years away from the stage, but yes, I believe I did. He gave me an Alan Bennett monologue - 'Miss Fozzard finds her feet', to perform, well, part of it, and then I chose Hamlet's, 'To be or not to be,' soliloquy. If Maxine Price can do it, I thought, why not me? Anyway, he really liked them, and he's putting me forward for some auditions, which could be anywhere in the UK - TV, adverts, theatre, films. Which is why I felt nervous about telling you. It'll mean I could be away from home quite a bit, if I'm offered anything. I can't afford to be too choosy. And money will be tight until I get work.'

I looked at Noah and he gave the faintest of smiles, and knew that being the twins' Dad would be more important than ever. I knew that he'd still have problems, and his gambling may or may not resurface, but I was living independently and forging my own life and career again.

Clara and Victor came forwards and together put their arms around me. 'You totally deserve it Mum,' said Clara. 'I've always thought you should go back to acting, and I can't wait to see you perform!'

284

39

Six Months Later
The Apollo Theatre - London's West End

I stood in the wing waiting for the auditorium lights to dim and the audience to hush. This would be my final performance playing Nora in Ibsen's, *A Doll's House*. It had been an exhilarating experience performing such a well respected and challenging role in the West End for twelve weeks, but I missed Clara and Victor desperately and couldn't wait to pack my bags and return home and spend time with them. I'd originally been cast as Nora's understudy, but in a bizarre parallel to when I started performing at Hull Docks Theatre nineteen years ago, the leading lady had been unable to continue at the start of the run after she lost her partner in a car accident. A dreadful loss for her, but a fortuitous opportunity to relaunch my acting career.

My fictional husband for the play's duration, Torvald, stood in the opposite wing and gave me a quick salute. I held the skirts of my dress and curtseyed in reply. I'd decided that Tomas who played Torvald had been perfectly cast for the role and really wasn't so different off stage as he was on.

Finally, the lights overhead illuminated the stage and the audience fell silent.

A stage hand placed a pile of Christmas parcels in my arms and I walked onto the stage humming, 'The Holly and the Ivy', as my petticoats swished against my legs. A porter followed behind carrying a Christmas tree and basket. He handed it to Helen, my maid.

'Hide that Christmas tree, Helen,' I said. 'The children mustn't see it before I've decorated it.'

When I turned to the porter to tip him, a single and loud cough from the audience echoed around the auditorium and interrupted my concentration. Instinctively, my spine went rigid and my scalp prickled. For some moments my mind reeled and I felt oddly misplaced and disorientated. The empty silence lengthened around me until I felt a gentle hand upon my arm.

'Nora, do you want to pay the porter?'

In an instant I returned to the boards beneath my feet, the presence of the other actors and the stage lights overhead.

I took out my purse from my pocket. 'How much?' I asked the porter.

During the interval, Tomas, who played Torvald knocked on my dressing room door, and standing squarely in the doorway with his arms folded, asked me why I'd chosen tonight of all nights to portray Nora as highly strung.

'You're making Torvald nervous,' he said, and I sensed his irritation.

'I'm sorry. I'll try to tone it down.' I didn't attempt to make any excuses.

When the audience had returned to their seats, talking and laughing after their interval drinks, I stood in front of the monitor backstage and scanned along as many rows and faces in the auditorium as I could. But I couldn't locate the face I half expected to see.

And at the end of the performance, when the audience applauded and gave us a standing ovation, I knew I was the only member of the cast who didn't deserve it. I'd managed to perform all of my lines without any further prompting, but I'd felt hyped up and on edge throughout.

After the final curtain, the Director came on stage to congratulate and thank us all.

'Well, Tess, I knew you were full of surprises, but tonight you had us all on the edge of our seats, quite literally.'

I glanced across at Torvald, with his chin jutting forwards and lips pursed. Evidently, he had not been so impressed.

'You brought the house down, dear, and of course so did everyone else. Bravo!' He held out his arms and clapped his hands whilst looking around at all the actors.

We applauded, too, and when we left the stage for the last time, one of the front of house staff, a young woman with jet black hair swept up in a ponytail, approached me holding a huge bouquet of lilies.

The girl flicked her fringe off her wide blue eyes. 'A gentleman left these for you at the start of the show.'

She held out the flowers and I took them from her.

'He's seen the show every night this week,' she continued. 'When he asked me about you on the first night I thought he must be your husband or boyfriend. But when I suggested he give you the flowers himself, he declined and said he wanted to surprise you, which made me wonder if you didn't even know he was here.'

The lilies looked exquisite, and lavishly presented with colourful ribbons and cellophane wrap. I searched amongst the flowers for a card.

'Did he leave his name?'

'No.' She shook her head. 'He had fairish hair and was quite old, but the older ladies thought he was a better looking Liam Neeson.'

Sweat broke from my pores and I realised my fear upon hearing that cough during the opening scene had been justified.

'Has he gone?' I said, trying to suppress the panic in my voice.

She inclined her head. 'He told me to tell you he misses you but that he'd see you later.'

'Where?' I took an involuntary step backwards and the bouquet of lilies fell from my hands. 'Where did he say he'd see me?'

'At the beach,' the girl said, and giggled. 'I told him there were no beaches down the West End, but he winked at me, flashed his eyebrows and walked away.'

40

The remains of the sun permeated the murky twilight and I called Digby back from the water's edge where the mist swirled in eddies over the waves as they hushed back and forth. Above the ocean the new moon had risen, a barely visible slither of silver, and I wondered for some moments what new beginnings it would bring beyond my meeting a fresh cast of actors when I began rehearsals for a production in Edinburgh.

I looked down at the damp sand at my feet and saw footprints, freshly made, that led back up the beach and in the direction of the rocks and cave where I'd found the drowned girl all those months ago. I peered closer at the footprints. Did I imagine that the imprints seemed familiar? Despite the horrors of the previous year, I hadn't been deterred from walking down here, but each sighting of the cave at the base of the cliff served as a stark reminder of that time.

After a second call, Digby scampered over, with tail wagging, and he proudly dropped a piece of driftwood at my feet. As I bent down to clip on his lead, my phone pinged in the back pocket of my jeans. It was a familiar tone, but one I hadn't heard for some months. I tapped on the screen to discover a message from an unknown mobile number. For some moments I felt unsure whether to open it, but I could see it had an attached video. Curiosity got the better of me and when I tapped the message my heart began to pick up speed even before I'd registered who the face on the screen belonged to. The woman's features might have been fuzzy, but I recognised the curly blonde hair and face as my own.

The message beneath the video said, "Bravo! Your most accomplished, and might I add, stimulating performance to date."

How could this be happening after all these months? My thoughts raced as the possible ramifications of this video twisted like splintered glass through my gut.

And yet, with hands trembling in horror at what I would see, I tapped the arrow and the video began to play. The image sharpened and I stared and listened as I watched myself on the screen, first undo the buttons of my silk nightshirt, then with a pathetic, coquettish smile, I pulled my shirt down over my shoulders and off my back. From this point on my performance sank to the level of embarrassing and explicit pornography as I caressed my breasts and then moved my hands down between my legs. Not one image or sound from Stefan who had been doing similar on the other end of the screen. The bastard!

As the images played before me, another message pinged.

"Wonderful to see you intimately, again... and again. And see how your audience adores you? 10K views on HeShehub.com and rising fast!"

What had been for me a beautiful, loving and intimate moment between two adults, had been distorted and twisted by him into something sordid, and publicly humiliating and damning.

I raised my eyes and looked around. I was alone here on an otherwise deserted beach watching myself, and the irony of this hit me full force.

My vision swam and my legs crumbled beneath me, as my dalliance with the devil rushed to the forefront of my mind.

Some time later, which could have been either minutes or an hour, such was my state of mind, freezing water washed over my legs and seaspray splashed my face. I raised my head and looked into the darkness, and as I scrambled to stand up another wave rushed forwards and made me lose my footing. I stumbled backwards, recovered myself and hurried away from the water's edge.

Still dazed and disorientated, I fumbled for my phone in my soaked pocket. I shook off droplets of seawater, unzipped my jacket and wiped my phone dry on my T-shirt.

I powered it on and after some moments the screen sprang to life.

Still working, and I let out a breath of relief. No further messages. The images from the video tumbled through my mind and a feeling of nausea returned. I walked away from the sea and back over the sand towards the lights on the pier.

Stefan, wherever he was, had got his revenge and I felt a wall of rage rise up inside of me. First thing I'd do would be to find a way to get the video taken down. I'd report it to the police, too.

I shivered from shock and the icy water upon my skin, and fighting back my tears, I hurried through the narrow streets towards home.

The cottage was dark and silent. The twins were at their Dad's new flat for the night and so I had the house to myself. I showered quickly and pulled on my robe, then sat on my bed and wondered what to do next as panic and rage rose and fell through me like tsunami waves.

My palms were damp with sweat as I opened Stefan's message and tapped his mobile number.

The dial tone rang out.

Would the bastard be too cowardly to answer?

And then he picked up.

I heard traffic noises in the background and then his voice.

'Tessa, darling. How wonderful to hear from you after all this time.'

I felt bile rise in my throat and my heart battered my ribcage.

My voice shook. 'We're tracking you, Stefan. The police have finally located you.'

The sound of traffic grew louder and rumbled through the phone.

'Impossible.'

But I heard the doubt in his voice.

'Don't look behind you,' I said with a steadiness that belied my fear.

I wanted to scare him and threaten his belief that he'd escaped conviction for his crimes.

With snake-oiled smoothness, he said, 'You're lying to me, again...'

His words were snatched away when a sudden and deafening noise came through the phone and I held it away from my ear.

Sounds I couldn't distinguish continued on and on amongst a squeal of brakes and scraping sounds.

'Stefan?'

I remained there holding the phone and heard voices, and people shouting. The commotion rumbled on.

'Stefan, Stefan?' I repeated, over and over.

Had he dumped his phone because he believed the police really did know his whereabouts? Or given the traffic sounds, had he flung his phone into the road?

I listened on, and after what seemed an age, a woman came on the line.

'Is anyone there?' her voice stuttered down the line.

'Where's Stefan? I was speaking to Stefan.'

There came a pause. And I could hear her breaths above more indistinct sounds in the background.

'I'm afraid,' she said. 'There's been an accident.'

My breaths came ragged and fast. 'Who? What's happened?'

She hesitated. 'Are you his wife - Stefan, you called him?'

'Not his wife. But I know him.'

'I'm so sorry,' she said again and she went silent for a few moments. 'The man you were talking to has been hit by a van. I believe he's dead.'

My breath juddered in my throat. 'He's dead? Are you certain?'

'Yes, I'm so sorry. Someone's called an ambulance.'

And as I tried to digest her words, I said quietly, 'Don't be sorry. He deserved it.'

And when I heard the sound of sirens blaring in the distance, I couldn't make out if they were coming through the phone. I climbed off the bed and walked to the window, and as I lifted the catch and opened it wide, the sirens echoed louder from the streets of the town.

I clasped the phone to my chest, and let out a sob, as shock and relief flooded through me.

The End

About the Author

Olivia Rytwinski was born in Worcestershire and now lives in North Yorkshire with her family. She is a full time writer and previously worked in Marketing and education. To date, she has written four contemporary thriller novels - *A Family by Design*, set in the Scottish Highlands and published in 2017, *I Never Knew You*, set in rural Wensleydale, published in 2019, *Shadowlake*, set in The Lake District, published in March 2021, and her latest publication, *The Actor*, set in Whitby on the North Yorkshire Coast, published in 2022.

Olivia's writing and stories stem from her fascination with the workings of the human mind and how adult relationships and family dynamics evolve over time and struggle amidst all the pressures that modern society brings - and on top of this how we are all under the influence of our inbuilt biological drivers that shape our behaviours.

Olivia gives talks and presentations about her writing and her novels to community groups throughout Yorkshire - sharing her journey to becoming a published author.

Printed in Great Britain
by Amazon

86446898R00173